MISS JULIA STANDS HER GROUND

ANN B. ROSS

LARGE PRINT PRESS
An imprint of Thomson Gale, a part of The Thomson Corporation

Detroit • New York • San Francisco • New Haven, Conn. • Waterville, Maine • London

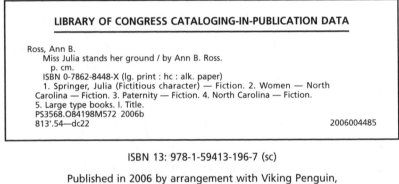

THOMSON

GALE

LIBRARY OF CONGRESS CATALOGING-IN-PUBLICATION DATA

Ross, Ann B.
    Miss Julia stands her ground / by Ann B. Ross.
        p. cm.
    ISBN 0-7862-8448-X (lg. print : hc : alk. paper)
    1. Springer, Julia (Fictitious character) — Fiction. 2. Women — North Carolina — Fiction. 3. Paternity — Fiction. 4. North Carolina — Fiction. 5. Large type books. I. Title.
PS3568.O84198M572 2006b
813'.54—dc22   2006004485

ISBN 13: 978-1-59413-196-7 (sc)

Published in 2006 by arrangement with Viking Penguin,
a division of Penguin Group (USA) Inc.

Printed in the United States on permanent paper.
10 9 8 7 6 5 4 3 2 1

This one is for the booksellers,
librarians, and readers
who have been
Miss Julia's loyal friends
since the first book
was published.

Acknowledgments

My thanks to Dr. William M. Surver, of Clemson University, and to Dr. Robert H. Dowdeswell, Henderson County medical examiner, for answering my questions about DNA and exhumations. My thanks, also, to Kathryn Wells, attorney and fellow sports fan, for her time and expertise. They all told me much more than Miss Julia needed to know, and in condensing the information, I may have made some errors. If so, I am the one at fault.

Chapter 1

"Hazel Marie?" I walked up a couple of stair steps, craning my head to see if she had heard me. "Hazel Marie, are you up there?"

I could hear her footsteps as she came out into the hall and poked her head over the bannister. "I'm here, Miss Julia. Come on up."

"I'm trying," I said, using the handrail to pull myself up the stairs, and thanking the Lord that I didn't have to do it a dozen times a day. To be free of that arduous climb and perilous descent was the result of having moved down to Hazel Marie's old room on the first floor, once Sam and I were firmly married.

Hazel Marie had said the exchange of rooms was to give us privacy, and it did that, but I now think that she was more concerned with the preservation of life and limb. *My* life and limb, that is, since I wasn't getting any younger, which was more apparent every day I lived, what with stiffening joints and wobbling limbs and people deliberately mumbling instead of speaking up as they should.

I finally gained the second floor and followed her into the room that Wesley Lloyd Springer and I had shared for forty-something years. *Shared* doesn't exactly give a clear picture of what went on there, however, because it's true that we slept in the same bed, but that joint enterprise had been more like two strangers who happened to end up next to each other on a train trip. He, however, had reached his destination, while I was still traveling.

But that was neither here nor there, for many things had changed since my first husband shucked off these mortal coils, and I'd learned to stand up for myself and do pretty much as I pleased.

"Whew," I said, relieved to sink down into an easy chair by the front window. I caught my breath and surveyed the changes in the room. "Hazel Marie, you've done a lovely job in here. I wouldn't recognize it as the same room, and it pleases me to be able to say that."

"Oh, I'm so glad you like it. I just love it." Hazel Marie turned slowly around, her eyes shining with pleasure at what she and Opal Nixon, Abbotsville's correspondence course decorator, had wrought. The room

10

was done in pink, and when I say done in pink, I mean pink wallpaper, pink bedding, pink carpet, pink upholstery, and pink fixtures in the bathroom. But to give the two of them credit, there was nothing frilly or girlish about the decor. It was elegant, with gold fringes and gilt mirrors and gilt picture frames and a great deal of texture in the use of silk and taffeta and plush this, that, and the other.

It wouldn't have been my choice, but then, I'm much more conservative and traditional in my decorative choices than Hazel Marie. So I was happy that she liked it and, since the room was quite unlike the rest of the house, comforted by the fact that hardly anybody else would see it.

"Hazel Marie," I said, heaving a sigh to indicate that I had something more on my mind than bedroom decor. "I am just sick at heart over Little Lloyd."

"Oh, I am, too." She slumped down into the matching pink velvet chair to my right. "I couldn't get to sleep last night, I was so upset. He tried so hard to be brave, it nearly broke my heart, and we had to pretend that it wasn't such a big deal."

I nodded, recalling how I, too, had tossed and tumbled, aching half the night over that child's tears he'd tried so valiantly

11

to hide. "Well, of course it isn't a big deal in the cosmic scheme of things, but it is for him. But, I'll tell you, Hazel Marie, I'd rather have a deep disappointment myself than for him to have one. I would do anything in the world to protect that child."

"Oh, me, too." Her eyes filled with tears and she sniffed before looking around for a Kleenex. "Excuse me, I better get some toilet paper."

She came back from the bathroom wiping her eyes with a few squares of pink Cottonelle tissue. "What can we do, Miss Julia?"

"I don't know. I've gone over in my mind any number of wholesome activities that might help him get over it, but nothing jumps out at me. I've even thought of offering to build a new gymnasium if the coach would reconsider."

"I think they play soccer on a field."

"I hope so. It'd be cheaper."

Hazel Marie took her seat again, her face streaked with tears with more on the way. "And I'd tell you to do it, if I thought it'd work. But it wouldn't. He just wanted to be good enough for the coach to choose him, and he wasn't. That's what hurts him so much."

"What we have to do, Hazel Marie, is

aim him for next year. All is not lost because he didn't make the team this time. After all, this is the first year he's tried out for any kind of athletic endeavor. I think the coach just saw that he's small and frail looking, and didn't look any further. I know he feels it's the end of the world now, but let's look into some camps or lessons so he can learn the game."

"I've already called for some brochures for a soccer camp." Hazel Marie bit her lip and looked off into the pinkish distance. "You know, I was relieved, and I think he was, too, when he didn't make the football team. I don't know why he went out for it in the first place. But, soccer? That's where the little, wiry kids ought to be able to shine. If they had half a chance."

I nodded in agreement, but objectively speaking, Little Lloyd was certainly smaller than your average middle-school student, and he wasn't what I'd call especially nimble on his feet. I wouldn't say clumsy, just a little uncoordinated in his movements. On the up side, though, he was as smart as a whip, quick to grasp and process every lesson he was given, and many that he just picked up by himself or by listening to me.

But that didn't help the child's feelings

at the moment. He'd tried to put a good face on it, saying that soccer only lasted a few weeks during the fall, and that he'd aim for the tennis team in the spring. His bravery just tore me up, especially since he wasn't exactly an Andre Agassi on the court, or a Chris Evert, either.

"Well," I said, putting my hands on the arm of the chair and pushing myself up out of it, "this isn't helping matters, and I don't know what will. But that coach just better stay out of my line of sight. I'm ready to give him a piece of my mind."

"Me, too. But coaches are a law unto themselves, and they pick the ones who can help them win." Hazel Marie dabbed at her eyes again, then cocked her head to the side. "You know, when I was in school, we had clubs like the Future Farmers of America. I bet Lloyd could be in something like that."

"Lord, Hazel Marie, that child's not interested in farming." I turned at the door and looked back at her. "But if they had a Future Accountants of America, that would be more up his alley. He's a whiz at numbers, you know."

"I know. I just wish he wasn't so set on sports." She caught her bottom lip in her teeth, and then, frowning, asked, "Miss

Julia, did you know that Episcopalians pray an awful lot?"

"Oh, I expect they're about the same as the rest of us, and pray when they need to. Why?"

"I think they do more than that," she said. "I saw this special book they have over at Binkie's the other day. I thought it was a Bible at first, but it was just full of all kinds of prayers for everything you can think of. Psalms, too."

"That's real interesting, Hazel Marie. Maybe they have one for . . ." A door slammed downstairs, and my heart flipped in my chest. "That's Sam," I said, smiling as I did every time he came into the house. "Have you ever noticed how loud men are? They're always slamming and banging and stomping around, like they have to let everybody know where they are."

She managed a rueful laugh. "I think they do it just to stir things up. J.D., for instance, is like a whirlwind. When it's just you and me and Lillian, the house is so quiet and peaceful. But let one of them come in, and it's like everything wakes up."

"Julia!" Sam's voice carried up the stairs, and I hurried toward it.

Meeting me at the foot of the stairs, he put his hands on my shoulders. I lifted my face toward him, expecting his usual greeting, but was taken aback when I didn't get it. Turning me toward our room, he said, "Let's go back here. I have something to tell you."

His voice was so full of ominous portent that I opened my eyes and immediately headed toward the back hall, him following every step of the way.

He shut the door behind us. "You better sit down, Julia. This is going to upset you."

"I'll take it standing up. What is it?"

"Well, I've got to sit down." And he did, taking one of the easy chairs by the double windows overlooking the back yard. "I just had a visitor. I don't know how he tracked me down to my house, but he did."

Sam spent most mornings and some afternoons, now that he was retired from the practice of law, over at his house, using his study there as an office as he worked on a history of the legal doings of Abbot County. It gave him something to fill his time, and he enjoyed going through legal records, old court cases, looking up early attorneys and judges, and analyzing indictments, convictions, and sentences of our local criminal population, which occasionally had included a few of those same attorneys and judges.

"Who're we talking about?" I asked,

somewhat disturbed that our marriage might be open to question again. "I'll tell you this, Sam, I'm not going through another wedding ceremony. Two of them ought to be legal enough in anybody's book."

"No, no," Sam said, with a brief smile. "I think we're safe on that score." He took a deep breath and glanced out the window. The leaves on the dogwood trees were already turning red, and he seemed to take an inordinate interest in their various hues. "You remember Brother Vernon Puckett?"

"Do I remember him?" I asked sharply. "How could I forget after what he put us through?" I took the chair across from Sam, fearing that anything to do with Hazel Marie's itinerant uncle who went from evangelistic telecasts to tent meetings to selling Bibles door-to-door could only mean trouble for somebody. "What did he want?"

"I'm still trying to figure that out." Sam rubbed his fingers across his mouth, then went on. "He said he didn't want anything but to put matters right. Said the Lord had spoken to him and put a burden on his heart. And that meant that he had to get up and act before a great wrong was allowed to fester and ruin a whole lot of lives."

"Shoo," I said, waving my hand. "The Lord speaks to that man more than anybody I've ever heard of. It doesn't mean a thing. He wants something, that's a given, and when has he ever not wanted his hands on Little Lloyd's inheritance? That's in the back of his mind, mark my words."

"Maybe so. But if what he said is true, there's no way in the world he'd have a chance at it. That's what has me puzzled. He'd be better off to just let things slide, *if* he knows what he's talking about."

"Well, what was he talking about?"

Sam leaned over and took my hand. "He said, Julia, and I don't believe it for one minute, but he said that Lloyd is not Wesley Lloyd's child."

Chapter 2

"That is the most ridiculous thing I've ever heard!" I sprang from my chair and started pacing, just so agitated I couldn't stand it. "Not Wesley Lloyd's child? Why, Sam, the boy's his spitting image, and I, who had every reason in the world not to believe it, couldn't deny it from the minute I laid eyes on him."

"I know, Julia. Not one soul's ever doubted it, not even Wesley Lloyd himself. After all, he tried to leave his entire estate to the boy on the night he died."

"Tell me about it," I said, getting a quick surge of the anger I'd felt when I thought my husband had cut me out all together. Well, actually he *had* cut me out, but because he'd not known that a wife can't be left destitute in this state, I'd gotten my half in spite of him and his last-minute, handwritten will on a piece of Hazel Marie's pink stationery.

I whirled around to face Sam again. "What does that trouble maker hope to gain by coming up with such a cock-and-

19

bull story at this late date?"

"I have no idea. Like I told you, he said he didn't want anything but to set things right. Said he couldn't live with himself to keep such a secret while his niece and bastard nephew took advantage of you."

"Oh," I groaned, collapsing in the chair and holding my head in my hands. "Poor Hazel Marie. Her uncle will do anything to hurt her, and this just takes the cake." I looked up at Sam. "She's not taking advantage of me, Sam. Nor is that child. There's not a more honest, more open person in the world than Hazel Marie Puckett, and why her sorry uncle wants to come in and stir things up, I don't know." I sprang up again, too disturbed to sit still.

"Come over here and sit on my lap," Sam said. "We'll figure something out."

I waved my hand at him. "I don't have lap sitting on my mind. Just what does Brother Vern plan to do with this *information* of his? Face Hazel Marie with it? Tell the child? Tell the whole world? And, come to think of it, why did he tell you? Why not me? I'm the one who, according to him, is being taken advantage of."

"You're not going to like this, but he said he bypassed you because I'm the head of the household." Sam's eyes betrayed a twinkle, as a smile played around his mouth. "Maybe you didn't know this, Julia, but you're now under submission to your husband and should be protected from grave matters such as this."

I thought the top of my head would blow off at the arrogance of that know-it-all self-proclaimed preacher. Sam might be the head of the household in the Biblical view of things, but I had to be reckoned with, too. "I'll show him who's under submission! The idea." I marched up to Sam and stood over him. "And what did you say to that?"

"Fill in the blanks, Julia." He took my hand and pulled me closer. "Let's just say that when he left he had a new understanding of what marriage is. At least, this marriage. Now, let's put our heads together and think how we're going to handle this."

"Well, I'll try." I took a seat again, and tried to organize my spinning thoughts. Taking a deep breath, I said, "Maybe it'll all blow over if we wait him out." But then I couldn't help the bitter edge that came into my voice. "Now that he's confessed his suspicions, maybe the Lord'll stop burdening his heart, and let him get some sleep."

Sam shook his head from side to side. "No, he said that this whole situation is a parable about the fruits of evil intentions — Hazel Marie's evil intentions, you understand — and that it's incumbent upon Christians to speak up and speak out, and unveil those who would deceive for monetary gain — I'm quoting here. Then he went into a long discourse on Satan as the Great Deceiver, and how Satan's and Hazel Marie's true colors had to be revealed." Sam stopped long enough for me to blink my eyes back into my head. "He's writing a tract about it to hand out at his meetings. Oh, I didn't tell you, he's in the printing business now. And he's making an infomercial to run on the local cable channel to sell a book he's working on, as well as tapes of his sermons." Sam smiled again, but there wasn't much joy in it. "He thinks the tale of Hazel Marie's trickery and subsequent comeuppance, which he plans to engineer, will win souls far and wide."

"How can he *do* that? He doesn't have a shred of evidence to back up his claims." I leaned toward Sam, expecting him to tell me we had nothing to worry about. "He doesn't, does he?"

"Not that he told me. He did hint

around, though, that he knows who Lloyd's real father is."

"*Is?* Somebody who's still around?"

Sam nodded. "That's what it sounded like."

"Then where is he? Why hasn't he made himself known? And what about his parental responsibilities?" I sat back in my chair. "I don't believe it for a minute."

"I don't either. But, Julia, be prepared. Brother Vern is convinced of it, and he intends to spread it around."

"Slander, that's what it is. I'll sue that man till he has to beg on the street. I'm not taking this sitting down, Sam, you can be sure of that." So I got up and started pacing again. Then I thought of something else. "Hazel Marie is his niece. His own flesh and blood, and so is Little Lloyd. How can he tear them down like this?"

"He thinks his relationship to them makes his parable more powerful," Sam said with a wry smile. "He said that he couldn't exhort others to follow God's leading until he'd straightened out his own kin."

"The man is crazy," I said, as firmly convinced as I'd ever been of anything. "Sam, I'm telling you that he has something against Hazel Marie, and he'll do anything he can to hurt her. Remember when she and Little Lloyd first came to live with me? Brother Vern tried every trick in the book to get the child away from her. Even tried to have her declared an unfit mother." I paused, recalling the troubles we'd had with the sweaty, heavy-breathing preacher, which included deceiving me and kidnapping Little Lloyd. "But that was to have himself named the child's guardian, so he'd have access to Wesley Lloyd's estate. But *this,* there's no profit in it for him at all. The only thing he can get out of it is to shame Hazel Marie and deprive the boy of his rightful inheritance. All he wants to do is hurt them. And I want to know why."

"I expect it'll come out sooner or later," Sam said. "But for now, we need to decide how we're going to handle whatever he comes up with."

"Well, what do you think we should do?" Not for the first time since our marriage, I felt some relief in not having to decide everything myself. "Should we tell Hazel Marie?"

Sam hesitated, then said, "If he proceeds with publicizing his accusations, we'll have to."

"Oh, Lord, I hate the thought of her being subjected to all that shame and worry."

"So do I." Sam rubbed his hand across

his face. "But as far as I can see, there's no need to burden her with it unless we have to. Maybe we ought to just keep it to ourselves as long as we can."

I thought about that for a few minutes, wondering how I could ever keep such a perilous threat to myself. I knew that the knowledge of it would simmer below the surface of my mind, until I wouldn't be able to look Hazel Marie in the eye and pretend that all was as it should be. So I said, "Would it be all right if I just told her that her uncle is back in town? You know, so it won't be such a shock if she finds out what he's doing?"

Sam smiled. "Whatever you think, Julia. I'm just saying that downplaying it as much as we can would be better for all of us in the long run."

Then, struck with a sudden thought, I sat up straight in my chair. "Listen, Sam, she may never even hear of his tract or his preaching. We don't associate with the kind of people who're willing to listen to four hours of ranting and raving under a tent out in the county." Our friends and associates went to mainline churches where the preaching lasted no longer than thirty minutes, and even then they got restless after twenty.

Sam shook his head. "Some people will hear of it, though. And it'll get around eventually. That's why I want to deal with him directly, and make him put up or shut up."

"Oh, Sam," I said, falling back in the chair and burying my face in my hands. "You know what I just thought of? He's saying that Hazel Marie was promiscuous, that she was seeing someone else at the same time Wesley Lloyd was visiting her every Thursday night when he was supposed to be working at the bank."

Sam nodded. "I know. And he's also saying that she deliberately deceived Wesley Lloyd, telling him it was his child, and he believed her."

"Well," I said, raising my head, "I don't doubt he'd believe her. Wesley Lloyd Springer couldn't have imagined that anybody would try to fool him. Nor could he have imagined that she would prefer someone else to him. The most arrogant man who ever lived. Except for Brother Vernon Puckett, that is. But what I can't believe is that Hazel Marie would lie about such a thing. I can't and I don't believe it. Even if Brother Vern dredges up another boyfriend, concurrent with Wesley Lloyd, I will still believe that Hazel Marie knew who the child's father was. But to question her basic goodness, to even imply that she's lived a lie all this time, Sam, it will absolutely do her in. And that child! Think what it'll do to him to hear such an attack on his mother. Oh, Sam, I can't stand it."

"All right, Julia, here's what let's do." Sam got to his feet, then began pacing in front of me. "Let's hold off a while before telling Hazel Marie the details — no need upsetting her until we know more." He cut his eyes at me and went on. "I'll leave it up to you about telling her he's in town. In the meantime, I'll get back with Puckett and see if he can back up his claims. If he can't, or won't, we'll think about having him prosecuted for slander and, if he publishes anything, libel." Sam stopped and looked long and hard at me. "Of course, you realize that if it comes to that, he'll have a ready-made audience for his claims."

"Oh, Lord, yes. And the newspaper'll cover it, too. How can we stop him, Sam? We've got to do something."

Sam cogitated for a moment, then he said, "I think what may work is for us to string him along and let him think we're taking his claims seriously. We'll tell him that we're disturbed that the boy may be getting something he's not entitled to, and we want to work with him to find the truth."

"I wouldn't work with Vernon Puckett if he was the last man on earth." I was thoroughly steamed at the thought, then thought better of it. "How would we do it, if we did?"

"DNA, Julia. By pretending to at least halfway believe Puckett, we'll get him to produce the man he's claiming to be the father. Then we'll compare his DNA with Little Lloyd's, and that should settle it right there."

"Oh, Sam, thank goodness. I knew you'd come up with something." I smiled at him as my heart lifted, for I'd watched enough television to know a good deal about forensic science. I had no doubt in the world that Little Lloyd's DNA would match no one's but Wesley Lloyd Springer's. How could it not? They were as alike as two peas in a pod.

Chapter 3

With that settled, I congratulated myself again for having married a man with such a good head on his shoulders. And one who took my concerns seriously and who was willing and able to do something about them. I declare, when I compared Sam Murdoch with Wesley Lloyd Springer, which I couldn't help but do since they were the only husbands I'd ever had, Sam beat him by a mile in every way you could think of.

So now that I was married to a good man — one who would look after my interests — I was determined to rein myself in and not run ahead of him. I wanted to be a helpmate to Sam. Or a helpmeet for him. Whichever translation was correct, that's what I was trying to be. But it was awfully hard to take a backseat.

"All right," I said, rising from my chair again. "I'll leave it in your hands, Sam, and wait a while before upsetting Hazel Marie. But I don't know how long I can keep it to myself."

"Just hold off a few days," Sam said with that cautionary tone he often uses to slow me down. "If I can find out what Puckett's up to, I'll hold his feet to the fire. When he has to back up his claims, it may all blow over, and Hazel Marie won't ever have to know."

"Well, I'll try. But I want it settled." I bit my lip, thinking of how I'd like to hand out a little comeuppance, myself, but to Brother Vern, not to Hazel Marie. "But, whenever and however we tell her, I don't want that child to get even a hint of what's going on."

"Absolutely not, Julia. He doesn't need to know a thing. At least at this stage."

I'd started out of the room on my way to help Lillian get dinner on the table. But at Sam's final words, I stopped and turned back. "What do you mean, at this stage? If we stop Brother Vern with this DNA test, there won't be any further stages."

"Well," Sam said, walking over to stand next to me, "even if this mystery man's DNA doesn't match Lloyd's, that won't settle the question of the boy's paternity. And once the question is raised, the only way to absolutely and positively disprove Puckett's claims is to compare Lloyd's DNA with Wesley Lloyd's, and how're we going to do that?"

"Oh," I said, brought up short by the un-likelihood of drawing blood from a dead man. "Then we'll never be sure, will we? Of course, *I'm* sure, and I'm the one who counts as far as the estate is concerned. But, Sam, unless we put this to rest once and for all, there'll always be some people who'll wonder, won't there? The suspicion that Little Lloyd's not a Springer could follow that child for the rest of his life, to say nothing of how it'll besmirch Hazel Marie. Oh, Sam," I moaned, leaning my head against his shoulder, "I've never wished Wesley Lloyd back among the living, but I could surely wish it now if we could get one little drop of blood from him."

"There're more ways to test DNA than through blood, Julia," Sam said, as he put his arm around my waist. "But I'm not sure just what, or what condition it has to be in. I'll do some research, though, and find out. If Brother Vern forces us to it, we may have to request an exhumation. Are you ready for that?"

My head popped up from his shoulder. "You mean dig him up? Lord, Sam, no! Surely we won't have to do that. Let the man rest in peace. Although for my money," I said, with a sniff, "he doesn't deserve a minute of it. Not that I bear a grudge, you understand. I just resent the fact that I can't ever seem to be free of him."

"You're free of him, Julia, and you've got me to remind you of it every day."

"I know, Sam, and I'm more grateful than you know." I took his arm as we went toward the kitchen, me thinking all the while of how comforting it was to have a good and capable man to lean on.

By the time we got through the dining room, though, I was reminding myself that as trustworthy as Sam had always proven to be, he could be a little slow getting things done. Always telling me to calm down, wait and see, or let things run their course. That wasn't my way by a long shot. I'd been an obedient follower all the days of my first marriage, never stepping out of line, and always reacting instead of acting on my own instincts. The few years between husbands, though, when I was free to do as I pleased, had shown me that my instincts were invariably correct.

Well, maybe not invariably, but nine times out of ten they'd led me on the right path.

So it was not my intention to sit around for days on end while Sam waited for

Brother Vern to show his hand. I mean, it was all well and good for Sam to handle the major problems — it was a relief to have him do it, in fact — but I could be a help to him in little ways. Like warning Hazel Marie to stay away from tent meetings, for example.

My intent had been to get Hazel Marie alone in her room right after supper and tell her what we were in for — not all the details, of course, but enough to prepare her for what might lie ahead. All I'd have to say was that Brother Vern was back in town, and she'd know to start girding her loins. So to speak.

Instead of planning a quiet evening at home, though, she'd hurried through her meal so she could go play a game that some of the younger set had taken up. I'd never heard of such entertainment before and, when she told me what went on at those bunco parties, I felt it my duty to make it clear how much I disapproved of gambling of any kind.

"Oh, it's not really gambling," Hazel Marie had said. "It's just a way to get together and have some fun."

"I can think of better ways to have fun," I told her. "And besides, gambling is illegal in this state."

"It is?" Hazel Marie frowned, then she laughed. "Well, if they raid Miriam Hargrove's house, you'll bail me out, won't you?"

And off she'd gone, as free of worry as if I'd never warned her of the dire consequences of wagering money. You let sin gain a foothold, and it'll take over your whole life.

So I had to lie in bed all night with the knowledge of Brother Vern's threat simmering in my head. It had about reached a boil by the next morning as I waited in the kitchen for Hazel Marie to make an appearance.

Since it was a Saturday, Sam and Little Lloyd were making their weekly visit to the hardware stores, during which they rarely bought anything, but seemed to enjoy thinking about what they might purchase.

Lillian was piddling at the counter, and I was at the table making out a grocery list, and trying to put my mind onto the menus for the coming week. I put down my pen when Hazel Marie, still in her bathrobe, pushed through the kitchen door.

"Morning, everybody," she said, heading for the coffee pot. "Lillian, I'm not going to mess up your kitchen with another breakfast. I just need some coffee."

"You better eat something," Lillian said, worried as always about everybody's digestive systems. "You need to put some meat on them bones."

Hazel Marie just smiled, poured her coffee, and came over to the table. I opened my mouth to suggest that she and I go upstairs, but before she had her chair pulled out, she started talking. "Miss Julia, you'll never guess what I heard last night about the Denhams."

"Dub and Clara? I can't imagine those two doing anything worth talking about. Which would you rather have with chicken, rice or potatoes?"

"Oh, rice. Now, listen, Miss Julia, Clara's left him."

I looked up at her. "Who?"

"Dub."

"Where'd she go?"

"That's just it. Nobody knows. Apparently, she came home from work a few days ago, slapped some papers down in front of him, and walked out with two suitcases."

"I can't picture Clara Denham slapping anything down, as meek and mild as she is."

"I'm just telling you what I heard, and everybody's saying that she'd taken it as long as she could, and just finally snapped.

Maybe it got better in the telling, because it doesn't sound like her. I mean, she's so meek and mild."

"Well, she is a librarian."

"Yes, and what is Dub? Just a big blob as far as I can see."

I was intrigued, in spite of the urgency I was feeling to tell her about her own looming troubles. But Sam had urged delay, I reminded myself, so I nodded in agreement. "That man's been on disability for as long as I can remember. He hardly cracks a lick at a snake."

Lillian, who couldn't help but hear our conversation, walked over to the table. "Mr. Dub, he work some 'round tax time at that place they open up for people who need help with they figures. Miz Edwards, what live on the street over from me, she use him last year, an' she say he do yo' taxes an' not even listen to what you say."

"Dub Denham," I said, "has never been known for his social skills. He's the last person I'd ever ask to a dinner party."

"I should say!" Hazel Marie agreed. "Have you ever seen him eat? I sat at the same table with him at the last church supper, and it was awful to watch him shovel it in." Hazel Marie stopped and sat up straight. "Come to think of it, Clara always stays in the kitchen. Maybe that's why she left him. She couldn't stand to watch him eat."

"Reason enough," I pronounced. "I read, one time, about this fastidious woman who was newly married, and at her first dinner party, she served soup as the first course. It just did her in when her husband, normally a well-mannered man, made loud, slurping noises when he ate it. Well, instead of saying anything to him and risk hurting his feelings, she just never served soup at her table again."

After a moment of quiet as we thought about that, Hazel Marie said, "What did she do when he ordered it at a restaurant?"

"Well, I don't know, Hazel Marie. But, let me tell you, if you followed that method with Dub, he'd starve to death." I tapped my pencil against the list I was making, trying to stop thinking of Dub's poor table manners. "You know, Hazel Marie, I haven't seen either of them in church lately. Not that I've been looking for them, but still."

"I saw her after Sunday school a couple of weeks ago, coming out of the young marrieds class." Hazel Marie squinched up her mouth. "They've both got to be in their fifties. Wonder why they go to that class?"

"Now you know we Presbyterians aren't like the Baptists, who make it their business to keep up with everybody's birthdays. They make you move to another class whenever you pass a milestone, which, I'll tell you right now, I'd rather not have the public recognition of."

Hazel Marie nodded, then got up for a coffee refill. While her back was turned, Lillian put a slice of coffee cake at her place, mumbling, "She better eat something."

When Hazel Marie sat back down, she propped her chin on her hand and said, "Have y'all ever noticed how fat men wear their pants?"

My head jerked up. "What?"

Lillian started laughing. "I never heard such."

"No, I'm serious," Hazel Marie said, "and thinking about Dub reminded me. When women put on weight, they just get rounder and rounder. But men get this big ole pot belly. You know, like Dub has. And some men pull their pants up over it, which means they have to buy a longer belt to fit, and that hikes everything up, so they end up with high waters. But other men wear their pants down below their stomachs, and that gives them baggy seats with the crotch hanging down around their knees." She frowned, giving it serious thought. "I wonder how they decide. I mean, why some men go for over the stomach and some for under."

I stared at her, amazed at the things that people take up to think about. "I admit, Hazel Marie, that I've never given it much thought."

"Well," she went on, stirring her coffee absently, "when they decide to go over or under, I guess it could say something about their personalities. But I don't know what."

"Neither do I." I prepared to rise and suggest we walk upstairs, where I intended to warn her of our impending troubles.

"Oh, my goodness," Hazel Marie said, springing from her chair, "look at the time. I better jump in the shower and get myself dressed. I have a million things to do today."

And with that, she was gone, and I'd missed my chance again.

Chapter 4

Just as Lillian was taking the yeast rolls out of the oven that Saturday evening, Mr. Pickens strolled in, smiling in the easy way he had, knowing he was welcome at any time. It was a wonder to me, though, how he always managed to get that welcome at dinnertime. I hurriedly set another place at the dining room table, while Hazel Marie and Lillian greeted him as enthusiastically as if he hadn't been with us three nights running over the past week.

"I'm so glad you're back," Hazel Marie said, clinging to his arm. "Did you have a good trip? How was Atlanta?"

"Didn't see much of it," he said, smiling down at her. "It was just a good place to meet. Better than having to go all the way to West Palm Beach to see him. But when an old friend needs help, you do what you can."

"Oh, I know," Hazel Marie said. "And you were so good to go see about him."

"Quite commendable, Mr. Pickens," I said, hoping that it had indeed been a him and not a her. "Is your friend sick?"

"Frank Tuttle? Not exactly." Mr. Pickens shook his head, then frowned. "Things aren't working out for him here lately, but he's a good man. Best investigator I've ever known."

"Well, I'm glad you could help him," I said, not really interested in another private investigator. "Lillian, if you're ready, we'll go to the table."

Sam and Little Lloyd showed their pleasure in Mr. Pickens's return, for he was good company. He could keep us entertained, if not with his teasing manner, then with stories of his long involvement with law enforcement of one kind or another. He did seem to have settled down now, though, what with having his own investigative agency, to say nothing of his attachment to Hazel Marie and his addiction to Lillian's cooking.

As I sat at the foot of the table, picking at the food on my plate, I was doubly grateful for Mr. Pickens's carryings-on. I would've been unable to keep a lively conversation going, as burdened as my mind was with the secret that I had to eventually share with Hazel Marie. She looked so happy, as she gazed with shining eyes at that black-eyed, black-haired, and black-mustached Mr. Pickens, that pity for what was hanging over her head nearly overcame me.

"You're awfully quiet tonight, Miss Julia," Mr. Pickens said, turning his intense gaze on me.

"I haven't been able to get a word in edgewise," I said, somewhat tartly, but with a smile, trying to give back as good as he handed out. "Besides, Lillian's meat loaf is so good, I'm giving it my full attention."

"It is that," he agreed, but his lingering look told me that he'd noticed my preoccupation. He was not a trained investigator for nothing.

"Lloyd," Mr. Pickens said, finally letting me off the hook, just as Lillian pushed through the swinging door with another basket of hot rolls. "Lillian's doing her best to get me fat, because she knows I can't resist anything she cooks. It's a conspiracy, is what it is, so pass the butter."

Lillian snorted at his foolishness, but she liked it, and him.

"So, Lloyd," Mr. Pickens went on, "let's shoot some baskets as soon as I can crawl away from the table. Want to?"

Little Lloyd's eyes lit up, since anything Mr. Pickens suggested was fine with him. "Yessir," he said, eagerly. Then his face fell. "I'm not very good at it, though."

"I know what your problem is," Mr. Pickens said in an offhand way, as if problems were a dime a dozen. "Your goal's too high. It's at professional height, and it ought to be a foot or two lower for your age. Sam, if you've got a ladder, we can fix it and get in a few baskets before it gets too dark."

"Sure," Sam said. "We can do that. I should've realized it was too high myself."

Little Lloyd frowned, as he looked hopefully at Mr. Pickens. "Is it really too high? I mean, it's not because I'm too short?"

"Nope," Mr. Pickens said, buttering a roll with infinite care. "If you're going to be ready for the season, you need to practice with the goal at the official height for your age." Mr. Pickens's black eyes glanced up at him, a smile beginning at the corner of his mouth. "Besides, bringing it down gives me an advantage, and I'm going to take you on, bud."

Little Lloyd laughed out loud for the first time since the soccer coach broke his heart, and I could've hugged Mr. Pickens's neck. He was a good man, in spite of his frisky nature and aversion to domestication.

Listening to this exchange and marveling at how sensitive Mr. Pickens was to the

43

child's athletic needs, especially after his failure to measure up to soccer standards, it occurred to me that one way to put a worry in perspective was to be overwhelmed by a bigger one. So, though I'd let myself be troubled because Little Lloyd hadn't won a place on the team, how important could that be now that his place on the Springer family tree was being questioned?

But not by me. From the first time I'd laid eyes on the boy, I'd known there could be only one person responsible. But now, the child's paternity had to be proven all over again. His legal rights had to be established beyond question, and his mother's reputation salvaged, or else they both would become social outcasts. Financial ones, too.

And the thought of it just tore me up. Here I'd exerted all my considerable social influence to get Hazel Marie accepted by my friends, my church, and the entire community, and it had paid off. She was now a valued member of my set, which, frankly, was the most envied set in town. And, if you could overlook her attachment to that devilish Mr. Pickens, the details of which I tried not to think about, she had since lived an exemplary life.

I couldn't help but wonder what Mr.

Pickens would think if he knew of Brother Vern's accusations. It doesn't matter what anybody says to the contrary, I knew that once an accusation is made concerning someone's morals, no matter how false or how thoroughly disproved, the taint of it never goes away. Would Mr. Pickens look with doubtful, rather than loving, eyes on Hazel Marie and her son after this?

Well, I thought, as I stabbed my fork into a helping of Lillian's cheese casserole, he'd have some nerve if he did. Mr. Pickens had been involved in more than a few less than savory associations himself, and if he got all self-righteous about false accusations toward Hazel Marie, and possible indiscretions in her youth, I certainly intended to remind him of his own not so youthful ones.

I started clearing the table while the others went outside to adjust the basketball goal over the garage door. Hazel Marie turned on the yard lights as she hurried out with a tape measure to make sure that the men attached the goal at the correct distance from the ground. Sam and Mr. Pickens, with a great deal of laughing and banging around, dragged a seldom used ladder out of the garage, while Little Lloyd drove me crazy, bouncing a ball on the paved driveway.

I shuddered to think of Sam up on a ladder, trying to manhandle that heavy goal, and I didn't want to watch his exertions. Nor Mr. Pickens's, either, who'd never shown the least indication of being handy around a house. It was a wonder to me that those two grown men insisted on doing work that neither of them was qualified to do.

Lillian began rinsing dishes and putting them into the dishwasher, glancing at me as I went back and forth from the dining room, bringing in plates and silverware. "Don't you want to see how they doin'?" she asked.

"No, I don't want to see either of them break his neck. Sam ought not to be climbing a ladder at his age."

Lillian craned her neck to look out the window. "Mr. Sam, he holdin' the ladder. It's that Mr. Pickens what's up it."

I didn't respond, busying myself with getting out dessert plates for Lillian's apple pie. I could feel her frowning looks aimed my way as I did it.

"What's the matter with you?" she finally asked. "Here, I been waitin' an' waitin' for you to make out yo' Christmas menu so I can be thinkin' 'bout all that cookin'. An' look like you always thinkin' 'bout something else. An' look like to me, you not actin' right."

I stopped and leaned on the counter. "Oh, Lillian, I can't think about Christmas menus right now. It's too early, and for all I know, we may not even have Christmas. There's something weighing on my mind, and I'm just heartsick about it. It could change everything."

She turned off the faucet and faced me. "Somethin' wrong with Mr. Sam?"

"No, oh, no. Sam's fine." I took my lip in my teeth, pondering the wisdom of unloading on her right then, even though Hazel Marie was still in the dark. I'd always unburdened myself to Lillian, and just because I now had a husband throwing a ball around in my driveway was no reason to stop confiding in her. "It's Brother Vern, Lillian. He's back and making trouble like we've never seen."

Her mouth dropped open. "You mean that preacher what stole our boy out from under us an' put him on the TV?"

"The very one. And it's beyond belief what he's come up with now. I am so distressed I don't know what to do."

She put her wet hands on her hips, and

demanded, "What he doin'?"

"He's saying . . ." But I had to stop, for the ballplayers were coming back inside, laughing and slamming doors and arguing over who had won a horse, of all things. The four of them came in looking flushed and excited and healthy. And wanting dessert, so I whispered, "I'll tell you later. But keep it to yourself for now."

She gave me one of her frowning looks, cutting her eyes at me from under her brows, then she nudged me out of the way and began to serve the pie.

At no time during the evening did I have a chance to get Hazel Marie alone, which was just as well for I didn't need a houseful of people when I disclosed a subject of such magnitude. As it turned out, she and Mr. Pickens decided to go off somewhere by themselves, leaving Little Lloyd with Sam and me.

After Lillian left and the boy went upstairs to his room, I climbed the stairs for the second time in two days.

Knocking on the jamb of Little Lloyd's open door, I said, "Am I disturbing you?"

He looked up from the book on his desk and smiled. "No'm, I'm just reading about Lewis and Clark. Did you know they took a dog with them? His name was Seaman

48

because he was such a good swimmer."

"Well, I declare. No, I didn't know that." I sat down in a chair next to his desk and tried not to stare too intently at his face. "I knew they took an Indian lady with them, but I never could pronounce her name."

"Sacajawea," he said, which sounded fine to me. Then he went into a long discourse about the expedition, where it started, where it ended, and how long it took, while I watched his facial expressions and hand motions, looking for traces of his heredity.

I was trying to reassure myself that Wesley Lloyd had left his mark. And, I'll tell you, it was a different way of looking at the child. For the few years he'd been in my care, I'd tried every way I knew *not* to see Wesley Lloyd in him. Every time he did or said something that reminded me of my faithless husband, I'd averted my eyes and closed my mind, determined to forestall seeing any inherited reminders. I'd looked for Hazel Marie in him, and deliberately denied what was as plain as the nose on his face.

Now I had to alter my thinking, and in order to protect the child, search for evidence of his resemblance to Wesley Lloyd Springer.

It really wasn't difficult, when viewed with unbiased eyes. There was the same wispy hair that, bless his little heart, would begin to recede in middle age, and the thin face with a fair complexion, spotted now with freckles, and the hazel eyes that were neither one color nor the other. And his short stature and slight frame — all spoke of familiar characteristics. It was only when the child smiled or laughed that his own sweet and benevolent nature shone through. At those times he exhibited nothing at all of Wesley Lloyd's rigid and arrogant spirit.

So, if it came down to offering proof, I'd have to make sure that Little Lloyd refrained from smiling, keeping at all times a belligerent frown on his face. That way, nobody would question who had fathered him.

"Did you want me for something, Miss Julia?" Little Lloyd asked, and I realized that he'd finished giving me a history lesson while I'd continued to peer at his facial features.

"Oh," I said, straightening up and averting my eyes from his little pinched face. "No, I just came up to see how you were doing, and to see if you need any help with your homework."

He ducked his head and smiled. "No'm, I don't need any help."

"Well, if you did, I was going to offer Sam."

Then we both laughed, for I'd tried in the past to do seventh-grade work, and failed miserably. They teach things differently than they did in my day.

I stood up and patted his shoulder. "Don't stay up too late. You need to be in bed soon."

Chapter 5

"Sam," I said, entering the living room where he was reading the paper. "All anybody has to do is look at that child, and there'll be no doubt as to who his father was. As much as I've tried to deny it, there's just too close a resemblance. I used to hope he'd outgrow it, but now I have to hope he won't."

Sam folded the paper and held out his hand to me. I gladly took it and sat beside him. "You know," he said in a warm, comforting tone, "I was afraid of stirring up all this turmoil for you, and for Hazel Marie, when I knew Puckett would have the devil of a time proving anything. I almost didn't tell you."

"Sam!" I jerked my hand away and almost hit the ceiling. "Don't you *ever* not tell me anything that affects me and mine. I declare, I can't believe you'd even contemplate such a thing."

"But I did tell you, didn't I? And together, we're going to handle it. Right?"

I sat on the edge of the sofa, my back as

stiff as a board. "Don't slide off the subject, Sam. I don't like the thought of it, I don't like it a little bit. The idea of you even thinking of shielding me, why, that's exactly what Brother Vern was doing by going to you." I switched around to glare at him. "And, I'll tell you this, his idea of marriage is different from mine, and you'd better make note of it."

Sam laughed, which he always did when I got on my high horse. "Come here, woman," he said, pulling me close. "I promise that I'll never keep anything from you. I haven't yet, and I won't in the future. But you have to let me do a little protecting every now and then. What else is a husband for?"

I rested my head on his shoulder and smiled. "Oh, I can think of a few things. But," I said, jabbing his chest with my finger, "the minute I think you're holding something back that I need to know, you are going to hear from me."

I don't know what time Hazel Marie came in during the night, but she was certainly slow and sleepy looking as she readied herself for church the next morning. Sam and Little Lloyd were up with the birds, as usual, and fixed their own breakfast. Then they walked across the street to the church on the corner to attend Sunday school. It was Sam's turn to teach the old men's class, and Little Lloyd was assigned the opening prayer for his middlers' class.

I rarely missed Sunday school, having been a member of the Lila Mae Harding class since before the woman died and had the class named for her. But on this morning, it was my plan to use the hour to sit down and talk with Hazel Marie. With the house quiet and empty, I figured it would be a good time to tell her how Brother Vern was about to disrupt our lives. Then we would go over to the church in time to attend the worship service. We could pray for strength and grace to weather the storm, as well as ask the Lord to bring down vengeance on the head of that meddling troublemaker.

Fully dressed and ready to go, I tapped on Hazel Marie's door. "Hazel Marie? You have a minute?"

She stuck her head around the door, looking bleary-eyed and only partially dressed. "I can't get a thing done this morning," she complained, pushing back her damp hair. "I don't know what's the matter with me. We've missed Sunday

54

school, haven't we?"

"Yes, but it's no great loss. Mildred Allen is teaching, and she won't do a thing but read from the lesson book. We can do that ourselves." I took a seat in my usual chair in her room and went on. "Can I help you get ready?"

"Oh, no'm, I'm just trying to get myself together." She rubbed her eyes and yawned. "I better brush my teeth." Then she went into the bathroom and turned on the water.

Plainly, this was not working. I waited for her to return, but she went into her newly constructed dressing room and began to slide clothes hangers around. "I can't ever decide what to wear this time of year," she called. "It's too warm for anything heavy, and too late for summer things."

"You need some transitional outfits," I called back. "Something that'll do for this in-between weather."

"Oh, good. I can go shopping." She gave a light laugh, but didn't reappear in the bedroom.

I waited while she put on a blouse and skirt, hoping that she'd exercise some speed so that I'd have time to bring up the matter that was weighing so heavily on me.

"Hazel Marie, as soon as you're ready, I need to talk to you." Maybe that would light a fire under her.

"Ma'am? Sorry, I didn't hear you."

"I said . . ." But by that time she was back in the bathroom, running the hair dryer, so I gave up. Raising my voice over the racket, I called, "I'll meet you downstairs."

We slid into the pew, taking our places between Sam and Little Lloyd just as Pastor Ledbetter entered the sanctuary behind the choir on their procession down the center aisle. Sam held the hymn book out for me, and I began mumbling the words. As we sat down, he raised his eyebrows and cocked his head toward Hazel Marie. I shook mine and whispered, "I couldn't tell her. She was too busy getting ready."

He leaned close and whispered back, "Just as well, because I'm having second thoughts about telling her at all."

I frowned at him, but it was neither the time nor the place to raise questions. Pastor Ledbetter had started the service, and I had to appear to pay attention.

The thought of our impending peril was enough to keep my mind far from the pastor's preaching, but gradually I began to notice something else going on in the congregation. I caught LuAnne Conover's eye from her place across the aisle, as she smiled at me in a curiously knowing way. Then when we stood for another hymn, Helen Stroud leaned from the pew in front of us and whispered, "We're all praying for you."

Then, bless Pat, if I didn't notice two other women nodding and smiling directly at me in what I took to be an encouraging way, and Margaret Easley, who was sitting behind us, patted my shoulder as one of the deacons started the collection plate down our row.

Something was going on, and all I could think of was that Brother Vern had started his tell-all campaign already. Lord, surely not this soon. Why, he'd not given us time to refute his claims, or do any tests, or threaten a lawsuit, or anything.

I bowed my head, hoping that they'd all assume I was in a state of prayer. I was, but I was also trying to hold myself together. All I wanted to do was get out of there and be safe in my own home, along with Hazel Marie and Little Lloyd, and Sam, of course, far from whispers and knowing glances. We just had to put the brakes on that meddling snake-oil preacher, and if it meant digging up Wesley Lloyd Springer, I was about ready for a shovel.

Before I married Sam, it had been my custom to bypass the bottleneck in the vestibule when the service was over and slip out the side door. I felt no need to shake the pastor's hand just to let him know I'd been in attendance or to tell him I'd enjoyed his sermon, when nine times out of ten, I hadn't. And on that subject, a sermon that had the fires of hell as its topic wasn't all that pleasant to contemplate in the first place, although any number of people will go out of their way to tell the pastor they'd gotten enjoyment from it.

But the days of evading the press at the main door were over, for I'd married a gregarious man who liked nothing better than to greet and socialize with everybody he met. So, we shuffled along with the crowd toward the pastor in his black robe who stood at the door, smiling as he accepted accolades for his performance. And, wouldn't you know, but just as we drew near, Adelaide Simpson, who'd crippled a dozen people in the line with her walker, held up everything to tell the pastor the latest on her pool-playing son who never visited her.

I wanted to pinch her and tell her to

make an appointment if she needed counseling, but my attention was diverted by Sarah Manning, who whispered, "We're all with you, Miss Julia."

Before I could respond, the crowd separated us, and I had no opportunity to ask her what they were with me *in*. But her comment shook me, because the only thing I was in was trouble with Brother Vernon Puckett, and nobody was supposed to know about that.

When finally we were able to approach Pastor Ledbetter, he reached past me to shake Sam's hand, in spite of the fact that mine was extended in plain sight. I withdrew my hand and moved on out the door.

"Oh, Miss Julia," the pastor said, just as I thought I was on my way. "I'd like to have a little chat with you. Would you be available this afternoon?"

It took me a moment to gather my wits, for every previous time that the pastor had wanted a little chat, it had been to correct and admonish me. And on this day I was in no mood to subject myself to such a session again.

I glanced at Sam, whose eyebrows were slightly raised, indicating that he was at a loss, too. "Sam and I will be home all afternoon," I said, trying to be hospitable.

"You can drop by any time that's convenient with you."

"If it's all the same to you," he said, meaning that it didn't much matter whether it was or not, "it would be better to discuss this in my office. About three o'clock? And, Sam, if you don't mind, this is something between Miss Julia and me." He smiled his ingratiating smile, and went on, "I'm sure she'll confide in you, and have the benefit of your advice and good sense."

I drew in my breath sharply, about to announce in no uncertain terms that I could count on my own personal good sense. But we were overtaken by the crush of people anxious to get home to their Sunday dinner, and out the door we went. I took Sam's arm as we started down the sidewalk, holding it tightly as I fumed over the pastor's words.

"Wonder what that's about?" Sam mused, guiding me around a root that had penetrated the sidewalk.

"There's only one thing he could possibly want to talk to me about, and that's Brother Vern and his fairy tale of Little Lloyd's ill-gotten gains." And with that thought, I stepped out right smartly, already preparing myself to do battle with another man who had done his level best once before to grab a share of the Springer estate. Even then Pastor Ledbetter had raised questions about Little Lloyd's paternity, asking how I could be sure that Hazel Marie wasn't playing me for a fool. And all because at some point, and for some unknown reason, Wesley Lloyd had hinted around to the pastor that he planned to make the church his primary beneficiary, with a lifetime trust for me. Which meant that I would've been a supplicant to Pastor Ledbetter and his faithful session for my livelihood.

The best thing Wesley Lloyd had done, although it hadn't seemed that way at the time, was scribbling out that last-minute last will and testament, leaving everything to the child he knew to be his own. He'd cut out both me and the church, but since the church wasn't his widow and I was, I got what was coming to me anyway. Namely, half.

And I intended to hold on to it, while keeping the other half safe for Little Lloyd and out of the hands of the likes of Brother Vernon Puckett and Pastor Larry Ledbetter.

Chapter 6

"I've a good mind not to go," I said, glancing at my watch as it neared three o'clock. Sam and I had been enjoying our day of rest, sharing the Sunday paper in the living room, while Hazel Marie and Little Lloyd were off somewhere with Mr. Pickens.

Sam grinned, looking at me over the paper that he read from one end to the other. "You defying the preacher now?"

"He needs defying. The idea, wanting to talk to me but not to you. I think I resent that."

"Now, Julia, you'd be even more up in arms if he insisted that I come along, when he really wanted to talk to you."

"Well, tell me this, what does he have to say that's so secretive that it can't be discussed right here? He just wants to have the trappings of authority that his office gives him. I know him. He's either going to try to correct me about something or talk me into doing something. And I am not going to direct the Christmas pageant this year, I don't care what he says."

Sam laughed. "Tell him you're too busy with me to take on anything else."

"Oh, you," I said, smoothing my hair in front of the Chippendale mirror over the butler's desk. "Well, tell me this, what am I going to say if he brings up Brother Vern?"

Sam lowered the paper again, letting it rest on his lap. "Don't discuss it with him. Just smile and tell him that I'm taking care of it. Plead ignorance, then get up and come home."

"I hope I can do that," I said, turning away from the mirror, having done all I could to make myself presentable. "But he always draws me into an argument, in spite of my good intentions. Oh, Sam, what if he already knows everything that Brother Vern is saying? What if he intends to accuse Hazel Marie of immoral activities? Or go after Little Lloyd's inheritance, like he did once before?"

"Julia," Sam said, reaching for my hand, "let's don't put the cart before the horse. I doubt Ledbetter knows anything about Brother Puckett. And if he does, you come get me."

"Well, all right," I said, taking a deep breath, "but you better not go off anywhere. I want you here where I can find you."

And with that, I took my pocketbook and started out for the church across the street.

Entering through the backdoor that the pastor had left unlocked for me, I walked down the short hall that led into the Fellowship Hall under the sanctuary. I tried to tiptoe along, fearful of breaking the unnatural quiet of the building.

I kept looking over and around my shoulder, slightly spooked by the heavy silence. In spite of the bright afternoon outside, the shadows in the dimly lit Fellowship Hall made me scurry along toward the pastor's office, my Naturalizer heels tapping on the tile floor.

"Pastor Ledbetter?" I called, not wanting to sneak up on him and scare him half to death.

As I rounded the corner that led to his office, I could see a light coming from Norma Cantrell's center of command. The only good thing about coming in on a Sunday afternoon was the fact that I wouldn't have to deal with the pastor's arrogant secretary.

I raised my hand to knock on the open door just as Pastor Ledbetter appeared there. "Miss Julia, come on in. I've been waiting for you."

"I'm right on time," I reminded him. "So you couldn't have been waiting long."

"No, no," he said, giving me a welcoming smile that was much too hearty for the little chat he'd promised me. "I didn't mean that at all. I came early to work on a sermon or two. Come in, have a seat." He waved his hand at one of the two damask-covered wing chairs in front of his desk.

I took a seat and rested my pocketbook on my lap. Looking around at the paneled walls, built-in bookcases, and plush carpeting that needed vacuuming every day of the week, I couldn't help but think again of what it all had cost. Take that paneling, for instance, it wasn't your inexpensive Home Depot laminated boards. It was the real thing, and better than what was in the homes of nine-tenths of his congregation.

I happened to have seen the budget expenditures for the refurbishing of this office to the pastor's specifications, and I'm here to tell you, the thought of it made my blood boil every time I was reminded of it.

Pastor Ledbetter surprised me by taking the other wing chair rather than going behind the desk to his executive chair. That new tactic put my guard up even more, as I figured he'd been reading some article on the new trends in pastoral counseling techniques.

"Now, Miss Julia," he said, steepling his fingers and bringing them toward his mouth. "There's a little matter that's recently come up, and I thought the best way to deal with it is for you and I to come to terms. Privately, that is, before it gets out of hand."

Well, right there, I felt a shiver sweep through my system. It sounded as if Brother Vern had gotten to him, and I could've put my head down and cried. Over and above that, his oh so genteel use of the term *for you and I* made my skin crawl.

"If anything's about to get out of hand, Pastor," I said tightly, though slightly untruthfully, "I don't know one thing about it."

"I'm sure that's true. At least, I've been assured that you're not in on it." He stopped tapping his fingers against his chin, and gazed directly at me. "But it has to do with you, and that's why you're the one to stop it before it gets too far along."

What in the world did he want me to do? I had no control over Brother Vernon Puckett, although if I had any, I wouldn't hesitate to use it. But if the pastor expected me to disown Hazel Marie and Little Lloyd before the gossip got going good, he was going to have to keep on expecting.

By this time, my back had gotten so stiff, I knew I'd have trouble getting out of the chair. Gazing right back at him, I said, "How am I going to stop what I don't know anything about? And if you think that I should talk to Hazel Marie, well, I'm going to do that already. And that's all I'm going to do. Sam'll take care of the rest."

He frowned. "What rest?"

"Why, you know. If it comes to providing legal advice, Sam'll take care of that."

He sprang from his chair, a look of sheer amazement on his face. "My goodness gracious alive, Miss Julia, we don't want it to go that far! There's no call for Christians to be suing each other. No, no. Why, it would fracture the church and damage our witness beyond repair." He began to pace the plush carpet, making a path of tracks all across it.

He came to a stop and looked off in the distance. "But maybe you should talk to Hazel Marie. She may be able to help, even though as far as I know she's not involved."

"Not involved! Why, Pastor, if she's not involved, I don't know who is."

"I expect they thought she was too close

to you to keep it a secret."

"Well, I admit she's not the best person to confide in if you want something kept quiet. She doesn't mean to tell, it just comes out before she knows it. But, Pastor, she has to be told sooner or later, since she'll suffer so much from it."

Pastor Ledbetter looked at me as if I'd been speaking in tongues, something he wouldn't tolerate in any shape or form. "She'll suffer? No more than any other member of the church, which is why all you have to do is say no, and stop this divisive movement in its tracks."

"Then we're in agreement, Pastor. And you can't possibly want to stop it any more than I do. But as far as it being divisive, what in the world does the church have to do with it? I mean, this only concerns me, Hazel Marie, and Little Lloyd, so I'll thank you to keep the church out of it."

I thought his eyes would pop out of his head. "How *can* the church stay out of it? It will change everything! In fact, nothing's been the same since that petition landed on my desk."

I sank back against the chair, finally realizing that the pastor and I were talking at cross purposes. And not for the first time, either.

Blowing out my breath, I asked with some relief, "What petition?"

He turned and walked back across the room, running his hand through his hair in agitation. He needed to stop that little habit, since his hair was becoming noticeably thinner.

Then he looked up and began to tell me what I already knew. "Miss Julia, you know what turmoil the Presbyterian Church, U.S. — what was once called the Southern Presbyterian Church, or the PCUS — has gone through ever since the Northern Presbyterians took us over. Now, in spite of my efforts to lead this congregation to higher ground, we're a part of the PCUSA."

"Lord, yes, and I never could keep them straight. I'm never sure which set of initials we belong to now."

He walked back to stand behind the chair he'd vacated and rested his hands on the back of it, trying, it seemed, to get himself under control. "And you'll remember that one of the biggest obstacles to the merger was our differences concerning the role of women in policy-making groups."

"Yes, I remember. You didn't think that women should be elders or deacons, because that meant they'd have to speak up in church, which Paul advised against, and because they were likely to disagree with the way men have run the church for, lo, these many years."

"Well," he said, stiffening and nodding sharply, "yes. But it's not just what *I* think. My stance is based upon the clear Scriptural teachings that a woman should not be permitted to usurp authority over a man. And, furthermore, we are told that a deacon should be the *husband* of one woman. It can't get any plainer than that. Deacons are supposed to be men."

I kept my peace, even though the issue was elders, not deacons.

He rubbed his hand over his face, then calmed himself down. "But you'll remember that a number of our southern churches pulled out of the merger and either formed another Presbyterian denomination or petitioned to join an established conservative denomination rather than permit women to have positions of authority."

"Yes, and I remember that you wanted to do the same, but you couldn't get the votes to let you do it."

He bowed his head in tacit agreement, but his hands tightened on the back of the chair. "True, I did want to lead our church out. But when the vote failed, I felt that we could remain in the merger and simply ignore the more egregious rulings of the General Assembly. I thought that this congregation would follow my leading, in spite of what was dictated, and keep women out of our session and diaconate. And it has, right up to this point. And that's where you come in."

Chapter 7

"Pastor," I said as strongly as I could, "if you're asking me to support another vote to split this church asunder, you'll have to look elsewhere, because I will not do it. If your conscience won't let you stay in whatever initialed denomination we're now in, then you should go, and go alone. But don't try to take all or any part of the congregation with you. We're happy where we are, and as long as the new General Assembly doesn't bother us, we won't bother it."

He bowed his head, but I couldn't tell if he was praying for strength or conceding defeat. But then he lifted his head, and I saw he was doing neither. "That's exactly the problem. The General Assembly *is* bothering us. They've opened the floodgates, and a few liberals with radical ideas have rushed in right here in our congregation. The only way I know to stop them is to ask you, no, beg you, to refuse to run."

"I don't know what you're talking about."

"I'm not putting this very well, am I?"

Frankly, he wasn't. In fact, I'd never seen the pastor quite so distraught. I could've felt for him, if he hadn't long ago exhausted all my compassion.

"Try again," I said, "and tell me how in the world I'm involved with the antics of the General Assembly."

"Look at this." He strode behind his desk and took several pages from a folder. Waving them in the air, he said, "This is a petition, signed by practically every woman in the congregation."

"*I* didn't sign it. I don't know anything about it."

"I know you didn't," he said, shaking the papers. "Don't you think I haven't studied every signature on the thing? And that's another problem, which makes it illegitimate in the first place."

With that word, I stiffened again. I was not going to listen to any aspersions cast against Little Lloyd. But before I could open my mouth, he was ranting on.

"Before any name can be put on the ballot, that person has to acknowledge his willingness to run and to serve if elected. And since they didn't get your permission beforehand, I'm within my rights to just ignore it." He slapped the papers down and ran his hand through his hair again.

"Except I can't. There're too many names, too many people supporting you. The only thing to do is to plead for your understanding of what this will do to the church, and ask you to refuse."

"I still don't know what I'd be refusing."

"The session, Miss Julia!" His voice caught in his throat, as he almost strangled over the words. "They want your name on the ballot when we elect elders next month."

"Well, my word." I collapsed against the back of the chair, stunned almost as much as he was. "I've never thought about . . ."

"I know you haven't," he said, as a conciliatory tone crept into his voice. "I know this isn't your doing, for you are as traditional as the day is long. There's no way that you would want to be the first to break with tradition and create strife in the church. We've always had men on the session, and I just can't see you leading a new wave of modernism."

"Nor can I," I mused, half to myself.

Relief flooded across his face. "Good! So we can just tell these ladies that you aren't willing to run, and be done with it."

I held up my hand. "Not so fast, Pastor. I'd like to know who all has nominated me."

"Oh, I don't think that would be wise. Suffice it to say that there are enough signatures to make you a strong candidate. But I think it best to just file this away, since you're refusing the nomination."

"I didn't say that."

His face fell. "You didn't?"

"I don't think so. I need to study on this a while. It comes as a shock, you know."

"I think," he began, then cleared his throat and tried again. "I think you should talk it over with Sam. And pray about it long and hard. You may not realize what a hornet's nest a woman elder would stir up."

Oh, I thought I did, especially in the session itself. And I couldn't help but smile at the thought. On the other hand, to accept the honor simply to show our arrogant preacher and the smug old men on the session a thing or two was hardly sufficient reason to take on such a heavy responsibility — and it a spiritual one, at that.

So I turned it over in my mind for a few minutes, gradually realizing that I was more interested in the political aspects of the nomination than the spiritual ones. "How many supporters do I have?" I pointed to the pages on his desk.

"A fair number," he reluctantly admitted. "But of course, when it comes down to it, not all of them will vote for you. They may change their minds."

I kept thinking. "All of them women?"

He tightened his mouth. "Most of them."

"Uh-huh." So some men had signed the petition, too. Interesting. "I tell you what, Pastor, I need to think about it. As you've told us many times from the pulpit, becoming an elder is a high honor, one that requires a strong spiritual foundation, great integrity, and the Lord's leading. I didn't ask for this, never even considered it, but here it is anyway. I feel a little like Moses, who was minding his own business and taking care of his sheep when a bush flared up in front of him. So I need to be sure what the Lord wants me to do."

I thought he would choke then. "The Scriptures are clear!"

"Yes, I know. But I'm neither the husband of one wife nor of many wives. But then, I haven't been nominated for the diaconate anyway, have I?"

If he wanted to stand on a literal reading of the Bible, I was more than willing to take him on.

I was so full of the news that I practically ran across the street. Throwing the door open, I rushed into the house, slinging my pocketbook aside as I went.

"Sam," I called as I rushed by, "where's the church directory?"

Not waiting for an answer, which would've been slow in coming since I'd disturbed his Sunday nap, I dashed through the dining room and into the kitchen. Pulling out the drawer under the telephone, I snatched up the directory and headed toward the living room again.

Sam met me, but I veered around him and took a seat on the sofa. "You'll never guess what the pastor wanted," I said, as I opened the directory. "Come help me, Sam. Oh, I need a pen."

"There's one right beside you." He pointed to the lamp table. "I was doing the crossword puzzle until I nodded off."

"Come sit down," I said, patting the sofa. "We need to get some campaign statistics."

Sam smiled, somewhat bemusedly, and took a seat. "What campaign are we talking about?"

I had to laugh, so delighted to have the upper hand over the pastor. I know that doesn't speak very highly of my spiritual state, but Larry Ledbetter had made me squirm so many times in the past that I couldn't help but take a little pleasure in the changing tides.

"Oh, Sam, the pastor is beside himself because — hold on to your hat — I've been nominated for the session. Can you believe that?"

"Sure I can. And you'd be good at it, too. You'll do it, won't you?"

I opened my mouth to answer, but was brought up short as I recalled my determination to follow his lead as the head of the household. "What do you think I should do?"

"Why, Julia, whatever you want. That's a decision you'll have to make. How do you feel about it?"

I brushed that aside with a wave of my hand. "I don't know yet. I told him I'd think about it, which certainly didn't reassure him. But, look, Sam, I want to count how many women there are on the church roll. He showed me several pages of a petition, but he wouldn't let me look at it. Just said it was mostly signed by women."

"So you want to see how many members are women?" Sam was always quick to understand my methods.

"Yes. I want to know what percentage of the total membership is made up of women. Of course," I said, with a sideways look at him, "he did admit there were a few men who'd signed it, too. Did you know anything about it?"

"Nope. But I would've signed it, if I had."

Well, of course one would hope that one's husband would be supportive, although I knew from experience that one's husband couldn't always be counted on. I patted his hand, grateful for his trust in me as a spiritual leader.

With Sam's help I went through the directory, counting the number of women and men who were church members, and eligible, therefore, to vote in the upcoming election.

When we finished, I looked at him with a merry glint in my eye. "No wonder the pastor is pulling his hair out. Women outnumber men by almost two to one. If they all vote for me, why, I'd be an elder without needing a recount."

Then, as the threat posed by Vernon Puckett rushed to the forefront, I closed my eyes and sighed. "Oh, Sam," I said, leaning my head back as the directory slid off my lap, "I can't let myself get all exercised over this. I already have my hands full with Brother Vern. Besides, why in the world would I want to give up an evening or two every month to sit around arguing with a bunch of old men?"

"Especially when you could sit around here arguing with one old man?"

I opened one eye and smiled at him. "And we don't have to put up with the pastor like the session does." I sat up straight then with another heavy sigh. "This elder business has come up at the most inopportune time. Ordinarily, I wouldn't at all mind becoming a thorn in the pastor's side. But I don't see how I can, what with all the upset and turmoil Brother Vern's bringing down on us."

"Don't completely discount it, Julia," Sam said. "Give it some serious thought before you turn it down. Apparently a lot of people want you on the session, which means they think you'll give them a voice in what goes on."

"Oh, they'd have a voice, all right, if I did it. But not everybody in the church would like hearing it. Well," I said, rising, "I don't have to make a decision today. And, who knows, you might fix Brother Vern's little red wagon in the next day or two, and I'll be ready to take on something else."

I began to gather the newspapers together, stacking them for the recycling bin. "Tell me the truth, Sam," I said, stopping with a pile in my arms. "You do think you can put that matter to rest, don't you?"

"It depends, Julia," he said, getting up to stand beside me.

"Oh, don't say that! I don't want to hear it if you're having doubts."

"All I'm saying is, we don't know what Puckett has up his sleeve. Until we know that, I can't promise it'll all be behind us in a few days." Sam took the papers from me. "Here, let me do that. Have you said anything to Hazel Marie?"

"I can't get her alone long enough to tell her anything. But in the morning I'm going to do it if I have to tie her down. She has to be prepared for the rumors and gossip that could undo everything I've done for her."

"Well, don't say too much," Sam said, turning me toward the kitchen. "But do tell her I'm keeping an eye on him."

"I will, and I know that'll give her comfort. I declare, Sam, I get so indignant when I think of how some people just live for the latest gossip. You'd think they had better things to do."

Sam pushed open the kitchen door. "Let's not start worrying before we have to. And to get your mind off of it, I'm going to fix you my special Sunday evening omelet."

Well, who was I to refuse such an offer? Having never before seen a man busy himself in a kitchen, my mood was considerably lightened. Even so, I was still stewing over the thought of the avid gossipers who would lick their lips at anything new and sensational they heard about Hazel Marie. Or me.

Gossip has been the bane of my existence, and I just had no use for those who indulged in it.

As Sam beat a number of eggs in a bowl, I began to set the table. Then, remembering the news that Hazel Marie had told me, I said, "Oh, Sam, I forgot to tell you. Guess what Hazel Marie said she heard about Dub and Clara Denham."

Chapter 8

"Hazel Marie," I said, looking up at her as she started down the stairs the next morning. I was determined to waylay her, so I'd been waiting in the hall for her to put in an appearance. "You've been so busy lately that it looks like I have to make an appointment just to talk with you. As soon as Little Lloyd is off to school, I want us to sit down so I can get something off my mind."

"We're both busy this morning, Miss Julia," she said, "so maybe you better tell me now."

At my questioning look, she smiled and said, "We have circle meeting this morning over at Marlene Easton's. Did you forget?"

"Oh, my goodness," I said, running my hand over my forehead, done in by my forgetfulness. "Yes, I'd forgotten. Hazel Marie, I tell you, my plate is so full right now that it's a wonder I remember my own name." Then, looking up at her, I went on. "Let's not go. I really need to discuss something with you."

"Oh, Miss Julia, I'd skip it if I could. But

I'm supposed to give a report on the child we've been assigned at the children's home. They sent a list of what the little girl needs for Christmas, and I have to pass it around so our members can sign up for what they want to get her." She began heading for the kitchen, where Sam and Little Lloyd were finishing their breakfast. "And Helen says I have to lead a prayer, too. And every time I have to pray or speak in front of people, I get so nervous I can't think about anything else. But this afternoon, let's sit down and have a long talk, okay?"

I mentally threw up my hands. If it wasn't Mr. Pickens or a gambling game, it was the church that was filling her days, and, since I'd been the one who'd opened doors for her, I had nobody to blame but myself that she had so little time for me.

As soon as Marlene greeted us, and we'd stepped into her spacious and modern living room, I suffered my usual spell of vertigo. I declare, when you build a house on the side of a mountain, you should be careful of having floor-to-ceiling windows. I always felt I'd slide right off the floor and go tumbling down the mountainside, but I guess if you reside in one of those cantilevered houses, you eventually get used to living on the edge.

Some dozen or so women were milling around in Marlene's living and dining rooms, talking together and partaking of coffee cake, toasted pecans, and coffee. Hazel Marie and I put our pocketbooks by chairs in the circle that Marlene had set up in the sparsely furnished living room, and joined the group around the table. I was immediately greeted by my campaign supporters, eager to talk now that they'd turned in their petition to the pastor.

"You're going to do it, aren't you?" Leona Miller asked, her coffee cup teetering on a dessert plate.

"We're all for you," Miriam Hargrove said, putting a hand on my arm. "As far as I'm concerned, it's past time for a woman to be on the session."

"Three cheers for our candidate!" Mildred Allen moved close to me as I tried to get to the table, almost mashing me into Hazel Marie. Mildred was a heavyset woman with thyroid problems who could never judge the amount of space she required.

As others came up, congratulating and encouraging me, I tried to remain noncommittal, telling them that the surprise nomination deserved serious thought that I'd not yet had time to give it.

"But you'll be so good," Helen Stroud said. "We really want you to run."

Emma Sue Ledbetter, the pastor's wife, had absolutely nothing to say. She tried, though, but her eyes welled up in her typical response to anything that distressed her. And anything that distressed the pastor played havoc with her, too.

LuAnne Conover peeked around the centerpiece on the table and smiled at me, but she was noticeably silent on the subject of my run for the session. LuAnne had been my friend for ages, but that didn't mean she'd cross the pastor for my sake. I wished I'd gotten a look at the names on that petition.

Hazel Marie latched on to Kathleen Williams, asking her what was going on that she didn't know anything about. I saw her smile get wider as Kathleen filled her in on the crisis that was about to hit the church with a woman's name on the ballot.

Tonya Allen, Mildred's daughter who was once her son, and as level-headed as they come, came by as I filled my plate. "I don't know who started this, Miss Julia, but we all realized that we need a woman on the session. And you were the unanimous choice, because we know you always speak your mind."

"Yes, well, I've never been accused of reticence." I smiled at her, thinking to myself that Tonya would be better on the session than any of us. She could see both sides, don't you know. But Pastor Ledbetter would have to be physically restrained if anybody nominated her.

Helen, who was either the chairman or the president of most every group I belonged to, called the meeting to order, so we took our seats and balanced coffee cups and napkins on our knees. She thanked Marlene for having us, dealt with a few routine matters consisting of reminders and announcements, then called on Hazel Marie for her report. I was the only one, since I was sitting next to her, who knew how nervous Hazel Marie was as she passed around the list of Christmas gifts for our chosen orphan.

"If you'll bring your gift to our December meeting, all wrapped and everything, with her name on it, I'll take them to the church," she said. "Then somebody will take them over to the children's home a week or so before Christmas."

"What if we want to get something that's not on this list?" Miriam Hargrove always had to be different.

"That's all right," Hazel Marie said.

"But let's be sure and get these things first. You'll notice that it's mostly things the little girl needs, like sweaters and socks and gloves, but I think it'd be nice if we got her something to play with, too.

"Now," Hazel Marie went on, her voice faltering with nervousness, "let's bow our heads in prayer."

I did, but cut my eyes up at her as she opened a sheet of paper where she'd written out her prayer beforehand. Some people do that, you know, which is perfectly acceptable, but most Presbyterians think it shows a higher state of grace if you wing it. But Hazel Marie's prayer was stunning in its beauty and eloquence. And its brevity. I was so proud of her that I patted her arm in commendation after she said amen and sat down.

As Helen went on with her agenda, Hazel Marie sat back, visibly relieved to have her duty over and done with. Soon, Helen turned the meeting over to our Bible leader, who of course was Emma Sue. Unfortunately for her, but eye opening for me, the lesson was on Lydia, the seller of purple in the city of Thyatira. Wherever that was. Apparently, Lydia opened her heart to the Lord and her home to Paul and Luke, and brought her whole household into the community of faith, which seemed to me to indicate that women could be spiritual leaders as well as men. But, not surprisingly, Emma Sue didn't see it that way. According to her, the account of Lydia was a lesson to us of women's role as providers of hospitality.

"We should be ready, day or night," Emma Sue said, "to open our homes to all those who preach the Gospel. That's why I keep my pantry and freezer filled and fresh sheets on the guest room bed."

Well, they Lord, I sighed to myself, if I'd wanted housekeeping tips, I'd have stayed home and watched Martha Stewart.

Finally, though, the circle meeting was over, and we all stood to gather purses and slip into light coats against the nippy December weather. Emma Sue pushed through the crowd around us and grabbed Hazel Marie's arm.

"Hazel Marie," she said, her eyes brimming with tears. "Thank you so much for that beautiful prayer. It was so moving, and it expressed exactly what was in my heart."

I beamed in pride, but Emma Sue had to spoil it by going on. "Your deep spirituality came through, and I want to ask you to forgive me for not realizing what a lovely

Christian you've become."

Hazel Marie's face turned red at the rush of compliments on her praying skills, and she mumbled her thanks to Emma Sue. Then, pulling away, she said she'd meet me outside.

As I thanked our hostess and walked out toward Hazel Marie, LuAnne Conover accosted me on the front walk.

"Julia, wait up," she said, puffing a little as she hurried toward us. "Hazel Marie, you gave an inspiring report about our orphan, and I'm going to get her two gifts. Now, why don't you run on and heat up the car for Julia while I talk to her a minute?"

Hazel Marie lifted her eyebrows in response to this dismissal, but she smiled and walked on. LuAnne was not the most tactful person in the world, but we were fairly used to her bossy ways.

"What is it, LuAnne?" I asked, pulling my coat close against a sudden gust of wind. "It's too cold to stand out here long."

"Well, I just wanted to tell you, now that you've seen the petition, that you might not be able to go by it." She pulled me aside as some of the other circle members edged past us on their way to the cars

90

they'd parked in Marlene's drive. We smiled and waved and responded to farewells. LuAnne waited for them to get out of earshot, while I wondered whether or not to admit I'd not seen the signatures on the petition.

"Now, Julia," she said, leaning in close, "I know you know that I signed the thing, but I have to tell you that I'm not going to vote for you. I think you deserve to know that before you make your decision."

"Well, why in the world did you sign it?"

"Because I was put on the spot and because everybody else was signing it, and I didn't want to be left out. But here's the thing, Julia, I am your friend, your best friend, and I don't want you to get the wrong idea just because my name's on a petition."

"So you're my friend, but you won't support me, is that right?" I was well acquainted with LuAnne's ability to come up with some convoluted thinking, but this was stretching friendship to the breaking point. "May I ask why not?"

"Because I don't believe in women elders," she said, nodding her head firmly.

"You mean you don't believe women elders exist? Because I know any number of churches that have them, and I can introduce you to a few to prove it."

"I *know* they exist, Julia," she said, with the patronizing air of one speaking to a nitwit. "But that doesn't mean I believe they ought to. They cause nothing but trouble, and you know it. Why, all you have to do is sit on any committee of women, and all they do is fuss and get mad and talk about each other."

"My goodness, LuAnne, you're talking like women are a separate species, calling them *they.* It's we, I mean us, that you're talking about."

"No, I'm not. I'm talking about women who step outside themselves and try to run things. That's a different class altogether, and one we're told not to be a part of. So, you'd do well to consider carefully all the ramifications before you decide to run." She frowned and lowered her voice even more. "I'm sure I'm not the only one who feels this way."

"No, there's Pastor Ledbetter and Emma Sue who would agree with you. And I'm sure I don't know how many others. But, LuAnne, I'll tell you this, if I decide to run — and that's a *big* if — I would expect everyone who signed that petition to vote for me, and that means you, too."

"Julia, I just told you . . ."

"I don't care what you just told me. I expect you to stand by your promise, and your signature on that petition is the promise of a vote. You can't say one thing and do another, LuAnne, it doesn't work that way."

She drew herself up and sniffed. "Well, I'm just telling you the way it is. And you know me, Julia, I am honest to the core and I stand on my convictions. I would think you'd want to know how I really feel. And think of this: Nobody knows how anybody else votes, so for all you know, I may vote for you, and I may not. Besides, I know that underneath it all you don't really want to be an elder, do you?"

"If I decide to run, LuAnne, I would expect to win. And if I have to do it without you, then I will. Now, Hazel Marie's waiting, so I have to go. Thank you for sharing this with me." And I took myself off, leaving her feeling self-righteously honest, if a trifle told off by her best friend.

Chapter 9

Hazel Marie chattered all the way home, beside herself with excitement over my possible run for the session. I mostly sat and listened, holding on to the armrest, as I usually did when she drove. Now that I had her alone in the car, I couldn't bring myself to tell her about Uncle Vern. Hazel Marie lived in the present more than anybody I'd ever known. She viewed the world with eager expectancy, which was a marvel to me, since the world had not treated her all that well. Until I came into her life, that is. Or rather, until she came into mine, and I kept her in it.

I hated that she had to be told that something was threatening not only her well-being, but Little Lloyd's, too. And that kept my tongue still and my mouth closed. That, and being too close to home to get it all said and dealt with.

"I know the pastor won't like it," Hazel Marie said, glancing at me, then quickly back at the street. "But that's never stopped you before. I think it's just what the church needs. We could use a little shaking up. Why, Miss Julia, you'll be representing half the congregation."

"More than half, Hazel Marie."

"That's what I mean. Anyway, I'd love to be a fly on the wall at the session meetings when you're there. I bet those old men won't know what to do with you." She laughed with delight.

"I haven't said I'd do it."

"Oh, but I think you should. It's perfectly all right now, and you know our church is way behind the times. A lot of churches have had women elders for ever so long, and nobody thinks anything about them now."

"I know, Hazel Marie, change has been in the air for years, but the Bible hasn't changed. And, you have to admit, that Paul was pretty specific about who should be deacons and elders and bishops, and it certainly wasn't women."

"Well, but in those days women didn't go to school or get out in the world. It's different now, and I think if Paul was living now, he'd be singing a different tune."

She turned into our driveway, came to a stop, and put the car into park. "Anyway," she went on, "whatever I can do to help, just let me know."

I opened the car door, but didn't make a move to get out. "Hazel Marie, don't get too worked up over this, because I'm inclined not to do it. For one thing, I have a lot on my mind right now and don't have time to fiddle with it. And for another, I'm not convinced that we should go against the Bible, even if parts of it do seem out-of-date and a little on the unrealistic side. I mean, if we all did what it says, then every last one of us would sell everything we own and take off for the mission field. And if that happened, who'd be here working so they could contribute to the mission fund for our support? So, I know we have to take a few things with a grain of salt." I started to climb out, but turned back to her. "My problem is, I don't know where to salt and where not to."

As we walked into the house, I felt more and more apprehensive about telling Hazel Marie what I had to tell her. I didn't know how she'd take it, and I wanted to have plenty of time and space for her to get it out of her system if she blew her top. As she might well do. I knew I would in her place.

"Don't forget, Hazel Marie," I said reluctantly, as we entered the house. "I want to talk with you right after lunch. I'll come up to your room where we won't be interrupted."

"I'm looking forward to it. We can discuss how to get the word out for your campaign, and I want us to decide about Christmas, too. You know, kinda go over who's going to get what for who. It's only a few weeks away, and I'm already getting excited."

I didn't say anything, just nodded. But it seemed to me that we ought to get closer to Christmas before we started worrying about gifts. Of course, nobody else did, for Christmas decorations had been up in the stores since Halloween. And about the same time, those Budweiser horse commercials had started airing, making Hazel Marie teary-eyed one minute and ready for shopping the next.

As it was nearing lunchtime, Hazel Marie and I went to the kitchen, where we were both brought up short. Little Lloyd was sitting at the table, all hunched over, nibbling on a piece of dry toast.

"Lloyd!" Hazel Marie cried, running over to him. "What's wrong? Why aren't you in school?"

"I'm sick, Mama." And he did look peaked, all white and washed-out looking.

Lillian walked over to the table. "That

school called while y'all was at yo' circle meetin', an' I went an' picked him up. The teacher say he th'owed up in the class."

Little Lloyd nodded his head. "Right in the middle of social studies."

"Has he got a fever?" I put my hand on his forehead, which felt warm, but as my hand was cold, I couldn't be sure. "This child ought to be in bed."

"Yessum," Lillian said. "I was 'bout to take him upstairs, but he say he so empty I thought he need something on his stomick."

"Come on, honey," Hazel Marie said, helping him up from the chair. "Let's get you to bed. Miss Julia, do you think I ought to call the doctor?"

"No, Mama," the boy said before I could answer. "I don't need the doctor. I feel better now, and besides, I wasn't the only one to get sick. Barry Peterson threw up, too, and Saralynn Hargrove thought she would, but she didn't. And her daddy's the doctor, and she didn't call him."

"Why don't you wait a little while, Hazel Marie," I said. "Put him to bed and take his temperature, and let's see if this toast stays down. He needs some fluids, too. It sounds like something's going around at school, and it may just be a twenty-four-hour bug."

"Come on, sweetie," Hazel Marie said, her arm around the boy's shoulders as she walked him out of the kitchen. "I'll tuck you in and sit with you. Maybe you can sleep a little while."

"Yessum," he said, sounding weak and pitiful as they left the kitchen.

Well, there went my serious conversation with Hazel Marie. But first things first, and the state of Little Lloyd's alimentary system certainly came first.

I don't know how the child got any rest, for if I wasn't going in to check on him, Lillian was bringing up trays of soup and whatever else she thought he needed. And Hazel Marie sat by his bed all afternoon, dozing in a chair when he napped.

An hour or so before dinner, I tiptoed up the stairs again to see how he was doing. As soon as I looked in, Hazel Marie came out into the hall, pulling the door closed behind her.

"He's asleep," she whispered. "I think he's a little better now. But he still has a fever, and he hasn't eaten anything. I forgot to tell you, Miss Julia, but I was supposed to go over to Tina Doland's house tonight. I called her and told her I couldn't come, but Tina said she really wants me to be there. She has something special planned."

I pursed my mouth, thinking of Tina Doland, who was an active member of First Baptist, and was forever coming up with something for other people to do. "Go, if you want to. I'll watch Little Lloyd. Just remember that she probably wants to rope you into something that her church is pushing."

"I know." Hazel Marie nodded. "But she's asked a lot of people we know, and she said to tell you that you're invited, too. I didn't think you'd want to go, though."

"No, I don't. But, Hazel Marie, I thought you were making time for us to have a talk."

"Well, I thought so, too, but you know how Tina is. She just said that if I couldn't leave Lloyd, they'd bring the party here. I didn't know how to get out of it, so do you mind? She'll bring the snacks and every-thing, and we don't have to do a thing but get Sam out of the house, because men aren't invited." Hazel Marie gave me a worried look, then went on. "You might enjoy it, Miss Julia. If you're in the right frame of mind."

"What kind of frame of mind?"

Hazel Marie squinched up her face while her eyes moved in every direction but mine. "Uh, well, it's kind of a new kind of get-together. Like, well, a Tupperware party. You've been to those, haven't you?"

"Once," I said. "Which was enough. Frankly, I've never thought it appropriate to invite people to your home and expect them to buy something so you'll get something free."

"Oh, we won't get anything free. Tina might, because she's the official hostess, but we won't. I'm sorry, Miss Julia. I should've asked you first, but I think I'm stuck now. I just didn't know what to tell her."

"This is your home, too, and you don't need to ask me about every little thing. Besides, I know Tina can be a steamroller when she wants to be. But I'm going to excuse myself and let you handle it. I'll sit up here with Little Lloyd, and you can enjoy the party." I started to turn away, disappointed that my talk with her was being deferred yet again.

At least Little Lloyd was on the mend, so that was one less thing to worry about.

I reached the head of the stairs and stopped. "Hazel Marie, I know you'll feel obligated to buy something tonight, but you ought to check with Lillian first. She may not want any more plastic bowls."

"Oh, it's not that kind of party. I just

used that as an example."

"In that case, I might slip down and join you for a while. What kind of party is it?"

Hazel Marie's eyes darted around. "Um, well, they call it, well, it's called a passion party." She took in a deep breath, and gave me an earnest look. "But it'll be in real good taste."

"A *Passion* party?" I frowned, wondering what Mel Gibson and his cohorts had dreamed up now. "Why, Hazel Marie, we've barely gotten past Thanksgiving, and Tina's celebrating Easter? That's the most sacred time of the year, and I just don't think we ought to commercialize that."

Hazel Marie stared at me for a minute, then she doubled over, laughing. Glancing behind to see if she'd wakened Little Lloyd, she held herself in check and walked over to me, her eyes dancing with mischief.

Leaning close, she whispered, "It's not that kind of passion, Miss Julia. It's the *other* kind."

"I don't know what you're talking about."

"Oh, you do, too," she said, giving me a light tap on the arm. "And if you don't, I'm going to get J.D. to explain a few things to Sam."

Chapter 10

I dismissed Hazel Marie's indelicate remark, knowing how she enjoyed teasing me. She was getting as bad as Mr. Pickens, who lived to shock and embarrass me. Nonetheless, I felt it incumbent upon me to be in attendance at the party. Especially since Tina Doland had commandeered my living room to push her wares, whatever they were.

To tell the truth, Tina had never been one of my favorite people. At one time she had run with a fast and loose crowd, and her reputation had suffered for it. Her husband, Tommy Doland, worked for a large construction company of some kind, and he was forever winning trips to Las Vegas and Atlantic City, which just goes to show. Somewhere along the line, though, both of them had reverted to their earlier religious upbringing, and they'd done it with a vengeance.

Now, you wouldn't find a more active couple in any church in town. Whatever program or committee or slogan or activity

Dr. James Dobson or their Baptist preacher came up with, Tommy and Tina were right there in the forefront. I didn't especially like to be around them, if you want to know the truth, especially Tina, since I was on her call list for all her requests for donations. And I wasn't even a member of her church.

Besides, when you're proclaiming the benefits of a simple and godly family life, your mouth shouldn't be caked with lip liner, lipstick, and lip gloss. And if you're forever witnessing to the joys of submission to your husband, you shouldn't be wearing dresses too short and your pants too tight. Of course, Hazel Marie wore hers that way, but that was different. Hazel Marie didn't flaunt herself before other people's husbands the way Tina did.

Anyway, the word was out that whatever had changed Tina, it hadn't completely taken hold. But who am I to question anyone's spiritual condition? Maybe she'd had another conversion experience. Baptists are known for that, you know. And if that was true, I would give her the benefit of the doubt. I'd keep my opinions to myself until she proved otherwise. I don't believe in talking about people, anyway.

Still, I was more than a little uneasy

about the approaching party. I didn't like the high-handed way it had been moved to my house just to accommodate Hazel Marie, who was known to have plenty of spending money. That was enough to put me off, right there.

I just wished I knew what Tina would be selling. Anything called a passion party conjured up any number of possibilities, Hazel Marie's intimations notwithstanding, because that was too far-fetched for me to believe. Maybe Tina planned to introduce some new weight program that featured passion fruit as a calorie eater. Or maybe she was into physical fitness and had warm-up suits for sale. People who exercise a lot can be quite passionate about it, I understand. Then again, it could be a course on how to have a passion for winning souls, and she'd have study guides and books for sale.

That's probably what it was, since Pastor Ledbetter occasionally whipped up a sermon exhorting us to put some passion in our spiritual lives.

On the other hand, it was hard to tell what Tina had in mind, for our local Baptists could work up a missionizing fervor for just about anything. It always brought me up short to see something like *Workout with*

Jesus on a marquee in front of a church, because I just couldn't wrap my mind around a picture of him on a treadmill.

We hurriedly finished dinner before the party guests arrived, and Sam good-naturedly took himself off for the evening. I didn't think it was a good sign that men wouldn't be welcome, but then they generally weren't at an afternoon tea, either.

Little Lloyd was able to come to the table in his bathrobe, but he didn't have much of an appetite. Hazel Marie prepared a tray of iced ginger ale and soda crackers to put beside his bed, in case he felt like eating later on. As she ran to answer the first ring of the doorbell, I straightened his bed and propped up his pillows.

"We'll be right downstairs, Little Lloyd," I told him. "Just sing out if you need anything."

"I'm feeling a lot better," he said, pushing back his glasses with one hand and reaching for a book with the other. "But I slept so much today, I probably won't close my eyes all night long."

"Oh, I expect you will." I moved the lamp a little closer. "Don't read too long, now. You need to rest your eyes, especially while you're feeling poorly. Do you have enough blankets on your bed? I don't want you to get chilled. Next thing you know, you'd be down with pneumonia or something."

"Yessum, I'm warm enough." He closed his book with a finger left to hold his place. "You don't need to worry about me. I'm a whole lot better, and I'll probably go to school tomorrow."

"Well, we'll see. Call me now, if you start feeling bad again."

I walked to the door, then looked back at him sitting up in bed with the lamplight making a halo of his wispy hair. We smiled at each other, and I pulled the door closed behind me.

By the time I got downstairs, Hazel Marie had welcomed six or seven women and was opening the door for more. I knew most of them, and knew of the rest. Helen Stroud was there and Mildred Allen, but not Tonya, which I thought unusual since she generally accompanied her mother wherever she went. LuAnne greeted me with a flurry of hands and excited giggles.

"Julia!" she said. "I couldn't believe it when Tina called to change the party from her house to yours. Marriage has done wonders for you, because I didn't think you'd ever be a party to a party like this."

So LuAnne knew more about the merchandise than I did, which didn't allay my concerns as to its suitability in a mixed company of Baptists, Presbyterians, Episcopalians, Methodists, and a few Catholics, as this group was shaping up to be. It was just not done to proselytize from one church to another, and I hoped Tina would keep her enthusiasm under control and not offend anybody.

Moving through the crowd of women, I noticed that most of them seemed somewhat subdued, even shamefaced, with averted eyes and less than warm greetings to each other. Hazel Marie made an effort to introduce everybody, but she didn't know half of them. I think they were mostly independents of one kind or another.

Tina took her place in front of a card table and opened up a large black case on the table. As she organized her notes, I smiled at Miriam Hargrove and Kathleen Williams, who had just come in. They gave me a quick nod and took seats in the back of the room. It struck me that everybody had been remarkably closemouthed about this party at the circle meeting that morning. And with that thought, I realized that Emma Sue Ledbetter wasn't with us, though that didn't exactly surprise me. She wasn't very ecumenical in her thinking.

"Ladies," Tina said, bringing to a close the murmur of voices among those present. "Ladies, tonight I am going to introduce you to some products that will literally change your lives. But before I show them to you, let me remind you that we are blessed to live in a time of greater freedom for women, but don't get me wrong, I'm not advocating women's lib. I'm just saying that there's no reason in the world that women, whether married or not, shouldn't experience the full pleasure and richness of all our God-given senses."

Well, I couldn't argue with that.

"Now, don't worry." Tina said. "I'm not going to give you my personal testimony, but I am going to say that when I came to know the Lord, I realized that I had a real problem. What is a woman supposed to do? How is she supposed to act? What is free and open to her, and what is not? It all boiled down to one basic question: Is it permitted, or even possible, to be both saved and sexy?"

My eyes rolled back in my head, and I had a queasy feeling in the pit of my stomach.

"And to answer that question," Tina

went on, "the company I represent, Erotica Home Parties, for which I am your official passion consultant, has come out with a number of products that will open the doors of the Christian woman's sensual nature. Just as we are to reach our full potential mentally, physically, and spiritually, so God wants us to reach our full potential sexually."

I felt myself rearing back in my chair, as my mouth tightened to a thin line. There wasn't a sound in the room, for Tina had our full attention.

"Now, ladies," Tina said with a laugh, "there's no reason for you to be embarrassed at anything we talk about. We just have to remember that a woman's sensuality is natural. In fact, it is a God thing, and we're all in the same boat. We all have needs and desires that are God given, and all I'm going to do is help you fulfill them. And believe me, you will thank me for it, and if you don't, your husbands certainly will."

That got a ripple of polite laughter, but not from me.

"So let's start with something simple," Tina said, drawing out a pink plastic bottle with a multicolored label. She opened it and poured a thick, clear liquid into the palm of her hand. "This is our strawberry-flavored, organic massage oil and, ladies, it contains only edible oils from nature, and I stress edible. It creates a tingling sensation on the skin and tongue, and tastes delicious. Here, Janet, let me rub some on your arm so you can see how it feels." She did, eliciting an amazed expression from Janet as the oil began its work. Then Tina passed the bottle around and urged us to try it on ourselves. "Just imagine what this will feel like all over your body, and even better, imagine what it'll feel like on your husband's body. It's our Delicktable Massage Oil, and it will put zing into your lovemaking."

I drew back when the bottle came around to me, not wanting to touch the thing, much less rub its contents on my arm. But it had broken the ice, for the women were laughing and exclaiming, and losing much of their earlier reserve.

"Now, ladies," Tina called above the laughter, "I want to show you something that will start things off right from the minute your man comes in the door. If he comes home tired and cranky, just flash him with this." Out of her satchel came a strip of pink and black lace. She stretched it over her hands to reveal what I thought were bikini step-ins, but, Lord, there was no bottom to it.

Gasps of shock and what sounded suspiciously like delight rose around the room.

"And what about this?" Tina yelled, holding up what seemed to be black pantyhose. "Just flip your dress up when he starts complaining about dinner, and see how fast he changes his tune."

My word, the whole bottom and back end were missing. It was the most indecent thing I'd ever seen.

"Anybody want to model this for us?" Tina said, laughing. But not a soul volunteered, which didn't surprise me.

What did surprise me, as well as everyone else, was what she pulled out next. It took me a minute to identify the items, because I wasn't all that familiar with the real things, much less life-sized plastic models of them. Tina carefully placed an array of what she called Erotica Love Toys on the table. Each item had its own name, which she called out and urged us to write down so we could place our orders.

"This one is called the Jelly Rabbit," she said. "And this one is the Bell-Ringer, and here's the Double-Duty Boy. And you can get the pulsating variety or the vibrating kind, and, believe me, with one of these *no*body will be lying there thinking of England."

I could hardly get my breath by this

time, panting in outrage at the nerve of Tina Doland for lining up substitute male members on my card table in full view of everybody. I had to avert my eyes and fan my face. So realistic, don't you know, and right there in my living room, where cultured family life was carried on.

I want to tell you that I had never seen nor heard of anything so coarse and tasteless. But Tina kept on and on, assuring us that each one of the gently curved, lifelike, lubricated, and battery-operated plastic passion toys was used by the most genteel of women.

"Ladies," she said, "you haven't lived until you've tried one of these. Turn one on, and you'll turn *him* on, too."

I couldn't sit still any longer. "Hazel Marie," I whispered, leaning close. She didn't move. Her mouth was slightly agape, as she gazed in wide-eyed wonder at Tina's lifelike merchandise.

"Hazel Marie!" I hissed, finally getting her attention. "I'm going to see about Little Lloyd."

She nodded, absently, and I took myself off, unwilling to spend another minute in the presence of such lewd notions as were being introduced to our minds. No one paid my leaving any attention at all. They were all transfixed by what they were seeing and hearing, and the possibilities being opened up to them in the privacy of their own homes.

I tiptoed upstairs, resolved within myself to give Tina Doland a piece of my mind for going beyond the bounds of decency and good taste. Just as soon as I could do it without creating a public scene.

Chapter 11

When I heard the door close behind the last guest, I left Little Lloyd softly snoring and went downstairs. Hazel Marie shot me a worried glance, then quickly looked away to concentrate on folding up the card table. I didn't say anything, just started moving chairs to their normal places.

"Miss Julia," Hazel Marie finally said, as she straightened up and pushed a lock of hair out of her face. "I didn't know what Tina was going to do, and I'm so sorry that you had to see it and be offended and all. She told me that she was only going to offer helpful suggestions for closer relationships." She stopped and bit her lip. "I should've known something was up when she called it a passion party."

"I should've, too," I said, sighing, as I sat on the sofa. "It's unfortunate that we didn't. I declare, Hazel Marie, I didn't know such things were made, much less *used*. And for Tina to display them and offer them for sale like they were the most ordinary things in the world, well, it just did me in."

"Me, too," Hazel Marie admitted, as she took a seat beside me. "I was shocked, but a little fascinated, too. I mean, where else would you find such items? You couldn't just ask for them in a store."

"I don't know who'd want them. I'm sure Tina didn't sell a thing."

"Oh," Hazel Marie said with a smile, "you'd be surprised. She did quite well. You should've stayed to see who ordered."

"Just saying right out loud what they wanted? Oh, surely not, Hazel Marie."

"No, what Tina did was give each of us an order form. We just checked what we wanted and gave them back to her. She's the only one who knows who got what."

"That alone would disturb me," I said.

We sat quietly for a few minutes, our minds occupied with the evening's activities.

Hazel Marie took a deep breath. "I might as well tell you, Miss Julia, I ordered something, too. But it was just that massage oil, because Tina said it was good for dry skin, and I thought I ought to buy something. But you don't have to worry," she went on quickly, "it'll come in a plain brown wrapper, so nobody'll know."

"No need to explain to me, Hazel Marie. I understand how these home parties can put you on the spot." I let the silence stretch for a minute, then casually asked, "Who else placed orders?"

She giggled. "Practically everybody. And some of the ladies took forever because they were checking so many things."

"Lord, Hazel Marie, what kind of woman would want any of it?" I leaned my head back on the sofa, just undone that I now had a whole new array of indecent thoughts cluttering up my mind.

"You should've seen what Tina had for men," Hazel Marie went on, an awed tone in her voice. "I couldn't believe it. She showed us these ring things that go on a man's, . . . well, they're called pleasure rings, but seems like to me they'd really hurt. But the *names,* Miss Julia, you wouldn't believe the names of the toys she showed us. There was something called the Coochy-Coo and something else called the Hot Potato. I never did get what you do with them."

Since my mind couldn't seem to be swayed from further contemplation of those offensive items, I just gave in to it, and asked, "What about Mildred Allen? Did she buy anything?"

"Oh, Miss Julia, you should've seen her. She laughed and giggled and checked what looked like the whole form. She kept

117

saying she wished Tonya had come, since Tonya probably needed all the help she could get."

"Did she really? That is so tasteless, with everybody knowing that poor Tonya will have trouble finding a man. I'm surprised at Mildred. Who else, Hazel Marie? What about LuAnne? Did she get anything?"

"LuAnne was sitting behind Mildred, all scrooched up so I couldn't see what she was doing. But she sure took a long time doing it."

"I guess it was a good thing that Emma Sue didn't come," I said, with a rueful laugh. "She'd have been so shocked she'd never get over it."

"I don't think she was invited," Hazel Marie said. "And you noticed that the Baptist preacher's wife didn't come, either, didn't you? Tina's no fool. I can't imagine that her church really approves of these parties."

"Yes, but she tried her hardest to bring a Christian slant to what she was selling." I sat for a minute, thinking of how often commercial enterprises painted a layer of Christianity over their wares. It was enough to make a real Christian sick at heart.

I suddenly sat up. "Oh, my goodness,

Hazel Marie. Tina showed those awful things in my house, and that means everybody's going to think I condone using them. This is going to ruin my witness, and here I am, practically an elder."

"You mean you're going to run?" Hazel Marie asked. "Oh, I'm so glad. Everybody wants you to."

"I still haven't made up my mind. But if Pastor Ledbetter hears about what was flagrantly displayed in my living room, he might well have grounds to disbar me before I even get started."

A door closed in the back of the house, and we both turned toward it. "That's Sam," I said, smiling and getting to my feet. "We'd better defer this conversation. I wouldn't want to shock him."

She laughed. "I know what you mean. I can't wait to see J.D.'s face when I . . ." She came to an abrupt stop, her hand flying to her mouth. "Not that I would tell him. I mean, since we're not married or anything."

What went on between Hazel Marie and Mr. Pickens was one of those matters that I didn't want to know about. To ease her embarrassment, I said, "I expect Mr. Pickens knows all he wants to know, and he wouldn't need a party to teach him anything new."

"No," she said, shaking her head and laughing. "He's forever surprising me with what he knows." She turned away, her face reddening even more. "I didn't mean anything by that, Miss Julia, but I think I better go on to bed. I keep putting my foot in my mouth."

Later, when we'd been in bed for some little while, Sam said, "How was the party? Did you have a good time?"

"Let's just say I'll never go to another one."

We lay there in the dark, breathing together. I pulled the blanket up over my shoulders, noting how the nights were getting remarkably cooler. It was most pleasant having someone warm next to me. Then Sam turned over, letting a rush of cold air under the covers.

"Sam?" I said, as his breathing slowed, and I, myself, was about to drop off.

"Hm-m-m?"

"I'm glad we don't need any substitutes in this marriage."

"I am, too, Julia," he mumbled. After a minute or so, he raised his head and spoke over his shoulder. "What brought that on?"

"Oh, nothing. Just being thankful for what I have, and relieved we don't have to buy it at a Tupperware party."

It was midmorning on the following day when Sam called me from his house, where he'd been working on his legal history.

"Julia? Vernon Puckett just called. He's on his way over, and I thought you might want to be here, too."

My heart rate jumped up a few notches. "Is he bringing proof? Or what he *thinks* is proof?"

"I don't know what he's bringing. He just said we needed further discussion about the wool that's being pulled over our eyes."

"Oh, for goodness sakes." Brother Vern made me so tired, I had to sit down. "Did he say he wanted to talk to me?"

Sam laughed. "No, this is my idea. I think it's about time he faced you with his allegations. I want to see his reaction when he has to look you in the eye and say that Hazel Marie has lied to you."

"I'll be right over."

Sam met me at the front door and ushered me into his study, which badly needed some organization. Books were stacked on the floor by his desk, and old newspapers and county records were piled on chairs and stuffed into bookshelves.

"You need to let James in here to straighten up for you," I said, as Sam helped me out of my coat.

"I wouldn't let James in here for love nor money. Everything's just where I want it. Here, let me move these files." Sam cleared a space on the leather sofa for me to sit down. As he did, the doorbell rang, and we gave each other a significant look, preparing ourselves for what was to come.

As Sam went to the door, I couldn't sit still. Getting to my feet to greet Hazel Marie's uncle and tormentor, I mentally girded myself to hear him out. Then I'd know how to cut him off at the knees.

"Ah, Mrs. Springer," Brother Vern said as he entered the room, seemingly unsurprised to see me waiting for him. "Oh, I guess I'm behind the times. I hear it's Mrs. Murdoch now. May I extend my heartfelt congratulations to the both of you. Marriage is a gift of God, bestowed upon us to illustrate the love of Christ for his church, and I'm sure that your marriage is like unto a perfect example of it. Remember, though, that the family that prays together, stays together."

Not necessarily, I thought, as he took my hand in both of his and smiled in his unctuous way. He could've wished us well and left it at that, but, like many preachers, he couldn't pass up a chance to preach. Brother Vern hadn't changed much since the last time I'd seen him, except he wasn't wearing his white summer suit. He had on a navy pinstripe, although the pinstripes were a little wide for my taste. His red tie almost matched his face, flushed as it was from the windy day and perhaps from the weight he carried. His hair was blacker than I remembered it, bringing to mind thoughts of Grecian Formula, which I couldn't necessarily fault him for, considering Velma's efforts with my own head of hair. Still, it always takes me aback to see dyed hair on a man. Vanity is so unbecoming, especially when there're no highlights to make it look natural.

"Have a seat, Mr. Puckett," Sam said, as he and I sat on the sofa.

"Brother Vern," Brother Vern said warmly. "Call me Brother Vern, for all us Christians are members of God's family. Now, Brother Sam and Sister Murdoch, I know that I've brought a ton of worry down on your heads, but I couldn't let this state of affairs continue on unabated. None of us is gettin' any younger, and the time's a-comin' when the roll's gonna be called up yonder for every one of us, and I know you don't want to leave a mess down here behind you. But that's exactly what you'll do if you don't get it straightened out now. Why, I tell you, there'll be nothing but lawsuits and legal wranglin's the likes of which you can't even imagine if you let things go on as they are now."

"You'll have to be more specific than that," I said, determined to pin him down. I just was not going to let vague insinuations stand in for absolute proof, which I knew he couldn't possibly have.

He gave me a brief stare, his black eyes boring into mine, as if he was unaccustomed to being brought up short by a woman. But since we weren't in church, I was under no Biblical injunction to keep silence.

He breathed heavily and noisily, being so cramped up in the soft leather chair that he could hardly get his breath good. His thick thighs, which I tried not to look at, were spraddled out to make room for the extra pounds in his midsection.

"Brother Sam," he said, switching his attention to my husband, "this is weighin' heavy on my heart, and I just can't bring myself to discuss these, well, these licentious matters in the presence of a godly woman. If it's all right with you, I'd ruther meet in private." Then with a nod in my direction, he said, "No offense, ma'am."

I came right back at him. "Oh, but there is offense. If you have something against Hazel Marie, you'd better speak up now or forever hold your peace. I am the one who's affected, not Sam. And it's my decisions that you've questioned, so let's hear what you have to say."

I think he glared at me, but he quickly pulled himself together. "You'll have to forgive me, Sister Murdoch. I'm not used to discussing personal and, may I say, dissolute matters with the fair sex." He shot a beseeching look at Sam but got no help from that quarter. Then, with a rasping breath, he said, "But since you insist, I'll just tell you that, as hard as it is for me to say out loud, my niece was a loose woman in her young days. And I don't expect she's changed much, in spite of having the Lord's own wealth showered down on her through your good offices. But what she's up to now is neither here nor there. Back before that boy was born, she took up with whoever'd have her, and there was plenty who would. I praised the Lord when Mr. Wesley Lloyd Springer came in the picture, thinking he'd settle her down and keep her from jumpin' from one bed to the other. Not that I could wink at adultery, you understand, but that girl needed a firm hand." He paused, glancing toward me to measure the effect of his words. "Now, see, Sister Murdoch, I didn't want to have to bring up such hurtful things in front of you, but the facts is facts."

"Just keep on stating them. I want to hear it all." I didn't, of course, but I wanted to know what we had to deal with.

"Well, I know there was a certain man that kept showing up and turning Hazel Marie's head, both before and after she hooked up with Mr. Springer. And I have every reason to believe that that boy of hers was conceived in a motel somewhere, completely unbeknownst to the man who was supportin' her. And," he went on, gathering the strength of outrage as he did, "it just frosts me good for her to fool that good man, then lie to you and profit the way she's done from it."

"What would you have us do?" Sam asked benignly. I glanced at him, wondering if he was feeling the same turmoil that I was.

"Why, brother, make her face up to her lies! You can't let things go on like they are. She's takin' your good wife here for a ride! And I hate to see it." He bowed his head and shook it, as if in sorrow. "I purely hate to see you good folk done in by the likes of her. That kid of hers is nothin' but a by-blow, and here he's in line for Mr. Springer's estate that he don't have no claim to at all."

Sam and I let the silence grow after that outburst. Then I pulled myself up to the edge of the sofa and said, "All that may be, Mr. Puckett, but I have two questions. Where is your proof? And, what is your interest in the matter?"

"Ma'am, my interest is in settin' the record straight. As a minister of the Gospel, I can't stand by and let her get away with it. Why, I can't even imagine the torment I'll feel when you pass on and I have to watch her and the boy come into all that wealth, when they don't deserve nothing but the wrath of God, because the wages of sin is death, not high and mighty livin'."

Envy, I thought, just pure envy. As hard as he'd tried, he hadn't been able to get his hands on Wesley Lloyd's estate, so the thought of his own kin having it handed to them on a platter was more than he could stand.

I stood up, indicating that I'd heard all I cared to hear. "Thank you for sharing your opinions with us. When you can produce unassailable evidence of your claims, we'll speak again. Until that time, I'll thank you to keep this matter to yourself. Unproven allegations bandied about town can bring down the wrath of the legal system, as I'm sure you know. But for now, I've heard all I want to hear, so I'll bid you good day." And I left the room, my head held high and my temper barely in check, to seek the peace of Sam's old bedroom. I paced around the room, waiting for Sam to get rid of Brother Vern and come to me.

"Julia?" Sam opened the door and came in. "You all right?"

"No, I'm not all right. That man is evil, Sam, that's all there is to it. You noticed, didn't you, that he gave not one iota of proof. Just unjustified accusations, all to bring Hazel Marie down and punish her. It was all I could do to keep from smacking him out of that chair."

"I know, Julia." Sam put his arms around me. "But you stayed calm and didn't let him know he'd gotten to you. That may be his aim in all this, to shake your faith in Hazel Marie. I think he just can't stand for her to do well, while he's not and has little hope of doing any better."

"You may be right." I leaned my head

against his chest, then looked up at him. "Did he say anything after I left?"

"Just that the man he claims is Lloyd's father is a fine Christian now, with a family, and he'd hoped he wouldn't have to bring him out in the open." Sam patted my back and leaned his head against mine. "Somebody specific, Julia."

I could've cried, even though I didn't believe a word out of Brother Vern's mouth. All the same, though, he seemed determined to push this thing to its limit, destroying any and every body in his path.

"He could get somebody to lie for him," I said, trying to think of all the possibilities. "If that happened, it'd be a stranger's word against Hazel Marie's. I'd still believe her, but we'd be right back where we are now — not having enough evidence to put a stop to Brother Vern."

"That's right." Sam nodded, then breathed out. "You know what we may have to do?"

"Yes," I sighed. "Get out the shovels and prove him wrong."

Chapter 12

It wasn't long after our meeting with Brother Vern that I began to notice little niggles of doubt running around in my mind. I tried not to dwell on them, but they were there, rearing their ugly heads when I least expected them.

I retired to our bedroom one afternoon a few days later, having told Lillian and Hazel Marie that I wanted to plan my annual December tea. Actually, it didn't need much planning, since I generally had the same people and did the same thing year after year, but one must make lists when it comes to formal entertaining, and that's what I was trying to do.

I wasn't getting very far because, try as I might, I couldn't keep my mind on the task. Finally, I put down my pen and got up from the desk. Taking a seat in the armchair by the window, I forced myself to face the fearful possibility that Brother Vern knew whereof he spoke, and could back up his claims with depositions, sworn statements, and worst of all, the public unveiling of a participant in the deed that had produced Little Lloyd.

So I allowed myself to wonder how I would feel if Little Lloyd was disproved as Wesley Lloyd's natural son and rightful heir. I thought about that for a few minutes, and had a great sense of relief to realize that it wouldn't change my feelings for him all that much. Maybe not at all. I recalled, with a shiver, the revulsion I'd felt toward that wretched child when he first showed up at my house. It had been all I could do to tolerate an ever-present reminder of Wesley Lloyd's carnal knowledge of his mother.

Of course, I'd risen above all that by this time, but my heart lightened as I realized that I might appreciate the boy even more if he had no connection whatever to the old goat. After all, he'd never been kin to me to begin with. What was between the child and me had nothing to do with whose blood ran in his veins.

I sighed, though, thinking that the blood in his veins could have a lot to do with where his share of Wesley Lloyd's estate ended up. Lord, if Pastor Ledbetter got wind of this, he'd start putting in his two cents worth as to where that money should go. He was still convinced that Wesley

Lloyd had intended to include the church in his will.

He hadn't, though. And, worse than that, he hadn't included *me* in his will, and I'd put up with more from him than the church ever had. Well, I thought, as I leaned back in the chair, it hadn't mattered a hill of beans what my wandering husband had intended. What had mattered was that Little Lloyd and I had gotten what we deserved.

Except now, if Brother Vern could prove that the boy was not Wesley Lloyd's son, would some judge decide that when Wesley Lloyd wrote his last will and testament, he was a victim of fraud, making his wishes null and void? Would Little Lloyd's inheritance be taken away from him? And who would get it?

And what about Hazel Marie? I thought I could live with Little Lloyd being a stranger's son on his father's side, but I couldn't come to grips with the idea of Hazel Marie as a liar with malice aforethought. I could never in this world accept that she deliberately set out to deceive Wesley Lloyd and, in turn, Sam, Binkie, and me. Nor could I accept that she could live with me on a day-by-day basis and keep up the deception.

For one thing, she wasn't that smart — in a manipulative sense, I mean. You could always count on Hazel Marie speaking before she thought and leaping before she looked. It was impossible for me to picture her with narrowed eyes and grim determination setting out on a lifetime of lies, as she would've had to've done when she first learned she'd been put in the family way by somebody.

So there, Brother Vern.

Then another thought came suddenly unbidden: Could it be that she hadn't *known* who the child's father was? Maybe she'd honestly thought Wesley Lloyd was the one responsible.

Lord, I couldn't imagine being in such a fix. One man was more than enough for me, and the idea of two or three at a time was unthinkable. And I couldn't think it of Hazel Marie.

Oh, I could understand — just barely — that an untrained and uneducated young woman could take up with anyone who would put a roof over her head. The little that Hazel Marie had told me about her family painted a dismal picture of a girl growing up unloved and unwanted, dropped off and left with one relative after another. That's a prescription for promiscuity if ever I heard one. Young women with that kind of background end up looking for love in all the wrong places. . . .

I think a wise man said that one time. I could find it in my heart to overlook the indiscretions of her youth, even if they were carnal in nature. So if Brother Vern thought he could bring her down in my estimation by recounting all her sins, he could think again. I knew how she'd lived her life since coming under my influence, and that's what counted with me — her dalliance, if that's what it was, with Mr. Pickens notwithstanding.

I breathed some easier after facing all the possible repercussions of Brother Vern's claims, and realizing that I could handle them all with some semblance of serenity. Well, except for a few things. I couldn't handle the besmirchment of Little Lloyd's paternity, because that would follow him all his life. Bad enough that he had to live with the taint of illegitimacy, even worse if he never knew for sure who his father was, which would surely change his view of his mother. And I couldn't handle somebody else getting the child's estate, if it came to that.

I came out of my chair with a renewed determination to fight Vernon Puckett to a standstill. Pacing around the room, I decided that he had to be brought down before he brought us down. And the only way to do that was to prove beyond question that the child was the pure and unadulterated result of Wesley Lloyd Springer's procreative episodes.

Well, not exactly unadulterated, but you know what I mean. Besides, the child looked just like him. Nobody, not even Brother Vern could get around that.

Sam tapped on the door, then stuck his head in. "You resting, Julia?"

"How could I rest with all this turmoil going on? No, I'm trying to figure out how we can put a stop to Brother Vern."

Sam came in and sat on the side of the bed. "Julia, you're going to worry yourself sick. Come sit down, and let me explain a few things to you."

I did, although it was always a wonder to me that people would choose to sit on a bed when there were two perfectly good chairs for the taking. "I wish you would," I said.

"First off, Binkie and I went through the file again to look at Wesley Lloyd's handwritten will. The way he wrote it was: 'I name my only son, Wesley Lloyd Junior

Puckett' — with Springer in parentheses — 'heir and beneficiary of all my wordly goods.' That says to me that, sick as he was at the time, he foresaw some difficulty. He didn't just write 'my son.' He named the child, claimed him as son and heir, and specifically added his own surname, even though the boy was born out of wedlock. And another thing, Julia. We looked at Lloyd's birth certificate, and Hazel Marie gave him both names, Puckett and Springer. And she named the father, Wesley Lloyd Springer. It's written there, big as life, and no one's ever questioned it."

"Well, it's being questioned now. And what worries me is that it might not matter what Hazel Marie and Wesley Lloyd wrote down. Anybody can write whatever they want to. The question is: Will it hold up in a court of law?"

"It's not going to come to that, and if it does, a judge would rely on the intent of the testator. And we can prove by these documents that Wesley Lloyd's intent was clear — to leave his estate to this particular child."

"Yes, but Brother Vern claims that if Wesley Lloyd hadn't been deceived, he wouldn't have left the boy a red cent.

That's the whole point, right there. According to him, Wesley Lloyd only *thought* Little Lloyd was his son. And if he can prove to the satisfaction of a court that what Wesley Lloyd thought was wrong, where does that leave us?"

"Back to proving that the boy *is* his son. Listen, Julia, before Puckett pulls some man out of his hat who's willing to swear that he was with Hazel Marie around the time of the boy's conception, we need to do something. I don't want either her or the boy to have to be faced with this."

"That's what I've been saying. But what do we do?"

"I want you to think carefully." Sam took my hand in both of his. "Is there anything of Wesley Lloyd's that you've saved? An old hairbrush, a shirt that hasn't been washed, anything at all that we could try to get DNA from?"

"An unwashed shirt is the last thing I would've kept." A washed one either, I could've added.

"I'm reaching, Julia, trying to think of anything that might have epithelial cells on it. They'd probably be too old to test, anyway, so forget about that. What I'm saying, though, is that we want to try everything we can before resorting to exhumation.

That would be hard to keep from the whole town, including Hazel Marie and Lloyd."

"Oh, Lord, yes, it would, and we don't want that if we can help it. Let me think, Sam." I rubbed the side of my face, thinking back to the shame and fury that had overwhelmed me when I'd learned of my deceased husband's folly. I'd marched up to our bedroom, fired with determination to rid myself of everything that had belonged to Wesley Lloyd. Rummaging through the clothes hanging in the closets and stacked in the dresser drawers, I'd flung everything he owned into the middle of the floor. Shirts, three-piece suits, shoes, raincoat, overcoat, umbrellas, you name it, it went onto the pile. I remembered cleaning out the medicine cabinet, throwing out Wesley Lloyd's toothbrush, shaving implements, comb, hairbrush, clothes brush, lint remover, shoe polish, his Listerine, his Metamucil, his half-used box of Tuck's — everything that he'd even touched. I'd raked it all into the wastebasket. I'd cleaned out the drawers of the table on his side of the bed, throwing away a full box of Kleenex, the glass he'd kept his partial in, his clock, the gold pocket watch and chain that had been his father's, tiepins, and cuff links. Even his Bible and his Sunday School lesson book, giving them a particularly vicious spin since he'd read them so piously while living so wickedly. I'd even thrown away his eyeglasses, including his extra pair, doubly angered by the funeral director's asking if I wanted to bury him with his glasses on or off. I ask you, what was he going to look at?

Downstairs, I'd started another pile, emptying his desk of pens, papers, calendar, and everything else that Binkie hadn't needed for probate. Things I didn't even know what they were, I threw on the pile. If they were his, they went.

Then I'd walked out. "Lillian," I remembered saying as I passed her in the hall, "if there's anything you or anyone you know can use, take it. Whatever's left, burn. I don't want to lay eyes on any of it ever again."

"Yessum," she'd said, her eyes wide as she stepped back from my passing. She'd never seen me in such a state, since up to then I'd always been of a meek and submissive nature.

That cleaning episode had been a turning point for me. Getting rid of anything that reminded me of Wesley Lloyd had given me a sense of power and control

139

that I'd never had before, and it had made me the woman I am today. Of course, I'd kept the most obvious reminders of his transgressions — namely, Hazel Marie and Little Lloyd — but I'd had my reasons. Everything else I could do without and never miss.

Except now I'd've given an eyetooth for a single strand of hair from Wesley Lloyd Springer's head.

Chapter 13

"Miss Julia," Hazel Marie said, as she pushed through the door into the dining room where I was looking over my serving pieces in the sideboard, "Lillian's just made a fresh pot of coffee. Come on and have some with us."

I held up a silver chafing dish. "Do you think this needs resilvering? It's been used so much that it's about down to the brass."

"It takes forever to get that done. I wouldn't worry about it. Come on, Lillian's pouring now, and she's made some brownies, too."

I rarely eat between meals, but a chance to sit down with Lillian and Hazel Marie was most appealing. The house had settled into its morning quiet now that Sam had left for his home office and Little Lloyd was back in school. I declare, my heart was so heavy and my mind so fraught with fearsome speculations that I stayed tired all the time. Efforts to keep myself busy had been for naught, so I followed Hazel Marie into the kitchen and gladly took a chair at the table.

Lillian set a cup of hot coffee in front of me and passed one to Hazel Marie. Then she sat down and commenced spooning sugar into hers. "If you 'spectin' anything different for Christmas an' all yo' parties, you better let me know," she said, giving me a baleful eye. "It gettin' mighty late in the day to come up with something I never cook before."

"You can cook anything, whether you've done it before or not," Hazel Marie said. She passed the plate of brownies. "Here, Miss Julia, have one."

I did, but I had no appetite for it. "No changes, Lillian," I told her. "Let's have the same Christmas dinner we have every year. But, I want you both to know, I am cutting down on the parties. I see no need to entertain everybody under the sun just because I've always done it."

"No parties?" Hazel Marie reared back in her chair, shocked that I would fall down on our social obligations. "But, Miss Julia, everybody looks forward to them."

"I know, but that's a poor reason to do them. And the fact of the matter is, I just don't have the heart to go all out this year. I'm a married woman now, and the holidays should center around the family and not the whole town."

They looked at me as if I had taken leave of my senses. Lillian recovered first. "What you talkin' about? We don't center 'round no whole town."

"Well, the ones who count, we do. But even so, I just don't feel like having so many people this year."

Hazel Marie put her hand on my arm. "Are you sick, Miss Julia?"

"I don't know why everybody thinks I'm sick every time I want to do something different. I'm not sick, Hazel Marie, I just have my hands full. I'm still getting used to having Sam underfoot all the time." Then, thinking that I might've sounded less than happily married, I quickly added, "Besides, I don't know how I could have Mildred and her husband, much less LuAnne and Leonard at my table, knowing what they bought from Tina. I'd keep thinking about what goes on in the privacy of their bedrooms while I watch them eat at my table."

Hazel Marie started laughing, with Lillian demanding to know what was so funny. She was both shocked and thrilled when Hazel Marie told her about the passion party in our living room. That took them off on another tangent, which gratified me in spite of the questionable nature of the conversation. I didn't want Hazel

143

Marie prying more closely into my reasons for slacking off on our holiday entertainments. But the fact of the matter was, I was fearful of Brother Vern and what he might spring on us next. I wouldn't put it past him to suddenly appear at one of my elegant teas with an erstwhile intimately known man of Hazel Marie's acquaintance, an occurrence that would certainly put a damper on the celebrations.

"Law," Lillian said, still entranced by Hazel Marie's description of Tina's party. "What this world comin' to?" She got up from the table, taking her empty cup with her, and said, "I got to get up from here an' go to the store. We out of everything. Miss Julia, you got the grocery list ready?"

"There by the phone," I said, indicating the pad where we all jotted down items as we saw a need.

"I have to get busy, too," Hazel Marie said, following with her cup. Then she stopped and came back to the table. "I forgot to tell you. Guess what I heard about Clara Denham."

"Is she back with Dub?"

"No, and she probably won't ever be." Hazel Marie took a seat and leaned toward me, eager to pass on the latest news. "She's moved in with an electrician, of all things.

Nobody knows who he is, exactly, but seems he did some work on the ceiling lights in the library. And that's where she met him, right there over the reference desk."

"That doesn't sound very romantic to me."

"Well," Hazel Marie said, lowering her voice, "from what I hear, he is a honey and a half. Big and muscular, and as dark and handsome as George Clooney, only taller. I can't blame her, because that's my type, too. Anyway, they say he has a house out on the east side of town, and she's living there with him. Helen Stroud said that Clara looks like a new woman — she's had her hair streaked and highlighted, and she's gotten so bouncy and happy and all that they've had to take her off the reference desk and put her in a back office. And they say she's setting such a bad example that the library board is thinking of firing her."

"Well, my word, Hazel Marie. I guess her mistake was being so happy about it. If she'd acted upset about her marriage breaking up, her job would've been safe." I paused, then added, "Not that I approve of what she's done, mind you."

"I know, and you're right. What people look on as sin is not supposed to make us happy, but sometimes it does. Oh, my goodness, look at the time. I've got to get out of here. Victoria's Secret's having a sale, so I'm going to run over to the mall and check it out." She looked at me, her eyes sparkling with fun. "You want to go with me? Sam would love it."

"I haven't lost a thing at Victoria's Secret, and neither has he. Hazel Marie, I declare, you shouldn't let Tina's merchandise turn your head."

She laughed and assured me that she'd loved flimsy lingerie long before Tina began peddling her brand of underwear.

After they left I settled into one of the Victorian chairs by the living room fireplace, thinking that we might build a fire later in the day. Unfolding the newspaper that Sam had left neatly put together, I scanned the headlines, then turned to the obituaries to see if anyone I knew had passed on in the last day or two. LuAnne's husband, Leonard, always said he read the obituaries to be sure that his wasn't among them. It was his one joke and, since it had gotten a laugh the first time he said it, he kept trying for more.

Giving up on the paper, I leaned my head back, content to rest a while in the silence of the empty house. I nearly dropped off to sleep, even as I went over and over the wisdom of letting Hazel Marie know she was being accused of fraud, deceit, lying, theft, and sleeping around. Though, Lord knows why that particular activity was called *sleeping*. As far as I could determine, there was nothing restful about it.

I jerked upright when the doorbell blasted the peace and quiet. Mumbling to myself about unexpected visitors, I got to my feet and went to answer it.

Brother Vernon Puckett, big as life, was standing there with an ingratiating smile on his face. I didn't return it, just stood there holding the door, my face as rigidly unwelcoming as I could make it.

"Yes?"

"Miz Murdoch," he stated flatly, as if I didn't know my own name, "accept my utmost apologies for droppin' in on you like this, ma'am, but I had to strike while the iron was hot. Would you tell Hazel Marie I'm here? I need to see her, and she needs to see me."

"I'm sorry," I said, even though I wasn't. All I could feel was relief that she wasn't at home. And anger at the nerve of the man, showing up at my door when we'd been trying to protect her from him. "She's not in at the present. And I'm not sure when she'll be back. Probably be gone all day and up into the night. If you need anything, perhaps you should speak with Sam. He's over at his house."

The smile gradually left his face as he learned that his surprise visit had not netted the results he wanted. He stood watching me for a minute, expecting, I expect, that I would invite him in. I didn't. I couldn't bring myself to be cordial to him, so I stood my ground, hoping he'd take himself off my front porch and never darken my door again.

"Ma'am," he said, as his face hardened, "I've made a special trip here to counsel her, for the Lord is burdening my soul about her devious ways. I even went far out of my way just to bring her face-to-face with her past, which she's got to face sooner or later, and I don't know when I'll be able to do it again."

"Well, I can't help that. She's not here, and I'm not expecting her anytime soon." My teeth were grinding together by this time, wondering if he thought I could make her appear out of thin air.

"Then I guess I'll have to do the next best thing. Hold on a minute, ma'am, there's somebody I want you to meet." He stepped to the edge of the porch, put his two fingers in his mouth, and blasted out a shrill whistle. Aghast at what the neighbors would think, I watched, open-mouthed, as he waved his hand toward the shiny silver Cadillac parked at the curb. Then he turned back to me. "It's the man I been tellin' you about — Hazel Marie's partner in immorality and the daddy of that boy of hers."

I clasped the edge of the door, fearful of losing strength in my limbs. I wasn't ready to hear the intimate details, and if I'd had the strength to do it, I would've shut the door and locked it behind me.

But then I took courage, realizing that Brother Vern was now showing all his cards. I was about to be justified in my total belief in Hazel Marie. I knew the kind of man she liked — tall and broad-shouldered, dark and swarthy, a man's man — whatever that was — just like Mr. Pickens and, by all accounts, Clara Denham's electrician, which proved in my estimation that Wesley Lloyd had been an aberration brought on by necessity. Brother Vern was going to bring out his number-one exhibit, and that would put my worries absolutely to rest, since there was no way on earth that Little Lloyd resembled Hazel Marie's preferred type.

I stuck my head out the door to watch as

a man climbed out of the car and came down the walk. As he stepped onto the porch, I looked him over as my grip on the door grew tighter. He was of a slight build, barely taller than Brother Vern, which wasn't all that tall, with narrow shoulders and the beginnings of a paunch in his midsection. He wore a brown wool suit with, Lord!, black shoes and white athletic socks. A pocket saver full of Bics was in his shirt pocket. His hair was a nondescript sandy color, receding from a prominent V over his forehead. He wore a pair of gold-rimmed glasses and a thin mustache — the only discordant note — that took a squinch of the eyes to see. He gave me a brief, jittery smile, along with a deferential nod of his head, as he chewed gum in a fast and open-mouthed manner.

I just stared, standing there, frozen in my tracks.

I couldn't get a word out of my mouth, even when Brother Vern said, "Miz Murdoch, this here's Deacon Lon Whitmire, known to one and all as Lonnie. He had a close friendship with Hazel Marie." He nudged the man with his elbow. "Tell her, Lonnie."

Deacon Whitmire nodded again, licked his lips, and snapped his gum, as high color bloomed on his face. He jammed his hands into the pockets of his trousers and began fingering his change — a sure sign of nervousness in a deacon when he's called on by his pastor. I don't know how many times I've had to listen to the jingling of coins while one of our deacons stumbled through a public prayer.

This particular deacon cut his eyes at Brother Vern, then jumped when he got nudged again. "Long time ago," he mumbled, "before I come to know the Lord."

An errant breeze whipped across the porch, lifting a wispy tuft of the deacon's hair.

My mouth moved, but nothing came out. I clung to the door, feeling lightheaded and wobbly. Everything seemed to tilt, and I thought I was about to faint, even though I'd hardly ever done such a singular thing in my life.

With a mighty effort of will, I managed to say, "You'll have to excuse me. There's been some sickness in the house. I fear it's highly contagious."

With that, I slammed the door in their faces and took a tottering step toward the sofa. Sick to my soul, I collapsed on it, thinking only one thing: Deacon Lonnie Whitmire looked enough like Wesley Lloyd Springer to be his brother.

Chapter 14

I took to my bed, pulling the covers over my head and retreating from the world. When the others came in, expressing concern and offering help, I told them that I'd had a sudden onset of the malady that had afflicted Little Lloyd a few days earlier. All I needed was a little rest, but one by one in they came, bearing hot-water bottles for my feet and ginger ale for my stomach.

That was all well and good, but there is no easy cure for soul sickness. All along I had relied on the fact that Little Lloyd had such a strong resemblance to Wesley Lloyd that there could be no question as to his descent from a Springer. And now, suddenly, a veritable replica of my first husband, except for the mustache, had emerged, claiming to have had relations with Hazel Marie. I'd always heard that everybody has a double somewhere in the world, but I never expected to find Wesley Lloyd's duplicate popping up in the same county.

It was more than I could bear, because

my previously unshaken confidence in Hazel Marie was now badly undermined. I remembered telling myself that it wouldn't matter who the child's father turned out to be. He would remain special to me, regardless. But as the repercussions rolled around in my head, I realized that his paternity did matter, not only because his rights of inheritance hinged on it, but also because the kinship I felt toward him and his mother — which was based on trust and affection — would be irreparably damaged.

It was enough to make anybody ill.

Finally, after numerous trips to see how I was feeling by Lillian, Hazel Marie, Sam, and Little Lloyd — and during which I got little rest — the house settled down for the night, and Sam came in to prepare for bed.

"Can I get you anything, Julia?" he whispered, as he leaned over the bed.

I threw off the covers and pulled myself up against the pillows, surprising him with my sudden show of energy. "I need to talk to you, Sam. Are we alone?"

"Well," he said, turning his head to survey the room, "it looks like it."

"I don't mean in here. I mean, will anybody come walking in on us?"

He smiled an intimate smile. "The door's closed, and they know what that means." Then he sat on the bed and took my hand. "You sure you're feeling well enough?"

"You can just switch channels, Sam Murdoch," I said, snatching away my hand. "I have something to tell you that is beyond belief, and it's what has sent me to my bed this livelong day."

So I told him of Brother Vern's visit and the uncanny resemblance of Deacon Lonnie Whitmire to Wesley Lloyd Springer.

"It's about to do me in, Sam," I said, burying my face in my hands. "I've been depending on how much Little Lloyd favors Wesley Lloyd, and now that's gone right out the window. What are we going to do?"

"*We* are going to let me handle it. Listen to me, now." Sam pulled my hands away from my face, then he looked me in the eye. "You're making yourself sick worrying over this, and Vernon Puckett is not worth losing one night's sleep. I want you to let it go and trust me to take care of it."

He went on in like manner, assuring me that looks weren't everything, and that he intended to leave no stone unturned until he'd undeniably proven that Little Lloyd was who Hazel Marie said he was.

I finally let him go to sleep but, in spite of agreeing to leave it all in his hands, I could find no rest. At last I slipped out of bed, put on my slippers and a warm robe, and took myself to the living room. There, a few logs in the fireplace were down to glowing embers, so I carefully laid on another one. Drawing a chair up close, I sat in the darkened room trying to pull myself together. As the fire blazed up, throwing light into the room, I noticed several rolls of Christmas wrapping paper that Hazel Marie had left on the sofa. Christmas, I thought with a sinking heart, a time of joy and celebration. Or, at least, it should be. Not this year, though, thanks to Brother Vern and Deacon Lonnie, and because of them, maybe not for years to come.

The pitiful irony of the current situation suddenly struck me: It had been Christmastime when I came to value what I'd been given, and here it was Christmas again as I was about to lose it.

Since Hazel Marie and Little Lloyd had been with me, I'd come to look forward to the season and enjoy it ever so much, when once all it had done was make me sad enough to cry. I never did, of course, just girded myself with my usual stoicism and got through it the best way I could.

Wrapping my robe close around me, I allowed my mind to wander in a way that I rarely had the inclination for these days. I didn't often have the desire to dwell on the empty years of my first marriage, and would just as soon have put them out of my mind forever. But the past was being dug up, and here was Wesley Lloyd's ghost hanging over my head again. And if anybody could put a crimp in a person's enjoyment of Christmas, or any other time of the year for that matter, he was the one who could.

With Sam by my side, and Hazel Marie and Little Lloyd under my roof, I'd had every reason to think that my waning years would be filled with peace and contentment. I leaned my head against the wing of the chair, simply overcome with the awful dread of losing what had seemed at first to be my shame, only gradually to have become my treasure. Finding a crumpled Kleenex in my pocket, I held it to my eyes as images of that precious boy and how he'd come to mean so much to me began to flicker across the back of my eyes. . . .

Chapter 15

Christmas had never been what you'd call a joyous time for me, since Wesley Lloyd Springer, my husband of some forty-five years, hadn't had a joyous bone in his body. Each year we spent the holidays going to church every time the doors opened, and at that time of the year they opened every time we turned around. I declare, I got tired of it, but it wouldn't've done to mention it. Wesley Lloyd's temper grew shorter and his comments more abrupt as soon as people started hanging wreaths and stringing Christmas lights. And Christmas music? He snapped the radio off as soon as he came home every evening.

"I get enough of that racket downtown," he'd say. "I don't need to hear it in my own house."

Lillian, who kept to the kitchen when she heard his car in the driveway, turned her radio off before he stepped into the house. I know she enjoyed the Christmas music, for I'd occasionally hear her singing along with it during the day. When I went in to visit with her, we'd sit at the table and drink coffee while we shelled pecans or chopped citron and candied cherries, and talk together. With the smells of cinnamon and nutmeg, and the sight of cake layers cooling, and Lillian herself in a red apron, I felt as if I were in some Hallmark Christmas card scene. Until, that is, Wesley Lloyd came home each evening, and I had to be the lady of the house again. He didn't approve of consorting with the help.

He just didn't like Christmas. I'm not sure he even approved of it. According to him, Christmas celebrations in the form of trees, holly, gift giving, and caroling were late and deplorable English and German additions that took away from the true meaning of the season. All the so-called merriment did nothing but disrupt the routine of business, and true spirituality was all but lost in the secular, materialistic society we lived in — I'm quoting him.

"It's supposed to be a Christian holy day, Julia," he'd say to me. "And just look at everybody and his brother out spending money they don't have and buying things they don't need. I tell you, there ought to be a law."

You can see how that kind of attitude would tend to take the joy out of a person. Oh, we had a Christmas tree on the table in the front window, but only because he didn't want people passing by to think he was strange. Which, the further away from his demise I get, the more I realize he was. At the time, though, I didn't know any different.

We exchanged gifts, too, one apiece, because Wesley Lloyd did not approve of going overboard in any way, shape, or form. He'd been firmly against spending money on frivolous things, so we bought each other needful and useful items, things you had to have anyway. I'd gotten it in my head one year to give him something different, thinking he might get the hint that I'd prefer something other than a small kitchen appliance, which I never used anyway since Lillian did all our cooking. So I'd studied and searched and finally came up with a beautiful cashmere sweater for him, which meant that I'd had to dip into household money in order to afford it. I'll never forget the sick look on his face when he pulled it out of the box on Christmas morning. At first I'd thought he was ashamed because his gift to me of a flannel nightgown was nowhere near the level of a cashmere sweater. But it hadn't been that at all. As far as he was concerned, he'd followed the rules he'd set down that limited our spending on Christmas gifts, and I hadn't.

He let me know about it in no uncertain terms, and from then on I stuck to socks, gloves, and the occasional pair of Hanes boxer shorts.

So I can't say that I was expecting anything different that first Christmas I had Hazel Marie Puckett and Little Lloyd under my roof. To tell the truth, I expected it to be worse. After all, I'd had several months of serious jolts to my system, what with Wesley Lloyd's sudden and unexpected departure from this vale of tears and the even more unexpected appearance on my front porch of his longtime mistress and their peaked and unattractive little son.

With all that hanging heavy over me, I couldn't get in the Christmas spirit no matter how many times I went to church. In fact, it was all I could do to make it through each day. I was still having to steel myself against the whispers and stares and head shakes of all those who disapproved of the way I'd handled the mess that Wesley Lloyd had left me. I tried not to care, and most of the time I didn't, but then I'd catch a pitying glance thrown my way and I'd have to struggle with my anger at Wesley Lloyd and at Hazel Marie, as well as with my despair at that child who looked just like him, all over again. In the face of all the talk and the snickers behind my back, it took all the strength I could muster to hold my head high and keep up a Christian front, much less stir up any Christmas spirit.

Some days were easier than others, for I was learning that Hazel Marie had a sweet and open disposition. Naive and gullible was what it came down to. She had to've been, or she wouldn't have put up with a decade-long association with a married man. I still couldn't understand it, but then, I'd never had to worry about where my next meal was coming from nor been burdened with an out-of-wedlock child, either. Maybe if I'd been in her shoes I'd have taken whatever crumbs that came my way, too.

As for the child, well, at first, I could hardly stand to be near him. Nine years old, and as much like Wesley Lloyd as anybody could be. Every time I looked at him, so thin and pale and wispy haired, all I could see was his father, and be reminded of what his father had to have engaged in to end up with this reproduction of himself. Add a smattering of freckles, thick glasses that slid down his nose, and a hangdog look about him, and you can see why I wasn't exactly eager to clasp the child to my bosom.

Besides, the boy needed a firm hand. He needed instruction on how to look people in the eye when he spoke to them, how to sit up straight, how to shake hands, and, Lord help us, how to blow his nose. I tried to bring some order and discipline to his life, and to Hazel Marie's as well. That's what they had been sorely missing, but, living as they had from week to week on Wesley Lloyd's meager handouts, who could wonder at it? Wesley Lloyd had never been known as an overly generous man, a state of affairs that I was thoroughly acquainted with. He was tight as a tick, if you want to know the truth.

Of course, I was getting my own back by this time, for all the assets he'd spent a lifetime amassing and stashing away were just sitting there waiting for me when he keeled over. I take that back. *Half* of all his assets came to me, since he'd left an even bigger mess with a last-minute handwritten will that made the child wealthy and me destitute. It took Sam Murdoch, Binkie Enloe, and the state of North Carolina to make sure that justice was done and I got my due.

To my credit, when it was all straightened out, I found I had no resentment in my heart at what was put in trust for the child. I had come so close to being stripped of everything that the half I finally got looked as if it would last my lifetime. If, that is, I exercised good judgment and made careful use of it. Just knowing it was there eased my fears of an impoverished old age, and I intended to stretch it out in a prudent manner so that it wouldn't run out before I did.

Still and all, I felt a certain amount of buoyancy at the thought of having financial assets that were totally under my control, and nobody else's. But you don't immediately overcome the habits of a lifetime, especially when those habits had been constantly dinned into your head. And, as I felt some obligation to teach the child fiscal responsibility and frugality, it behooved me to set an example and make sure that he and his mother didn't let their sudden wealth go to their heads.

And, if I'm honest, I have to admit that more of Wesley Lloyd's attitudes and opinions had rubbed off on me than I realized.

Even though I'd disagreed with him more times than not, I'd kept my mouth shut and let him rant on about whatever was exercising his mind at the time. But, without realizing it, I'd gradually absorbed some of his viewpoints, in spite of myself.

Needless to say — but I will, anyway — I was shaken to my core when the extent of my absorption of his frame of mind was brought home to me during that first Christmas. But after my eyes were opened, I came to realize that I didn't have to put up with Wesley Lloyd any longer. I could have opinions, viewpoints, and attitudes of my own if I wanted to. And, boys, I wanted to.

It took me a while to get to that point, however, because I was still so wrapped up in my anger at Wesley Lloyd in spite of the fact that he'd been dead and buried some four months by the time that first Christmas rolled around. To say nothing of my bitter resentment toward Hazel Marie for her youth and beauty, even though she was bordering on forty and just this side of trashy looking. How could my husband have preferred her to me, who had led an exemplary life conforming to every dictate that issued from his mouth?

And that child! I can't tell you how it

ripped out my heart every time I looked at him. He was a pitifully poor substitute for the children I never had, but I intended to do my duty by him if for no other reason than the fact that I knew no other woman in the world would've opened her heart and home to her husband's bastard son.

Besides, it was the Christian thing to do, as anyone would tell you if they didn't have to do it themselves.

From the distance of a few years now, I could look back and see how wrong I was to project forty-something years of bitterness onto Hazel Marie and that innocent boy. Yet I still can't see how, given my temperament and my husband's betrayal of his marital vows, I could have done it differently. We all have to learn, you know, and that first Christmas with both of Wesley Lloyd's families — licit and illicit — under one roof was a learning experience from which I have yet to recover. Thank goodness.

Chapter 16

When the first of December rolled around and Hazel Marie received the first check from the child's trust account, she couldn't believe it.

"It just showed up," she marveled, looking intently at the check. "Just like that, it just came in the mail."

"That means Sam has the trust fund up and running," I said. "From now on, he'll see that you and the boy have enough to live on."

"Enough to live on?" She looked at me with those luminous eyes and said, "I've never seen so much money in my life. If all this keeps coming every month, I don't know what I'll do with it."

"I expect you'll find a use for it. Now, Hazel Marie," I said, using the subject to launch into a lecture on financial responsibility. "You should set up a budget and live within it. Open a checking account and start a savings account, if for no other reason than to teach your son how important it is to put aside something for a rainy day. Money requires careful and prudent management, and you need to exercise discretion in handling it. Don't go spending it here, there, and everywhere."

For a minute, an echo of Wesley Lloyd's words sounded in my head, but I brushed it aside. I had a responsibility here to give her sound advice, and if she had any common sense at all, she would pay attention to it.

"Well," she said, "the first thing I'm going to do is pay you room and board. Now that I can pay our way, I should do it and not expect to live off your generosity."

Well, my generosity had nothing to do with it. I wanted them in my house for the simple reason that having them defied the town gossips. It showed the town that I could do as I pleased, in spite of what was said about me, my dead church-going husband, and his clandestine activities. I wasn't about to hide my head in shame by pretending his mistress and his son didn't exist. Besides, everybody knew about them anyway — had, in fact, known about them long before I did. What good would it have done to pretend they didn't exist?

Hazel Marie didn't understand any of that, and I didn't intend to enlighten her. She thought that I was the kindest, most generous, and wonderful person she'd ever known, and she constantly told me so. I don't mind saying that it pleased me to hear it, even if I knew in my heart that I possessed none of those virtues. At least, in this situation.

"It's my pleasure to have you here, Hazel Marie," I said, which was nowhere near the truth, but I believe in being courteous even to the point of outright lying if the circumstances call for it. "There's no reason in the world for me to live alone in this big house, and you're doing me a favor by keeping me company." Then I added, "And Little Lloyd, too. This house has never had a child in it, and as he is of a quiet and malleable nature, he is a pleasure to have around."

"Maybe I ought to think about getting our own place," Hazel Marie mused as she smoothed out the check on her knee. "I mean, if this much keeps coming in, we could afford a nice apartment."

Right there, Hazel Marie proved how little she knew about money and how far it would go. The income from the trust would've afforded a good bit more than a nice apartment. So it was imperative that I not permit her ignorance to make her the prey of every gold digger and real estate agent that came along. It was up to me to instruct her in financial management in order to preserve the child's legacy from grasping hands. Not that I knew that much about money management myself, having been given so little opportunity to learn by Wesley Lloyd, but I discovered I had an aptitude for it that would've amazed and confounded him. Why, I'd been able to balance my household account every month since he'd been gone.

"Hazel Marie," I said, trying for a somewhat pitiful tone, "I hope you won't consider moving. I need someone around, well, in case I get sick or fall and break something. I'm not as young as I used to be, you know."

"Oh, Miss Julia," she cried, reaching over to put her hand on my arm, "you know I'll look after you. Afer all you've done for us, being so good to us and all, I'd do anything in the world for you."

Not especially liking to be touched, I lifted my arm and brushed back a strand of hair. "Thank you, Hazel Marie, that's quite reassuring, but unlikely to be necessary. The truth of the matter is, I'd just like you to stay here for the company. It gets lonely, you know."

"Well, if you really want us to stay, I

think I ought to pay something toward our upkeep."

Frankly, I did not want another boarder, having already accepted one at Sam's insistence. Deputy Coleman Bates had moved into my upstairs guest room that opened off the back sunporch not long after I'd buried Wesley Lloyd. "So I won't worry about you being alone, Julia," Sam had said, as if he ever had.

But somebody else paying rent? No, thank you, I was not running a boardinghouse. Still, I appreciated Hazel Marie's concern that she not camp on my doorstep, expecting to be taken care of. And it occurred to me that she'd be exhibiting an admirable sense of responsibility if she paid her own way.

"One hundred dollars a month," I said. "If you feel that strongly about it."

"But that's not nearly enough. I think it should be more, since more groceries have to be bought, and we use hot water, and I don't know what all."

"No, that's plenty," I said, and resolved in my mind that the extra money would go to Lillian who, when you came down to it, was the one who'd have more work to do. "I want you here as guests, and company for me." Besides, I suddenly realized, if

Hazel Marie paid the going rate for room and board, she might take it in her head to go and come as she pleased, whether I approved or not. And that wasn't what I wanted.

But the fact of the matter was, I didn't know what I wanted, except to keep the child and his mother close, and I had no idea why I wanted that. Maybe to keep rubbing salt in my wounds so the pain and anger wouldn't subside. But that was too uncharitable of me to even consider. So I didn't.

Hazel Marie got up from her chair by the front window and said, "I think I'll walk downtown and deposit this check. Then I can write one to you for the months we've been here, and one for December, too."

"No, just start as of this month. No back pay is necessary. Now, Hazel Marie, remember to fill out a deposit slip and endorse the back of your check."

She nodded. "Yes ma'am, I know."

Well, I hadn't, so how did she? It still griped my soul that Binkie Enloe, my attorney, who was less than half my age, had had to instruct me on how to manage my own money. Well, Wesley Lloyd's money but, in spite of his intentions to the contrary, he'd not been able to take it with him.

I tightened my mouth, but Hazel Marie didn't notice. She said, "I used to close out the cash register when I worked at Pat's Convenience Store. Other than that, I've never had much to do with banks, which is kinda ridiculous when you think about it. I mean, at my age and all. But then, I've never had enough to have any use for a bank."

"Just deposit that, then you can write a check for cash to have walking around money. And you can write checks for anything you want to buy." I stopped and thought for a minute. "Hazel Marie, you do know to enter the amount of the checks you write in your checkbook, don't you?"

"Yes, ma'am, I do. And I know I have to subtract each time, too. I don't think that's going to bother me, because it doesn't look like this'll ever run out."

I smiled tightly. "You'd be surprised. Why, your personal monthly maintenance bills will mount up before you know it."

"My maintenance bills? You mean, rent and food, things like that?"

"No, I mean what it takes for your own personal grooming. Things like hair care, manicures and pedicures, and such."

A delighted smile spread across her face. "Really? I can do all that?"

"And you need new clothes and so does

the child. What I've purchased for you both is not enough. You might want to think about buying a car in the next few months, too."

She looked at me, her eyes shining. "A car," she said, as if it would be a dream come true, as it undoubtedly was. "I would love to have a car, and be able to come and go whenever I want to."

"Be careful with that kind of thinking, Hazel Marie. There are many places you shouldn't want to go to. We're known by the company we keep, you know."

Her eyes widened. "Oh, I wouldn't want to go to any place I shouldn't. I'm just talking about being able to take Lloyd to school and pick him up without asking you to do it for me or borrowing your car. And being able to run to the store for you or Lillian. You know, not having to be dependent on anyone else."

I understood what she was saying, but I didn't know her well, and who knew but what she'd want to hang out in roadhouses or bars or whatever. Not that we had any bars in Abbotsville to speak of, but this was not a woman who was accustomed to patronizing libraries, concert halls, or art museums. I needed to keep my eye on her so she wouldn't be profligate with her child's inheritance.

"Oh, Miss Julia!" Hazel Marie's face lit up with a sudden idea. "I know what else we can do."

"What would that be?"

"Let's have a wonderful Christmas! Oh, my goodness." In her excitement, she began fanning her face with the check. "This will be the best Christmas ever. I won't have to tell Lloyd that Santa Claus didn't get his letter, or make up some story about another little boy who needed a gift more than he did. I can get everything he wants for the first time in his little life."

Now, have you ever heard anything so foolish? I just shook my head, because that was exactly the kind of rampage I'd feared. She was going to take that money and go crazy with it.

"Hazel Marie," I said, "I hope you don't mean that. That child has to learn that he can't have everything he wants. It's not good for his character. And don't tell me he still believes in Santa Claus. He's nine years old, for goodness sake."

"Oh," she said, frowning as the light faded from her face. "You may be right." She looked at the check again and said, "Well, I guess I better go put this in the bank."

Chapter 17

I heard no more about Christmas for some few days after that, and to tell the truth, I thought no more about it either. There was still so much to do to get Wesley Lloyd's estate settled, and it seemed that I spent days at a time in Binkie's office, looking through deeds and bills of sale, and first one thing and another. We went through lockboxes and file cabinets and, as more and more assets came to light, I wondered where my mind had been all those years when Wesley Lloyd was amassing such wealth. *And* keeping another woman. *And* begetting a child, the thought of which kept me so unsettled I could hardly pay attention to what Binkie was telling me.

"Look at this, Miss Julia," she said, turning a ledger toward me.

"What is it?" I asked, following her finger as it went down a list of names.

"I'm not sure," she said, frowning. "Oh, I see what it is. It's a list of loan transactions. See, here's the rate of interest charged on each one and the monthly payments due. And this is the total owing on each loan. Wait a minute." She began flipping through the pages, comparing them with the names on the first list. "Yes, I thought so. This is the master list, and these are the amortization schedules for each one."

"Oh, then it's bank business," I said, no longer interested, even if I'd known what she was talking about. Wesley Lloyd had owned one of the few independent banks left in the state. But since I had no desire to learn the banking business, Binkie was in the process of negotiating its sale to one of the major institutions that was always looking to buy up something with the money they'd accumulated from deposits, certificates of deposits, car loans, and home mortgages.

"No, it's nothing to do with the bank." Binkie pushed her reading glasses up into her curly hair. "It's a record of private loans."

A rush of fear surged through me. "You mean I owe all this?"

Binkie flashed a quick smile. "Nope. You don't owe a thing. They owe you." She leaned again over the ledger, pointing to a number of names that I recognized. There was Horace Allen and Dr. Walter Hargrove and Pete Williams and Ronnie Crenshaw and Jim Hardison and that new dentist in town, Dr. Bradley, and, my goodness, a bunch of others.

"They owe me?"

"Yes, and it's perfectly within your rights to call these loans in so we can settle the estate. But since you don't need it, you'd be better off just continuing to receive the monthly payments until the loans're paid off."

I sat back in my chair, warmed by an unexpected feeling of well being. Half the town, it seemed like — at least the half that I knew — was indebted to me. I hesitate to admit it even now, but for the first time in my life I knew what it was to have the upper hand, and I liked it. I could even feel a little warmth toward Wesley Lloyd for all the work he'd put in, but most especially for his not being around to stifle my enjoyment of the results.

"All right," I said, trying not to let my pleasure show too much. "Let's do that. But I don't understand, Binkie. Why did these people borrow from Wesley Lloyd? Why didn't they just go to the bank if they needed money?"

"Lots of reasons. Some of them may have been over-extended at the time.

Others may not've been a good loan risk or maybe they didn't have sufficient collateral and would've been turned down. And I'll bet, if I looked all these up, that Mr. Springer charged something like a quarter or a half point less interest than the bank." Binkie glanced up at me, then went on. "Private loans are a good source of income for those who can afford to make them. Of course, you do have to be selective and know who you're lending to, but a lot of people do it."

I leaned over the ledger, memorizing the names of those who owed me money. Then I noticed something else. "These interest rates, Binkie, why are there different amounts?"

She smiled. "Interest rates fluctuate anyway, but these probably depended on who wanted the loan, how badly he wanted it, and how much Mr. Springer could get away with charging."

I took a deep breath at the thought of Wesley Lloyd's sharp business dealings. "You mean he was a usurer."

"Well, I wouldn't say that exactly, but he obviously knew when somebody really needed money. I see a few here who I know have been in a particularly hard spot, and, let's just say, he took advantage of their need."

"Then why don't we renegotiate these loans and make the interest rate the same for everybody? Say, a quarter under the current rate, whatever it is. I'd sleep better at night, knowing I wasn't taking food from anybody's mouth."

Binkie grinned up at me. "Hardly that. But you could even cancel them, if you wanted to."

I reared back in alarm. "Let's not go that far." I shook my head. "No, when you borrow, you have to pay back. It's not good to get something for nothing, and I don't intend to be the cause of anybody's character being ruined."

"Okay," she said, but for some reason, she tried to hide a smile. "I'll make a note to notify these folks of the rate change, as well as your intent to continue the loans. You're going to relieve a lot of minds, Miss Julia. They'll be worried about the loans being called in, so I expect they'll be grateful to you for not doing it."

"Well, I should hope so," I said, feeling quite satisfied with myself. I was now in a position to grant relief to the hard-pressed and reveal myself to be both gracious and charitable. I just hoped those debtors appreciated it.

I got home later than usual that evening

just as Lillian was ready to serve dinner. Hazel Marie and the boy had waited for me, as they should've, and we went into the dining room together. I sat at the head of the table with the others on each side of me, across from each other. The table was pleasing to me, with its white cutwork placemats against the polished mahogany and the lighted candles in the candelabra. It's important to carry on with the daily routine, especially after a family tragedy, which we'd all experienced and I was still suffering from. Wesley Lloyd had always insisted that the evening meal be served with silver and crystal and fine china, and I saw no reason to discontinue that custom. The child and his mother both needed to learn that meals should be taken in a refined atmosphere, and not on a hit-and-run basis like you see on television, with people eating in cars and talking with their mouths full.

I shook out my napkin and placed it across my lap. "Little Lloyd," I said, "you may return thanks for what we're about to receive."

"Yessum," he whispered, as we bowed our heads. Then he proceeded to mumble the old standby. "God is great, God is good. Let us thank him for our food. Amen."

"Thank you. We're ready for Lillian now," I said, and tinkled the tiny silver bell by my plate.

Lillian entered with a platter of roast beef and vegetables. She offered it to me first, as I'd instructed her to do, so that our guests could see how it was done. Still, she had to help both of them fill their plates.

I noticed as we began to eat how their eyes kept cutting over to me, watching to see how I handled my knife and fork, when I took a sip of water, and where I put my butter knife. I didn't mind, for they both needed to learn correct table manners.

"Little Lloyd," I said to break the heavy silence, "it's customary to discuss the day's events at the dinner table. But remember that such conversation should be light and entertaining and conducive to good digestion. Would you like to share anything with us?"

The child ducked his head, causing his glasses to slide down his nose. He murmured, "No, ma'am. Thank you, anyway."

"Come now, surely there's something you can tell us. You can start any subject at all and, chances are, your mother and I will have something to add to it. So give us a topic of interest to you, anything but religion and politics, both of which are apt to cause disagreements and subsequent internal upsets."

He turned a pleading face toward his mother, hoping, I was sure, to be rescued from my attention. She was equally intimidated, so he had no help from that quarter. I disliked putting the child on the spot, but, if we were ever to have a comfortable relationship, we had to learn to converse together.

"Perhaps something amusing happened in school today," I prodded him.

With another desperate glance at his mother, he hunched his shoulders, took a deep breath, and spoke to the tabletop. "Well, this one boy in my class had to go to the bathroom real bad and the teacher said he'd already been and couldn't go again. And he started wiggling and squirming, and he got real red in the face, and the teacher said, 'Willis, you do not have to go to the bathroom, so quit putting on,' and he said he wasn't putting on, he was putting out."

Lillian, who had just walked in with a basket of rolls, laughed out loud, and Hazel Marie sputtered so bad she had to put her napkin over her mouth. I permitted myself a polite smile, although it was all I could do to keep from falling off my chair.

"Well, you certainly avoided religion and politics," I said, when I could keep a straight face. I had no wish to kill his spirit, but I didn't want to encourage such unsuitable dinner conversation either. "But perhaps we should add another forbidden subject."

Lillian walked over to him and said, "Take one of these here rolls, baby. You done entertained these folks enough, so you eat while we see how good they do."

Lillian had already lost her heart to the child, and I feared she'd spoil him rotten if his mother didn't do it first. I thought it well that there was at least one person in the household who cared about the proper rearing of a child. Train up a child in the way he should go, and when he is old he will not depart from it, so saith the experts, as well as Solomon, who said it first.

As Lillian removed our dinner plates before serving dessert, she surprised me by speaking of a subject that was usually discussed in our weekly planning sessions. "Miss Julia," she said, standing by Little Lloyd's chair, "December already here, an' we don't have us a Christmas tree yet. This chile need one an' so do you an' ever'body in the house, includin' me. I know you mournin' Mr. Springer, but he . . ." She stopped and put her hand on the child's shoulder, perhaps to bolster her courage. "You know he love Christmas, an' I know he want you to keep on keepin' on with the usual. An' prob'ly a little more."

I looked sharply at her. She knew as well as I did that Wesley Lloyd Springer had despised Christmas and all its trappings, so I didn't know why she'd stand there with no expression on her face and tell a bald-faced lie. But then, she cut her eyes down at the child, who was looking expectantly at me.

"Well, I suppose," I said, resigning myself to the inevitable. "Yes, I suppose with a child in the house, we should make an effort to celebrate the season. Hazel Marie, if you'd like to take my car tomorrow, perhaps you and Lillian could go pick out a tree."

"Can I go? Please, can I?" Little Lloyd was exhibiting more animation than I'd seen in the few months I'd known him, a matter of concern to me, for my tolerance of unruly children was all but nonexistent.

"Of course, you can," his mother said. "Lillian, if it's all right with you, we'll pick him up after school and then go find a tree." She turned to me. "Where should we go? When I was little, we'd get our tree from a field or out in the woods, but I wouldn't want to take your car off the street."

"I should say not," I said. "Go to the nursery on North Main and pick out a good one."

"They're awfully expensive," she said, frowning. "They grow them special, you know."

"Yes, I know. But if you're going to have a Christmas tree, you might as well have a nicely shaped one, two or three feet high. I don't want a straggly, crooked tree with half the branches in nubs. Lillian, you know the kind we usually get."

"Yessum, but . . ."

I turned to Hazel Marie. "Lillian will clear off the lamp table in the front window, and we'll put it on that. The box of ornaments is in the basement, clearly labeled. I'll leave the decorating to you."

Little Lloyd's eyes shone as he looked at his mother. "A real Christmas tree," he said. "I'm going to like that a whole lot better than what we got in a box at Wal-Mart's."

My word, I thought, an artificial Christmas tree, the most tasteless thing I could imagine. The child desperately needed training in the finer things of life, and a real Frazier fir covered with ornaments was as likely a place to start as any. Of course, if it'd been left up to me, I'd've gone to bed and stayed there until Christmas was over and done with.

Now, all this time later, I squirmed and twisted in my chair, but no rearrangement of position could relieve the discomfort in my soul as I recalled the pinched and ungenerous woman I'd once been. Rubbing my hand across my face, I reminded myself that a lot of things start out a far cry from what they end up being. In a lot of cases, the end results are remarkably better than the way they start out — penicillin, for one, and bacon for another. And perhaps Julia Springer Murdoch, for a third.

Taking a deep breath, I realized that our present troubles might not be quite as bad as the ones I'd already come up against. And overcome, I might add.

Except they wouldn't stay overcome. Here was Brother Vern back again, this time with a Wesley Lloyd look-alike claiming to be Little Lloyd's natural father. And, of course, it wasn't a stretch to consider that he just might be. I had no illusions as to Hazel Marie's morals. I knew when I first laid eyes on her and that child what she'd been up to. I might be old and old-fashioned, but I knew where children came from and how they get here.

But I had changed and so had she. Yet, here I was, reliving those early days again. . . .

Chapter 18

Late the following afternoon, as I was studying some figures that Binkie had given me, I heard cars pull up in the driveway and doors slamming. The sound of voices and the child's laughter disrupted my concentration.

Christmas, I thought, as my spirits dropped. Something to be endured if I could stand it. Closing the folder, I sighed and resolved to put on as good a face as I could. No need to let everybody and his brother know the pain and anger that kept my chest so tight I could hardly breathe.

The commotion grew louder as Lillian, Hazel Marie, and Little Lloyd and, I then determined, Deputy Coleman Bates entered the house with a great deal of talking, laughing, and what I can only describe as high and boisterous spirits. It made me tired just to hear them.

"Miss Julia!" Deputy Bates called with great exuberance as he came into the living room, bringing with him a blast of wintry air. I declare, the young man always over-whelmed me with his good nature and good looks, augmented by his dark navy uniform and the law enforcement odds and ends strapped around him.

"Man, it's lucky I happened to see every-body at the nursery," he said, with a wide grin. "I was on my way home when I saw them. Can you believe they'd picked out the tiniest tree on the lot? But I fixed that. We got a tree you're going to love. Lillian said she didn't think you had a stand big enough for it, so I got us one. Where do you want it?"

I was taken aback by this rush to judg-ment, but I managed to indicate the front window. Before I knew it, Lillian had re-moved the lamp and the other accessories on the table, all the while avoiding my eyes. Deputy Bates picked up the table and carried it out of the room, then he rear-ranged the chairs that had been on either side of it. All this while Hazel Marie and the child were bringing in armloads of sacks and bags from the car. Then they sat cross-legged in the middle of the floor and commenced removing and unwrapping one ornament after another, along with strings of lights and ropes of tinsel.

"Lillian," I said, "where did all this stuff come from?"

"Uh, well, ma'am, when Deputy Bates say he gonna get us a decent-size tree, I knowed we needed more'n that box you got in the basement."

"It's all right, Miss Julia," Hazel Marie said. "I bought them. It's a good investment, you know, because we can use them year after year."

The child held up a multicolored ornament. "Look, Mama, it's a little tiny sled." And he began digging into the sacks again.

I held my peace, but I was dismayed at the needless expenditure. I arranged myself in one of the Victorian chairs by the fireplace, settling in to watch but not to participate. Sometimes you just have to tolerate what's going on.

Pulling my cardigan closer as Deputy Bates told the child to hold the front door open, I watched with amazement the entrance of the largest Frazier fir I'd ever seen.

"Hope we don't have to cut this off," Deputy Bates said, his face red with exertion and cold. He manhandled the huge thing into the living room, leaving needles all over my Oriental, and stood it upright in the front window. It reached all the way to the ceiling.

Ten feet tall, I thought to myself, and

costing a fortune for every foot. I rested my forehead on my hand and tried to think pleasant thoughts.

"Oh, no," the child cried, "there's no room for the angel on top."

"Sure there is," Deputy Bates said. "I'll snip a little off the top, and she'll sit up there as pretty as you please."

In their excitement, they had forgotten that I was not in the habit of heating the outdoors. "Close the door, please, Little Lloyd."

"Oh, yes, ma'am. I'm sorry."

"Tell you what," Deputy Bates said, as he headed toward the open door. "There's a pile of wood behind the garage. I'll bring some in and start a fire."

"Oh, yes," Hazel Marie said, still sitting on the floor while she tested the strings of lights. "A fire in the fireplace will make it all the more like Christmas."

I sat up straight, preparing to voice my disapproval, but Lillian caught my eye with a fierce glare, and I subsided. After that look I decided that the mess an open fire would make couldn't be much worse than the one they'd already made.

As Deputy Bates brought in logs and kindling and set himself to laying a fire, Lillian and Hazel Marie began putting the lights on the tree.

"As soon as we finish with this," Hazel Marie said to the child, "you can help us put the ornaments on. Won't that be fun?"

The child laughed as the colored lights illuminated his face. I sighed, thinking that too much excitement surely could not be good for him. I drew myself closer to the fire, grateful for the warmth it was beginning to put out, but wondering how I'd let my neat, quiet house get so far out of hand.

"Look," Lillian sang out, as she glanced out of the window. "Here come Miss Binkie."

She hurried to the door and opened it to receive Binkie Enloe. Her arms were filled with packages wrapped in shiny paper and adorned with bows and holly.

"Merry Christmas, everybody!" she said.

"Merry Christmas! Merry Christmas!" Little Lloyd was beside himself, almost dancing up and down. "Did you bring presents? For us?"

"They sure are," Binkie said, stacking them on the floor and adding to the disorder in the room. "Coleman called me from his car and told me you needed something under your tree. So here I am!"

"You can go under my tree anytime," Deputy Bates said, taking her coat and looking at her with admiring eyes.

I rolled mine, disapproving of such blatant displays of affection.

"Come help us, Binkie," Hazel Marie said, climbing up the stepladder that Lillian had brought from the kitchen. "We have so many ornaments, it'll take all night to get them on."

"I'm helping," Little Lloyd said. "Everybody's helping, except Miss Julia, and she's watching."

They all turned to look at me. "Yes," I said, putting on a good face for their sakes. It was not my habit to throw cold water on the pleasure of others. "And I'm enjoying it ever so much."

Lillian hung an ornament, then said, "I got some soup I'm gonna heat up. I think I bring it in here so you can eat it by the fire."

I opened my mouth to protest. Food in the living room? Wesley Lloyd would've been outraged, the thought of which closed my mouth.

"By the fire! By the fire!" Little Lloyd said, as he jiggled around with excitement. "Oh, Mama, this is shaping up to be the best Christmas we ever had."

His mother looked at the child with loving eyes, and Deputy Bates put his arm around Binkie. "It sure is," he said.

I turned my head and gazed at the fire. The best Christmas ever? Maybe for some, but, for me, Christmas was just another lonely time to get through, as it had been for an untold number of years.

Chapter 19

Mildred Allen's Christmas tea was a staple of Abbotsville's social calendar, as mine had been up until that year. But I had no heart to do any entertaining, even if it had been acceptable as, clearly, it was not, with Wesley Lloyd barely cold in his grave.

In fact, I'd had some qualms about the propriety of accepting Mildred's invitation, and had half a mind to stay home. I would've been well within my rights as a grieving widow to send my regrets. And there was another reason I almost stayed home. I was vexed to my soul that Hazel Marie had been left off the guest list. The invitation had been addressed only to me, even though Mildred was obviously aware, as was everybody in town, of the fact that I had a houseguest. The lack of an invitation to Hazel Marie was a clear snub, although I didn't for a minute think that Hazel Marie recognized it as such. I expect she would've been astounded, as well as thrilled, if she had received one.

But I decided to go for two reasons.

One, they would talk about me even more if I wasn't there, and, two, I didn't want them to think I was prostrated with grief over the loss of a man who didn't deserve one restless night, much less a whole year of honoring his memory.

"Hazel Marie," I said, as I readied myself for a public outing, "I don't know what to wear. This fall has been so busy that I've not done my usual seasonal shopping."

She was sitting in the easy chair in my bedroom, watching as I searched through the hanging clothes in my closet. I'd invited her in to use my address book for the Christmas cards she wanted to send. I, myself, was sending none.

"Well," she said, tapping a ballpoint pen against her cheek. "It's a Christmas party, so something red would be pretty."

"But not at all appropriate," I said, somewhat testily. "I am in mourning, you know." Then I could've bitten my tongue off, for I almost said, "as you should be, too."

The subject of Wesley Lloyd's relationship to each of us was something that we both steered clear of. It was easy most of the time, for Hazel Marie had such an innocence about her that it took an effort on my part to think of the two of them having physical congress. Until I looked at that child, that is, which I tried to do as infrequently as possible.

"Oh, yes, you're right," she said, immediately contrite. "I guess black would be appropriate, then."

"Well, not that much in mourning," I replied, thinking that if black was the color of mourning, what would be the color of anger. "It is a party, after all. Maybe gray?" I laid a gray woolen on the bed and studied it.

"That's nice," Hazel Marie said with little conviction.

"What about this?" I pulled out a beige crepe and spread it beside the gray dress.

"Um, I don't know. That beige won't do much for you. You know, with your coloring."

I stared at her, wondering what kind of coloring I had and what she knew about such things.

"May I look?" Hazel Marie approached my closet as I stood aside. Then she pulled out an emerald green wool dress that I'd worn once two years before, then decided the color was too vivid for my taste. "This is it," she said.

"Much too bright," I said, although it did look better than I remembered.

"Come look in the mirror," she said,

holding it up in front of me. "It's perfect for you, and it's a Christmas color without being red. Besides, it makes a statement."

I didn't know what kind of statement she had in mind, but she was right when it came to the one I wanted to make. Let them talk, I decided. I'd wear the green and defy any of them to say one word about it.

I parked down the block behind the other cars, then walked up the wide brick walkway, lined with miniature boxwoods and winter pansies, to Mildred Allen's Federal-style house. The afternoon was gray with lowering clouds, and the Christmas lights on the tree in the window and on the garland over the door looked especially welcoming. I made an effort to gather myself before facing the nicest ladies and the biggest rumormongers in town.

"Oh, Julia," Mildred said as she stood in the door greeting her guests, "I'm so glad you came. I was afraid you wouldn't, you know." I declare, the woman was getting wider by the day. She had always been heavy-set — big boned, she called it — but in the long, bright red dress she was wearing she looked monumental.

"Why wouldn't I come? I always have," I said as I handed my coat to her maid.

"Well, but you know," Mildred whispered, engulfing me with the scent of Shalimar. "That child and that woman. Everybody's so *interested,* and you might not be ready to talk about them." She laughed. "I know I wouldn't be."

"You might," I responded, "if you got to know that *woman.* As soon as people begin to remember their manners and invite her to places, they'll know how sweet and kind she is."

My intention was to rub her face and everybody else's in my shame so I wouldn't have to endure it alone, but it went right over Mildred's head.

"I tell you, Julia, you are the most forgiving woman I know. I admire you ever so much. Now, go on in and have some tea. Emma Sue is pouring — I had to ask her, you know, or her feelings would've been hurt. Oh," she said, turning away from me, "here comes Helen Stroud. Can you believe what she's wearing?"

I wandered through the hall, glancing into the spacious living room where a fire glowed on the hearth, and continued across to the table in the dining room. As with everything in Mildred's house, it was perfectly appointed. A silver service was at one end, while candelabra and a spectacular Christmas centerpiece in her silver epergne were in the middle. People — my friends and long-time acquaintances — spoke to me, then quickly huddled with their heads together as I passed on.

With tight lips and straight shoulders, I walked to the head of the table where Emma Sue Ledbetter was ensconced behind the teapot.

"Hello, Emma Sue," I said. "Are you ready for Christmas yet?"

"Oh, Julia," she said, her eyes widening as she looked up at me. The lemon slice she held on a fork fell into a cup of tea, splashing the tray. "I didn't think you'd be here. I mean, I didn't think you'd feel like coming." She reached up and grasped my arm. "I've been praying for you and, well, your whole situation. But the thing is, Julia, I need more information so I can pray specifically for your needs. Would you like some of us to come over and have a prayer session with you?"

"I think not, Emma Sue. I'm doing what we're told to do and going into my closet to pray. And there's not enough room for anybody else. I'll have tea, please, with lemon and two lumps of sugar."

"I'm just trying to help, Julia," she said, her lower lip trembling, the presage of a spurt of tears.

"I know, Emma Sue, and I appreciate it. But I'd really prefer not to be the subject of either group prayer or gossip, no matter how beneficial the one might be."

"*Julia!*" LuAnne Conover interrupted us, which was a mercy, for Emma Sue had made me feel so uncharitable I might've backslid all the way out of the church. LuAnne came bustling up and hugged me, in spite of the fact that she knew good and well that I was not the hugging kind of friend. I almost spilled the cup of tea Emma Sue had handed me.

"Careful, LuAnne," I said, cringing at the thought of a tea stain on the winter white suit with gold buttons she was wearing.

"Why didn't you call me?" LuAnne said. "I would've picked you up and we could've come together. Oh, I should've called you. I just assumed you wouldn't want to come."

"You look lovely, LuAnne," I said, ignoring the reason behind her assumption. "You've had your hair done, haven't you?"

"Yes, do you like it?" And, before I could say I did, she went on. "And how about this suit? It's a knockout, isn't it? I got it at Marilee's. You ought to go in there, Julia, she's got the cutest things. Come on," she said, taking my arm, "let's go mingle. You've been holed up too long, what with all that's happened. I know everybody'll want to talk with you."

LuAnne drifted from group to group, with me in tow, talking and laughing and socializing as only she could do. She was good at it, and I began to feel more comfortable just by being with her. No one said a word about my situation, although there were a lot of comments about how they'd been thinking of me, how glad they were to see me out and about, and how they'd been intending to drop by but hadn't gotten around to it.

A little before our designated hour was drawing to a close, I wandered away from LuAnne, who was engaged in a brisk conversation with Helen Stroud about the best way to winter over African violets. Knowing that Mildred had staggered her guest list so that another group would soon be arriving, I edged my way to the stairs to retrieve my coat from her bedroom.

As I entered the room and began searching through the pile on the bed, I heard voices through the slightly ajar door of the bathroom. Intent on finding my coat, I paid little attention to the conversation until I heard my name mentioned. Unable to help myself, I perked up.

"Did you see Julia Springer?"

I immediately recognized the voice of Kathleen Williams, a young woman who was active in community benefits and fundraising, and who was a member of every do-gooder organization in town.

I pulled out my coat and turned to leave, but the voice of Miriam Hargrove, the doctor's wife, stopped me. "Yes, I did, bless her heart. I feel so sorry for her. Can you imagine what she's going through?"

"Oh, I know," Kathleen said. "It's just pathetic. Let me borrow your brush a minute."

Feeling my face burn with mortification, I draped my coat over my arm and started to tiptoe out. But then Kathleen went on.

"You know, if you think about it, it's funny, too. I mean, think about having somebody living with you who's slept with your husband. Wonder if they sit around and discuss his bedroom techniques."

As their laughter bubbled up, I turned around, furious at being the subject of gossip. My first thought was to sling open the door and let them know I'd heard them. I knew they'd die of embarrassment, but I also knew that the confrontation would add one more juicy item to be spread throughout the town.

So I stood for a minute, vacillating between facing them down and turning away in shame. Then, recalling a certain ledger in Binkie's office, I made a decision.

With coat on and purse in hand, I marched myself downstairs and toward the front door where Mildred was receiving thanks for her lovely tea from others who were leaving.

When my turn came, I said, "Mildred, thank you for having me. Everything was beautiful, as always. But I want to tell you, and I hope you'll pass the word to everybody else, that I will not be attending any other social activity unless Hazel Marie Puckett is invited, too."

Mildred's face showed her shock, then it hardened as she shook her head. "I'm sorry you feel that way, Julia."

"Oh, you won't be the only one who's sorry," I replied, smoothing on my gloves. "Ask Horace what he thinks about cutting me off and slighting my houseguest. You might also tell Kathleen Williams and Miriam Hargrove to discuss it with their husbands, too. There are several others I could name who, I assure you, would want my wishes to be respected. Thank you again for a lovely time."

And I left, knowing that the telephone lines would soon be humming, and that there would be many heated discussions between husbands and wives that evening. The thought of it lifted my head and straightened my shoulders. I stepped along right smartly, determined to put to good use my newly discovered position as creditor to half the town.

Chapter 20

Before the week was out, Hazel Marie and I were inundated with invitations. Even the postman commented on the amount of mail we were receiving, and Hazel Marie was beside herself with excitement.

"Oh, Miss Julia," she cried as she opened two more invitations, "everybody is *so* nice. I mean, they don't even know me, and they're inviting me to everything. I can't believe it. Look, here's one to a cocktail party at Dr. and Mrs. Walter Hargrove's, and another one to a luncheon at Mildred Allen's. And she just had a tea! My goodness, she gives a lot of parties, doesn't she?"

"Oh, yes," I said, somewhat dryly, as I looked through my own invitations. "Mildred's one of the town's biggest party givers. We have a number of other invitations, too, so much so that it looks as if we have something to go to almost every day up until Christmas. Now, as for this cocktail party, we'll certainly forego that. Miriam Hargrove knows better than to ask me to a function where alcohol is the centerpiece."

"Whatever you think," Hazel Marie said, her face flushed by her sudden popularity. "I just had no idea that people did so many fun things during the holidays."

Nor did I, but I didn't mention it. I knew why there was such a spate of dinner parties, luncheons, cocktail parties, coffees, receptions, and open houses, and it certainly wasn't because people loved to entertain all that much. I smiled grimly, thinking of all the women scurrying around to plan some sort of last-minute event with an anxious husband breathing down their necks.

Hazel Marie looked up from her stack of invitations and said, "What do you wear to all these things? I mean, these functions?"

Oh, Lord, I thought, from what I'd seen of Hazel Marie's scanty wardrobe, she had absolutely nothing suitable. "We need to go shopping," I said. "We'll do that first thing tomorrow. Now, Hazel Marie, enter each of these invitations on your calendar, so you'll know when and where, and so you won't accept two things at the same time. Put those we're going to refuse in a separate pile, and we'll write all the regrets and acceptances tonight. That reminds me. We need to order you some engraved stationery. We'll do that after Christmas. I have some plain sheets that you can use until then."

"Oh, there's so much I don't know about such things," she said. "I hope I won't make a mistake, but I probably will. I know I'm kinda ignorant, but I don't want to embarrass you. You'll tell me when I do something wrong, won't you?"

That willingness to learn pleased me beyond all bounds, and I assured her that I would let her know how best to conduct herself.

When we entered the small boutique on a side street off Main, I thought to myself that there wasn't a bit of difference between a boutique and a shop, except a few airs. It was nicely furnished, though, with soft music playing and even softer lighting so the customers would look their best. Marilee, herself, hurried to greet me as soon as we walked in the door, asking what I was interested in today and all but ignoring Hazel Marie. She changed her tune right smartly when I told her that Hazel Marie was the one in the market for a number of outfits for the Christmas social scene.

I took a seat in a spindly French chair

and prepared to give my opinion on the suitability of Hazel Marie's choices. We were the only customers at the time, so as soon as Hazel Marie tried on one dress or ensemble, as Marilee called them, she came out and stood before the three-way mirror, so I could pass judgment.

"Not at all appropriate, Hazel Marie," I gasped, as she walked out in a long-sleeved black dress whose neckline was cut all the way down to her stomach. I had to avert my eyes.

From the look on her face, I think she liked it. But she quickly came out of it and tried on another that provided the coverage I had in mind.

"Marilee," I said, "what do you have that would be appropriate for a luncheon? And let us look at some dinner suits, too."

Marilee was eager to please, taking clothes off the displays and running to the back to bring out some that had not yet been offered for sale. I noticed that Hazel Marie leaned toward the tight and the colorful, while I was determined that she choose the loose and the subdued. Not only was that my personal preference, but I knew that if she paraded around in eye-catching outfits people would talk about her even worse than they already were.

It took all morning and then some, but we were finally able to come to terms on what Hazel Marie should purchase. In fact, I had less trouble with her than I did with Marilee, who had quickly understood the type of attire that Hazel Marie preferred. The woman kept showing her one little number after another, none leaving much to the imagination. I finally had to put my foot down.

"Hazel Marie's not going on the stage, Marilee," I told her. "She's going to luncheons and dinner parties. Now show us something decent."

When the decisions were made and Marilee handed me the bill, I was staggered. I had known that a half-dozen outfits would not be inexpensive, but my word, I hadn't realized they would come to so much. Nonetheless, I wrote a check without a qualm and hardly a tremble of my hand, for Wesley Lloyd had always insisted that I dress in a manner appropriate to my position as his wife. "Quality, not quantity, Julia," he'd said more than once.

"Miss Julia," Hazel Marie whispered while Marilee wrapped our purchases, "maybe we shouldn't get all this. I didn't know they would cost so much."

Well, I hadn't either, but there was more

at stake here than a check, no matter how hefty. Since I was her social sponsor, it behooved me to see that she make a good showing. In fact, the impression she made would reflect more on me than on her.

"Appearances are important, Hazel Marie," I said, keeping my voice down so Marilee wouldn't hear, and repeat what she had heard. "Unfortunately, we are judged by how we look, and I want you to look your best."

"Yes ma'am, I appreciate that, but, well, I know you're careful with your money, and I hate to see you spend so much on me. Couldn't I at least pay part of it?"

"No, I want to do this for you," I said, while a scary thought flashed through my mind: If I'd let her do the buying, there was no telling what she'd've come home with.

We left with a number of boxes, then had to drive over to Asheville to find the right kind of shoes. I let her have her way when it came to that, but I'm here to tell you that three-inch heels would not have been my choice.

"I can't wait to wear my new clothes," Hazel Marie said, as we were driving home. "I've never had anything like them, and they're not at all what I usually wear.

But I know they're right because you helped pick them out."

I nodded and said, "You'll look lovely, I'm sure. But the important thing is, you'll know you're properly dressed. That gives a woman confidence, right there. Any remarks that are made will be about how well you're turned out."

She turned and looked at me for a minute. "They'll make remarks?"

"It'll just be pleasant chitchat. You know, comments about the weather, if you have your Christmas shopping done, and so forth. Just social conversation. You won't need to worry about it. You'll do fine."

"Well, I don't know," she said, frowning. "I've never been to a ladies' luncheon before, or a tea." She paused, then turned to me again. "What do you talk about at a dinner party?"

"Same things. The trick is, Hazel Marie, learn to ask questions before they ask you any."

"Like what?"

"Oh, ask about their hobbies, their children, how long they've lived in Abbotsville, are they ready for Christmas. That sort of thing. And, of course, if you're talking to your hostess, you say nice things about her house, the food she's serving, tell her you like her dress, even if you don't."

"I hope I can remember all that."

"You will. Just remember, when you compliment somebody that person will always think well of you. The compliment doesn't even have to be true, and she may even know it's not true, but it will make her feel good."

She nodded and looked out the side window of the car, thinking, I supposed, about her debut into Abbotsville society, such as it was.

After a while of silence, I bit my lip as a disturbing thought niggled at my mind. "Hazel Marie," I said, "if at any time when we're at these functions, anyone says anything to you that distresses you in the least way, I want to know about it."

She turned to look at me, her eyes wide, as if she couldn't imagine such a thing happening. "What would they say?"

"Probably nothing, but what you have to watch for are these women who can make a slighting remark with a smile on their faces, so that you don't know if they really mean it or that you even heard right." I smiled grimly, remembering a few instances. "We have a number of experts at that kind of thing, so you just smile right back at them. Then let me know who they are and what they said."

"Maybe I ought not go to any of the parties," she said, a worried look on her face. "I don't know what I'll do if anybody says something ugly to me."

"Nobody will. It's just a few who might try to get in a dig or two. On the whole, though, they're quite well mannered, and you can rest assured that they'll be on their best behavior. You'll enjoy meeting them." My concern was not about an out-and-out insult but one of those snide remarks that Hazel Marie might not even recognize. "Besides, I'll be right by your side, and I guarantee you'll have a good time."

And, if she didn't, I thought to myself, somebody was going to have a loan called in, and then we'd see who was having a good time and who wasn't.

Chapter 21

So, with Christmas bearing down on us, Hazel Marie and I went to one social event after another. I must say that the woman conducted herself reasonably well, given the fact that she worried herself to death before each one. She would get so wound up with excitement and nervousness that on one or two occasions, her stomach acted up on her before we left the house. All in all, though, I was pleased with her performance in the homes of the elite of Abbotsville. She was so openly happy to be included that even the most aloof hostess couldn't help but warm toward her.

I introduced her around and stayed close while certain ladies went overboard to make her feel wanted and welcomed. I would've given a penny to've overheard the less than gracious conversations between those ladies and their husbands beforehand. In general, though, I was satisfied with Hazel Marie's reception and felt that she was well on her way to being socially acceptable on her own.

Of course, it didn't hurt that Hazel Marie was the equal of any woman at any place we went as far as her attire was concerned. Seeing how she was watched and stared at, I was doubly glad that I'd caught her in time to suggest some caution about the length of the skirts on her new clothes. As soon as we'd gotten them home, she'd pinned up the hems on every one. But, thank goodness, I saw what she was doing before she threaded a needle, and was able to talk her into a halfway decent length. Not that she was difficult to talk into anything; all she needed was to have some impropriety pointed out, and she readily concurred.

She was, in fact, so eager to please that I didn't have the heart to unleash the angry criticism that threatened to boil over every time I thought of what she'd once done with my husband. Well, not just once, obviously.

The only reservations I had, as we went from one event to another, concerned the amount of makeup she wore and that brassy head of hair. There wasn't much to be done about the color of her hair, because even Velma, who is not the most conservative hairdresser around, said she wouldn't touch it with a ten-foot pole. "It's already colored to within an inch of its life," she told me. "And if I do anything else to it, it might all fall out. Wait till it grows a little, and I'll see what I can do."

As for the makeup, I didn't know enough about beauty products to make any suggestions, although I wanted to. Hazel Marie loved color, and she put it on her eyes, her cheeks, and her mouth. And for a dinner party, she dusted gold powder all over her face. Not one soul said a word to her or to me about her showgirl appearance, but I was struck by the number of married men who seemed to want to engage her in small talk. My mouth stayed so tight all through one dinner I could hardly get a fork in it.

Even though most folks kept their mouths shut about Hazel Marie's looks, I must admit that Emma Sue Ledbetter opened hers a little. She sidled up to me at Helen Stroud's coffee and murmured, "Julia, I know you'll take this in the spirit it's meant, but your friend would have a better testimony if she didn't wear so much eye makeup."

I looked at Emma Sue, studying the plain face that had never known the least dab of makeup, and said, "Eye makeup, whether her amount of it or your lack of it, is the last thing on my mind, Emma Sue."

"Well," she said in the hurt tone that was

so familiar to anybody she spoke to, "I'm just trying to be helpful."

All in all, my crusade to force Hazel Marie on my friends and acquaintances worked exceedingly well. Hazel Marie never learned what had opened the doors of the finer homes to her, and I didn't intend to tell her. And if any of my friends and acquaintances harbored resentment toward me because of it, well, that was just too bad. Let them take it up with their husbands for getting into debt with Wesley Lloyd in the first place. None of it was my doing, for I had been neither a borrower nor a lender. I just used what was handed to me, as anybody would.

Actually, our two-week social whirl paid dividends at home, as well. No longer were there heavy silences at our dinner table with Hazel Marie and Little Lloyd casting anxious glances at me. We had plenty to talk about, and talk we did. Hazel Marie told Lillian, and she told the child, and she retold to me everything that happened at each event. She told us who all attended — those whose names she could remember — what was served, what the houses looked like, who had complimented her on her outfit, and on and on. She was like a child, starry-eyed and thrilled at her good fortune in being included in the celebrations of the season.

And the child followed every word that issued out of her mouth, equally caught up in his mother's happiness. It was like a new world had opened to them, and I didn't doubt but that it was. I occasionally found myself joining in with the rehash of the day's occurrences, laughing with Hazel Marie as she told of Mamie Harris's cat, who'd jumped up on LuAnne's lap and made her teacup fly across the room.

"I shouldn't've laughed, Lloyd," Hazel Marie said, her eyes sparkling with the memory. "But everybody else did, especially when the cup landed upside down on the toe of Mrs. Broughton's shoe. She was so surprised that she kicked it, and it went sailing through the air, and, would you believe, Mrs. Harris caught it, one-handed. And it didn't break or anything. It was real funny, except tea was flung all over the place."

The child was just as entranced with his mother's social life as she was, and gradually he began to offer comments on the occurrences at school. Before I knew it, we no longer seemed to dread the gathering around the dining table, but rather to look forward to it.

It became my habit each evening, after

Lillian had gone home and the others had retired for the night, to sit alone in the living room before going to bed myself. Deputy Bates had apparently appointed himself the keeper of the flame, for each day he laid a fire, which we enjoyed while Lillian prepared the evening meal, and I continued to appreciate as the house quietened for the night.

I found that I liked to turn off all the lights except those on that expensive Christmas tree, and sit by the fire to mull over the untoward events that had shaken my life to its core. As our social season began to wind down, I was more often than not left with a bitter taste in my mouth, and it was especially acidic when I was alone in the darkened living room. I was of two minds about the way I'd inserted Hazel Marie into my life and my social circle. On the one hand, it gave me a strong sense of power for having forced my will on those who had either pitied or laughed at my wretched situation. Especially so since I'd rarely been in a position to have a say in anything, much less have occasion to ride roughshod over anybody who didn't please me. But on the other hand, the whole thing hadn't given me the lingering pleasure I'd thought it would.

Maybe vengeance should not have been mine. Maybe a meek heart was better than a proud one. Still, if I'd continued in my meekness, accepting whatever anybody wanted to dish out, I might as well have resigned myself to having Wesley Lloyd reach out from the grave for the rest of my life.

Sitting there, feeling the fire warm my near side, I wished to my soul that Christmas was over. It was all too much for me, what with Hazel Marie's happiness, and the child's excitement, and my own awful exertion to pretend that I shared their anticipation.

Ah, well, I thought, leaning over to poke at the fire, to do good is its own reward, although I'm here to tell you, I had yet to see any. Pastor Ledbetter often sermonized on the rewards awaiting us in heaven, but, with such a bitter heart eating away at me, I could've done with a few prizes to lift my spirits in the here and now.

Chapter 22

And speaking of Pastor Ledbetter, I was getting sick and tired of the way he ignored Hazel Marie and Little Lloyd. He hardly ever looked at them, just stood in the pulpit and let his gaze sweep right past them as if they were too insignificant to catch his attention, despite my having seen to it that they were in church every Sunday morning that rolled around, and had put the child in Sunday school and taken Hazel Marie to my own class. She was much too young for the Lula Mae Harding Class that I attended, but I knew she wasn't ready to go it alone in one of the young women's classes. And I certainly wasn't going to suggest that she join a class for couples.

So, here were two regular attendees, both of whom dropped something in the offering plate when it went around, and the leader of the flock acted as if they didn't exist. It was enough to make me grind my teeth.

Of course, I'd known all along that Pastor Ledbetter was a sore loser, since preachers in general are as accustomed to getting their own way as any other corporate leader. And he had lost big and publicly when he'd tangled with me over Wesley Lloyd's estate, and it must've pained him considerably to see that illegitimate and very wealthy child sitting in a pew each Sunday, staring up at him with his mouth hanging open. I know the pastor heartily disapproved of my association with the child and his mother. I expect he would've preferred that I keep them hidden away just as Wesley Lloyd, his most ardent supporter, had done. It was my deep suspicion that the pastor had known something of Wesley Lloyd's secret life but had turned a blind eye as long as his pledges and contributions kept coming in.

But perhaps I wrongly accuse him. I just know that he was not happy with me, in spite of the hefty pledge envelopes I put in the collection plate, and in spite of my seeing that Little Lloyd dropped in his quarter every Sunday, which I must point out was considerably more than a tithe of his weekly allowance.

None of that was appreciated by the pastor, but on the last Sunday before Christmas Day, he truly outdid himself. Maybe a lot had to do with the fact that he did not preach a sermon. Instead, various young people read from the Scriptures in between hymns and carols by the choir, all going on behind a group of children who presented a nativity scene. It was your typical church pageant, with the prettiest blonde child cast as Mary and a boy with a pasted-on beard as Joseph. The angel had a bedsheet draped around her and a tinsel halo on her head. The whole thing would've been better staged at night when the sanctuary was too dark to see clearly the shepherds' ratty bathrobes and the dish towels wrapped around their heads.

But these were children, so you have to overlook a lot and appreciate their efforts. Which I did, but none of it affected me much until they digressed from the Scriptural narrative and added a little drummer boy scene, with Little Lloyd as the little drummer boy himself.

I hate to admit this because it seems so maudlin, a distasteful sentiment to my way of thinking, but I was so moved that tears sprang to my eyes before I could get hold of myself. Hazel Marie latched onto my arm when he appeared, and both of us had to dab at our eyes throughout the presentation.

We watched with bated breath as the child marched slowly down the center aisle with a toy drum hanging from his neck, that stirring song on a record player accompanying him. He approached the manger and knelt to offer the only thing he possessed — the ability to play his drum.

Well, of course, the child couldn't play a blessed thing, but he tapped the drum a few times when the choir director pointed at him, and our imaginations did the rest. But the whole scene with that child, unacknowledged and hidden away by his father, portraying the poorest of the poor just struck me as the most pitiable and heart-rending thing I'd ever seen.

I soon got over it, especially since one of the three kings almost knocked over the manger, and by the time the benediction was pronounced, I'd regained my usual composure.

Later, as Hazel Marie and I were heating up the food that Lillian had prepared for our Sunday lunch, I said, "Do you know who directed that little pageant?"

"Edna Worley, I think. She's Lloyd's Sunday school teacher, so I expect she had a hand in it." Hazel Marie gathered a handful of silverware and started toward the dining room.

"Hazel Marie," I said, reaching for an oven mitt, "I think it'd be easier to eat here in the kitchen. I mean, it's just us, so there's no need to be so formal."

Hazel Marie stopped and smiled at me. "I think so, too. And easier to clean up."

I nodded, wondering if I were letting slackness overtake my usual customs. Wesley Lloyd would never have eaten in the kitchen. Everything had to be just right and as formal as it could get to please him.

All the more reason, I thought with a tightening of my mouth, to do it differently. Besides, with a child in the house, and one who had performed so satisfactorily, there was every reason to ease off a little. Casual living has much to recommend it.

When we were gathered around the kitchen table, and our plates had been filled, I said, "Little Lloyd, who was it that cast you as the little drummer boy? Or did you volunteer?"

"No, ma'am, I didn't volunteer. Miss Worley just told us what we had to do, and we did it."

My word, I thought. Edna Worley might be unmarried and childless, but she certainly knew her child-raising techniques. That just confirmed to me that you didn't have to bear a child of your own to know how to raise one.

"Mama," Little Lloyd said, hurriedly

swallowing what was in his mouth. "Can I get Miss Worley a Christmas present? A lot of the kids brought her one this morning, but I didn't."

"Oh, Lloyd," Hazel Marie said, immediately concerned. "I'm so sorry. I didn't even think of her."

"Well, I didn't either," the boy said. "And I still wouldn't have, except she told everybody after the pageant was over that I was the best drummer boy she'd ever had. So now I'd like to get her something real nice."

I was immediately on my guard, readying myself to head off any infelicitous spending. "It's not necessary, Little Lloyd, to give everybody you know a gift," I said. "A nice note in your own hand would be more than sufficient."

He ducked his head, and those heavy glasses slid down his nose. "Yes, ma'am, I guess so."

"But," I said, relenting somewhat, "perhaps something small and thoughtful would be appropriate."

"What did the other children give her?" Hazel Marie asked, which I thought entirely germane to the situation. One must keep within the bounds of custom.

"Well, she got a lot of candy, and somebody gave her a book of devotions, and somebody else gave her a gift certificate for pizza. But Ben Sommers gave her some earrings like little tiny stars, and she really liked that. So that's what I want to give her. But I want to give her some dangly ones, Mama, like what you like."

Hazel Marie's face lit up, and she opened her mouth, I knew, to agree that dangling earrings would be the perfect gift. I beat her to it. "Little Lloyd," I said, "it is entirely inappropriate to give such a personal and expensive gift. She would not expect it, and you should be careful not to go overboard in spending for any one person. If you give Miss Worley something expensive, you will only embarrass her, because she is not in a position to reciprocate. And, even if she were, she could hardly play favorites by giving you a gift and not any of the others. Just remember, it's the thought and not the gift that counts."

"Yes, ma'am," he said, his attention firmly fixed on his plate. "I'll try to remember."

Hazel Marie was silent for a while, then she said, "Lloyd, we'll think about it and then go shopping for her. I expect we can find the perfect gift without too much trouble. You have one more day of school, then we'll have three whole days before

Christmas to come up with something."

"Okay. I mean, yes, ma'am."

Of course, I knew my lecture on fiscal responsibility put a crimp in their high spirits, but I knew I was right, so I didn't let it bother me too much. Besides, the child was in line for a considerable inheritance, and he needed to have the polish and finesse of a gentleman in order to carry it off responsibly. There is nothing worse, to my mind, than sudden wealth descending on a person who doesn't know any better than to conduct himself in the tackiest and most tasteless way possible.

Startled, I suddenly cocked my head, thinking I'd heard a footstep upstairs. Quietly sitting upright as I prepared an acceptable excuse for being up so late, I waited to see if someone was coming to check on me. After several minutes of listening to the house creak and the furnace click on, I decided that the sleepers were slumbering on undisturbed.

Stiffly and gingerly, I rose from the chair and tiptoed into the kitchen, feeling my way through the dark rooms. A cup of coffee would've hit the spot, but I settled for a glass of water, then made my way back to the warmth of the chair by the fireplace.

That little boy . . . How poorly I had treated him! I hung my head in shame, remembering how he had never shown me anything but wide-eyed admiration and a constant desire to please.

Chapter 23

The following morning the three of us took our places at the dining room table. As Lillian came in with a plate of toast, I lifted my head and glanced around.

"What's that I smell?"

"It's cookies in the oven," Lillian said, and glared at me. "*Chris'mas* cookies."

Well, for goodness sake, I thought, as she flounced back to the kitchen, what in the world is wrong with her? I ask a simple question and all I get is a hard look and a short answer.

No one else said a word, which suited me fine. The evening meal was the time for polite conversation, but the morning one was made for silence. That had been Wesley Lloyd's dictum, and over the years I had come to subscribe to it. I would concentrate on my breakfast, while he ate and read the newspaper and stirred his coffee. And stir his coffee and stir his coffee, until it was all I could do to keep from stabbing his hand with a fork.

But after more silence, Little Lloyd ventured to speak, although so quietly that I barely heard him.

"Mama?"

"Yes, honey?"

"Today's the last day of school."

"Yes, I know. The Christmas holiday starts tomorrow. Are you excited?"

"Uh-huh, I sure am."

Silence descended again, with only the clink of silver against china to disturb the peace. Perhaps it was because I hadn't joined in the conversation, which was just as well, since the only thing that it had occurred to me to say was that the child didn't sound too excited. And that was just as well, too, for I've noticed that excitement in a child soon escalates into rowdiness, which I could do without.

As Hazel Marie was putting on her coat to drive the child to school, I stepped into the kitchen to talk over the week's menus with Lillian. She had two pans of cookies cooling on racks. She frowned at me as she pulled off a length of cellophane wrap. Little Lloyd and his mother came through on their way to the garage, the child listing to one side from the heavy book satchel on his shoulder.

"Here, baby," Lillian said. "I 'bout got these cookies ready for you." She placed a stack of cookies on the cellophane, gathered it together, and tied the package with a red ribbon. "You give these to yo' teacher, an' tell her Merry Chris'mas. An' they's a whole pile of 'em waitin' for you when you get home."

The child smiled so big that it changed his entire face, making it somewhat palatable. If, that is, you could overlook those two front teeth that were all out of proportion to his size. I wondered if we should have something done about them.

"Oh, thank you, Lillian," Hazel Marie said. "I appreciate this so much, but I wish you'd let me bake them."

"No'm," Lillian said, with a smile. "I don't let nobody do no cookin' in my kitchen but me."

"Good thing," Hazel Marie said with a giggle. "I'm not much of a cook. I know his teacher will love these and be thankful that I didn't bake them. Come on, Lloyd, we'd better get going. See you in a little while, Miss Julia. I'm going downtown after I drop Lloyd off, if that's all right."

"Of course," I said, but of course I wasn't too happy about it, since I knew she was going to spend money.

Little Lloyd started out the door, then turned back to me. A hint of the smile lingered on his face, but there seemed to be something wistful in the look he gave me. Surely I misread it, though, for the child had everything anybody could want. He gave me a tiny wave, then followed his mother on out.

"Now, Lillian, we need to . . ."

"I know what we need to do, but don't look like you do," she said, surprising me so bad that I had to take a step back.

"Why, what do you mean?"

"I mean it almost Chris'mas, an' you need to get yo'self busy doin' something 'bout it. Who you gonna get presents for, anyway?"

"Well, I was planning to give the paperboy a dollar bill, but I just don't have the heart to think about anything else."

"Now, you jus' listen to me." Lillian propped her hands on her hips and stared me down. "They's nothin' under that tree in yonder but what Miss Binkie bring. You need to get some Chris'mas for that little chile, and for Miss Hazel Marie, and for Deputy Bates. It ain't right for you to pull them down jus' cause you don't feel like doin' nothin' but mope around here all day. And what about Miss Binkie? That girl been helpin' you all this long time, an' you ought to be gettin' her a present, too."

"I pay her, Lillian. She doesn't expect a gift on top of that."

"She got you one," Lillian came back at me. "I know, 'cause I done looked at ever' one of 'em. An' what about Miz Conover? You an' her always give presents. What you gonna do 'bout her?"

"I thought I'd wrap up a loaf of your banana bread for her. You still have some in the freezer, don't you?"

"Yessum, I do. But that mighty poor givin', seem to me, since I know she come in here with something store bought for you."

I waved my hand. "Yes, and it'll be bath powder, like it is every year."

"Don't matter what it is. She take the trouble to go an' do something for you, an' you can't even bring yo'self to think about a little chile, what lookin' for Santy Claus to come in here 'bout three days from now." Lillian stopped and drew in a deep breath. "Miss Julia, I know I don't ever talk to you this way, an' I hope you won't hold it against me. But it look like to me you have a better Chris'mas yo'self if you make a better Chris'mas for somebody else."

She was right. She'd never spoken to me in such a way before, and I was just before being mortally offended by it. But I am not one to reciprocate in like manner, so I thanked her for her advice and went upstairs to be by myself for a while.

I sank into the easy chair in my bedroom and rested my head on my hand. Lord, everybody was after me about something every time I turned around. If it wasn't Binkie wanting my signature on a piece of paper, it was LuAnne wanting me to get out of the house and do something. Now, Lillian was on my back about shopping for Christmas, when all I wanted was to be left alone.

Well, no, I guess I didn't, else I would've sent Hazel Marie and that unfortunate child packing long before this. I hadn't realized what a burden they would be, for if it wasn't Christmas it would be Valentine's Day and Easter Sunday and Mother's Day and birthdays and first one thing after another. All requiring, according to custom, some recognition in the form of gifts and presents and the spending of money. Before I knew it, I would be scraping the bottom of the barrel, without a penny to my name. What no one seemed to realize was that I was on my own now and, if the money ran out, what would I do?

I rubbed my forehead and sighed from the depths of my soul, thinking back to the barren years with Wesley Lloyd. He hadn't believed in acknowledging any of the milestones of life, except Easter, of course, by going to church, which made it no different than any other Sunday. Birthdays, I thought with a pang, were barely worth his attention. Every year on mine he would hand me a check for fifty dollars and tell me to buy something I wanted. And he would always — and I mean, every year that rolled around — say, "Don't spend it all in one place."

It had taken me years to get over being disappointed and to stop hoping for things to be different. At first, I'd decorated the house for each occasion, planned special meals, did my best to make special days special. He hadn't appreciated any of it, often not even noticing unless I interrupted his routine. Is it any wonder that I'd given up and taken on his sour disposition? Now I didn't know if I could rekindle any of the hope and expectation of a special day that I'd once known. I wasn't even sure that I wanted to.

But Lillian had shaken me up. I *should* make an effort. I knew that. I just didn't know where the energy for the effort was going to come from.

Maybe I'd go downtown and see what I could find.

I reached for a pen and paper to make a list. *Lillian,* I wrote first. Well, a check would be the thing for her, something she could use and would appreciate. That was easy enough.

LuAnne. Body lotion, since she was into bath articles.

Binkie. She needed something for that mop of hair, but I didn't know what it could be. So body lotion for her, too, and I could kill two birds with one stone, or rather two gifts at the same counter.

Deputy Bates. What would a law enforcement officer need? Nice leather gloves with a warm lining? No, too expensive, and he probably already had some. A box of candy. That would do it, and I could pick that up at the drugstore.

Sam? Should he even be on the list? We'd never exchanged gifts before, so should I start something that neither of us would want to continue? And it might embarrass him, since he wouldn't have anything for me. On the other hand, he had been of inestimable help in straightening out Wesley Lloyd's two wills, and I suppose I owed him some recognition. Another box of candy with a nice note of thanks. In that way, he wouldn't feel obligated to run out and get something for me.

I breathed out another long sigh. Now for the difficult ones.

Hazel Marie. The woman could use everything, so much so that it'd be hard to decide what she needed most. More body lotion? She'd be thrilled. Well, I gave her credit, she'd be thrilled with anything. Maybe body lotion plus a box of bath powder, just to show that I made more of an effort for her than for LuAnne, although I wasn't sure that would be wise. Maybe the cosmetics counter would have a gift package that came free with purchase when I bought lotion for Binkie and LuAnne. They do that on occasion, you know.

That child. What in the world do you get a nine-year-old boy? A Monopoly set? No, that took a number of players, and I didn't want to be roped in. Tinker toys? Absolutely not. Who wants those things scattered all over the living room floor? There were numerous things advertised on the television — action toys, electronic toys, and you-name-it toys. As far as I was concerned, though, none of them were suitable. A gift for a child ought to be educational and have some lasting value. Well, it was beyond me.

No, it wasn't. Forget toys. They weren't worth the money it'd take to buy them. Nine times out of ten they'd fall apart before they were out of the box.

A book, maybe. Except I didn't know what he liked to read. Something practical, then. I thought of pajamas, a sweater, socks, gloves, and on and on, until I began to realize that I was thinking of things that I would've given Wesley Lloyd.

That stopped me, so I folded the list and put it in my purse. I'd had enough of thinking about Christmas. As for the child, I'd just give his mother a check and ask her to buy something that he needed. She could put my name on it, and that would be that.

I closed my pocketbook with a snap, and said under my breath, "There, Lillian. I hope you're satisfied."

Chapter 24

Two days later I tapped on the open door of Hazel Marie's room, the downstairs one that used to be a guest room no one ever used, and peeked around the jamb. "Hazel Marie?"

"Oh, wait!" she said, and I heard a great rustling of paper. "Just a minute, Miss Julia. Don't come in yet, or yes, come on in but close your eyes." She giggled, while I waited with some impatience. "Okay, you can look."

I stepped into a room that might've been hit by a cyclone. Wrapping paper, ribbon, boxes, shopping bags, and bits of Scotch tape were all over the bed and the floor.

"I'm wrapping presents," she said.

"So I see," I said, surveying the damage. "I expect you've found that the wrappings can cost as much as the gifts, and some-times more."

"They sure can, but I'm being careful. I got all my wrapping supplies at Eckerd's, so I didn't spend all that much." She quickly took an armload of boxes off the easy chair, and said, "Sit here, Miss Julia. Would you like me to wrap something for you? I can do all of yours, if you want me to."

I sank into the chair and said, "No, I don't have anything to wrap yet. And it won't be much when I do. I declare, Hazel Marie, from the looks of this room, I'd say you've about bought out the town."

"Oh," she said, looking around as I had done. "I didn't think I had, but I guess it looks like it. I tried to exercise some discretion, just like you told me, but, Miss Julia, I can't tell you how much fun I've had, getting things for the people I love and not having to worry about paying for them."

I almost rolled my eyes, disappointed but not at all surprised. That money was burning a hole in her pocket, just as I'd thought it would.

"Be that as it may," I said, "I just came in to tell you that, as much as I hate doing it, I'll be going out for lunch, so you and Little Lloyd and Lillian will have to manage alone for a couple of hours. I may do a little shopping while I'm out, too."

"Oh, that'll be so much fun. I'm glad you're going out, and to tell you the truth, I've been worried that you haven't had time to do any shopping. Tomorrow's

Christmas Eve and the last shopping day before Christmas."

"Yes," I sighed, "I know. It'll probably be wall-to-wall shoppers today, too. I've never waited this long before, but I've had a lot on my mind this year."

"Can I help you? I'll be glad to do some of it for you."

Lord, I thought, no way in this world would I give her an excuse to hit another department store, but I said, "No, thank you, I'll manage."

Her eyes sparkled as she said, "It has to be a secret, doesn't it? It's no fun if people know what they're getting. Oh, Miss Julia, Christmas is the most fun in the world, and this one is the best ever."

"Well, we'll see." I got to my feet, preparing to leave. "By the way, where is Little Lloyd? He's been so quiet all day, it's like he's still in school."

"He's up in his room, working on something." She cut her eyes at me, smiling slightly. "He's got a secret project, and he's taking real pains with it. He better finish it today, though, because I'm taking him tomorrow so he can do his Christmas shopping."

I tried my best not to let my eyes roll back, but all I could think of was more money going out for little reason. Would the Christmas shopping frenzy never end?

"Well, I'll leave you to it." I started toward the door, then turned back. "I'm meeting Sam Murdoch for lunch, and . . ."

"Oh! Mr. Sam? Oh, Miss Julia, I'm so glad. He is just the nicest man, so kind and thoughtful. And he's real handsome. For his age, I mean." She looked at me, as something seemed to dawn in her widening eyes. "Oh, are you and him . . . I mean, are you two . . . ?"

"Whatever you're trying to ask, Hazel Marie, the answer is no. I've known Sam Murdoch for years, and his wife was a friend of mine before she passed some years back. I'm sure he has some business to discuss, but I wouldn't even do that if there was any way I could get out of it." I stopped and pulled myself together. The idea of even suggesting something between Sam and me was beyond my comprehension. Believe me, I was not in the frame of mind to grapple with any more problems, least of all, that kind of problem. "Now, is there anything you want me to tell him? Or ask him? Anything you don't understand about the trust fund?"

"No'm, he's explained everything real well, already. But, Miss Julia, I think you and

Mr. Sam would make a real nice couple, so you ought to think about it. I mean, he's so good looking, and you're a handsome woman. You're just made for each other."

I stopped in my tracks, absolutely stunned. Me? A handsome woman? I started to say something in return, but I couldn't think of a thing.

"That reminds me, Hazel Marie," I said, anxious to change the subject. "We need to make an appointment to have Little Lloyd's eyes checked. Those glasses won't stay up, and he needs new ones that fit." I started out the door. "I'm going upstairs and put my feet up for a little while. And, well, I thank you for what you just said, but Sam Murdoch is not interested in me, nor I in him."

To tell the truth, as I thought about this disturbing conversation up in my room, I'd never given much thought to Sam Murdoch. Other than, of course, the fact that he'd been Wesley Lloyd's attorney and a member of our church and a distant friend who'd come to my rescue when I thought I'd been reduced to living on Social Security and food stamps.

But anything else? No. One thing was as sure as I was sitting there, I had no intention of putting myself under submission to another man as long as I lived.

Chapter 25

Not that Sam was interested in me either, and I could've switched Hazel Marie to within an inch of her life for putting the thought in my head. Of all the things I could do without, it was some foolish notion about romantic entanglements. I was long past such things, if I'd ever been there in the first place.

After a while, I laughed at the idea and got up to ready myself for a business lunch that wouldn't come close to what Lillian would serve. Ordinarily, I would've insisted that Sam come here but, with two extra people in the house, I could understand why he wanted to have a serious discussion in another place.

I put on my coat, gloves, and hat, then told Lillian where I'd be.

"Mr. Sam not coming to pick you up?" she asked. "It still pretty cold out there, an' if he invite you, he ought to be givin' you a ride."

"He offered, Lillian," I told her, somewhat vexed that I had to explain myself to everybody in the world. "But I prefer to walk. I'll meet him at the tea shop. Then after lunch I'll do a little shopping on Main Street."

"Bout time," she grumbled, turning back to the sink.

Sam was waiting inside the door when I got to the tea shop. He smiled as soon as I stepped in, and, I couldn't help it, I smiled back. He *was* a handsome man, there was no doubt about that, and I wondered why it hadn't occurred to me before. Actually, I was undone that it had occurred to me at all, but that's what happens when someone puts an idea in your head.

As he took my coat, I couldn't help but notice how tall he was, how thick and white his hair, how broad his shoulders, how capable his hands, how confidently he spoke to the waitress who led us to the table he'd reserved, how his hand felt on my back as we wended our way, how pleasantly he greeted other diners as we passed, how he held my chair and made sure I was comfortable, how pleasant his manner, and how his blue eyes shocked me when he smiled.

And how such unwanted and preposterous thoughts were cluttering up my mind.

I declare, I was so self-conscious to be sitting alone with and across from a man who was not my husband that I could hardly get my napkin unfolded. Shaky hands, you know. All my social confidence seemed to have drained away, and I couldn't bring myself to look at him. That, unfortunately, caused me to glance around at the other diners, who were making it clear that they had an inordinate interest in us. I'd probably get a few phone calls later on, telling me that I'd been seen in the company of Sam Murdoch. As if I needed to be told what I was doing.

The waitress handed us menus and said, "May I take your drink orders?"

"Just water for me," I replied, accustomed by Wesley Lloyd to putting nothing extra on the bill on the few occasions we had eaten out.

"Wouldn't you like some tea, Julia?" Sam asked.

I shook my head. "Water's fine."

"Coffee?" he urged. "Wine? Come on, Julia, have a *drink*."

"You know I don't drink."

"More's the pity," he said, with a teasing smile, then ordered coffee for himself.

This business meeting was hardly getting off to a felicitous start. Offering an alcoholic beverage to me, right there in front of God and everybody, took my breath away. It was a shock to me to learn that Sam tippled, having assumed that everybody I knew lived by the same rigid regimen that Wesley Lloyd had insisted on. Of course, Wesley Lloyd hadn't followed it himself, so now I was having to adjust my thinking about everybody else.

"Now, Julia," Sam said, after his coffee had come and we'd given our orders for lunch. "I want to know how you're doing."

"I'm doing fine. Thank you for asking." I folded my hands in my lap and made sure my posture was correct. "Well, we might as well get to it, Sam. What did you want to discuss?"

"You."

"Me?"

"Yes, I've been concerned about you, Julia. I know you've not had an easy time, and I'd like to help if I can."

"That's considerate of you, Sam, but I'm managing all right." I fiddled with my fork, glanced up at him, then quickly down. "It's just . . . well, there is one thing that worries me, and I don't much know what to do about it."

"Tell me." And he looked so interested in what I had to say that I couldn't take my eyes from his for the longest time.

Then I cleared my throat and went on. "It's Hazel Marie, Sam. Wait, now, don't get me wrong. She is just as easy to get along with as, well, as you are, but she doesn't have any sense of the value of money. I declare, she's throwing it away like it grew on trees. I've spoken to her about being frugal and careful in her management, but it goes in one ear and out the other. You need to talk to her, Sam. It's your responsibility to preserve that trust fund for the child."

Sam frowned. "What's she doing? Giving it away? Buying things she doesn't need?"

"That's exactly it." I leaned across the table, so I wouldn't be overheard. "You should see the pile of stuff she's bought for Christmas. She's going to spoil that child until his character is ruined for good."

"Julia, listen now," Sam said, his kind face seeming to give my concerns the value they deserved. "What we have to realize is that Hazel Marie has never had any superfluous money in her life. Barely enough at times to cover the necessities. So, sure, she may go overboard a little while she's learning to manage it."

We were interrupted by the waitress, who set our plates before us. I hadn't been sure that I could eat with Sam watching every move I made, but I was so intent on making sure he understood the problem that I didn't give it another thought.

"I understand that, but when is she going to learn? And what if she runs through the fund before she does?"

"No," Sam said with a smile. "She can't touch the fund. Nobody can, except me and Lloyd when he reaches maturity. No, Julia, she is staying well within her monthly income. In fact, and this may make you feel better, she's opened a savings account and is putting aside part of it. For a rainy day, she told me."

"Well." I was somewhat taken aback, both surprised and gratified that the woman had taken some of my advice to heart.

"Well," I said again, then leaned toward him again. "If that's the case, how can she afford to buy so much for Christmas?"

"As long as she's not spending more than she's getting, and I assure you she's not, then I say let her enjoy it however she wants."

Enjoy, I thought with some disdain. Money was not for enjoyment. It was for security in your old age and freedom from worry about paying your bills. And it was for making people do what they wouldn't ordinarily do, which was to invite Hazel Marie to their social functions.

Now that was an eye-opening thought. Maybe having one's way was the kind of enjoyment money bought. Then I put that thought away as unworthy of a practicing Christian.

"What're you thinking about, Julia?" Sam asked, looking as if my thoughts were not only interesting, but valuable.

"Oh, it's not important but . . . Well, let me tell you what I did, which, at the time, gave me a great deal of enjoyment." Then I told him how I'd managed to introduce Hazel Marie to Abbotsville society.

Sam's eyebrows shot straight up. "You did what?"

"I held their feet to the fire and, Sam, you should've seen the invitations come rolling in." I smiled. "We were the most popular women in town."

Sam gazed at me, a smile playing at the corners of his mouth. "You amaze me, Julia. I didn't know you had it in you."

"There's very little you know about me."

"I certainly thought I did. We've known each other forever, seems like." He laughed. "It's just that I never thought you could be so, well, forceful."

"Huh," I said. "You haven't seen anything yet. Now that I don't have to answer to anybody but myself, I'm going to be as forceful as I want."

"Good for you," Sam said approvingly. "I always thought there was more to you than the dutiful wife everybody else saw."

"You did?" It had never occurred to me that Sam gave me any thought at all, much less that he'd wondered what was below the surface.

Sam nodded, studying me with eyes filled with enough warmth to embarrass me.

"Well," I said, as I fiddled with my fork. "I'm a little ashamed of myself now. I probably shouldn't've done it, but I figured that if I had to put up with the Puckett woman, they had to, too."

"Don't worry about it. I happen to know that most of those loans were made to people who'd gotten in over their heads from buying more than they could afford. So it serves them right. Besides, I like Hazel Marie. She's a sweet, unspoiled young woman, and they'll learn to appreciate her when they get to know her."

He likes her? And she thinks he's handsome. My Lord, I thought, I had personal knowledge that Hazel Marie was attracted to older men, as they were to her. Something heavy and overwhelmingly sad fell on my heart. I wanted to go home.

"Julia," Sam said, and to my everlasting surprise he reached across the table and put his hand on mine. "Don't worry about Hazel Marie. I'm watching out for her and the boy. It's you I'm concerned about. I want you to get a little fun out of life. I know you haven't had much before this, but now that you have the wherewithal, I want you to enjoy it. I'd like to see you kick up your heels a little, and I'm hoping you'll let me do a little of that kicking with you." He smiled at me, and did something between a rub and a pat, or maybe both, to my hand.

Fearing that someone would see, I slid my hand away from his and put it in my lap, trying to appear unruffled by his touch.

"Kick up my heels? With what? I have to be careful, Sam, and watch my pennies. Wesley Lloyd's estate could run out, you know, and then where would I be?"

He threw back his head and laughed so that the people at the next table looked around at him. Then he lowered his voice and said, "Run out? Hasn't Binkie shown you how much there is?"

"Well, yes, and I know it seems a lot, but you never know."

"My goodness, woman," he said, shaking his head. "You could spend a thousand dollars a day for the rest of your life, and still have plenty left over. And furthermore," he said, shaking his finger at me in a nice way, "you need to start spending some of it."

"I do?"

"Yes, you do. What is money for at our age, anyway? Who are you saving it for? Enjoy it, Julia, get some fun out of life for a change."

"Well, I'll think about it, but having fun is hardly at the top of my list. Now, I have to get home, Sam. Thank you for lunch, and for listening to my concerns. I thought you had some business matters to discuss, but I guess what we've talked about qualifies." I began to gather my things, then stood.

He stood, too, and whispered, "We'll have to do this again. I have a lot to talk to you about."

I just nodded my head and concentrated on getting around and past the tables without running into them.

As he followed me to the door, I stunned myself by turning to him and saying, "Why don't you come over Christmas morning and have breakfast with us? I'm sure Little Lloyd would love to see you, and Deputy Bates and Binkie'll be there, too."

"I accept," he said, without even having to think about it, which was much too quickly for my comfort. "I'll be there early to see what Santa brought. And I may even bring a little Santa myself." And, I declare, I think he winked at me.

After turning down his offer of a ride, I walked home, practically in a daze. I was so taken up with the unnerving twists and turns in our conversation that shopping for Christmas completely slipped my mind.

Leaning over to lay another stick of wood on the fire, I smiled to myself. It had never entered my mind that I'd end up married to Sam Murdoch. Oh, I'd been attracted to him early on, but at the time I was so far from wanting another husband that I hadn't recognized the symptoms. I'd thought I was coming down with something.

Wrapping my robe more tightly, I sat back in the chair wondering what Sam had seen in me. I'd been a sour old woman then, filled with bitterness and anger, yet he'd been able to look beyond those unattractive qualities. And now, of course, he'd gained a woman of heart and of courage, one who was his equal in spirit and generosity.

At least, that's what he told me.

Chapter 26

I had to give Lillian some excuse for coming in without a package to my name, so I told her I would have to finish up tomorrow, leaving the impression that I'd at least started, and perhaps had left a few bags in the trunk of the car.

"You shouldn't ask questions about Christmas gifts, Lillian," I said primly. "Secrecy is what it's all about."

Then I retired to my bedroom, sat in the easy chair, and put my feet on the hassock. I leaned my head back, going over in my mind everything that had been said — and done, for my hand was still warm where Sam had touched it.

Every time I recalled the way he'd looked at me, and touched me, and said he wanted to see me again, something perilously close to a loss of breath occurred. I knew I was being foolish to dwell on such notions, making me no better than half the widows in town who lost their heads every time a man spoke to them. It was a settled fact that I had read more into Sam's actions and words than he'd intended, so why was I entertaining such foolish notions? All I had to do was look in the mirror and know that my frivolous days were long gone.

I was a long married woman and a recent widow, for goodness sake, and had never in my life turned my eye toward any man other than my husband. Although considering the diversions my husband had engaged in, maybe I should have.

But it had never been my way to stray off the beaten path, regardless of the motivation. Nor would it be my way now, even though I was legally and morally free to pursue any adventurous enterprise that happened to appeal to me.

"Oh, for goodness sake," I said aloud, fidgeting in the chair. I had let my mind wander along forbidden and uncharted pathways. "What is wrong with you?" I asked myself. Let one man smile politely in my direction and here I was, entertaining romantic nonsense.

First thing you know, I'd be as bad as Hazel Marie.

Sam was merely being kind to the wife of an old friend and nothing more. To read something into nothing was a sign of old age and failing perceptions. Silliness, actually, and I did not intend to let myself lapse into such a state as that.

As I started to rise and busy myself with practical matters, I heard a tap on my door.

"Yes?"

"It's me." Little Lloyd's voice was so soft I could barely make out what he was saying. "Can I, I mean, may I come in?"

"Of course you may."

He opened the door and stood waiting, hesitant, it seemed, to fully enter the room.

"Well, come on in," I said, wondering what business the child could possibly have with me.

He edged in and walked over to my chair, one hand behind his back. "I have something for you."

"A Christmas present? You can put it under the tree with the others."

"No, ma'am. It's something you can use before Christmas. I'm going to get you another present to unwrap."

"What is it, then?"

"You might not like it."

"I won't know until I see it, will I?"

I declare, getting anything out of the child was like pulling teeth.

He brought his hand from behind his

back and thrust a little homemade booklet at me. I took it, turned it this way and that, giving it a good examination. It seemed to be made from several notebook pages, cut in fourths, and tied on one edge with Christmas ribbon. On the front in the child's crooked handwriting was: MISS JULIA'S COUPON BOOK.

"A coupon book?" I asked. "I don't know what that is."

"It's like you use at the grocery store when you buy something and don't have to pay much for it."

I had never used a coupon in my life and only entered a grocery store when Lillian was too busy to go.

I frowned at the booklet, wondering what he expected me to do with it. "How does it work?"

"You tear out a page and give it to me when you want me to do something for you. See," he said, turning to the first page, "right here, it says BRING IN THE MAIL. When you give that to me, I'll run out and bring in the mail. Even when it's raining or snowing."

"Well, that's nice. What else do we have?"

"The next page says EMPTY TRASH CAN. So when the trash can by your desk needs emptying, I'll do it for you." He sniffed and pushed up his glasses.

"Are you getting a cold?"

"No'm, I don't think so." He turned to another page. "See this one? When you give me this page, I'll clean out your car. Sweep it and wipe off the dust and whatever else it needs."

"That will be helpful. What's on the next page?"

He turned the page. "BRING IN FIRE-WOOD. That means when Deputy Bates is gone or if he forgets."

"Indeed. I'll certainly appreciate having a constant supply of firewood."

"And this one," he went on, still in that soft, whispery voice. "This one says BRING IN THE NEWSPAPER, but that's not just for one time. That's kind of like a promise to do it every morning."

"Well, I like that one. But you have to do it early, or Lillian'll get it before you do."

"Yes, ma'am, I know. Now this one says SIT UP STRAIGHT, and it's a promise, too, because I forget sometimes. So now you won't have to tell me, just show me that page and I'll do it."

"This is all quite commendable."

"Look at this one." He turned a page and showed me where it said BRING YOU A BLANKET WHEN IT GETS COLD AT NIGHT.

I took my lower lip in my teeth, unable

to think of a suitable comment. I looked at the written promise, slanted across the page, thinking of this child climbing out of a warm bed to bring a blanket to me in the middle of the night.

"That's very thoughtful," I managed to say, although I did wonder how I would wake him out of a sound sleep without getting up myself. In which case, I might as well get my own blanket. It was, however, the thought that counted.

"The last one is more like a promise, too, but I don't think I'll have to be reminded to do it. I'll think of it all by myself."

I turned to the last page and read ASK GOD TO MAKE ME A GOOD BOY. I closed my eyes, smitten to my soul, and truly rendered speechless.

"See, Miss Julia," he said, leaning and rocking on the arm of my chair, which I could've done without. "See, I know you want me to be a good boy, and I'm trying really hard."

"I know you are," I said, having to blink my eyes and clear my throat. "You are a good boy, Little Lloyd, as good as anyone could want. Although," I hastened to add, "we all need to be aware of the need for improvement. And that includes me, as well. Perhaps we both could ask God to make us better than we are."

"Yes, ma'am."

"Now, you should run along and get ready for dinner. Lillian'll be calling us in a few minutes." I took the booklet from him and glanced through the pages again, struck with his efforts. On each page, there was a drawing, carefully colored in, relating to the subject matter. This was the secret project he'd devoted the previous entire day on. And he had done it for me.

As he turned to leave, I said, "Little Lloyd."

"Ma'am?"

"This is the best present I've ever received, and I thank you for it."

His face lit up with a smile that transformed it before my eyes. If I could keep him smiling, he would never again remind me of his worthless father.

When the child was gone, I sat still, holding the booklet and feeling overcome with tenderness, a sentiment most unusual for me. The care that the child had lavished on the pitiful-looking booklet affected me powerfully, and, after the way I'd undoubtedly misread Sam and gone off into a frenzy of daydreaming, well, all I can say is that everything was contriving to play havoc with my nervous system.

Chapter 27

Later that night, on the eve of Christmas Eve, I sat again in the living room by myself, enjoying the warm glow of the dying fire and the colored lights on that beautifully shaped and decorated tree, which now seemed worth every penny it had cost. I picked at the pleats on my dress while my thoughts wandered all over the place. I had essentially lived alone all my life, in spite of the fact that Wesley Lloyd had resided in the same house. So, I was not accustomed to having anybody, especially a child, make demands on my emotions. Yet, that was exactly what had happened. Here I was, getting all warm and dewy-eyed, thinking of Little Lloyd laboring with painstaking intensity to make a coupon book for me. And I knew his mother had not suggested it to him, nor even known what he was doing, for I'd asked her about it. No, he had come up with the idea on his own and followed through until he had it exactly as he wanted it. That shows strong character, right there.

Thinking of the child's thoughtfulness, I

was so moved that I had to get up and walk to the window. The streetlight appeared to waver as the wind blew tree limbs in front of it. A cold night to be alone and lonely. I shivered, in spite of the warmth of the room, seeing myself as a sad and lonely old woman with a heart as cold as the north wind and as grasping as another Ebenezer Scrooge. I pressed the coupon book to my breast, as something broke and crumpled inside of me. Leaning my forehead against an icy window pane, I thought of that child asking God's help to be good. Lord, that's what I needed, worse than he ever would. Without realizing it, I had become so much like Wesley Lloyd that all I could think of was how to protect and hoard my wealth, dribbling it out penny by penny, holding on to it as if I could take it with me. He hadn't been able to, so why had I thought I could?

A line of poetry or scripture or something began running through my mind: And a little child shall lead them. One had certainly led me. With that, I took a few deep breaths, then turned and went into the kitchen to use the phone.

"Binkie?" I asked when she answered.

"Hi, Miss Julia. You want to speak to Coleman?"

"Why, no. Why would I?"

She giggled. "Because he's over here, watching television. I thought you might be wondering where he was."

"Binkie, you know I'm not in the habit of checking up on Deputy Bates. Now listen, I know it's late, and you have guests, so I won't keep you long. What I want to know is how much money I have."

She didn't answer right away. Adding things up, I supposed. Then she said, "Overall? Or readily available?"

"Both, eventually. But right now I want to know how much I can spend in one day and not wish I had it back next year or five years down the road."

"Well, let's see. Your household account . . ."

"No, not that," I said. "We need to eat, you know."

"I know. I was just listing things off. You have three money market accounts that you haven't touched. Remember those small checkbooks I gave you? You can write three checks a month on each one. Look at the balances, there's plenty in all of them."

"Binkie," I said, somewhat plaintively, "I don't know what you mean by plenty. I may want to spend a good bit, but I have a great fear of it running out."

"Are you planning to go to New York or to Paris to do this spending?"

"Certainly not. I'm just going downtown and shop for one day."

"Tell you what, Miss Julia," Binkie said, her voice taking on a professional firmness. "You go on and spend however much you want. There's no way in the world you could do much damage in downtown Abbotsville in one day."

"Really?" I had always heard of having a light heart, but mine suddenly lifted off.

"Really. And enjoy every minute of it."

"I believe I will. Yes, I do believe I will."

After hanging up, I got down on my hands and knees, searching through the packages under the tree to see how many gifts Hazel Marie had for Little Lloyd. Not enough, that was plain to see. I declare, you would think his mother of all people would've done better by him.

I was up bright and early on Christmas Eve, long before anyone else. I had things to do and barely enough time to do them. After dressing, I went down to the kitchen, put on the coffee, and sat down to make a list of the bare necessities for a boy's Christmas. Then I dialed the phone.

"Sam? Are you up?"

"Just barely, Julia. What's wrong?"

"Not a thing. You said if I needed anything to let you know, and that's what I'm doing."

"I'm at your service, ma'am," he said, with what seemed to me a suspicious amount of levity. "What can I do for you?"

"I need a truck. Can you get one?"

"A truck. You mean a semi or something like a pickup?"

"A pickup will do. If we need to make two trips, we'll do it."

Sam was quiet for a moment, then with what sounded like a suppressed laugh, he asked, "Do I dare ask why?"

"I'm going Christmas shopping, and I need your help if you're available. I can't drive a truck, for one thing."

"Well, I'm certainly available, and I think I can prevail on James to let me borrow his. He'll be here in a little while to start breakfast."

"Good, but don't wait around for breakfast. I want to get there before the shelves are empty, so we need to get an early start. I have too much to do to be waiting around half the morning."

"I'll be there within the hour."

That was not soon enough for me, but I had to accept it. I knew my car would not hold what I intended to buy, so I was at the mercy of a truck and a driver. So I poured a cup of coffee and tried to stem my impatience.

Before long, Hazel Marie pushed through the kitchen door, wrapped in a woolly robe and fuzzy slippers against the chill of the morning. She pushed back her frowzy hair and stared at me with bleary eyes.

"Are you all right?" she asked. "I heard you come downstairs, and thought something was wrong."

"No, I'm fine. It's early, Hazel Marie. Lillian's not even here, so why don't you go back to bed?"

"But you're already dressed and everything. What's going on? Can I help?"

"No, I'm just going shopping with Sam. It's the last shopping day before Christmas, you know. Now, Hazel Marie, I've looked under the tree, and there's simply not enough under it for that child. What did you get him? I don't want to duplicate anything."

She blinked her eyes, then said, "I got him a new car coat, which he needs real bad. A sweater and some pullover knit shirts. A couple of books, and a Game Boy. You know, it's a kind of electronic toy. And

I got him a few games to go with it. I wrapped everything separately so it would look like a lot. But I was real careful, Miss Julia, not to go overboard."

I let out an exasperated breath. "That is poor doings, Hazel Marie. It is Christmas, you know, and we need to do better than that. But don't run out and get anything else, because I'm going to take up the slack."

She opened her mouth to say something, but nothing came out. So she just stared at me as if I'd said something completely incomprehensible. Which I had not. As far as I was now concerned, it was perfectly understandable to give that child a memorable Christmas.

A noise in the driveway took our attention, and Hazel Marie went to the window just as a motor backfired. "Who in the world? Why, it's Mr. Sam in some old rattletrap of a truck."

I got up from the table and put on my coat. "Finally," I said. "Now Hazel Marie, you can have my car for a little while, but I might need it this afternoon after we get through at Wal-Mart."

She turned to look at me, surprise on her face. "I didn't know you shopped at Wal-Mart's."

"I don't, ordinarily. But it meets my

present requirements, so I'll give them my business. Tell Lillian that I'll be in and out all day."

I hurried out to meet Sam on his way to the door. The wind whipped my coat around me, and I cast a hurried glance at the lowering clouds. Bad weather in the offing. That was all I needed on this day, when I had so much to do.

"Let's go, Sam," I said, heading him off, as he seemed intent on going inside. Then I stopped in my tracks. That truck had seen better days a long time ago. There was a large rust spot on the fender, and the front bumper had been wired in place. A long crack ran across the windshield, and a piece of cardboard filled the space where the passenger window had been. Sam had left the motor running, and the whole thing was shaking and shimmying with alarming portent.

Sam grinned as I viewed our conveyance. "It's not much," he said, "but it'll get us there and back."

"Well, beggars can't be choosers, I guess. How do I get in the thing?"

Sam walked around to the passenger door and helped me up onto the duct-taped seat. "My word," I said, "are you sure it'll hold together?"

He laughed and went around to crawl under the steering wheel. "It runs better than it looks. Now, where to, madam?"

I looked straight ahead, not wanting to see his reaction to my destination. "Wal-Mart. And I can do without any comments."

He laughed. "Wal-Mart, it is then."

I declare, it was trial to try to carry on a conversation in that noisy contraption, but I managed to tell him what I wanted to get for Little Lloyd. The truck shook so bad as we traveled to the edge of town that our voices trembled like we both had St. Vitus dance.

It was a mortal relief to park in the huge lot that was already half filled with shopper's cars. Half the county must've had the same idea I'd had.

As Sam helped me out of the truck, I said, "Now, Sam, there's one, no, two things I want you to do. First, keep that old man they have at the door from coming at me with open arms. I'm going to smack him if he lays a hand on me."

Sam threw back his head and laughed. Then he took my arm as we threaded our way across the parking lot. "I'll watch him like a hawk."

"And the other thing is," I went on, "I don't want you to say a word about what I buy. Binkie said I could spend whatever I want, and that's what I aim to do."

"Not a word," he promised. "I'm just along for the ride."

As we went through the automatic doors at the entrance, all I could think of was that the place reminded me of a beehive. The aisles were fraught with glassy-eyed shoppers propelling overladen carts like they were the only ones in the store.

"Well," I said, casting an anxious eye around for that masher who was paid to feel up every woman who walked in the door. "If you have any suggestions as to what a nine-year-old boy would want, I'd like to hear them. But first, let's head for the bicycles. Where do you think they'd be?"

"We'll find 'em," Sam said as he took my arm, and together we plunged into the turbulent crowd.

Chapter 28

Sam was ever so much help, and I congratulated myself for having the foresight to engage him in my Wal-Mart foray. He knew what little boys would like, which was natural, I supposed, since he'd once been one. He knew the exact size and style of bicycle that Little Lloyd needed, including a basket and a bell on the handlebars, matters that I'd not even thought of. I did think of a sled, though, and we got that, too, in case it snowed. Then we cruised the toy shelves, and Sam pointed out the toy soldiers, Star Trek figures, and this, that, and the other that would thrill any small boy.

"A flashlight, Sam," I said. "Every boy needs a flashlight. And a camera, too. Help me look for them."

By that time, we'd filled one cart and I'd roped in two clerks, who were supposed to be working but who could never be found when you were looking for something. I set one of them to pushing the bicycle behind us, and sent the other to procure a second cart for our additional purchases. Finally, when both carts were almost full, we began to wend our way to the front of the store.

"Hold up, Sam," I said, before we got to the checkout line. "I think a television set would be nice. One he can have in his room for his very own. Oh, wait. Do you think that would be a hindrance to getting his homework done?"

"I expect his mother'll lay down a few rules. And from what I've seen, he's a conscientious little soul, so I doubt it'd ruin him. You might also think of a boom box."

"A what?" But I didn't really care what it was. If it was suitable for a neglected and needy child, I'd get it. "While we're here, I want a television for Deputy Bates, too. There's no need for him to have to go all the way to Binkie's when he wants to watch something."

"Uh, huh," Sam said, smiling as if to himself. "I expect that'll keep him home, all right."

"And some leather gloves with a warm lining. I may have to go to a men's shop for those, because I want something nice. You should see how chapped his hands are."

We had the two carts full and teetering with boxes by that time, and one tired and dragging clerk pushing a bicycle in and around the aisles behind us.

"Oh, for goodness sake," I said, as we once again headed for the checkout line. "A boy needs a ball of some kind. What would you suggest, Sam, a baseball or what?"

"Already covered. I've got him a baseball and a glove. I'm looking forward to showing him how to season and mold the glove to his hand. Binkie's got him a basketball, and Coleman has a hoop hidden away somewhere. He's concerned that you won't let him put it over the garage."

"He shouldn't be. I don't care what he puts up, as long as it's something the child wants."

Sam gave me a sidelong glance, but I kept my eyes straight ahead and on the next piece of business. I had long prided myself on being fiscally conservative and getting the most for my money. But my careful management was no cause for pride, since it had gone unappreciated anyway. Watching my money had been a case of have-to, for Wesley Lloyd had doled it out in driblets. I had learned penny-pinching from a master.

Well, times had changed, and so had I. And if Wesley Lloyd didn't like it, he could take it up with whoever was in charge of wherever he was. As for me, I didn't know when I'd enjoyed anything as much as this all-out shopping for Christmas presents.

I stopped in the aisle and let other shoppers sidle around me and my entourage of carts and clerks. "Let me consult my list, Sam, and see if I've forgotten anything."

His eyebrows went up at the length of my list, wondering, I expect, what had gotten into me to turn a tightfisted woman into a generous and bountiful giver of gifts.

"Don't say a word, Sam. It's better to give than to receive, you know."

Sam just smiled and said, "I agree, Julia. What's next?"

"Well, I think I've done all the damage I can do here. Let's get this paid for and out to the truck. Then I have a few other stops to make."

With all we had to purchase, we took up several spaces in the checkout line, which got us some ugly looks. I declare, people ought to have more of the Christmas spirit, even if they have to wait a few minutes. Everybody was in such a hurry, and I had to straighten out the clerk in charge of the bicycle when he wanted to prop it by the counter and leave.

The sum total for two carts full and a bicycle came to an astronomical amount. No wonder some people had to join Christmas

Clubs and save all year to buy Santa Claus for their children. Nonetheless, I wrote out a check and signed my name with a flourish. If you have it, use it and enjoy it, I always say.

"Now, Sam," I said, when the back of the truck was loaded and we'd climbed into the cab. "I need a place to hide all this. It won't do for Little Lloyd to see it before tomorrow morning."

"We'll take it to my house. I'll just put the truck in the garage, and we'll leave everything in it. James can drive my car home this afternoon, and I'll bring the truck to your house in the morning."

"Oh, that's good. But listen, Sam, you have to get there early. I want everything under the tree before that child gets up."

"You're talking real early, Julia. He's likely to be out of bed before sunrise."

"You think?"

"Absolutely. Every kid wants to get up early to see what Santa Claus left." He maneuvered the truck into the flow of traffic and we headed back into town. "Tell you what. Why don't I bring it over about midnight or so? We'll have plenty of time to unload and get it arranged around the tree."

"Yes, let's do that, if you don't mind staying up that late."

Sam cut his eyes over to me, giving me an indulgent smile. "I think I can manage. And, Julia, if Lillian has any eggnog made, I'll bring a little something to go in it and we'll raise a few to the season."

"Sam," I said, with a reproving look.

He laughed. "Wouldn't hurt."

"You know I don't indulge."

"Well, you certainly have this morning," he said, cocking his head toward the pile of goods in the truck bed. "I'm proud of you, Julia. You're going to have a happy little boy tomorrow."

"Indulging a child is different, Sam, from tippling out of bottle, and you know it. Drop me off at my house, if you will. I'll get my car and go downtown to finish up."

"Want me to go with you?"

"That's not necessary, thank you. I have to go to a few ladies' shops and such as that, for Hazel Marie, Binkie, and Lillian. Oh, and for LuAnne. Then I'll be through, except for wrapping, which I'll probably be doing half the night."

Sam pulled into my driveway and, stopping him from getting out, I managed to slide out of the seat by myself. "I'd invite you in, Sam, but you need to get this truck out of sight before that child sees what's in the back. Besides, it sounds as if it's on its last legs. I just hope it gets you back here tonight."

I started to close the door, then was brought up short by my failure to thank him. "Sam, I can't tell you how much I appreciate all your help. I'd've never gotten it done, and done so well, without you, and I thank you."

"It was my pleasure, Julia. I had a lot of fun watching you turn Wal-Mart inside out."

I never knew when Sam was teasing, but all I could think of as I walked to the side door was his description of our shopping trek. With a sour twist of my mouth, I thought, *Fun.*

Well, on second thought, maybe that's what it'd been. I knew I had a feeling of great satisfaction, as well as tired and aching feet. But maybe that's all part and parcel of having fun.

Lillian started in on me as soon as I stepped in the kitchen. "Where you been? Did you get any breakfast? You gonna break in two, you don't eat something."

"I have things to do, Lillian. Time is about to get away from me, and I just came in to get the car keys. If Hazel Marie has the car, I guess I'll have to walk downtown."

"No'm, she back. Her an' Little Lloyd

got they shopping done a little bit ago. Set down at the table. I got some soup for you an' a sam'wich. You gonna eat 'fore you leave this house again."

"Well, my goodness," I said, shocked by a glance at the clock. "I didn't realize we'd been gone so long. Hurry then, Lillian, I've got to get my shopping done before the stores close."

"You got all afternoon, but if you'd of listened to me, you wouldn't be running 'round at the las' minute like you doin'."

Don't you just hate it when somebody tells you something you already know?

After hurriedly eating, checking my list as I swallowed, I got in the car and drove downtown. I might as well have walked, in spite of the bitter cold, for I had to drive around the block three times before finding a place to park. Then I had to walk almost as far to get to the jewelry store.

"I want a string of pearls," I told the young woman behind the counter. "Real ones that they dive for in Japan, not your imitation kind."

"Oh, yes, ma'am," she said, quick to recognize a knowledgeable customer. "Right over here. What did you have in mind, exactly?"

"A traditional type of necklace, about

sixteen inches or so in length, and a nice size to the pearls."

"What about this one? These are lovely." She held up a necklace that was the right length, but the pearls were of a size more suitable for a young girl's first string.

"No. I want something appropriate to a more mature woman. Let me see those right there." I pointed through the glass counter.

"Oh, these are outstanding," the young woman said. "See, they're graduated from about five millimeters up to eight and nine. Any woman would be thrilled to have them."

I knew Hazel Marie would be, although she wouldn't know one millimeter from another. "I'll take them," I said. "And I'd like them wrapped, if you would."

"Yes, ma'am. I'll get right to it."

"Wait, I'm not through. I want something else. Something dangly and a little on the flashy side."

The salesgirl's eyes lit up. She knew she had a live one. "I know just the thing," she said. "Come over to this counter."

Before I finished, and while I was there, I selected a trinket or two for Binkie. Then, falling victim to the salesgirl's enticements, I couldn't resist a heavy gold charm bracelet for Hazel Marie. I chose several gold charms of one kind or another to go on it. "If you'll attach these to the bracelet and wrap everything separately," I said, "I'll run do a few more errands. I have to have them this afternoon, though, so don't close up till I get back."

I left, feeling inordinately pleased with myself. I knew Hazel Marie would love the bracelet, since it not only dangled, but jangled, too. She wouldn't appreciate the necklace half as much, but she would learn to. Every woman needs a good string of pearls.

By the time I finished my shopping and got home, I was so full of the Christmas spirit I could hardly drag myself into the house. I declare, it's good that Christmas only comes once a year, else I wouldn't be able to put one foot in front of the other.

Chapter 29

I was so tired, in fact, that I had to lie down after we returned from the Christmas Eve service, knowing I'd have to be up again till all hours when Sam came over. I couldn't sleep, though, for I was about as excited as Little Lloyd. He had entertained himself most of the evening by scrambling through the gifts under the tree, trying to guess what was in them.

"Mama! Here's one for you," he cried. "And it's from Miss Julia. And another one, too! Goodness sake, wonder what's in them?"

I expect he was somewhat disappointed by not finding anything addressed to him from me, but that didn't deter him from looking at every wrapped box again and again. It was too bad that a bicycle or a sled couldn't be conveniently wrapped, but I intended to put everything out and let it appear that Santa Claus had left them.

"Mama?" Little Lloyd said, sitting back on his heels as he surveyed the paucity of packages under the tree. "Do you think

Santa Claus knows where I live now?"

"Oh, honey, I'm sure he does," Hazel Marie said, trying to allay his fears. "He won't forget you."

She cast a questioning glance at me, fearful, I supposed, that I had given no thought to the child's expectations. I had a powerful urge to defend myself by telling them that Santa was on his way in a pickup truck. But Christmas is for secrets, so I curbed the impulse.

"Well," the boy said, as he nervously pushed up his glasses. "I just thought my letter might've got lost again, and he wouldn't know where to find me."

"I sent him a letter, too, Little Lloyd," I said, hesitating before ascending the stairs. "So I expect he'll find you with no trouble at all. Now, what time do you expect to get up?"

"As soon as my eyes open," he said, although from the excitement shining in them, I figured he'd have difficulty closing them for any length of time.

"You'll need to get in bed early, then. Hazel Marie," I said, turning to her, "I've invited Binkie and Sam, and told Deputy Bates that we're expecting them all for Christmas breakfast. I told Lillian that she shouldn't come in, but she wants to see what Santa leaves under the tree. They'll all be here early, so we should get on to bed."

"Yes, ma'am. I hope we can get to sleep, but I'm not sure I can, I'm so excited. Come on, Lloyd, you need to leave out some cookies and milk for Santa."

Cookies and milk, I thought. There were so many little traditions that I'd either forgotten or not known about, never having had a child in the house. But I was not too old to learn, and I intended to do so.

I didn't go to bed, just let the others assume I had by going to my room and curling up fully dressed in a chair. But I must've dozed off in spite of myself, for I was awakened by the sound of that rattly truck pulling into the driveway. "Oh, Lord," I thought, as I jumped up and smoothed my hair. "He's going to wake that child."

I tiptoed across the hall and closed Little Lloyd's door, then hurried downstairs in my bedroom slippers, hoping to make as little noise as possible. The house was dark as pitch, and I had to feel my way to the backdoor to let Sam in.

"Sh-h-h," I said. "They're both sound asleep, so we have to be quiet."

"I'm quiet as a mouse, Julia. Where do you want it all?"

"Why, it has to go under the tree, of course. Wait, I tell you what. Let's bring it in the front door. That way we won't have to go through the house and bang into things."

It took several trips between truck and living room to get everything unloaded and set up around the tree. By the time we finished, I was pretty well frazzled, but Sam had gotten into the spirit of our conspiracy and kept shushing me every time I wadded up a plastic bag.

"I can't help it, Sam," I said. "We can't leave these things in a Wal-Mart sack. The child can read, so he'll know they didn't come from the North Pole."

"I just don't want him to come tiptoeing down the stairs to see what the clatter is," Sam said, and grinned at me to see if I got his reference. Which of course I did.

That shiny new bicycle and sled gleamed in the reflected glow of the Christmas lights. When we had everything arranged just so, half the living room floor was filled with things that would make any child's eyes come alive with delight.

Then my spirits fell as I thought of something. "Sam!" I almost wailed. "I forgot to get an electric train. You know, a Lionel, if they still make them. Little Lloyd would be thrilled to see one running on the tracks under the tree. Would anything be open this time of night?"

"Julia, it's after midnight, so nothing but a few gas stations and convenience stores. Why don't you save that for his birthday?"

"Oh, good idea," I said, feeling a great relief that my lapse could be rectified. "When is his birthday?"

"Sometime in February, I think. I expect he'll let you know in plenty of time to get a train."

I nodded, then began to feel the consequences of a day on my feet, as well as the satisfaction of having spent the time well.

"What a day," I said, as Sam and I took a seat across from each other in the Victorian chairs beside the fire. "I've never shopped so much or spent so much in my entire life. But I must say, it's been a pleasant experience."

I poured two cups of Lillian's eggnog from the silver pitcher and handed one to Sam. "Unspiked, Sam. I hope you can stand it."

"I think I can manage," he said, his blue eyes sparkling in the light of the fire. "Especially in such good company."

My face felt warm as I tried to think of some innocuous reply. Thank goodness, I didn't have to, for we both lifted our heads as the sound of Deputy Bates's patrol car pulling in took our attention. We soon heard him come in the kitchen and begin tiptoeing through the house toward the living room.

"Well, hey," he whispered, as he came in with a great deal of squeaking leather from his deputy sheriff's paraphernalia around his waist. "I didn't expect anybody to be up. My lord, looks like ole Saint Nick's already been here. Is there room for mine?"

He lifted a white board with a basketball net attached to it, while Sam hurried to clear a space for it.

"Would you like some eggnog, Coleman?" I asked.

"No'm, thank you, but if you don't mind I'll make like Santa and have the milk and cookies some little elf has left out."

"Oh, good. I was about to offer it to Sam, because I certainly couldn't eat it. Sam, there're more cookies if you'd like some."

"I'm perfectly content, Julia, with what I have, and what I hope to get one of these days." He smiled at me, as Deputy Bates looked from one to the other of us, a knowing grin creeping across his face.

"I better get to bed," Deputy Bates said. "Binkie said she'd be over at the crack of dawn. She can't wait for Lloyd to see what all he got." He started out of the room, then poked his head around the dining room door. "Don't stay up too late, now."

Chapter 30

What can I tell you about that Christmas morning? Little Lloyd came running down the stairs, calling for his mother and me. "Hurry, hurry," he called. "I know he came. I heard reindeer feet on the roof last night. Hurry, Miss Julia. Mama, hurry up."

I followed him down the stairs, somewhat more slowly due to the meager amount of sleep I'd had. Hazel Marie appeared in her robe from the downstairs hall, and we both came up against the child, who was standing stock still in the door to the living room.

"Mama?" he said in a quavery voice. "Mama, did Santa Claus get mixed up?"

"Oh, my goodness," she said, holding her hand against her mouth as she got her first glimpse of the array around the Christmas tree.

The child stood there, trembling all over. I could see that wispy hair quivering with the fine tremors of his body. He seemed unable to move, so I patted his shoulder and urged him on.

"It's all for you," I said. "Santa told me that it was high time for you to have a good Christmas."

And then he flew to the tree, excitement jumping in his voice as he said, "Look, Mama. Look at this. I didn't know I was going to get this." The first thing he went to was the bicycle, which gave me an inordinate amount of pleasure.

It wasn't long before Deputy Bates came downstairs, looking half asleep. Then Binkie came in with her usual high spirits, wishing us a merry Christmas, then getting down on the floor with Little Lloyd to look through his presents.

Sam joined us then, his arms filled with packages, and his presence made the day even brighter. I was so glad I'd gotten him that clear blue cashmere sweater to match his eyes. I intended to watch his reaction closely when he opened it, like a test, you know.

He passed with flying colors, but it would be inappropriate to repeat what he whispered to me when he put it on. He wore it the rest of the day, and every day afterward until it had to go to the cleaner's.

Hazel Marie lost her breath when she opened the jewelry boxes I had gotten for her. I've never seen anyone so thrilled with anything in my life as when she put on the pearls.

"Oh, they're so pretty," she gasped, fingering them at her throat. "I just love beads."

I rolled my eyes just the least little bit, determining to set her straight on the difference between beads and South Sea pearls.

But, just as I'd thought, it was the charm bracelet that really capped her Christmas. She put it on, then ran at me with open arms. "Oh, Miss Julia, thank you from the bottom of my heart. I've always wanted one. I just love it."

She hugged me tight, as I thought I'd be more careful in my purchases from then on if they elicited such exuberance. For the rest of the day, the bracelet jangled and clanked on her arm. I think she made some extra moves just to hear it.

Binkie loved the dangly earrings I got for her, as well as the gold bangle bracelet. She hadn't expected to be so well rewarded for the help she'd given me, but I believe in being generous. I never did learn what Deputy Bates had given her, for they had exchanged gifts the night before in the privacy of her apartment. She seemed mightily pleased with whatever it was, though. In the same manner, I am reserving the right to keep to myself what Sam gave me. It's nobody's business if it was something no lady should accept from a gentleman friend. Let us say that in general I received an abundance of completely useless and impractical gifts, and I treasured each one of them.

Lillian was almost as excited as Little Lloyd when she arrived and saw the proliferation of gifts under the tree. Before long she was crawling around under the tree, helping the boy examine first one thing and another. She turned to look up at me, nodding to indicate her satisfaction with my efforts.

But I wasn't through. "Lillian," I said, "that box over in the corner is for you."

Her eyes lit up, as she and the boy ripped the paper off a television set. "Oh, sweet Jesus," she cried. "It's a teevee, an' one of them big 'uns, too. Where we gonna put this in the kitchen, Miss Julia?"

"It's not for the kitchen. It's for your home, Lillian."

Tears shone in her eyes, but she quickly wiped her face and said, "I better get these folk their breakfast."

She soon came back with a tray of coffee

and sweet rolls, while Sam and Deputy Bates began picking up the empty boxes and the mile-high pile of discarded wrapping paper.

The rest of the day consisted of consuming more food than anyone has a right to eat, although we managed, and sitting around the fire, talking together and listening to the exclamations of Little Lloyd as he discovered the ins and outs of each gift he'd received. Deputy Bates and Sam wanted to put up the basketball hoop, but a cold rain had started, so they had to defer their plans. It was just as well, for one of them might've fallen off the ladder, and wouldn't that have put a cap on the day?

When our guests left after a light supper of leftovers, I climbed the stairs so tired out I could hardly manage them, yet so full of the Christmas spirit that I was sorry the day was over. We were such a disparate group, it was a wonder that we'd enjoyed each other so much. But I decided not to question it. It was enough to know that I had brought pleasure to each one of them, not the least being that child.

I collapsed in my easy chair, too spent to ready myself for bed. I didn't even turn on a lamp, content to sit in the dark and experience the fullness of my heart.

There came a tap on my door, and a muffled voice asked, "Miss Julia? May I come in?"

"Yes, come on in."

Little Lloyd opened the door and slid silently over to my chair. "I want to tell you a secret," he whispered. I had to strain to hear him.

"What is it?" I whispered back.

He leaned close, so that I could feel his soft breath against my face. "I know there's not a real Santa Claus."

"How do you know that?"

" 'Cause he never brought me a lot of toys till we came to live with you."

"Who do you think brought them, then?"

He ducked his head and looked up at me over the top of his glasses. A smile started at the corners of his mouth and spread across his face. I smiled right back at him, and, at that moment, something was signed and sealed between us.

As he leaned on the arm of my chair, smiling at me, I thought to myself that Wesley Lloyd should be pitied for his cold and stingy ways. He had never known what it was to truly enrich a child's life. Money's not everything, you know.

The child bent over and whispered, "Don't tell Mama, okay? She thinks he's real."

"We won't tell her, then. It'll be just between the two of us. Now, you better get to bed. Maybe it'll clear up tomorrow and you can ride your bicycle. But not in the street, just in the driveway. And you have to wear your helmet every minute you're on the thing."

"Yessum, I will. Night-night, Miss Julia."

"Sweet dreams, Little Lloyd. Sleep well."

He slipped through the door, then turned again to me as the hall light backlit his slender figure. "This has been the best day of my whole life."

"Mine, too," I said, and leaned my head back as he closed the door and the room was engulfed in darkness again.

I smiled to myself, more at peace than I'd been since Wesley Lloyd's unexpected departure and the equally unexpected arrival of the two who'd turned my life upside down. This day had proven to me that all things work together for good to those who give of themselves and their assets.

With a sigh of complete satisfaction, I considered all that I had accomplished, simply with a little unrestrained outlay of funds that Binkie had assured me I would never miss. Making a child and his mother, as well as a few others, happy is what the season is all about, isn't it?

Besides, Christmas had always been my favorite time of the year, even if I hadn't known it until this one rolled around. And, if I had anything to do with it, this was just the first of what that little boy had called the best day of his whole life.

Chapter 31

I came awake with a start when the last log broke into embers, and light flared in the room. I don't know how long I'd sat there, but it was now up into the wee hours of the morning, long enough to put a crick in my neck from leaning against the chair wing.

It was past time to be in bed, and I wondered why Sam hadn't missed me and come looking to see where I was. Well, some people can put aside worries and sleep like babies, but it doesn't work that way with me. Carefully placing the screen in front of the fire, I tiptoed back into the bedroom and eased into bed so as not to disturb his rest.

My feet were like blocks of ice. I edged them up close to Sam's without touching them, not wanting to shock him so bad he'd rise up out of bed. Then, inch by inch, I moved my feet closer to his warm ones, gradually inuring him to the drastic change in temperature. He moaned and moved his feet, giving up his warm place — a pure pleasure for me.

By morning, I was feeling the effects of sitting up half the night, but of course one does not stay in bed half the day to make up for it. So, by the time Sam and Little Lloyd were off to office and school, I was dragging, my mind still so full of *what if*s and *should I*s and *shouldn't I*s that I didn't know whether I was coming or going.

Easy enough to have told Sam in the dead of night when I was at my lowest point that I would stop worrying and let him take care of the mess. I expect that is exactly what Pastor Ledbetter and his ilk would counsel me to do. More than once, the pastor had told us that marriage creates one person out of two. That sounded mystical and romantic, if your mind is so inclined, and if you don't care that the newly created person retains the mind, will, and abilities of only the husband.

But how many wives actually give up themselves to their husbands? Not many that I knew. Take LuAnne Conover, who couldn't do anything but complain about Leonard. I'd never heard her say a kind word about him, and she did all the thinking — and the talking — for both of them. And Mildred Allen kept Horace on a tight rein, deciding when he could spend her money and when he couldn't. Then there was Helen Stroud, who seemed to have a happy marriage, but she'd been known to put her foot down and have her way.

And look at Emma Sue Ledbetter, who, more than anyone I knew, submitted herself to her husband. That woman had never had a thought or opinion of her own in her life. She just replayed, sometimes in a garbled form, whatever the pastor thought or opined. And what was the result? Why, I was convinced that the effort it took to restrain herself showed up in the tears that constantly threatened and frequently leaked out of her eyes.

As much as I admired and cared for Sam Murdoch, I had a mind of my own that didn't need somebody else doing its thinking for it. So, stop worrying and leave everything to him? Not on your life.

In fact, I was thoroughly vexed with myself for even considering such an unnatural turn of events. He'd known what he was getting when he married me, and it certainly wasn't an Emma Sue Ledbetter.

So I immediately took up where I'd left off and started worrying again. And in the midst of it, it came to me that there was one way to either put my mind at rest or else open a real can of worms — I could just ask Hazel Marie. Except how do you pose a question to someone about who they'd been on intimate terms with? It wouldn't do to simply ask if she'd known Deacon Lonnie, because she might have — in a perfectly normal and innocent way. So an affirmative answer wouldn't tell me anything. Besides, she'd want to know why I was asking, and what would I say then?

I could be blatant about it, and ask if she'd ever been on a date with him. But a yes answer to that wouldn't tell me what I wanted to know. Even in this day and age, going out could mean nothing more than seeing a picture show together.

I rubbed my forehead, trying to figure out how to approach her. There was just no way in the world I could flat-out ask Hazel Marie about having Biblical knowledge of any man at all, even though Little Lloyd was living proof that she'd had some with somebody.

I made my way to the kitchen, relieved to find it empty. I could hear Lillian walking around upstairs, and the sound of her and Hazel Marie in some lighthearted conversation. Pouring a cup of coffee, I sat at the table, pondering my next move.

And the longer I sat there, the more determined I became that the next move had to be mine. Sam was counseling patience, saying that we needed to draw Vernon Puckett out and see what he could prove.

Well, I'd seen his proof, and it was making me sick to my stomach.

The ring of the phone disturbed my planning session, and I hurried to answer it.

"Julia," Emma Sue Ledbetter said, the tone of her voice telling me that she was upset about something, "tell me it's not true."

Lord, my heart sank to my feet, fearing that Brother Vern had already started spreading the word.

"Tell you what isn't true?"

"What I heard about . . ." Emma Sue stopped and blew her nose not too far from the receiver. "Excuse me, I had to blow my nose."

"I know."

"Julia, I can't believe that you allowed that immoral party to be held at your house." She sniffed wetly, forecasting another blow headed my way.

"Oh, that," I said, a sense of relief sweeping over me. I drew up a chair and prepared for a long discussion of Tina's passion party. "Emma Sue, that was ages ago."

"It was last week!"

"Well, but time is relative, and it seems like a long time ago. But I agree with you, Emma Sue, if I'd known what it was going to be, I'd never have had any part in it."

"But you had it at your house, and what kind of testimony is that to all those young women who look up to you?"

"Oh, I doubt they give two thoughts to anything I do."

"Well, they certainly do!" Emma Sue was steaming up, and I cringed at what was coming. "Julia, I am going to give you my best advice, based purely upon Biblical principles and my concern for you. You need to tell Larry that you can't run for the session, and tell him why. That way, you will be a witness to all those young women who might think twice before leading their husbands into such depravity again."

"I think it's too late for that, Emma Sue. They've already placed their orders. Now listen, I got roped into that party, and I left as soon as I saw what it was about. So I'm not the one you should be talking to. In fact, it might not be a bad idea for you to discuss this with Tina and her preacher's wife. Tina might listen to her. And, if I were you, I'd do it right away, because Tina's in a full selling mode, and she's having parties all over the place."

Emma Sue didn't say anything for a few seconds. Then in a quieter voice, she said, "That's a good idea. If all the pastoral wives get together on this, we can put a stop to it. Thank you, Julia, for pointing me in the right direction."

"I'm happy to do it. But, Emma Sue, a word of caution. You should be careful and not get the pastors involved. I know they're men of God, but they're men, too, and, I'm telling you, some of the things that Tina's selling are enough to turn the head of any one of them. And, like you say, we don't want them to get corrupted or anything."

"Oh, my goodness, no. Larry is so careful not to let strange thoughts enter his mind and distract him from a prayerful attitude." She paused again, and I let the silence draw out. Then she said, "That's why we don't watch a lot of television."

Thank you, Lord, I thought, after getting off the phone, for helping me divert Emma Sue toward the Baptists and away from me. I lifted my head as I heard Hazel Marie clattering down the back staircase.

"Hey, Miss Julia," she said, coming to a stop as her feet hit the kitchen floor.

"You're running a little late this morning, aren't you?"

"Just a little on the slow side, that's all. Come sit a while and let's talk."

She laughed and poured a cup of coffee. "We've been trying to get together for the longest, haven't we? I've been so busy with first one thing and another, but this is a good time." She glanced up toward the ceiling. "Lillian's changing the beds, so we'll have a few minutes."

She drew up a chair and sat across from me at the table. "I think we ought to talk first about what to get Lillian. What do you have in mind?"

"I'm not thinking of Christmas right yet, Hazel Marie." Then I took a deep breath and plunged in. "It's just that with my recent marriage, I have begun to think back over my whole life. It's been sort of flashing before my eyes, making me wonder about the choices I've made and what would've happened if I'd made different ones."

"Oh, my, you can't do that. It's too late to change the past, you know." She poured cream into her coffee and carefully stirred it. A frown creased her forehead, as she considered the subject. "What you have to do is just accept what's gone before, and try to do better today and in the future."

I nodded, beginning to understand how she could be so happy and lighthearted now, in spite of her earlier waywardness. Hazel Marie didn't allow guilt over past errors to ruin the present.

"How do you do that, Hazel Marie? I mean, how do you put the past and all its mistakes aside, and start each day fresh?"

"I just take the Lord at his word. He's forgiven me for the mistakes I made and blessed me with Lloyd in spite of everything."

Well, my word, I thought, the very thing I'd had pounded in my head from the pulpit almost every Sunday. Could it be as simple as that?

She leaned across the table, and said, "But you haven't made the mistakes I've made, so what's troubling you?"

"Oh, I don't know." I bit my lip, wondering how far I should go. "Well, marrying Wesley Lloyd, for one thing. I mean, without looking around to see who else was out there. I married the first man who asked me. And I keep wondering what my life would've been like if I'd met Sam first, and we'd had all our lives to be together. I expect you met a lot of boys and men when you were a girl, Hazel Marie, but what kept you from marrying one of them?"

Hazel Marie got real busy stirring her coffee again. "Miss Julia, I did go out with a lot of men in my young days, and I probably would've married any one of them if they'd asked me."

"I'm sure they conducted themselves like gentlemen. Or did some of them try to get fresh with you?"

She laughed, but her face turned a pretty shade of pink. "Lord, Miss Julia, they'll *all* get fresh if you let them." She studied her cup, as she turned it around in the saucer. "I kept hoping to find somebody who'd want a home and a family, like I did."

I nodded again, having known the feeling myself.

"But I didn't get either one till Lloyd and I met up with you, and you changed everything." She propped her chin on her hand and looked out the window. "I wasn't a good girl, I know that, and maybe I'm not much better now. But I'm in love with J.D., and that's never happened before." She smiled and shrugged. "A fat lot of good it's doing me, though."

"He'll come around," I said, though with little conviction, knowing Mr. Pickens's reluctance to marry again after trying it so many times with no success.

"I hope so. Well, I've got to get up from

here and get busy." Hazel Marie picked up her cup and took it to the sink. "Now listen, I don't want you moping around, having regrets over what could've been or should've been. We've all made mistakes, some worse than others, but all we have is today. You should just be happy that you and Sam have found each other. And count your blessings, because some people never find the right one." She smiled. "I mean, better late than never, right?"

I returned her smile, and nodded in reluctant agreement, but feeling some chagrin that Hazel Marie had ended up counseling me instead of the other way around.

As she headed for the back stairs, she turned back to me. "I'm glad we finally had this little talk, although it took us long enough to get around to it. But it was my fault for letting things interfere. Next time you want to talk, just sit me down and make me stay there."

"Thank you, Hazel Marie, I'll do that."

And as she hurried upstairs, I buried my face in my hands. I had done my best to find out the truth about Deacon Lonnie, without actually asking her. And I thought she'd answered my question, not only about him but about any number of others.

As distasteful as it was to consider, there was no wonder that Hazel Marie had thought Wesley Lloyd was a catch — who wouldn't after Lonnie Whitmire and the like? Of course, I'd thought Wesley Lloyd a catch, too, but that was before I'd had to live with him.

The funny thing about it, though, was that my heart went out to Hazel Marie even more. What a life she'd led, yet she was a good and decent person, warm-hearted and happy because she believed what she'd been told.

The faith of a child, I thought, and stood up abruptly. Brother Vern was not going to destroy her and that little boy. I was determined not to care who the child's father was. He was Hazel Marie's son, and that would have to be good enough.

But if Sam could prove a Springer connection by means of modern-day science, then so much the better.

Chapter 32

Sam came home earlier than usual that afternoon. He spoke warmly to Lillian as he passed through the kitchen on his way to the living room. Wondering what had brought him, I rose from my chair as soon as I heard his voice.

"Julia," he said, cocking his head toward the back hall. "Let's talk."

Without a word, I followed him to our bedroom, the only private place in the house. Turning to him, I couldn't keep the anxiety out of my voice.

"What is it? What's happened?"

"Nothing that helps, I'm afraid." He took my arm and led me to the bed, his favorite sitting place. "I've spent the day looking into Lonnie Whitmire, who he is and what he is. There's not much on record, and I didn't want to ask too many questions."

"But you found out something?"

He nodded. "Not much, but few a things. He grew up on the south side of the county, a little community called Wilkes Creek, and has lived there all his life, some fifty-two years. He's worked in retail for years, selling shoes at Belk's for a while, then moving into automobile parts at the NAPA store. For the past couple of years he's been with some kind of cut-rate store out in Delmont. As far as I can tell he's never been in trouble with the law. Well, he was fined for letting an inspection sticker on his car run out some years ago, but that's all."

"What about a family? Is he married?"

He nodded again. "Two children. Both grown and gone. I couldn't find anything on a wife, not even if he still has one."

"Oh, my," I said, dismayed at the report. "He sounds like a model citizen. I was so hoping that he'd be a chronic tale teller, and that nobody had ever believed a word out of his mouth." Then I grabbed Sam's hand. "But, wait. If his children are old enough to be on their own, that means he was already married when Little Lloyd was conceived. Doesn't that tell us something?"

"It tells us that he was no better than Wesley Lloyd. If," Sam said, with a sharp glance at me, "he was the one responsible. We don't know that he was."

"And," I said, picking up on his thought, "if he was, which I still don't believe, his claim to have come to the Lord since then wipes everything out." I sighed. "Hazel Marie was just reminding me how well that works. But what I don't understand is why he's willing to let Brother Vern dredge it all up again."

"I know," Sam said with a sympathetic smile. "But we've just scratched the surface. If we could dig deeper, interview his neighbors and talk to his coworkers — things like that — we'd have a better picture of the kind of person he is."

"Then let's put Mr. Pickens on him. He's used to digging up dirt."

Sam looked at me. "You want to let Pickens in on this? We'd have to tell him everything, you know."

"Oh, me, I don't know." I brushed back my hair in frustration. "I'd hate for him to know and Hazel Marie not. You know I wanted to tell her at first, but I've changed my mind now. She's so happy, looking forward to Christmas and all, and, like they say, ignorance is bliss. Oh, Sam, it is just a mess."

I rested my head on Sam's shoulder, thankful that it was there for me, and wishing I never had to move.

He rubbed my back in a distracted way. Then he said, "All right, let's keep Pickens in reserve for now. At least until we hear from Puckett again. But I'll tell you this, Julia: I don't like the fact that he just showed up at the door with Whitmire in tow. He may do it again when Hazel Marie's here, and I know you don't want that. If we just had something, anything, with Wesley Lloyd's DNA on it. . . ."

"Yes, and I've racked my brain to think of something, but it's all gone. I went into a frenzy, Sam, there's no other way to describe it. I rid myself of everything he owned."

Sam drew me closer and spoke against my hair. "What's done is done, Julia, so don't beat yourself up about it. Now, listen, I know you don't want to do it, but maybe we should go ahead and apply for an exhumation order."

I could no longer argue against it, so I didn't try. Just nodded and hoped it could be done without fuss or fanfare. All I could think of was Wesley Lloyd rising up out of his grave, demanding to know why I was spending his money on gravediggers.

Sometime in the middle of the night, I sat straight up in bed, snatched fully awake by an idea that was perfect in its simplicity. Sam stirred beside me, and I started to wake him and announce that I had the solution to our problem.

But then I eased back down on the pillow, smiling to myself. No, I would wait and present it to him when the results came in. Wouldn't he be surprised? I scrooched up to his warm back, so pleased with how my mind had kept on working in my sleep. I'd found a way to settle the matter once and for all, and there would be no need for a front-end loader at the cemetery to do it.

It was about time that I began to follow through on my own instincts. It's all well and good to say, as any number of well meaning but unrealistic Bible teachers have done, that a wife should step back and let her husband take the lead. But that didn't take into account all the instances of men who'd chosen intelligent and capable women to marry. Was such a wife then to bury her light under a bushel just because she had a marriage certificate? Was she supposed to shut down her brain because of it?

Well, I'd tried, and my trying time was over. Sam would just have to put up with a woman who could both think and act.

Anxious to follow through with my sleep-induced solution, I could hardly wait for daylight to come. But, as these things happen, I fell back asleep and had to hurry when I woke up again. It was imperative that I get there before office hours started. I didn't want to be slotted in between patients with a few minor complaints and have to struggle for the man's full attention.

It was all I could do not to give away my intentions while we had breakfast, but with Hazel Marie and Little Lloyd at the table, I couldn't have, anyway. So I tried to hurry everybody along.

"Lillian," I said, as I surveyed the table, "we're through here. Can I make Little Lloyd's lunch for you?"

"I don't need no help with this baby's lunch," she said, eyeing me suspiciously. " 'Sides, you may be through, but Mr. Sam still eatin' biscuits."

"Well, for goodness sakes, Sam," I said. "How many have you had?"

"Uh-uh-uh, Miss Julia," Little Lloyd said, wagging a finger at me. "It's not polite to comment on what one eats."

I had to laugh with the rest of them, but it was mortifying to have my own words thrown back at me. "You are right, and I apologize. Here, Sam," I said, passing the bread basket to him, "have another one."

"I believe I will," Sam said, smiling.

"Lloyd, have you heard the one about the Yankee visitor to the South who thought biscuits were called hot 'uns? Every time he finished one, somebody would pass the basket and say, 'Have a hot 'un.' "

Of course the child thought that was the funniest thing he'd ever heard. It was always a wonder to me how easily amused he could be. But Sam wasn't through.

"Did you hear about the three old men out walking one day?" he asked.

Little Lloyd shook his head, his eyes bright with expectancy.

"Well, the first one said, 'My goodness, it's windy.' And the second one said, 'No, it's Thursday.' And the third old man said, 'So am I. Let's go get a beer.' "

I thought the boy was going to fall off his chair, he laughed so hard. Lillian liked it, too, as did Hazel Marie, but it took her a while to get it.

As soon as everybody had cleared out, going their separate ways for the day, I put on my coat and told Lillian I had things to attend to. Then I drove to one of the medical buildings near the hospital, walked right in, and told the receptionist that I was there to see the doctor. And no, I didn't have an appointment, but she was to tell him that Mrs. Julia Springer Murdoch had an urgent need to speak with him.

She was nice enough, although she pointed out that others were there before me. I looked around at those who were sitting in the waiting room, but none seemed in dire enough straits that they couldn't wait a few minutes more.

At my insistence that the doctor be told I was there, the receptionist slid the glass partition closed and picked up the phone. I couldn't hear what she said, but she kept glancing at me while I tapped my fingers on the shelf where people paid their bills.

Finally she opened the partition and told me I should have a seat, that the doctor would be with me in a moment. Well, I didn't have a moment to spare, and besides, I didn't like the looks of anybody I'd have to sit next to. Who knew what they were suffering from or how quickly they could pass along their ailments?

So I waited on my feet, tempted to put a Kleenex to my face to ward off stray germs swarming in the air.

"Miss Julia!" Walter Hargrove held open the door that separated those waiting from those being seen, and gave me a pleasant welcome. "Come on in here, and let's see what's wrong with you." Then he cast a broad smile around the waiting room. "Be with you folks in a minute."

I followed the hulking man down a hall, past examining rooms to his office at the end. I was still trying to get over the bushy growth on his face, wondering what had possessed him to stop shaving. I realized that I hadn't seen him at church in a few Sundays, and thought maybe he'd stayed away until his beard had fully flourished.

He led me into his office, and motioned to a chair in front of his desk. Then he perched on the corner of the desk, and said, "Now, what's troubling you? Been some time since you've been in, hasn't it? I want you to make an appointment and let me give you a thorough workup. But let's treat the problem you're having now. Throat infections're going around, and they settle in the chest if left untreated. Open up. Say ah. How's Sam doing these days?"

I opened my mouth, obedient as always to authority, then quickly snapped it shut. "I'm not here for treatment, so put that thing down." I pointed to the flat wooden stick in his hand. "I just need some information, which I hope you can give me, and Sam's doing fine."

"Well," he said, smiling as he tossed the

stick into a trash can. "You're the first patient I've had who didn't have a complaint of some kind. What information do you need?"

"Do you remember when Wesley Lloyd had his gallbladder operation? It was some ten or so years ago, I think."

He put his fingers to his mouth, then thoughtfully began grooming the beard that had sprouted on his chin. "That was a while ago. But, yes, I remember diagnosing him and referring him to a surgeon. I forget which one."

"Well, you shouldn't have forgotten, because I distinctly remember that you were the assistant. And you were the one who told me afterward that Wesley Lloyd was doing as well as could be expected. Except I didn't know what to expect."

"Ah, yes." He smiled, though I could hardly tell it. "I remember now. It was Dr. Avery. He's retired now, and living in Florida, I think. As a matter of fact, that surgery might have been one of the last he did. My goodness, I haven't thought of Tom Avery in years. I expect he spends his days out on the water on that boat he always wanted. Unless he's dead, but I doubt it, because I would've heard."

"Dr. Hargrove," I said, recalling him to

the present, "I'm sure I don't care what the man is doing. I need to know if you still have them in your possession."

His eyebrows rose up as he looked at me. "Have what in my possession?"

"Why, Wesley Lloyd's gallstones. That's why you did the operation, isn't it? To take them out? I want to know where they are."

He laughed, whether in amusement or in surprise, I couldn't tell. "Why, Lord, Miss Julia, that's been more than ten years ago. I don't keep those things, and why would you want them, anyway?"

I waved away his question. He didn't need to know my purpose. "I expect they're on a shelf somewhere, soaking in formaldehyde or whatever you use to store such things in. Would you look? Or have your nurses look?"

He kept shaking his head and smiling, somewhat in a condescending manner, I thought. "No, we don't keep them. They're sent to the lab for analysis, along with the gallbladder. After that, they go to the patient, if he wants them. If not, they're thrown out. Incinerated, probably."

"Burned up? You're telling me that you treat human samples with such disrespect? I can't believe this."

"First of all," he said, lecturing me with

some amusement, "the word is specimen, not sample. And second, gallstones aren't living tissue. You haven't heard of anybody having a funeral for them, have you?"

I could've smacked him for having fun at my expense. Why do doctors assume that because you're old and never been to medical school, you don't have good sense?

Then he leaned forward. "Now, tell me this, Miss Julia, why this sudden interest in Wesley Lloyd's gallstones?"

I couldn't answer, so deflated at losing the opportunity to have those very gallstones tested for DNA. Thrown out! Burned up! The very idea of such careless handling of body parts undid me.

Then I perked up again. "You give them to the patient? Is that what you said?"

He nodded. "Sometimes. Occasionally, a patient wants them as a souvenir of the surgery. Though it beats me why."

"Did Wesley Lloyd want his? See if you recall giving them to him. I tell you, I need to track those things down."

"Miss Julia," he said, putting a calming hand on my arm. "How long have you had this on your mind?"

"Since last night. It came to me out of the blue. Or rather in the dark."

He gave me a long, studied look. "Why

don't we give you a good going over while you're here?" He rose to his feet and started toward the door. "Just sit right there and I'll call in a nurse to help you get undressed."

"I didn't come in here to get undressed or to have a going over, good or otherwise. I came to ask a simple question, and you've answered it, so I won't take any more of your time." I came to my feet and faced him. "But I'll tell you this, I think it's a shame the way you doctors throw things away. You ought to know that somebody might need them sometime. Now, I thank you for seeing me, but I have to be on my way."

I reached for the doorknob, but he stopped me. "I'm a little concerned about you, Miss Julia. If you don't want an exam today, maybe we could sit and talk a while longer. What else is worrying you, besides Wesley Lloyd's gallstones?"

"You don't want to know," I said, softened by his tone of compassion but unwilling to burden another soul with what I was carrying. Besides, doctors can gossip as well as the next person.

"Oh, but I do. We have lots of medications now that can calm the mind and relieve some of your symptoms. You should know it's not uncommon to have these little obsessions as we get on in years."

As his meaning became clear to me, I drew myself up and glared at him hard enough to freeze him solid. "*I'm* not the one with an obsession. Every time I come in here, *you* bring up my age. And I'm tired of it. I'm going to look for a doctor who isn't obsessed with the subject. Then maybe I'll hear something besides how old I am."

I opened the door and marched down the hall. When I reached the receptionist I slid a ten-dollar bill under the partition. "This should cover it," I said, "and, if it doesn't, you can bill me."

Then I left, thoroughly disgusted with the state of modern medicine. And no better off as far as Little Lloyd was concerned than when I'd first gone in.

Chapter 33

Halfway across the parking lot, headed for my car, I had another sudden thought, along with an equally sudden urge. Turning on my heel, I retraced my steps and went back into the office.

The receptionist looked up at me, a tentative smile on her face. "Do you want to make an appointment? I know the doctor wants to see you again."

"He can keep on wanting, because I've seen all I want to of him. No, I need to use your telephone, if you don't mind."

She hesitated, but then slid the window open and put a phone up on the counter. "This really isn't for public use, but if you won't tie up the line . . ."

"You can time me," I said, scrounging in my pocketbook for the card I kept with important numbers on it. Finally finding it, I dialed the one I wanted.

A familiar voice answered. "You got the Pickens Agency, Private Investigations and Discreet Inquiries. Go ahead."

That took me aback for a second. "Is this a recording?"

"Nope. You got the real thing. What can I do for you?"

"You can stay right there, Mr. Pickens. I'm coming over."

Finding Mr. Pickens's office in the strip mall several blocks from the interstate was not easy. I'd been there a couple of times before, but neither time had been recent. Everything had grown up so that I hardly recognized the place, what with rows of condominiums along the highway, new businesses, office complexes, and more cars than you could shake a stick at.

But I found it right where it had always been, which was a commendation for Mr. Pickens, since the businesses on both sides had changed hands. What was once a beauty supply store was now a shoe repair shop, and the erstwhile insurance office had become a bagel emporium.

I opened the door to his reception room and had to stop to take in the redecoration that Hazel Marie had done for him. The dark paneled walls were now painted a bright aqua, or maybe it was a teal, and mountain scenes hung on the walls instead of NASCAR posters. The same heavy sofa and matching chairs with wide, wooden arms lined the room, but *Field & Stream* had been replaced with *Town & Country* on the coffee table.

"Mr. Pickens?" I called, since he didn't have a receptionist to announce my arrival. "I'm here."

And there he was, coming out of the back office and down the short hallway toward me. "Come on in, Miss Julia. Good to see you."

He escorted me to his tiny office filled with one desk, two chairs, file cabinets, computer paraphernalia, stacks of papers, used coffee cups, and other kinds of clutter. "Sit right here, and tell me how I can help you." He pulled the client chair closer to the desk, got me seated, and went to his own chair. He put his arms on the desk, looked at me with a quizzical glint in his black eyes, and smiled. "I assume this is not just a friendly visit."

I declare, the man could melt a heart of stone and addle the mind of the most rational and determined woman. But I took myself in hand and kept my eyes on his and away from his broad chest and muscular arms, although I couldn't help but note the tail end of that unfortunate tattoo peeking out from under his rolled-up shirt-sleeves. And in the glare of the overhead light, I could see a sprinkling of silver in that black head of hair of his.

"No, it's business," I said, clutching my pocketbook in my lap. "I just need some information. I want to know how, well, more to the point, *where* one can get a DNA sample from somebody who's unavailable for testing."

His expression was a mixture of surprise, interest, and, suspiciously, humor. I could tell from the way his mustache twitched. He pushed away from the desk, turned sideways in the chair, and crossed one leg over the other. Propping one arm on the chair arm, he rubbed his mouth with the hand of the same arm. He looked at me sideways, the hint of a smile in his eyes.

"How unavailable?" he asked.

"Very, so don't even consider it. Look, Mr. Pickens," I said, leaning forward, "the only thing I could think of that might still be around was his gallstones. You know how some people save them? Well, but wouldn't you know, they've been thrown away and incinerated, so I have to think of something else. It just upsets me so bad that the doctor did away with them."

He waved his hand in a dismissive fashion. "Wouldn't've done you any good, anyway. Gallstones don't have DNA."

"They don't?"

"No, but tell me this. Why do you need an unavailable person's DNA in the first place?"

My eyes darted around the room, taking in the folders on his desk, the open file drawers, the overflowing waste can, the flourescent light on the ceiling, as I searched for an answer that wouldn't give away too much.

"Well, it's like this," I finally said. "I'm, ah, researching my family tree, and, since I have no living kin that I know of, I'm having a hard time of it."

"Okay," he said, nodding, as I felt a great relief that he was accepting my answer. "So, let's see, you want to figure out how you can get DNA from a deceased person without going to the source, namely, without digging him or her up — is that it?"

"That's it exactly. This is important to me, Mr. Pickens. I'm not just playing around trying to find a distinguished ancestor so I can put a family crest on my wall. Besides, the DAR has already established my credentials. It's just that, well, ..." I paused, searching for a seemingly legitimate reason for my interest. "Well, there's some question about one of my father's acquaintances."

There, I thought, sitting back in my chair, *that's close enough,* and hoping that my stern and rectitudinous father wasn't spinning in his grave.

"Okay," Mr. Pickens said, with another nod of his head. "DNA can last a long time, but it does degrade over time. It's found in what are called DNA receptors like epithelial cells, mucous membranes — any kind of body tissue — blood, of course, saliva, teeth, and bone."

"Teeth? I don't guess a partial would work, would it?"

He grinned. " 'Fraid not. Has to be real teeth."

"Oh, well, I threw that thing out anyway." Then, fearful that I'd said more than I intended, added, "When I helped my sisters close up the house." Then, realizing that I'd just admitted to living relatives, quickly tacked on, "They're both dead, too." And hoped to my soul that lightning wouldn't strike me down for such a blatant story.

"I declare, Mr. Pickens," I said, somewhat pitiably, "I guess I haven't saved anything of his. That's why I came to you, hoping that you could think of something I'd forgotten or hadn't thought about."

"I think you're out of luck, Miss Julia. But why do you care what your daddy did? I assume he's been dead and gone for some time now."

"Mr. Pickens!" I said with some asperity. "It's a matter of paternity."

Those black eyebrows sprang up. "Yours?"

"Of course not, and I'm surprised you would even think to question my lineage." I got to my feet, disappointed that my quest was not over. "I must say that I expected more from you, but thank you for your time anyway. How much do I owe you?"

He stood, too, as he should have. "No charge," he said, still with that twitch of his mustache that usually preceded a laugh. "Let me take you to lunch. There's a nice little place close by."

"No, thank you, I don't care for bagels. I need to get home. I've been gone all morning, and they'll all be wondering where I am."

I turned to leave the office, my mind racing now to come up with a likely story to tell Lillian and Hazel Marie about my morning absence.

But halfway down the hall, I stopped and swung back to Mr. Pickens, who was close on my heels. My breath caught in my throat at the vibrations or aura or whatever the current term was for the masculine magnetism that emanated from him.

Stepping back so that I could get out of range, and remembering my manners, I said, "I hope your friend in Atlanta is doing better. Mr. Tuttle, was it?"

"Yes, but it's Florida," he said. "He works out of Palm Beach, that area. He's managing, I think. Thanks for asking."

"Certainly. I knew some Tittles once, but it's probably not the same family. Now, Mr. Pickens, I must caution you. Please don't say anything to anybody about this little visit. None of them understand my interest in genealogy, and they'd just laugh at my pursuit of it. Can I trust you to keep this quiet?"

He stepped forward and put his arm around my shoulders, making me step out smartly toward the outside door. "Don't give it another thought. Let me know if there's anything else I can do."

I smiled and thanked him, but since he hadn't done anything to begin with, I didn't know why he was offering more of it.

"Miss Julia!" Hazel Marie popped up from the sofa and ran toward me before I'd gotten in the door good. "Guess what's happened. It's just awful."

I stood stock still, struck dumb by the fear that she'd heard about Brother Vern's accusation or that she'd actually heard it from the horse's mouth, specifically, that he'd been there in my absence.

Steeling myself to reassure her, I managed to say, "Oh, Hazel Marie, you can't believe everything you hear. You mustn't listen to gossip and ignorant speculations."

"Well," she said, frowning, "it's not that I *listen* to gossip, exactly, but sometimes I can't help but hear it." She stopped to consider the difference. "Especially when that's all anybody's talking about."

"Oh, my," I moaned, my hand fumbling for the back of the sofa to keep myself upright. "That's what I was afraid of."

Hazel Marie leaned toward me in concern. "Please don't get upset, Miss Julia. It's all right."

"Well, of course it's not all right, Hazel Marie." I took a deep breath, determined to face this as stoically as I'd done every other misfortune that had come my way. "But don't you worry. I don't believe a word of it. He's after something, even though we don't know what. But mark my words, that's why he's doing it."

"Oh, everybody knows what he's after. Because, see, they're saying that he said if he took away his wife, he's going to get recompensed."

I stared at her, wondering what in the world she was talking about. She seemed to be doing the same thing.

"Recompensed," she said, getting a far-off look on her face. "That means getting paid, doesn't it?"

I nodded, unable to speak as I tried to figure out whose wife Brother Vern had taken away and who was going to get paid for it.

"So," Hazel Marie said with a note of triumph, "that's why he's suing him."

The mention of a lawsuit nearly stopped my heart. My words catching in my throat, I said, "Who's suing who, Hazel Marie?"

She frowned again. "It may be whom, Miss Julia, but I can never keep them straight. Anyway, Dub Denham is suing that electrician. His lawyer's already filed papers and everything."

I didn't know whether to laugh or cry out in relief. It took me a moment to get on the same page, but when I did, I could only manage a weak, "Why?"

"For 'alienation of affections,'" she said, as a smile played around the corners of her mouth. "Come sit down, Miss Julia, you look wiped out. But have you ever heard of such a thing?"

"Well, yes, I've *heard* of it, but I didn't know anybody actually did it in this day and age."

"Well, Dub can and he is. For a half a million dollars, too." Hazel Marie caught her lower lip in her teeth, then she said, "I'd think a wife would be worth a whole million. Wouldn't you?"

"I don't know, Hazel Marie." I finally gained the sofa and eased myself down on it. "It would depend, I guess."

"Well, I mean, if you're going to sue somebody for something, looks like you'd go for a big, round figure. At least, I would, if it was me."

Chapter 34

The telephone rang early Sunday morning while we were scrambling around getting ready for church. It was Emma Sue, and she started right in with no apology for the early call.

"Julia? You know my toddler class has been bringing in pennies for their offering all year? Well, today I'm collecting them to get a Christmas present for one of the little orphan children. And the whole class will sign a poster with their handprints. Anyway, I'm going to have a bag full of loose pennies, and it'll be so inconvenient to take to the bank that way. So I was wondering if Lloyd would like to roll them for me this afternoon."

"He's in the shower now," I said, "so I can't ask him. But I expect he'll be glad to do it. You want him to pick them up after Sunday school?"

"Oh, no. I think the children in the nursery during the service will want to contribute, too. I'll have to collect from them, so I'll just bring the whole bag and the little thingies to roll them in to your house after lunch. I think Larry wants to talk to you, too, so we'll drop by later on. If that's all right."

Well, it wasn't, because I didn't want to talk to Larry. I knew what the pastor wanted to say to me, but I didn't know what I wanted to say to him. I'd about decided that I could pray till the cows came home, and I still wouldn't know what to do about running for the session.

So I sighed, and said, "Make it late this afternoon, Emma Sue. I think Hazel Marie is going out with Mr. Pickens, and they usually take Little Lloyd with them. And Sam likes his afternoon nap, especially during football season. He drops off as soon as a game begins and wakes up for the final few minutes."

We said our good-byes, and I began to finish dressing, just so vexed that I was going to end a potentially pleasant Sunday by wrangling with the pastor.

But at the time, I didn't know the half of it. Just as we got ourselves settled in our usual pew, four rows from the front and on the side aisle, we had to stand again for the processional hymn. The church was full and, while I mumbled the words to the hymn, I glanced around to see who all was there. With people standing and the choir processing along the center aisle, it was hard to pick out who was in their customary place and who wasn't.

As the tail end of the procession approached the altar, I thought my heart would stop. Following right behind Pastor Ledbetter, then sliding into aisle seats on the far side, were Brother Vernon Puckett and Deacon Lonnie Whitmire. They squeezed into the pew, making the Harden family slide closer together so that their shoulders were all bunched up. The smallest Harden child got shoved out of her place, and she let out a wail until her father put her on his lap.

It is just so inconsiderate to push into a pew that is already full, taking up space reserved for one's pocketbook and hymnal. But people do it all the time.

I poked Sam with my elbow. "They're here, Sam," I hissed. "What're we going to do?"

"Who? Where?"

"Over there. Look across the aisle and up one pew."

Sam's eyebrows went up as he located the unlikely visitors. Then he smiled. "Good," he said. "Maybe they'll learn something."

That just frosted me. The only thing I wanted them to learn was to stay away from us. But I didn't get a chance to say it, because the pastor was beginning the opening prayer.

When that was over, the church filled with the rustling of people taking their seats. Then we had to stand for another hymn. It was one I didn't know, which wasn't unusual, not being musically inclined, so I cut my eyes at Hazel Marie, hoping she hadn't seen who I'd seen.

But she had, for she was staring across the aisle as if she couldn't believe her eyes. The hymnal had all but slid right out of her hands. Little Lloyd looked up at her, then he glanced at me. He was too short, or at least I hoped he was, to see what had taken his mother's attention.

I had to do something, because the last thing I wanted was a confrontation in the narthex when the service was over. Who knew what Brother Vern would say to her and about her with everybody and his brother looking on and taking it all in.

"Sam," I whispered, leaning close to him, "we're leaving. Don't let them come to the house."

"How am I supposed to do that?"

"However you can. You're the head of

the household, so handle it."

Then I leaned across Little Lloyd, took Hazel Marie by the arm, and whispered, "Let's go. You, too, Little Lloyd."

Hazel Marie slid the hymnal into the bracket on the back of the pew in front of us and, with a dazed look on her face, turned with Little Lloyd to follow me out into the side aisle.

It always creates a stir of whispered speculations whenever anybody leaves the service early, but this time I didn't care. Besides, everybody was still standing, and if they were singing as they were supposed to be doing, hardly anybody would notice us. So instead of parading all the way to the back of the church, I led my little troupe to the door at the front that took us behind the chancel.

As soon as we were out of the sanctuary, Little Lloyd said, "What's going on? Why're we leaving?"

"There's somebody we don't want to talk to," I said, hurrying them down the stairs to the Fellowship Hall under the sanctuary and out the backdoor of the church. The sun was bright enough to make me squint, but there was no warmth to it. The wind whipped around us, swirling our coats and messing up our hair.

Ice crystals sparkled in the clear air, making it hard to breathe.

"Who?"

"I'll tell you later," Hazel Marie said. She had regained some color in her face, and was matching me stride for stride as we hastened down the frigid sidewalk past the Family Life Center and on toward home.

As soon as we got inside, I told Little Lloyd to go upstairs and change out of his Sunday clothes. "But, before you go, we might as well tell you that your great-uncle Vern was in church, and we didn't want to talk to him. Now, I know that wasn't very courteous of us, but you'll remember how troublesome he's been in the past. Your mother and I thought it the better part of discretion just to avoid socializing with him."

"Oh," he said, nodding. "I don't blame you. I don't want to socialize with him, either." Then his face brightened. "Now I've got all day to work on my science project. I'll call Charles and tell him we can get started collecting germs."

"Germs?"

"Yessum. We're going to see what kind of germs are on door handles at churches and schools and stores and things like that.

Then we're going to grow them and write a report."

"Well, you be careful with those things."

As he ran off upstairs, I turned to Hazel Marie. She was sitting in one of the Victorian chairs by the fireside with a pensive look on her face, frowning.

I sat down opposite her, wondering where and how to start. "It might be a good idea for you not to be here, Hazel Marie, in case they decide to visit. Why don't you go on over to Mr. Pickens's?"

"I can't. He's in Florida somewhere, seeing that friend who keeps having problems. Something to do with a case that has ties up here, I think. He won't be back till tonight." She glanced over at me. "Why would Brother Vern come to our church?"

"I haven't the slightest idea. He surely doesn't want to join. That man would never be happy just sitting in a pew. He needs a pulpit, and I thought he had one. We might as well face it, Hazel Marie, he was there for one reason and one reason only. And that was to aggravate us."

"That's what I think, too." She took her lower lip in her teeth, thinking it over. Then she said, "Who was that with him?"

I did a little frowning of my own. "Don't you know?"

She shook her head. "No'm. He did look a little familiar, though."

A little familiar? Would that mean that she'd never known Deacon Lonnie in an intimate manner? Or did it mean that there'd been so many she couldn't remember one from another?

Not wanting to pursue that unnerving line of thought, I got up and went to the kitchen. She followed, and together we reheated the meal that Lillian had prepared for our Sunday lunch. Before long, Sam came in from church, and the four of us gathered around the table. With Little Lloyd present, we skirted around the subject of Brother Vern, but Sam had told me as soon as he came in that he'd made it his business to get out before being accosted by him.

"He's not coming over here, is he?" I'd asked.

"He could, but if anybody rings the doorbell, let me handle it."

I nodded, but my mouth tightened. So far, the head of my household had not handled Brother Vern anywhere near to my satisfaction. And the only handling that would've satisfied me was to have gotten rid of him for good.

As soon as lunch was over, Little Lloyd

took his books and papers and left for his friend's house. Hazel Marie insisted on clearing the table by herself, saying that she needed to be doing something. She had been quiet and subdued all through the meal, spending her time stirring peas with her fork and gazing off in the distance.

My spirits sank to the bottom of my soul, as I watched her troubled expression. Was she afraid that her past was catching up with her? I mentally shook myself, thinking that, most likely, she was just shaken up from seeing Brother Vern again. We all have relatives who shame and embarrass us, although hardly any who are as capable at it as he was.

Sam thanked us for lunch, then headed for the living room and the Sunday paper. With my head spinning with one fearsome possible outcome after the other, I soon followed him.

"Sam," I said, "put that paper down and tell me what we're going to do. I don't like it that Brother Vern showed up at our church and brought that man with him. That is pure harassment. Or, no, it's intimidation, that's what it is. It may even be a threat."

"Julia," Sam said, folding a section of the paper, "I don't see how we can keep him from coming to church. He didn't make an effort to waylay me, so maybe he was just checking out Ledbetter's sermon. Puckett could use some pulpit pointers, if you ask me."

I waved my hand in dismissal. "That man thinks he could give our pastor some pointers. No, Sam, he was there to put Lonnie Whitmire on display. And listen, I asked Hazel Marie if she knew him, and she wasn't sure. What do you think that means?"

"Probably just what she said. Even if she knew him years ago, she might not recognize him right off."

I moved closer to him and lowered my voice so it wouldn't carry to the kitchen, where Hazel Marie was loading the dishwasher. Then I waited a few more minutes as I heard her going upstairs to her room. "But what if it means that she doesn't recognize him with his clothes on?"

"Why, Julia," Sam said, his eyebrows going straight up and a smile playing around his mouth. Then seeing that I was in no mood for frivolous remarks, he sobered up and said, "Let's not lose our trust in Hazel Marie. I know she can be a little scatterbrained at times, but believe me, she wouldn't forget something like that."

I nodded and kept my own counsel. But every time the wind rattled the windows or the furnace clicked on or the house creaked, my insides tightened up for fear that it was Brother Vern and Deacon Lonnie stepping up onto the porch.

Chapter 35

As the afternoon lengthened and no one came by to interrupt our day of rest, my eyelids grew heavier and heavier. It wasn't until Hazel Marie tiptoed into the living room and whispered my name that my head jerked up.

"Oh," she said. "Are you asleep?"

"Not really. Just resting my eyes."

Sam stirred beside me, sitting upright and rubbing his neck. That's the problem with putting your head back on a chair or sofa and taking a quick nap — your neck stiffens up on you. But Sam came awake with his usual smile, speaking to Hazel Marie and patting me on the knee. He was the most remarkable man — never waking up cranky or grumpy like some people I could mention.

Hazel Marie sat down in the Victorian chair across from us. She had changed into a sweater and a pair of jeans that looked as if they'd had twenty years of hard living, but were, in fact, the newest fashion purchase. "I had a nap, too," she said, covering a yawn with her hand. "Is Lloyd home yet?"

"I haven't heard him. But it's getting late, so maybe we should call him."

"Yes, I'll do that." She glanced at her watch, then said, "It sure gets dark early these days. I thought it was later than it is. I'll give him a few more minutes, then call him. Would you like me to start supper?"

Well, not particularly. Hazel Marie was good help in the kitchen, but you wouldn't want to leave her in charge of a entire meal. Not that I was much better, but between the two of us we usually managed fairly well without Lillian.

Sam said, "Why don't I fix my famous omelettes?"

"Oh, good," I said. "I was hoping you'd say that."

Hazel Marie laughed and rose from her chair. "I'll get the table set and call Lloyd."

As she started out of the room, the doorbell rang, and my heart did a flip in my chest. Hazel Marie veered toward it, saying, "I'll get it."

"No," I said, trying to launch myself off the sofa, while Sam was doing the same. "Hazel Marie, wait. . . ."

It was too late, for she was already at the door, opening it, and greeting whoever was there. I can't tell you the relief I experienced when I heard Emma Sue's voice and saw her as she appeared with Hazel Marie in the door to the living room. By that time, Sam and I had finally gotten to our feet, so we were standing to give her an exceedingly warm welcome. She walked in, canted over to one side with the weight of a large, brown pocketbook hanging from one shoulder.

"Emma Sue!" I said. "I declare, I'd forgotten that you were coming by. It's so good to see you. Here, have a seat. Would you like some coffee? Something warm? How have you been?"

"Fine, Julia." She gave me a sideways look, wondering, I supposed, at my effusive joy at seeing her. "Whew," she said, shrugging the pocketbook off her shoulder. She wrapped the strap around her hand, allowing the bag to dangle almost to the floor. "This thing is heavy as lead. It's filled to the brim with I-don't-know how many hundreds of pennies given by those precious little children. We can all take a lesson from their example of stewardship."

"Yes, well," I said, feeling that I needed no lesson in contributing to the church. "Toddlers are hardly the example I would choose. But you should've gotten the pastor to carry it for you. Isn't he with you?"

"He got held up at the hospital," she said, rubbing her shoulder with her free hand. "Doing visitations, you know. So I can't stay. I just wanted to leave these pennies for Lloyd. Is he here?"

Hazel Marie said, "He should be back any minute. He's working on . . ." The doorbell rang again and, as she turned toward it, I stretched out my hand to stop her.

"I'll see who it is," she said. "Do have a seat, Emma Sue, and I'll help you unload those pennies."

Sam, who so far hadn't gotten a word in edgewise, hurried after Hazel Marie, a worried look on his face. And rightfully so, for after I heard the front door open there was nothing but dead silence. Then the relentless voice of Brother Vernon Puckett greeted Sam in unctuous but insistent words that were the preface to doom and destruction for the rest of us.

"I know you have to run, Emma Sue," I said, anxious for her to be on her way. "Just leave your pennies, and Little Lloyd'll get right on them."

"Well," she said, turning to see Brother Vern, Sam, and Hazel Marie enter the room. I couldn't remember if Emma Sue had ever met Brother Vern, but at the moment I wasn't quite at my social best.

Brother Vern, ruddy of face and slightly windblown, strode into the room like he was not going to be deterred from his mission this time. From the imperious lift of his head and the squinched-up expression on his face, I could tell that he was bound and determined to say his piece regardless of what anyone thought.

He came up short when he saw Emma Sue. Sam quickly introduced them, saying that she and Brother Vern had a lot in common, both being in the ministry to varying degrees. I bit my lip, thinking it best that we get her out before Vernon Puckett said something that would shock Emma Sue to her core.

Before I could open my mouth, Sam gave me an intense look that made me realize that Emma Sue's presence might keep Brother Vern's lid on.

Emma Sue, unaware of the tension, held out her hand and smiled at Brother Vern. "It's so nice to meet you. I always welcome the chance to speak with a fellow worker in the Lord's vineyard."

Brother Vern deigned to nod his head in her direction, then proceeded to let her know that he did not consider her or her husband an equal laborer in anybody's vineyard. "Some people," he said, "are working the wrong fields, and them that till in rocky soil ought to know enough to pick up and go elsewhere." He raised a finger straight up, as if he were speaking from on high. "I tell you and I tell all these folks here that the wrath of God will not be delayed too much longer. It's gonna come down on 'em the likes of which nobody has seen to this day. Look to yourself, woman, and take heed."

Emma Sue's head snapped back and her eyes nearly popped out of her head. She was not accustomed to having her position as the wife of a minister of a mainline church being treated with such disrespect. And she didn't take a backseat to anybody when it came to following Biblical precepts.

I moaned to myself as I wondered how I was going to explain the unseemly behavior of a guest in my house. I looked over at Hazel Marie to commiserate with her, but she was standing stock-still, a stunned and mortified look on her face.

Sam put a gentling hand on Brother Vern's shoulder and said, "I'm sure everybody agrees that things are bad all over. Come on now, and let's have a seat. I'd like to hear about your print ministry. I'm working on a book, you know."

But Brother Vern was not to be sidetracked. "I'm not here to talk about that. Everybody and his brother is working on a book, and none of it fit to read. No, I'm here to find out what you're doing about the serpent that's nestling in your bosom. You've put me off long enough, and it's time, Brother, it's long past time to pluck that serpent out." Brother Vern stopped to take a breath and a step closer. "I tell you, Brother Murdoch, you got nothing but poison in your well, and you got to clean it out and I mean, *clean it out!*" And with that he spun around to face Hazel Marie, pointing his finger right in her face. His voice rose in the cadence of early morning radio preachers. "This woman . . . this, this harlot, has turned your head-ah. She has blinded your eyes-ah. She has in*sin*uated herself into your life-ah. This woman has eaten the forbidden fruit and borne a tainted issue-ah, and I got a witness-ah, that can flat out *prove* it. Brother, I'm tellin' you, she is wicked-ah and unholy-ah, and a blot on your testimony-ah. . . ."

He stopped again for breath, leaving a tense silence in the room. Every one of us was struck dumb by his withering attack on Hazel Marie, and in front of Emma Sue Ledbetter, too. Hazel Marie's face was as white as a sheet. She stood there, her eyes wide with astonishment and what may have been fear, as his words lashed her up one side and down the other.

And he wasn't through. "And I'm a-gonna tell you something else about this *Whore* of Babylon . . ."

Emma Sue sprang at him, screeching, "Don't you talk to her like that!" She pulled back her overloaded pocketbook by the strap and, with the force of a righteously angry Christian woman, swung it in a sweeping roundhouse. I felt the rush of air as the heavy bag whizzed right past me, and heard the thunk when it connected with Brother Vern's chest. The bag sprang open on contact, wallet, comb, Chapstik, car keys, notepad, three pens, two pencils, and hundreds of pennies came spewing out into his face, over his head, onto the furniture, and across the room in a copper-colored spray of coins. Emma Sue's momentum whirled her around, with the bag whipping along in a wide circle. Sam ducked as it swished past his head, showering Hazel Marie with a swath of coins and coin wrappers. Pennies spewed out here, there, and everywhere, some hitting with a metallic clank as they fell onto tables and chests, others tinkling melodically as they rolled along the floor into the far reaches of the room. Several of them landed off the Oriental, where they twirled like tops on the hardwood until they died down and clinked over.

Brother Vern grunted with the impact, took a step back, and, struggling to stay upright, tripped over his own feet. He sat down heavily on the floor, pennies falling from his shoulders and hair.

"Emma Sue?" I said in a quavering voice.

Sam took the pocketbook from her, picked up her wallet and car keys, then reached out a hand to help Brother Vern to his feet. "My goodness," he said, "we've got a mess here, haven't we? We'll be picking up pennies for the rest of the week. You need to have this strap fixed, Emma Sue."

Brother Vern was having none of it. He batted Sam's hand away and sat still, looking stunned and woozy. Less, it seemed, from the actual impact of the pocketbook than from the identity of the swinger of it. Finally, he began trying to rise, rolling over at first, then heaving himself up on his knees.

Emma Sue, still with fire in her eyes, put

her hands on her hips and, without so much as a glance at Sam, said, "There's nothing wrong with that strap, Sam Murdoch." Leaning over Brother Vern, she said, "You better understand, right here and now, that I am not going to listen to anybody talk to Hazel Marie like that." Then she pointed her finger in Brother Vern's face. "I don't care who you are or what you do. You are not going to come in here and say ugly things to my Christian sister. Not while I'm around, you're not. I'll have you know that anybody who can pray the way she can is spiritually head and shoulders above us all, and she does not deserve to be run down by the likes of you. Give me my bag, Sam, I'm going home."

She gave Hazel Marie a hug, and left with her head held high, slamming the front door behind her.

Ignoring Brother Vern's protests, Sam helped him to his feet and guided him toward the door, saying, "I think we've talked enough today, don't you? It takes a while to get our dignity back after a public fall. Why don't you give me a call when you're feeling better." And Sam ushered him out of the room and through the door. I heard his words fading away as he saw the shaken preacher out onto the porch and down the steps.

I started toward Hazel Marie to offer comfort and reassurance, but she backed away, wringing her hands. I declare, her face was so pale and her eyes so wracked with pain that she looked like a war-torn waif. I wanted to put my arms around her, even though I rarely get such an improbable urge.

"I need some time, Miss Julia," she whispered in a ragged voice. "Look after Lloyd for me."

"Of course," I said. "I'll call him."

But she was already on her way through the kitchen, and soon after I heard the backdoor close and her car start up in the driveway.

Chapter 36

Lord, who could've imagined such a scene? I couldn't, and I'd been an eyewitness to it. Sam came back in, and all we could do was stand and look at each other across the copper-covered room.

"Well," he said, with a twist of his mouth, "at least she didn't start crying."

"I don't know which is worse: Emma Sue in tears or Emma Sue enraged," I responded, crossing my arms and holding myself to stop the trembling. "I never thought I'd see the day when Emma Sue Ledbetter went on the attack. We sure saw a different side of her today, Sam, and, believe me, I'm going to watch my step around her from now on."

"Speaking of which," Sam said, waving his arm at the layer of pennies on the floor. "Watch where you walk. Don't want you to slip and fall."

"Yes, well, I guess we should start picking them up, but if I get down, I might never get up. Oh, Sam," I moaned, "forget about money on the floor. What I want to know is, what exactly did Brother Vern say? Did he come right out and say that Little Lloyd is not Wesley Lloyd's child?"

"He implied it, Julia, but in such round-about terms that nobody but us knew what he was saying."

"I think Hazel Marie knew, or guessed. Oh, Sam, that's why she flew out of here like she did. And what about Emma Sue? You think she understood what he said?"

"Emma Sue? No. All she heard were ugly words thrown at Hazel Marie, and that was it for her. As for Hazel Marie, I think she was just plain humiliated by her uncle's behavior."

"Well," I said, "she would be, of course. We've gone so long thinking he was out of our lives forever that it must've been a total shock to her. You know, he just walked right in and lit into her like nobody's business. It shocked me, too."

"It shocked all of us. Now, let's get something to eat." Sam walked gingerly across the layer of pennies, took my arm, and led me toward the kitchen. "Where did Hazel Marie go?"

"I don't know. She just said she needed some time." I got as far as one of the chairs by the kitchen table. I took hold of it as a sudden thought came to me. "Oh, Sam.

Maybe it's worse than that. Maybe she remembered Deacon Lonnie after all, and when Brother Vern started in on her, she knew what was coming next."

"Now, Julia . . ."

"No, wait. Maybe her leaving like that is an admission of guilt. Oh, my word, I can't bear the thought of it." I clung to Sam, just sick to my soul.

"Now, Julia, you're jumping to conclusions. Hazel Marie is tender-hearted, you know that, and she was ashamed at the way her uncle showed himself. I expect she's gone to J.D.'s for a little comfort."

I took a deep breath. "You're right. If he's home from his trip, that's exactly where she went, and I hope to goodness he gives it to her."

Sam smiled. "I expect he will."

I heard bicycle wheels squeal on the drive way. "There's Little Lloyd, and about time, too. Make out like everything's fine, Sam."

Little Lloyd came in, shedding his cap and coat, and propping his book bag against the wall. "Hope I'm not late. We really got a lot done. Charles's mom took us all around, even to the courthouse and a doctor's office."

"Why, those places aren't open on

Sunday," I said, as I put placemats on the table.

"Yessum, but we only swabbed the knobs on front doors, so they didn't need to be open. Then we transferred our samples to petri dishes with a growth medium in them. I sure hope we got some germs that'll grow."

Not being especially scientifically minded, I knew enough to caution him. "Be sure and wash your hands good."

By this time, Sam had bacon frying in a skillet and was cracking eggs into a bowl. Setting the table, I hesitated before laying a place for Hazel Marie.

Little Lloyd looked around, then asked, "Where's Mama?"

Sam and I exchanged a quick glance before I answered. "She's at Mr. Pickens's. I expect she'll be back after a while."

"Oh, okay," Little Lloyd said, seemingly unconcerned. "I didn't think he'd get back this early. He told me it might be midnight or later. I'm going to wash up."

As the child left for the bathroom at the back of the hall, I hurried over to Sam. "Oh, my goodness, Sam," I whispered, "what if he's not back? Where would Hazel Marie go?"

"I wouldn't be surprised if she had a key.

She's probably over at his house waiting for him." Then, as Little Lloyd came back into the room, Sam said, "I have a job for you, Lloyd, if you're willing. I need some help picking up about a ton of pennies off the living room floor. You want to help?"

He grinned. "Yessir, but how'd they get there?"

"Mrs. Ledbetter brought them. She wants you and me to count them and roll them in wrappers. But, in an unfortunate occurrence, she dropped the bag and it popped open. There're pennies everywhere."

Little Lloyd laughed. "Wish I'd been here to see that. I bet she bawled her head off, didn't she?"

Sam laughed, as I said, "Little Lloyd! Show some respect."

"Well, but she cries all the time. Everybody knows it, but I respect her anyway."

"Here it comes," Sam said, dividing his omelette onto three plates. "Everybody sit down."

After supper, the three of us adjourned to the living room, and Sam and Little Lloyd got down on the floor and began picking up coins. They brought them to the dining room table, where I was happy enough to sit and count them out into stacks. Although I must say that if a certain somebody had had the bright idea of collecting them, then that somebody should've been willing to see the job through herself.

I counted and stacked pennies from the piles that Sam and Little Lloyd kept dumping on the table, all the while listening for Hazel Marie's car in the drive.

Finally Sam stood up with a great creaking in his knees, and said, "Let's leave the rest, Lloyd. These old bones can't take anymore."

Little Lloyd crawled out from under a lamp table. "We've got 'em all except what's underneath things. I'll get them tomorrow."

They joined me at the table, and we wrapped pennies in companionable silence, although I fumed at having to finish up Emma Sue's project.

"Time for bed, Little Lloyd," I said, glancing at my watch. "And time to wrap this up. My hands are filthy. I'll be up in a little while to check on you."

He wished us both good night and went upstairs without complaining. He was such a satisfactory child, always cheerful and obedient, much like his mother.

"Where is she, Sam?" I whispered. "She ought to be home by now."

"Listen to yourself, Julia," he said. "It's only nine o'clock. When has she ever come home this early when she's with Pickens?"

"Well, I know," I said, sighing. "It's just that I thought she might call. To see if Lloyd got home all right, for no other reason." I pushed several rolls of pennies away from the edge of the table. "Lillian's going to throw up her hands when she sees this mess in the morning. We'll have to move furniture to be sure we've got them all. Sam," I said, looking up at him. "I'm surprised that Emma Sue hasn't called, either. Mark my words, she'll be suffering because she lost her temper, which is not the image she wants everybody to see. Sooner or later, she'll be crying on my shoulder."

"Tell her I'm proud of her, and if she hadn't taken a lick at Brother Vern, I was going to."

"Were you really?"

"I'd already taken a step toward him when that pocketbook came at me on her backswing. I ducked just in time, or I'd've been laid low, too."

We ended up laughing together, replaying the scene in our minds. But it didn't take long for me to straighten up as I thought again of the threat posed by Hazel Marie's uncle.

"He's not through, Sam. You know he's not. He's going to confront Hazel Marie with his so-called proof, and you know what? I think he wants an audience. I think he was glad Emma Sue was here, because he wants to embarrass and shame Hazel Marie."

"Maybe so, Julia. I am a little surprised he didn't bring that Whitmire fellow with him. And the more I think about it, the more I think he may have something else up his sleeve."

"Lord, I hope not. I can't stand too much more. Well, let me get up from here. I'll be back down in a few minutes."

I went upstairs and tapped on Little Lloyd's open door. He was sitting on the side of the bed, already in his pajamas, leafing through a book.

"Time to be in bed," I said. "School to-morrow, you know."

"Yessum," he said, swinging his feet up on the bed and scooting up to the head of it. "I know what I'm going to get Mama for Christmas."

I straightened some papers on his desk. "What?"

"A tattoo on my arm. With *Mom* on it."

I whirled around. *"What?"*

He threw his head back and went into a fit of giggles. "Just kidding," he said, hardly able to get his breath. "I got you good though, didn't I?"

"You nearly gave me a heart attack." I went over to the bed, and held the covers so he could slide under them. "Don't do that to me again."

"Okay, but what I think I'm really going to get her is another gold charm for her bracelet. Something to engrave my name on, like maybe, *From your son, Lloyd Puck*. . . uh, maybe just *Lloyd*."

"She'll love that. Now, say your prayers and turn off the light. Are you warm enough?"

"Yessum."

"Good night, then." I got as far as the door on my way out.

"Miss Julia?" he said, rising up from the pillow. "Is my last name Puckett or Springer?"

Oh, Lord, I knew this was coming sometime. I stood with my hand on the door, unable to turn and face him. It wasn't my place to explain such delicate matters to the child, but I had to answer him in some way. I took a deep breath and said, "Both." And hoped it would satisfy him.

"Well, but everybody I know has the same last name as their daddy, but I have Mama's for mine."

"Yes, well, families can get all mixed up, and it'd take a legal mind to straighten them out." *There was a thought!* "I tell you what, Little Lloyd, why don't you ask Sam, or maybe Binkie?"

"Okay, I will. Good night, Miss Julia. Tell Mama I'll see her in the morning."

I bade him good night again, and got out of that sticky situation as fast as my feet would carry me.

Chapter 37

"Sam," I said, hurrying over to him when I got downstairs, "you won't believe what that child just asked me. He wanted to know whether his last name is Springer or Puckett. He knows he's a Puckett and his daddy was a Springer." I sat down beside Sam, but couldn't put myself at ease. My nerves were tingling all up and down my system. "At least, I hope his daddy was."

"I'm surprised he hasn't asked before this," Sam said, a brooding look on his face. "He's too smart not to have thought about it. But that's for Hazel Marie to explain to him. Not us."

"Well, speaking of . . . I think I'll call Mr. Pickens and see if she's all right."

"I wouldn't do that, Julia." Sam put a hand on my arm. "It might be better to let her have this time with him. He'll calm her down and reassure her. I expect she'll be home in a few hours. It's still early, you know."

"Not for me, it isn't. I declare, this has been the longest and most upsetting day

I've ever had to endure, and I'm ready for it to be over."

Sam and I were getting dressed the next morning, although he was much more adept at it than I was. The events of the previous day were still having their effect, for I was so unsettled that I doubted I could recapture my normal serenity of mind. Sam was having no such problem. He was shaved and dressed in half his usual time, which was never very long in the first place.

"Julia," he said, while I was still trying to button my dress, "I've come to the conclusion that I've been remiss in dealing with Vernon Puckett."

That was a surprising admission. "I wouldn't say remiss, exactly," I said, looking up at him. "But maybe a little slow."

"Well, either way, it's coming to a screeching halt. I'm going to track him down today if it takes me all day. The idea that he would come into our home and verbally attack a woman under our protection is more than I can tolerate. I should've ushered him out yesterday before he got started. As far as I'm concerned, he is no longer welcome in this house."

"As far as I'm concerned," I said, my

spirits lifting at this pronouncement, "that's long been the case."

"I know it, Julia, and I've let you down by letting it get this far. But Puckett's going to know that I've had all I'm going to take from him." Sam headed for the door. "I'll be out and about all day, Julia, and it may be suppertime before I get back. Tell Hazel Marie that she doesn't have to worry about him any more."

"Wait, Sam. Did you hear her come in last night?"

"No, but I never do." Sam paused in the door on his way to the kitchen. "She's probably sleeping late, so I'll take Lloyd to school, then be on my way."

As we gathered for breakfast, Little Lloyd brought up his mother's whereabouts again. "I guess Mama's still sleeping. Her door's closed, so I didn't bother her."

"That was thoughtful of you," I said, relieved that she was safe in her bed even if I hadn't heard her come in.

"I hope she not sick," Lillian said, as she wrapped a sandwich for Little Lloyd's lunch. We'd had to get an extra large lunch box to hold all the food that Lillian packed for him, little of which, I suspected, actually got eaten.

"Oh, I doubt she's sick," Sam said in that easy way he had of calming everybody's fears. "Pickens has been out of town for a few days, so I expect it took them a while to get caught up. You ready to go, Lloyd?"

After they left, Lillian joined me at the table for a second cup of coffee. Even though I was more than pleased at Sam's determination to have it out with Brother Vern, I found myself increasingly edgy.

"I'm going up to check on her," I told Lillian.

I went upstairs, tapped on Hazel Marie's door, and, getting no response, I opened it to find a perfectly made bed with no sign that anybody had been in it. I nearly broke my neck hurrying back downstairs.

"Lillian! Lillian, she's not there. Oh, my goodness," I said, leaning for support on the edge of the table. "Where is she? What's happened to her?"

"Why, Miss Julia, I hate to have to tell you this, but I 'spect she spend the night with Mr. Pickens." Lillian stood up and guided me to a chair. "Now, you quit that carryin' on. She a grown woman, an' I guess she can stay out all night if she want to."

"You don't understand, Lillian," I said, breathing in gasps. "Brother Vern was here yesterday, and . . ."

And I proceeded to tell her some of what that meddling fool was up to and how he'd lambasted Hazel Marie in front of us all and how Emma Sue had knocked him for a loop and how Hazel Marie had run out and not been heard from ever since.

"Oh, my Law, . . ." Lillian moaned, flopping down on a chair. "That pore little thing, havin' to put up with such again. Where you reckon she at, Miss Julia?"

"She's got to be at Mr. Pickens's, and I don't care if she stayed all night with him or not. I'm calling him right now."

So I did, looking up his office number first, since it was high time for him to be at work. All I got was his answering machine, so I left a message.

"Mr. Pickens, call me as soon as you come in. And in the meantime, I'm calling you at home."

And I did that, too. His home phone rang for ever so long, as my hand on the receiver grew tighter and tighter.

"Yeah?"

"Oh, Mr. Pickens, you're there. Thank goodness, I thought I'd missed you."

"Who is this?" Mr. Pickens sounded as if

he were still in bed and not a little cranky at being disturbed.

"Why, it's Julia Murdoch. Wake up, Mr. Pickens, half the morning's gone and I need to speak to Hazel Marie."

There was a long silence on the line, in which Mr. Pickens was either yawning or going back to sleep.

"She's not here," he finally said.

"Now, listen, I know that you two want to keep me in the dark as to your personal lives, but I don't have time for such niceties. I don't care what you do or when you do it. So put her on the phone right now."

"Miss Julia," he said, sounding more awake by the minute. "Hazel Marie's not here."

"But she has to be! Have you looked around?"

"I didn't get in till about four this morning, but I think I would've noticed if she'd been here. Now, what's going on?"

"Oh, Mr. Pickens. She left here yesterday afternoon right after Brother Vern called her the whore of Babylon in front of Emma Sue Ledbetter, and Sam's gone to track him down, and she's not in her bed, and she hasn't been there all night, and we don't know where she is."

"I'm on my way."

★ ★ ★

"Oh, Mr. Pickens," I cried, practically throwing myself on him as soon as he stepped into the house. While waiting for him Lillian and I had done little else but wring our hands.

"Tell me again," he said, "and this time in detail. When did it all start?"

He put his hands on the back of a chair and leaned over it, his arms straight and stiff. Lillian sat hunched over the table, not even thinking to offer him something to eat — a clear sign of her distress.

So I began where it started, a week or so back, when Sam first told me that Brother Vern was back in town, carefully omitting the reason he'd come back — not wanting to ruin her reputation if I didn't have to — and ended with Hazel Marie's sudden departure. "And, Mr. Pickens, you wouldn't believe the awful things that man said to her, and right in front of the preacher's wife, too. She was so upset that she just took off, asking me to look after Little Lloyd on her way out. I thought she meant for the evening, but now it looks like she meant forever. And he doesn't even know she's gone, and how am I going to tell him?"

Mr. Pickens pressed his mouth together,

his black eyes studying the tabletop intently. "I'll check with Coleman first," he said, relinquishing his hold on the chair and heading for the telephone to call Deputy, I mean, Sergeant Coleman Bates at the Sheriff's Department.

Lillian and I stared at each other, hardly able to breathe, as we listened to one side of the conversation. Mr. Pickens explained to Coleman that Hazel Marie had been missing since the previous night, then asked about vehicle accidents and hospital admissions.

"He'll call back," Mr. Pickens said, hanging up the phone. "Now, think hard, Miss Julia, did she give you any idea of where she was going?"

"Don't you think I have been thinking? No, she didn't, because I thought she just wanted to clear her head after Brother Vern's rampage." In my distress, the words started tumbling out. "And, Mr. Pickens, I didn't start to worry until Little Lloyd went to bed. But Sam said he was sure she was with you, and even if you weren't home, she probably had a key and would just wait for you. And even then, I thought she'd come home sometime last night even though I didn't hear her, which I usually do, but not always. It wasn't until I saw her bed hadn't been slept in, then called you and found out she wasn't there, that I knew she was really gone. And, oh, Mr. Pickens, both of us were sleeping while our sweet Hazel Marie was out wandering around somewhere alone in the night."

I put my head down on the table and cried, wanting so badly to tell them the real reason behind Hazel Marie's flight from hearth and home. In my telling, I'd slid right over the question of Little Lloyd's paternity, letting Lillian and Mr. Pickens think that Brother Vern was only up to his usual mischief. I'd gone over and over in my mind exactly what the meddling fool had actually said the day before, and as far as I could determine, he hadn't come right out and named Lonnie Whitmire the child's father. But Hazel Marie had seen the two of them together, so she would've known what he was about to say. Why else would she have run from us?

"What I don't understand," Mr. Pickens said, "is why she'd be so upset. She's had to deal with her uncle before, so what made this time so different that she'd run off?"

"Yessir, tha's what I want to know," Lillian said, nodding solemnly. "Why she not slap him down like Miz Ledbetter do? Why she have to run away from all of us?"

I knew, but I couldn't bring myself to tell them that this time everything was different because Brother Vern was claiming a different father for Little Lloyd and accusing Hazel Marie of long-term deceit and deception, and that a great and awful dread was building up in me that this time she might be running from the truth.

Chapter 38

Mr. Pickens couldn't stand still. He paced the floor, slapping a fist into the palm of his other hand, his black eyes darting from one side to the other. "Where's Sam?"

"He's out looking for Brother Vern, and he still thinks Hazel Marie is safe in her bed. He doesn't know we don't know where she is, and I don't know where he is."

"He have a cell phone with him?"

"No, but wherever Brother Vern is, that's where he'll be."

"Okay. Here's my cell number," he said. "Call me if you hear from her."

"Where're you going?"

"To the sheriff's office to see Coleman. If Puckett's doing any street preaching, he had to get a license. It should have his address."

"I know he started a new business. Printing things, I think. But, Mr. Pickens, how is finding Brother Vern going to help find her? That's the last place she'd be."

"I know, but we have to start somewhere. And I want Sam to know she's missing. In the meantime, you stay here. . . ."

"I can't just sit here. I'm going with you."

"We've had this conversation before," he said, his face grim and determined. "You need to be here in case she calls, and if she does, call me on my cell. And I want you to do something else. I want you to call everybody Hazel Marie knows and ask if they've seen her."

"I can't do that," I moaned. "She wouldn't want everybody to know. Besides, if I tie up the phone, how's she going to call?"

"Leave five minutes or so between each call you make, and she'll get through. Now, I'm outta here. Lillian, make sure Miss Julia stays right where she is. I don't want to be looking for two missing women."

Lillian nodded at him, her eyes big with apprehension. Then she put her hand on my arm to keep me seated.

"All right, all right!" I snatched my arm away. "I'll stay." But I wasn't happy about it. It just did me in to have to sit and wait while the men were out doing something — and usually not getting it done.

Before Mr. Pickens's car, with its low

rumbling motor, had gotten out of the driveway, the telephone rang. My heart leapt in my breast and I nearly crippled myself getting to it.

I answered it with an eager, "Where are you?"

"Why, right here, talking to you," Emma Sue Ledbetter said, as my heart dropped like a lead balloon. "Who did you expect?"

"Oh, uh, I thought it was Sam, letting me know where to meet him for lunch." I shook my head at Lillian to let her know it wasn't Hazel Marie. "I have to get off the phone, Emma Sue. He'll be calling any minute."

"It's only ten o'clock, Julia. You have plenty of time to arrange a lunch date. But I won't keep you, I just wanted to apologize to you for my behavior yesterday."

"Don't worry about it, Emma Sue. If ever a man needed swatting, Vernon Puckett did."

"Oh, I didn't mean that. Jesus himself took a whip to the money changers in the temple, you know. No, I just couldn't stand by and listen to that man castigate Hazel Marie. She is just the sweetest thing, and so spiritual. We have to stand up for each other, Julia."

I didn't know what to say. Hazel Marie

was certainly sweet, I could attest to that. But if Emma Sue had known what Vernon Puckett was claiming, she would have to rethink her opinion of Hazel Marie's spiritual quotient.

So I said, "Uh, huh."

"No," Emma Sue went on, "I want to apologize for slamming your door when I left. There was no call for that, and you know I am not ordinarily that rude."

"Don't give it another thought," I said, shifting from one foot to the other in my anxiety. "Now, Emma Sue, I do have to go."

"Wait, Julia, I have something else to tell you. You know about Dub and Clara and that electrician, don't you? Well, did you know that Dub was fixing to sue him for stealing Clara's affections?"

"I've heard all about it, Emma Sue, but I don't have time for an update now. Besides, I think it's ridiculous for a man to demand payment for a wife who wants to go."

"Well, but, Julia, marriage is sacred, and it has to be preserved."

"But not by buying and selling a woman's affections, it doesn't. I can't be bothered with this now, Emma Sue, it's all so sordid."

"Well, anyway, they settled out of court, and Dub got seventy thousand dollars because he had them dead to rights."

"My word, Emma Sue, I heard he was asking five hundred thousand, and he settled for seventy? If I were Clara, I'd be insulted."

"Oh, Julia, you are such a liberal. And speaking of that, Larry is beside himself, wanting to know what you're going to do about the session."

"I haven't had time to give it a thought, Emma Sue. I'm still praying about it, though, and I'll let him know the minute I decide."

"You can't take too long. The election'll be here before you know it. What you ought to do, Julia, is get Hazel Marie to pray for you. She's come so far on her spiritual journey, and I just know she can guide you in the right way."

My eyes rolled back in my head. "I'll be sure and do that, Emma Sue. Now, thank you for calling, but, oh, someone's at the door. Talk to you later." And I hung up.

Lillian said, "Who's here? I don't hear no do'bell."

"Nobody, Lillian. I just wanted to get off the phone. Now, help me think who to call about Hazel Marie."

We spent the rest of the morning taking turns calling everybody in the Lila Mae Harding Sunday School class, the Tuesday morning circle, the book club, the bunco group, the PTA, and the dress shops downtown. It was hard work, for we couldn't just come out and tell everybody that Hazel Marie was missing. The whole town would've been out beating the bushes, if we had. So we went all around Robin Hood's barn to find out if anybody had seen her. A lot of little stories were told, like, Hazel Marie was on her way to the grocery store and we needed to add something to the list, but she'd said she had to run a few errands of her own beforehand, and had she stopped off at your house before going on to the store. We really needed a head of lettuce. Like that.

But nobody had seen her or heard from her. A lot of them offered to lend us some lettuce, though.

"Lillian!" I slapped my hand down on the table, struck with a new thought. "I don't know where my mind is. Kinfolk! That's where she is. She would go to family."

"Who her fam'ly?"

"Well, that's the sad thing," I said, deflating in a hurry. "I don't know a one. But let me think. I know that her mother passed on years ago, and I think her father remarried. I gathered that the new wife pushed her out of the house before she was old enough to take care of herself."

"She don't have no brothers or sisters?"

"I've never heard her mention any, so I guess not." I mused on that for a few seconds, saddened that I knew so little of Hazel Marie's early life. Hadn't wanted to know, if you want to know the truth. As far as I'd been concerned, her life had begun the day she first showed up at my door, mainly because I didn't want to hear the details of her connection to Wesley Lloyd. Now, though, I'd have given anything to know every last one of them.

"Anyway," I went on, then stopped again. "Lillian! There is one person we haven't called." I jumped up and hurried to the phone. "Etta Mae Wiggins! They've known each other for years."

I leafed through the phone book. "Let me see, she's probably at work, so I'll call there first. Here it is, Handy Home Helpers."

The woman who answered the phone was not the most helpful person I'd talked to, in spite of the name of her business. In fact, she was right on the verge of rudeness, saying that Etta Mae Wiggins had called in sick that morning, and she'd had to get somebody else to fill in for her at the last minute, and furthermore personal calls were not encouraged at a place of business. She wouldn't even give me Miss Wiggins's home phone number, so I had to look that up, too.

"Some people," I said to Lillian, as I listened to the phone ring and ring and ring some more. "She's not answering, Lillian, and no answering machine, either."

"Maybe she at the doctor's, if she sick."

"Maybe so. Well," I said, finally hanging up, "we'll have to keep trying. Miss Wiggins is our last hope, although I never thought a woman like her would be in such a position."

I did not care for Miss Wiggins. She was too outgoing, too perky, too flashy, and too familiar with Sam. But at the moment I could overlook every one of her faults if she could lead us to Hazel Marie.

Chapter 39

About that time, two long and anxious hours after he'd left, Mr. Pickens returned. Both Lillian and I hurried to meet him at the door.

"Have you found her? What did Coleman say?"

"Where she at?"

"Let me get inside," he said, for we'd waylaid him on the back porch, where it was too cold to stand around and talk. "No, I haven't found her. But no accidents and no admissions to the emergency room, thank goodness. Coleman got me Puckett's business address, but the place is closed up tight."

"Oh, Mr. Pickens," I moaned, standing aside but not too far away. "We've come up against a stone wall, too. Nobody's seen or heard from her, and Miss Wiggins is not at home or at work, and I'm at my wit's end, not knowing where to turn to next."

Mr. Pickens smeared his hand across his face. "I still don't understand why she'd take off this way. I thought she'd come to me if she had a problem. She knows I'd make it right for her."

Well, not always, I thought. There're some things that can't be made right by anybody, no matter how good their intentions, and nine times out of ten they're things out of the past that we've brought on ourselves. In spite of Hazel Marie's philosophy, we have to live with the consequences, and that's the fact of the matter.

I turned away so he wouldn't see the distress on my face. Everything that was happening seemed to lead to the conclusion that Hazel Marie had a secret, the potential revelation of which was now tearing her apart and sending her scurrying off to who knew where.

"You've not heard from Sam?" Mr. Pickens asked.

"No, and I'm about half mad at him for not staying in touch." I paused and reconsidered. "Of course, he doesn't know that Hazel Marie didn't come home last night. Maybe you ought to be looking for him, too."

"I'm going to," Mr. Pickens said. "I just stopped by to see if you'd heard anything."

"I would've called you. Now, don't stand around, Mr. Pickens, we need to find her before Little Lloyd gets home from school."

"I'm gone, then."

"Wait," Lillian said, "lemme fix you a sam'wich to take with you."

"He doesn't have time for a sandwich," I said, holding the door open. "He needs to be on his way."

And so he was. I stood by the door, my nerves so on edge that I could hardly think straight. Listening to his car back down the driveway, I decided that I couldn't sit around and wait much longer.

"Lillian," I said, "I'm going to Miss Wiggins's house, I mean, trailer. She'll have to come back sooner or later, and I can get more out of her face-to-face than I can over the telephone."

"Yessum, an' I'll go with you."

"No, somebody has to stay by the phone. Where's my pocketbook?"

"I don't know, an' you not about to go drivin' off by yo'self. We got enough people running 'round where nobody know where they be. An' we got that machine what say leave yo' number an' we call back, so I'm goin'."

"Well, so we do." It brought me up short to be reminded of the answering machine, mainly because I'd not given it a thought, hating to talk on one myself. And also, of course, because I wanted to speak directly to Hazel Marie if she called. But we'd waited all morning, and I was sick of it.

"Let me get my pocketbook then," I said.

I hurried out of the kitchen, snatched up my pocketbook from the dresser in the bedroom, and hurried back in, shrugging on a coat as I went. Lillian was doing something with peanut butter and crackers at the counter.

"We can't linger, Lillian. Get your coat and let's go."

Lillian stuffed the crackers smeared with peanut butter into a plastic bag, and followed me out to the car. "We can eat on the way," she said, settling herself into the passenger seat.

"I can't think about eating now." I raced the motor to warm it up, turned the heat on high, and backed out into Polk Street. Lillian grasped the armrest as I gave it the gas and we sped through town and out onto the state road that led to Delmont.

On the way, Lillian dug into the plastic bag and handed me two graham crackers sandwiched with peanut butter. "It won't hurt you none to eat this while you drivin'. Jus' keep yo' eyes on the road while you doin' it."

A short way on the outskirts of Abbotsville, I impulsively turned onto a side road that led us to a long, sloping, grass-covered hill lined with hemlocks and dotted with a few leafless oak trees. A tarred track curved away from the two stone pillars that indicated the entrance to Good Shepherd Memorial Park.

As we passed between the pillars, the tombstone-studded hill spread out before us. Lillian sat up. "What we doin' here? I thought we lookin' for Miss Hazel Marie."

"We are, and I know she's not here, so don't say a word. I'm just seeing if everything is as it should be." I swung the car onto the lane that bisected the cemetery, following it to the top of the hill where the Springer family plot was outlined by a dry stone wall. One tall moss-covered tombstone marked the resting place of Wesley Lloyd's father, a lesser one, his mother.

I slowed the car and peered through the window. "Look at that, Lillian. Why in the world did I let them put that double tombstone over Mr. Springer?" I pointed to the wide granite marker that had SPRINGER engraved across the top. An engraved line down the middle divided the stone into two halves. One half was etched with Wesley Lloyd's name and dates, along with the words WELL DONE, GOOD AND FAITHFUL SERVANT.

"Lord, Lillian, I'd forgotten about that. Mr. Springer arranged for it long before he passed, and I was in such a state at the time that I told them to go ahead and put it up. And just look at it."

My own name and birth date balanced Wesley Lloyd's on the other half of the tombstone, and beneath the blank space for the date of my passing were the words LOVING WIFE.

"The arrogance of the man!" I fumed. "That thing has got to go. There's not a way in the world I'm going to be buried beside anybody but Sam."

"I still don't know what we doin' here," Lillian said. "We didn't bring no flowers or nothin'."

"Flowers don't last long, especially in this weather," I mumbled, still eyeing the site while my mind was on the logistics of getting an earthmover in there without destroying a fifty-year-old wall. Not that I particularly cared, because whether we exhumed Wesley Lloyd or not, and even if it tore up the entire burial plot, I was going to get that double marker removed. After we got through with Wesley Lloyd, he could just lie there under a single gravestone, alone forever. I'd show him a "loving wife."

Wanting out of the place, I sped up, but Lillian was still mumbling at my lack of respect for the dead. "Lots of people put plastic flowers on they graves."

"Lord, Lillian," I said, turning to look at her. "Mr. Springer would come flying out of there if I did that." Besides, I was more interested in what was *in* his grave, namely the same DNA as Little Lloyd's, not what was on top of it. "We better go."

"Yessum, an' I don't know why we up here in the first place. You don't never tend to his grave nohow."

"Lillian," I said, somewhat exasperated, as I took a side lane that would lead us back to the main road. "His grave is well tended because I pay a tidy sum every year for what they call perpetual care. Although how long perpetual would last if I missed a payment, I don't know. But I'm not about to come out here and pull weeds every time it rains."

"We s'posed to look after the dead," she said under her breath.

"Well, I'm more concerned about the living. Now let's get on to Miss Wiggins's place."

"Wasn't me wantin' to stop at no graveyard."

I let her have the last word, because she

didn't know the interest I now had in getting in and out of a particular grave site. Trying to make up the time, I sped along the highway toward Delmont. But wouldn't you know, we caught the only red light. I cleared my throat of lingering peanut butter and tapped my hand on the wheel, waiting for the light to change.

Before long, we were through the town and out on the road again, watching for the left turn onto Springer Road.

"I haven't been out here in I don't know when," I said, as I made the turn. A horn from an oncoming pickup blasted us and the driver shook his fist. "People can be so uncivil when they're behind the wheel. He could see I had my blinker on. Let's see, Lillian, the trailer park's on your side, so watch for it. We ought to be fairly close."

We went over a slight rise in the tarred road and saw the trailer park on our right. A dozen or so trailers, looking bleak and forlorn under the gray sky, lined the narrow gravel drive. As I made the turn, I took note of the neatness of the place, a far cry from the way it had looked when I first learned that it was part of Wesley Lloyd's estate. Even though I had little use for Miss Wiggins, I congratulated myself for elevating her to the managerial level. With her bossy ways, she was making the tenants toe the line and pick up their trash.

"Watch out!" Lillian yelled, grabbing the dashboard with both hands.

I slammed on the brakes and gasped for air as the seat belts jerked us upright. "Lord!" I yelled back as the car skidded on the gravel, ending up nose to nose with another car on the way out. Gravel spewed up around both cars, and I could hear my heart pounding away at the close call.

"Look, Miss Julia!" Lillian yelled again. "It's her!"

"What? Oh, my goodness, it is!" I opened my door and started out of the car, almost strangling myself on the seat belt. Fumbling to unsnap it, I said, "Watch her, Lillian. Don't let her leave."

But Hazel Marie wasn't going anywhere. By the time I got around to her door and looked through the window, her head was resting on the steering wheel.

Lillian, who'd followed me, peered over my shoulder, looking in at Hazel Marie. "Lord Jesus, she ain't hurt, is she?"

The door was locked, so I knocked on the window. "Hazel Marie! Are you all right?"

She looked up at us, her eyes red-rimmed and teary. Then she slowly opened the door and stepped out. Lillian pushed me aside and wrapped Hazel Marie in her arms.

"Law, Miss Hazel Marie, we been worriet sick. Where you been? Why you not come home where you s'posed to be?"

Hazel Marie stared at me over Lillian's shoulder. Her eyes seemed to be filled with fearful questions. Did I know? Did I suspect? Did I want anything more to do with her?

We looked at each other for several seconds while my mind went a mile a minute. As Sam had pointed out, everything Brother Vern had said had been couched in such ornate and oratorical flourishes that only those in the know would've caught his meaning.

And I was in the know. But, for Hazel Marie's sake, I didn't have to be.

"Hazel Marie," I said, reaching out to pat her arm, "don't you worry about that uncle of yours any more. Both Sam and Mr. Pickens are after him with a stick. He is not going to be around to embarrass you in front of Emma Sue or anybody else. You don't have to run off and hide your head. Everybody has relatives they'd rather not have, so you just hold your head high. He may shame you with words, but he can't touch you any other way."

She stared at me for a while longer, then gradually a look of gratitude filled her eyes with more tears. "Oh, Miss Julia," she said, moving away from Lillian and flinging herself at me. "I was so afraid . . . I thought you'd, you know, believe all that stuff he said."

"There, there," I mumbled, patting her back, somewhat unnerved to have her clinging to me. "Who could understand him? I know I couldn't, nor any other preacher when they get on their high horses."

She stepped back then, wiped her eyes with the sleeve of her sweater, and sniffed loudly. She tried to laugh, but made a poor showing of it. "I'm about to freeze," she said. "I left so fast yesterday that I forgot to get a coat."

"Well, let's go home," I said, noticing now how the wind was whipping up under the low clouds. "We've all been quite beside ourselves with concern for you."

Hazel Marie straightened her shoulders, sniffed one more time, and said, "Not yet. I have to do something first. Etta Mae helped me see that I have to face him down. We talked all night, and now she's about half sick and had to go to the doctor.

But I'm not waiting for her. I'm going to nail that man's sorry hide to the wall all by myself."

"No, you're not," I said. "I'm going with you, but let's go home first. I'll pull over, and you lead the way."

"I think I jus' miss something," Lillian said, looking from one to the other of us. "Whose hide we gonna be nailin'?"

Hazel Marie's eyes took on a hard glint, and between clenched teeth, she said, "Lonnie, that lyin' hypocrite, Whitmire's."

Chapter 40

As I followed Hazel Marie's car on our way home, I thought of all the backflips I'd done to keep her from knowing about Lonnie Whitmire. Somewhere along the line she must've recalled more than a familiar face. I hated to think what that might be, but I wasn't about to let her get away from me again.

Pulling into the driveway behind Hazel Marie's car, I took up as much room as I could to prevent her from flying out of there again. Lillian had ridden back with her — another device to keep our wayward girl in line.

As we got into the house, Hazel Marie said, "I need to take a quick shower and change my clothes. I've been in these since yesterday. Then I'm going after Lonnie." She started toward the stairs, then whirled around. "What time is it?"

"A little before one," I told her. "Hazel Marie, do you know where this Lonnie Whitmire is?"

"Etta Mae told me. I want to get this

done before Lloyd gets home." And out of the room and up the stairs she went.

Lillian turned to me, leaned close, and whispered, "Who that man she goin' after?"

"Somebody she used to know." I whispered back, realizing that I'd not kept Lillian up to date. "He's hooked up with Brother Vern and is just a tool in his hands."

"Law, look like he want to be more'n that." Then, with a sudden frown, she asked. "You say tool or fool?"

"Both. It's like this, Lillian. Brother Vern's using him to hold Hazel Marie's past over her head, only she's had enough of it, and so have I. Except I'm not supposed to know what's going on, so don't say anything."

"No'm, but you be better off, you don't keep it all to yo'self. You want somethin' to eat now?"

"Lord, Lillian, I can't eat anything at a time like this. I've got to be ready to go when she is." Hearing the shower running above us, I said, "Maybe a quick sandwich."

Then recalling the answering machine, I hurried over to it. The light was blinking, so I waved for Lillian to come over.

"Look, Lillian, we have a call. Make sure I'm doing this right so we don't lose it." I gingerly pushed the Play button and waited while the thing rewound itself. "I hope it's Sam saying he's on his way home."

"Maybe it Mr. Pickens."

Either one would've done, but it was Pastor Ledbetter. "Miss Julia?" His deep voice came over the machine with such authority that I almost picked up the receiver. "I'd like to come over this afternoon and get this matter settled. I'm sure with a little praying and counseling, you'll see that for the peace and order of the church, you'll want your name omitted from the election slate. I thought I'd hear from you before this, but . . . Well, I'll see you later today and we'll talk."

"Oh, for goodness sake," I said. "I don't have time to worry with him. See, Lillian, that's the problem with these machines. People can reach you even when you're not here, and that means you can't get out of anything."

"Well, maybe you be gone with Miss Hazel Marie when he come, an' you get out of it that way."

"Call him back, Lillian, and tell him today is not convenient. Do it after we leave."

She started shaking her head, as she headed for the counter to make sandwiches. "No, ma'am. Uh-uh. Not my place to be callin' yo' pastor an' gettin' you outta talkin' to him. That's yo' business, not mine."

"Well, they Lord, Lillian. If I call him, he'll keep me on the phone for an hour. By the time he gets through, he won't need to come over. Well, . . ." I threw up my hands, "he'll just have to take his chances. Now Lillian, tell me what Hazel Marie said in the car. Did she say anything about what happened yesterday, what upset her so bad and all that? I mean, I know Brother Vern is enough to upset anybody, but was it anything in particular?"

"No'm, she don't say much. She jus' hunker down over the wheel an' drive like nobody's business."

"Yes, I noticed. I could hardly keep up with her. But surely she said something. You know, why she was gone all night and what she's planning to do now."

"No'm, she jus' ast me to watch out for Little Lloyd, case she don't get back 'fore he come home. An' I had to say I would, but I sho' hate to stay here while y'all out nailin' that man's hide to the wall." She put a plate of sandwiches on the table.

"You want milk or tea?"

"Coffee. Lillian, I declare, you should've *asked* her. Started her talking, so we'd know something."

"It not up to me to be doin' such as that. 'Sides, you the one wants to know, so you ast her."

I rolled my eyes as I bit into a ham and cheese sandwich. "All right then," I said. "I will. But don't blame me if we end up at that Whitmire man's house with Hazel Marie running wild and me not knowing how to handle it."

"Don't worry, I won't," she said, in such a complacent manner that I almost choked on the sandwich.

Hearing Hazel Marie clomping down the stairs, I hurriedly finished my lunch and jumped up from the table. She bounded into the kitchen dressed in fresh jeans, another heavy sweater, and ankle boots. Her hair was combed and her makeup freshly applied. She jabbed her arms into the sleeves of a three-quarter-length coat, which she had assured me was the "coat of the season" this year, and she was ready for action.

"If I don't get back in time," she said, hurrying past the table on her way to the door, "tell Lloyd I'll see him."

"Just one minute, young lady." I grabbed my coat and pocketbook. "You're not leaving without me."

"An' you need to eat somethin'," Lillian put in.

"Etta Mae fixed a big breakfast," she said, scooping up my keys from the table. "I'll take your car, Miss Julia, if you don't mind. You didn't leave me enough room to get out."

"Lillian," I said, struggling to get into my coat, "when Sam and Mr. Pickens get here, . . . Hazel Marie, wait!"

She was out of the house, hell-bent for my car, and I had to run to catch up. She stood by the open door of the car, her hair whipping in the wind, and watched as I caught up with her.

"You don't want to be a part of this," she said. "It's something I need to do myself. I'm going to have it out with him, and it's likely to get pretty nasty."

"What? I can't get nasty, too? I'm going, Hazel Marie, so resign yourself. I'm not about to let you face that man without me." I stood on the other side of the open door, holding onto it so she couldn't get in and lock it.

She stared at me, her eyes watering in the cold. Or maybe just watering. "I don't think you know what this is about, Miss Julia, and I don't think you want to know. Lonnie Whitmire is somebody I knew years ago. I didn't recognize him yesterday in church, because he's really changed. He used to have a little wispy beard on his chin."

"Well, he still has wisps, only not on his chin. But, Hazel Marie, I don't care who you used to know. If he's bothering you now, let me help you put him in his place. Or we can sic Coleman on him."

She finally broke her gaze and looked down, leaning her head on the cold metal of the door. "It's more than that, Miss Julia. He's hooked up with that uncle of mine, who'd do anything in the world to put me down in your eyes." She sniffed, then rubbed her nose. "When I realized who he was, I knew there was no telling what they'd be saying about me."

"Lord goodness, Hazel Marie. You think I'd believe a word out of the mouth of either one of them?" I caught my own mouth with my teeth, thinking frantically. She didn't know about Brother Vern's visitations to Sam and me. She didn't know that he'd brought Lonnie Whitmire, looking for all the world like Wesley Lloyd Springer, right to our very door. She didn't know that Sam and I knew that Brother Vern had thrown Little Lloyd's paternity up for grabs. As far as she knew I was completely in the dark, and I intended to let her keep on thinking that way.

It didn't bother me a bit to pretend ignorance. In fact, I didn't turn a hair as I lied through my teeth. "I don't know what you think Brother Vern said yesterday to make you run off that way. All I heard was the same old ranting and raving he's always done. For my money, it was nothing new, even if he did drag Deacon Lonnie to our church. So you knew him. So you even dated him a while, if you did. That's nothing that should bother you now. Lord," I went on, "I'd hate to have some of my old suitors show up in church. Considering what some of them were like, I'd be embarrassed to death, just like you were."

She turned her head but didn't lift it, just cut her eyes up at me, like she wanted to be sure I meant what I was saying. "But what if maybe they were saying ugly things about you," she whispered. "And you couldn't prove they weren't true? What about if that happened?"

"There's always a way to prove the truth, if it even needs proving. And I have the means to find it." I didn't mention that it might involve hiring a backhoe or a front-end loader. "Now," I went on, as I started around the car, "let's go find Lonnie Whitmire and stop whatever he's been cooking up with Brother Vern."

She slid into the car while I got in the other side. She sat there for a few minutes, mostly staring out of the windshield, but darting an occasional sideways glance at me. "I wish you wouldn't, Miss Julia. Go with me, I mean. He could say some awful things about me. He's done it before." She clasped the top of the steering wheel with both hands, then leaned her head against them, hiding her face. "I don't want you to hear what he's going to say. You won't think much of me after that."

"Let me tell you something, Hazel Marie," I said. "If what I think of you could be changed by what a stranger says, then I'd be a sorry friend to have. And another thing, the times you most feel like hiding away in a closet are exactly the times you ought to hold your head up high and stare down your detractors.

"Now crank this thing up," I said, shivering in my coat, "I'm about to freeze to death."

Chapter 41

I make it a practice to give advice whenever I see that someone needs it, so I was pleased that my little pep talk seemed to put some steel in Hazel Marie's backbone. She sat up, cranked the car, and peeled out of the driveway so fast that I had to grab the armrest.

"You know where we're going?" I asked.

"Etta Mae told me where he works."

Her mouth was set in such a firm line that I wondered how she got the words out. I tried a few more conversational stabs, mentioning the number of cars on the road, Little Lloyd's report card that would be coming out soon, and how cold it had gotten. But she wasn't in the mood for chitchat, so I finally subsided, realizing that she had her mind set on one thing, and it wasn't the state of the weather.

Looking around and noting the turn she had made, since it had nearly snapped my head off, I said, "We're going to Delmont?"

"He works at the American Dollar store there."

"Well, I say. I've never been in one of those, but you see them all over. What does he do?"

"Manager, I think."

I couldn't get any more out of her, so I entertained myself by looking out the window. I was trying to keep a serene demeanor, but taking deep breaths and tapping my fingers on the armrest probably didn't come across as the most unruffled indicators of my state of mind. I didn't want to let on that I was torn up inside with fear of what Lonnie Whitmire was going to say and with worry of what she was going to do.

"You know, Hazel Marie, it used to be that we had five-and-dimes everywhere you looked. But you don't see them anymore. Now it's just dollars and Penney's."

I think she nodded, but I couldn't be sure, because she whipped us into a parking lot that ran in front of a strip mall on the east side of Delmont. She pulled up in front of the American Dollar store, threw the car in park, and out the door she went. I had to hurry to keep up.

Lord, the inside of the store was a wonder. It was long and narrow, with rows of shelving running the length of the store, and all the shelves and the floor under them were packed with every consumer item you could think of. And each one of them selling for a dollar? I'd have to come back some day when I had time to shop.

Hazel Marie walked right up to the stout woman at the cash register, unheedful of the customers lined up to check out. "I need to see Lonnie Whitmire. Where is he?"

The woman, who was moving as slow as Christmas in the first place, gave her a sullen glance but kept turning a garment around and around, looking for the sale price. "You'll have to get in line." She nodded at the three customers who were waiting.

But Hazel Marie didn't have standing in line in mind. "You could've told me what I want to know in the time it took to tell me to get in line. Now, get him out here or I'm going through this store like Sherman through Georgia."

The woman stopped her search and looked up, her face going slack. She stepped back from the counter and came up against the cash register. "I'm calling the police."

"Call them. I don't care," Hazel Marie said, slapping her hand on the counter. "Just get Lonnie out here, and we'll see who needs the police."

"Mr. Whitmire," the woman mumbled, correcting Hazel Marie. "He's in the back. In the office. But he can't be disturbed."

"Huh," Hazel Marie said, with a switch of her shoulders. "We'll just see about that."

She took off, heading down one of the aisles with me right behind her. There was so much merchandise stacked on the floor that we couldn't walk abreast even if I'd been able to keep up with her. I declare, I'd never seen so much stuff crammed into one store. There were grocery items, toys, clothing on circular racks, cleaning supplies, grills, gardening tools, and I don't know what all. And probably every last one of them made in China or Japan or Hong Kong, right there on display in the American Dollar store.

Hazel Marie wasn't interested in the merchandise. She headed straight for a door in the back with a sign saying Employees Only and pushed through it. I was two steps behind her, but we were brought up short by stacks of boxes and cartons waiting to be opened. Flattened boxes and packing materials littered the floor, at least what I could see of it, for the light was dim and the windows crusted with grime.

Hazel Marie didn't let any of that delay her. She began weaving in and out of the stacks of cartons until we saw an office cubicle enclosed with glass panels in the back corner. Inside it, Deacon Lonnie, with his shirt unbuttoned at the neck and his tie pulled down, sat behind a desk. He had his sleeves rolled up, and he was scratching his head with the hand that held a cigarette. Lord, if I hadn't known better, I'd have thought it was Wesley Lloyd Springer sitting there.

Hazel Marie took a bead on the man and threw the door open, slamming it back with such force that the whole office shook from the impact. Then she barreled in, startling Lonnie Whitmire so bad that he sprang from his chair, toppling it over and flipping the cigarette out of his hand and up in the air. He brushed frantically at his white shirt as the sparks flew.

"Why, why," he sputtered, snatching up the cigarette and burying it in an overflowing ashtray. "What's the meaning of this? You can't just come barging in here. . . ." Then recognition spread across his face, and he began backpedaling. "Why, Hazel Marie Puckett. Long time no see. Uh, what're you doing here?"

"You *know* what I'm doing here," Hazel

Marie said, her face scrunched up so bad that even I took a step back. She put her fists on his desk and leaned over it toward him. He stepped back until he was stopped by the wall.

"Why, I don't have any idea, but it, uh, sure is nice to see you again." Lonnie Whitmire's eyes were darting all around, looking for a way out. But he would've had to get past Hazel Marie first, and then me. And I was standing in the door.

"You won't think it's so nice by the time I get through with you." Hazel Marie shoved the desk, sending it closer to Mr. Whitmire. "I want to know what you've been telling that uncle of mine. What've you been saying about me?"

"Why, Hazel Marie," he said, shrugging his shoulders and turning his palms up, like he didn't know what she was talking about. "I don't know what you're talking about." But his face was red, and he couldn't look her in the eye, so he certainly did.

"Yes, you do, you lyin' polecat." Hazel Marie was so mad that spit was flying out of her mouth. Lonnie Whitmire cringed out of firing range. "So let's hear it. Just tell me right now, right to my face, if you've got the nerve. Which you don't.

And you never did. You were always a sneak, Lonnie Whitmire, and that's what you've been doing to me. Sneaking around and telling tales and lying about me and giving Uncle Vern another stick to beat me over the head with."

"Now, Hazel Marie, you know I wouldn't do that," Lonnie said, pleading innocence just as any tattletale will do. "You and me, we had us some good times once upon a time. You know we did."

"I don't know any such thing!" Hazel Marie shoved the desk another inch or two. "I don't know where you get off, thinking a couple of movies and a hamburger add up to some good times."

Hearing her confirm that she had been out with him, I sagged against the door.

"Now, Hazel Marie," he said, with just the hint of a smirk. "You know it was a little more than that."

"I don't know any such thing! Now you listen to me, Lonnie Whitmire," Hazel Marie told him, as she trembled so bad she had to hold onto the desk. "Whatever ideas you've put in my uncle's head, you better get them out, and get them out *now*. I'm not going to put up with it, and you can put that in your pipe and smoke it."

"But I didn't . . ."

"Yes, you did, too! There's no where else he could've gotten it. And I don't care if he misunderstood or if he made it out to be more than you said or what. It came from *you,* and you better get it straightened out. And I don't mean maybe, either."

Hazel Marie straightened herself up, crossed her arms over her heaving bosom, and glared at him. Her hot anger seemed to dissipate, and her voice grew low and cold. "You don't want to take me on, Lonnie, I promise you. I have powerful friends in this town, and one of them is standing right behind me."

I pulled my shoulders back, put a hard glint in my eye, and tried to look powerful.

"Mrs. Julia Springer Murdoch," Hazel Marie went on, "can buy and sell you and this store, too. And if you don't put a cork in Vernon Puckett, you're going to find out that I mean what I say."

"Why, sure, Hazel Marie," Lonnie said, all too eager now to pacify her. "Sure, I'll do that. It was just a little misunderstanding, that's all it was. But I'll set him straight, bet your boots, I will." An appeasing grin spread across his face as he pulled out a handkerchief and patted his forehead. "Would you ladies like something to drink?"

Hazel Marie snorted, but delicately. "I wouldn't have a drink with you if you were the last man on earth. Come on, Miss Julia, I've had enough of this."

She charged toward the door, making me step lively to get out of her way. Then she whirled around and threw one last threat at him. "I'm watching you, Lonnie, and if you want to work in this store and live in this town, you'll mind your own business."

She headed out through the stockroom and banged open the door into the store, with me right behind her and Lonnie right behind me. As she strode up an aisle, her arms swinging and her boots clomping with every step, Lonnie stopped and flung out the last word. "Fine, but you're both crazy! I don't care what that uncle of yours promises, it ain't worth the aggravation!"

Hazel Marie was halfway up the aisle and paid no attention. But I did, and I understood right then that Brother Vern had paid for Lonnie's testimony. That's called suborning perjury, if I'm not mistaken.

And with that uplifting thought I hurried after Hazel Marie, all the while marveling at how she'd stood up for herself. She was marching up that aisle, holding her head so high that it brushed a blue stuffed animal off a shelf. She grabbed it and sent it winding with no thought of where it would land.

I ducked and plowed on after her, but I had to pick up my pace right smartly to keep her in sight.

Chapter 42

"Oh, *no!*" Hazel Marie slammed on the brakes, bringing us to a jolting halt in the middle of Polk Street.

"What? What?" I gasped, as the seat belt almost cut me in two.

"Look, just look at that," she said, easing off the brakes and pointing to the shiny silver Cadillac parked in front of our house.

"Oh, my goodness. Keep going, Hazel Marie, and maybe he'll leave. "

"I can't. Lloyd'll be home from school any minute, and I don't want him near Uncle Vern."

"You're right. I didn't think of that. Hazel Marie, we have got to get rid of him." Scanning the driveway and the street, and seeing no familiar cars, I went on. "And wouldn't you know that neither Sam nor Mr. Pickens is back, so it's up to us."

"Up to me, you mean. He's my problem, and I'm going to deal with it." Then she shot me a frowning glance. "Why would J.D. be here?"

"I called him, looking for you. And now he's out trying to find you."

Her eyes rolled back in her head, a gesture I thought quite uncalled for under the circumstances.

She pulled the car into the driveway and went tearing through the backdoor. By the time I got into the kitchen, all I saw was the door to the dining room still swinging from her passage.

"What she fixin' to do, Miss Julia?" Lillian said, wringing a dish towel.

"There's no telling, Lillian. She's on a rampage, and I for one don't want to get in her way. How long has Brother Vern been here?"

"I don't know. Not too long, but he say he stay 'til y'all get back."

"Why in the world did you let him in? I declare, Lillian, we could do without this."

"What you want me to do?" she demanded, turning up her hands and glaring at me. "He come right in soon as I open the door. Didn't ast me nothin'. Jus' walk right in, an' say he come on the Lord's business. How I gonna stop a man what workin' for the Lord?"

"Oh, Lillian, you know you can't believe anything that man says. Brother Vern can't tell the difference between the Lord's work and his own. They're one and the same to him."

I tiptoed to the door to the dining room, hoping to hear what Hazel Marie was saying to Brother Vern. Or him to her, whichever it was.

"You better stop that," Lillian said.

"Hush. I just want to be available if I'm needed." But I couldn't hear a sound, so I straightened up and asked, "You haven't heard from Sam?"

"No'm, nor Mr. Pickens, neither. I wisht one of 'em come on back here. I don't like that man in the house with jus' us. He might do something."

"Oh, he won't *do* anything, Lillian, but he could sure *say* something."

I shuddered at the thought of the words that Brother Vern could be saying to Hazel Marie, and at what those words could mean to Wesley Lloyd Springer, whose eternal rest might have to be temporarily disturbed.

"Lillian," I said, walking over to her so I could speak softly. "I want you to prepare yourself. We might have to do something so unheard-of that you won't believe it."

"What?" she whispered, her eyes getting bigger.

Then we both turned at the sound of a

basketball bouncing in the driveway. "Little Lloyd's home! Hurry, Lillian, get your coat and waylay him. Take him to the store. Tell him anything, just don't let him come in. Here's the keys to my car. Now hurry before he comes in."

She got her coat from the pantry, took my keys, and started for the door. "How long I got to keep him away from here?"

"Until that car parked out front is gone. If you come back and it's still there, remember something you forgot and go back to the store."

"Law," she said, on her way out the door, "that mean I got to 'member to forget something."

I watched out the window as she spoke to Little Lloyd and saw him put away his ball. Then he threw his book bag in the backseat and climbed willingly into the car with her. Such an agreeable child, never a minute's trouble. But, oh, how his problematical origin troubled me.

When the car was out of earshot, I stood in the empty kitchen, listening as hard as I could, but there was no sound from the living room. I paced a few steps, wondering what to do.

After about two paces, I could stand it no longer. I pushed through the door into the dining room and marched myself into the fray. Hazel Marie was going to get my help whether she liked it or not. Even though I'd seen her take on some pretty formidable people in my time, she was no match for Brother Vern.

So I didn't have any qualms about going forward, and it was a good thing I didn't. As soon as I stepped into the living room, I could see that she needed all the help she could get. She was sitting bent over herself in one of the Victorian chairs, her face buried in her hands and sobbing. Brother Vern stood over her, murmuring on and on, so softly but insistently that as close as I was, I couldn't make out what he was saying.

The Oriental rug deadened my footsteps so that neither of them heard my approach. I stopped right behind Brother Vern, finally picking up what he was drilling into Hazel Marie's head.

"Girl, you know you sinned an' you're still sinnin'. You got to repent and confess, and do it so everbody hears and knows the kinda life you been leadin'. You been away from God long enough, and what kinda mother does that make you? You're an evil influence on that boy with your lyin' and deceivin' ways, livin' all your life with first one man and then another, and if you want to make it right and undo all you've wrought, you'll come clean, Hazel Marie."

It was remarkable to me, after having heard Brother Vern in full preaching mode when his voice could shake the rafters, to now hear this persistent drone, meant only for Hazel Marie to hear. And hear she was, for he had her so browbeaten and down-trodden, that she was all hunched over, her shoulders shaking and the tears flowing. In a matter of minutes the steel that had shored up her backbone enough to lay Lonnie Whitmire low had been taken right out of her by Brother Vern.

"Repent and confess," he went on, leaning closer to her. "Repent and confess, girl, that's all you gotta do."

"Yessir," she moaned between sobs. "I know I do, and I'm sorry. Sorry for everything."

"Sorry don't cut it," he said, as he put his hand on her head and mashed down on it. "You have to give up this easy life you got. That's the wages of sin, and we all have to suffer the consequences. But you don't have to worry about the boy, I'll see he's taken care of, and I won't let you go without, either. It won't be like you got it now, but it'll be enough so you won't have to go takin' up with another man. Cause I'm tellin' you, Hazel Marie, you got to put away fleshly thoughts and needs and all that wantin' in your heart. They already got you in enough trouble. You ought to be thinkin' of livin' a life of scrimpin' and savin' and sacrificin' from here on out to make up for the kinda life you been livin'."

I'd heard enough. Brother Vern was still unaware that I was behind him, so I leaned over and raised my voice right in his ear. "What is this?"

He nearly jumped out of his shoes, springing back with his mouth open and a startled look on his face. "Lord amighty, woman, don't sneak up on me like that!"

"I don't sneak up in my own house, and I'll thank you not to take the Lord's name in vain in my presence." Turning to Hazel Marie, who had half risen from her chair, I said, "Hazel Marie, this man's done all the damage he's going to do. I want you to go upstairs and lie down. I'll be up in a minute, just as soon as I see Brother Vern out."

"Miss Julia . . ." She could barely get the words out between the shuddering sobs and gasps. "I'm sorry, I'm sorry . . . I didn't . . ."

"It doesn't matter. Whatever he's said to

you, it doesn't matter."

She sidled away from me, cringing as she passed Brother Vern, and scurried out of the room. By the time I turned my attention to Brother Vern, he'd regained his composure and was puffing himself up again.

"I'm here to tell you, sister, that sin always matters, don't matter whether we know it or not." He pointed toward the door through which Hazel Marie had gone. "That woman has run a ringer in on you, and you been taken in by him and her, too. That boy that's been livin' under your roof and partakin' of your generosity and become known as the son and heir of your husband — your first husband — is no more kin to him than I am."

"You are wrong, Mr. Puckett." I looked him in the eye and stood my ground. "That child is a Springer through and through, and nothing you say will make it any different."

He pursed his mouth and shook his head. "It's a sorry thing when a woman won't be led by the admonitions of a man of God, so let me lay it out for you plain as I can. Hazel Marie used to flit from one bed to the other, right up to the time Mr. Springer took her in hand. But, and this is a big 'but,' " he said, raising a finger in front of my face, "there was somebody else in the picture. And that somebody else was Lonnie Whitmire, and *he* fathered that boy, not Mr. Springer, may he rest in peace. So there it is, plain and simple."

"Not so plain and simple at all," I said, glaring at him. "Where's your proof, Mr. Puckett? Just because a man claims a child doesn't mean the child is his."

Brother Vern's face turned red, whether from the delicate subject matter or from anger, I couldn't tell. With a knowing smirk, he said, "A man knows when the seed he's cast has taken root."

"No, he does not," I said, coming right back at him. "All a man can do is cast and hope. Or hope *not,* as the case may be. If the only thing you have to go on is an old wives' tale like that, you might as well pack it in."

"Listen, Miz Murdoch, I know I'm tellin' you what you don't want to hear, but Deacon Lonnie is willin' to swear that the boy is his and . . ."

"You better check with your deacon. I happen to know that he's just been aggravated into having a change of heart. You'll be hard-pressed to get him to swear to anything."

That news brought Brother Vern up short, but he shook it off and plowed ahead. "I already got him notarized. He'll stand up and swear he is."

"And Hazel Marie will swear he's not. So who do you think I'll believe? And I'm the one who counts."

"No, ma'am," he said, shaking his head in a sorrowful manner, "you are not. Now listen, I already talked to a lawyer, and that boy is Mr. Springer's true and legal heir, they ain't nothin' nobody can do about that, and it don't matter that Mr. Springer was sufferin' from a delusion, can't nobody take a nickel away from the boy. That will's as good as gold, and it don't matter who his father was, or is. Legally, the money's his'n. I mean, it will be when he's old enough. The real problem is his mother, the one who's lied and deceived and taken you in. *She* don't deserve nothin'. And she's been brought to her knees about it, too, ready to repent and confess and take herself out of the way of raisin' that boy."

So that was it. I could feel my eyes narrow and my breath starting to pick up speed. "And who do you think deserves to raise him?"

"Well," he said, spreading his hands, "ain't it plain? His mother's the next of

427

kin, but I got her on lying and perpetratin' fraud and being a loose woman, so it falls to me to step in. I'm that boy's great-uncle, and that makes me the *next* to the next of kin."

It was all I could do to stand there and keep a semblance of equanimity, but inside I was steaming and ready to blow. But before I could let him have it, he kept on talking.

"Now, I've give this a lot of thought, and here's what I'm thinkin' of doin'. We'll just let that boy keep on thinkin' his daddy was Mr. Springer, God rest his soul, there ain't no need to muddy up the waters. We'll just keep all this under our hats, so he won't get mixed up. And Lonnie won't be a problem. He don't want to take on a half-growed kid at this late stage, so don't worry about him. Ever'thing'll go right along like it's been doin', only Hazel Marie'll have to step down as one of the trustees."

"Wait a minute," I interrupted. "What do you know about the trustees?"

"I know Brother Sam and that lady lawyer, Binkie whoever, and Hazel Marie are the trustees for that boy till he comes of age. It's a public record. But Hazel Marie's not fit for the job, so as the next closest kin, I'm the natural one to take her place. And I believe I can make a good case to a judge for doing just that."

Lord, I thought, as a stab of fear hit me hard, put that way, he just might.

Chapter 43

I leaned against the door after closing it behind Brother Vern and tried to make sense of what he'd said. His parting shot was that he'd be in touch with Sam to make arrangements.

And where was Sam? He'd been gone all day without a word as to where he was or what he was doing. And Mr. Pickens was in the wind as well, both of them out scouring the countryside, while everything had blown up in my face right here at home.

Pushing away from the door I prepared myself to undo what Brother Vern had done to Hazel Marie. From what I'd heard, he had beaten her down until she had thrown in the towel and given in to him. And I wasn't going to have it. Brother Vern a trustee? Over my dead body, or Wesley Lloyd's, as the case might be.

I climbed the stairs, intent on giving her enough gumption to stand up to him. With even Brother Vern convinced that Little Lloyd's inheritance couldn't be touched, I could put that out of my mind. All that remained was Hazel Marie, and if she had deliberately lied or even if she wasn't sure who the child's father was, I just didn't care. At the moment, at least.

When I went into her room, I expected to find her in bed or cowering in a chair or maybe on her knees, but she was doing none of that. Her back was to me, as she leaned over to fill a suitcase lying open on the bed. Her face was blotched from crying, and she held a wad of Kleenex in one hand as she folded a sweater.

"Hazel Marie," I said, "what are you doing?"

"Packing. I'll be leaving in a few minutes."

"Leaving! And just where do you think you're going?"

She turned away as her shoulders shook with a new flood of tears. "I don't know," she said between sobs. "But I can't stay here."

"Of course you can. This is your home. Listen to me, Hazel Marie. I don't know who you were before you came here, but as far as I'm concerned your life began the day you moved in. And I don't care what Vernon Puckett says or Lonnie Whitmire, I know you and I believe you."

"It doesn't matter," she said, wiping her

eyes. "I can't prove who Lloyd's father was, so it's just my word against his. People will believe what they want to believe."

"But that's just the point, Hazel Marie. I want to believe you, and I do. And so does Sam, and so does Mr. Pickens and Lillian and your son, too. There is no need in the world for you to turn tail and run. You ought to know that your word carries more weight than his. After all, you were there and he wasn't."

"But he'll make a big scene and hire a lawyer and make Sam and Binkie put him in my place, and, and . . ." She stopped to blow her nose. "And Lloyd will hear all he says about me, and he'll hate me, and everybody'll look down on me, and it'll just be awful." She took a rasping breath and tried to pull herself together. "As soon as I get settled, I'll send for Lloyd, if you don't mind looking after him for a little while."

"Oh, no, Hazel Marie, you can't do that." The thought of losing her was bad enough, but the possibility of losing that child sent me into a tailspin. "I can't stand this. Please, come over here and sit down. Let's talk this out. There's no reason for you to run off. You'll just be playing into Vernon Puckett's hand if you do that.

Come on now." I took her by the arm and led her to one of the chairs by the window. "Listen now, there're a few things you don't know. Brother Vern came to Sam several days ago and told him this cock-and-bull story about Little Lloyd's natural father. Neither of us believed him then, and we don't believe him now. So we've been thinking about it longer than you have, and we've come up with a few things we can do. Are you listening to me?"

She nodded, but she wouldn't look at me.

"All right, first off, we'll demand a DNA test from Lonnie Whitmire, and that will prove beyond a shadow of a doubt that Little Lloyd is not his child."

She raised her head, and I saw the first glimmer of hope in her eyes. "It will, won't it?" There was something like awe in her voice, and I have to admit that her reaction reassured me more than I can say.

"Absolutely. And where will Brother Vern and his claims be then?"

"Oh, Miss Julia," she said, as she buried her face in her hands again, "he'll just come up with somebody else. Because it's still just my word against his."

"Then there's only one thing to do." I closed my eyes tight, hating to think it, much less say it. But I did. "We have to dig up Wesley Lloyd and test his bones or whatever's left of him."

Hazel Marie gasped and pulled away from me. "Dig him up! Oh, that's awful." Then she gave her eyes a final wipe. "Can we do that? I mean, how would we do it?"

"Don't worry about it. Sam and Binkie'll take care of the legalities, and hiring the diggers and the testers and whatever else we need. And as soon as Sam gets back here, if he ever does, we'll start doing whatever has to be done. In the meanwhile, you start unpacking, because you're not going anywhere. We're going to put this matter to rest once and for all, even if the dirt has to fly."

Whatever qualms I had previously had about disinterring Wesley Lloyd were now gone. Oh, I still hated to have to do it, especially since it'd make the local headlines, but I was considerably relieved that Hazel Marie was eager to have it done. If there'd been any doubt in her mind about who Little Lloyd's father was, she'd have tried to talk me out of it. Wouldn't she?

"But," she said, her eyes wide, "what would we tell people? I mean, it would get around, and everybody'd want to know why we did it."

"We'll tell them it was for health reasons," I said, thinking fast. "Hint around about pollution of the ground water or something, then say no more. They'll think something was wrong with the burial, and believe me, they won't want to know the details of that."

"Oh, my goodness," she said, beginning to see a light at the end of the tunnel. "If we could do it, that would settle everything, wouldn't it? I wouldn't ever have to worry about anything Vernon comes up with again." She stood up, a smile beginning on her poor, ravaged face. "Oh, Miss Julia, thank you for being willing to go that far for me."

"Think nothing of it," I said, with a wave of my hand. "People are dug up for one reason or another all the time. We live in a modern age, Hazel Marie, and we might as well make use of it. Now, I'm going downstairs to try to get Mr. Pickens and Sam back here so we can put things in motion."

I started for the door, but she called me back. She'd slumped down in the chair again, hiding her face. "Miss Julia, there's something else."

"Oh, Lord," I said, feeling another cloud of dread close over me. I walked over to her and collapsed in the chair beside her. "Hazel Marie, this is no time for true confessions. If you think that testing Wesley

435

Lloyd won't help us solve this mess, just tell me now before we disturb him. Anything other than that I don't want to hear."

"No, oh, no. I want you to disturb him, I really do. It's just that I do have something to confess, but it's not about him. It's about Emma Sue."

"What does Emma Sue have to do with this?"

"Well, nothing, really. It's just that I've been feeling real bad ever since she said I was so spiritual. Because I'm not."

"Now, Hazel Marie, none of us are as spiritual as we'd like to be or ought to be. Just accept the compliment and go on about your business."

"But I did something I shouldn't've done, and I can't let her go on thinking I'm something I'm not."

"I can't imagine what you did, Hazel Marie. I certainly haven't noticed anything. What was it?"

"Well, you know that prayer I gave at the circle meeting? Well, it wasn't mine like Emma Sue thought it was. I couldn't ever come up with something that good by myself, so I used somebody else's."

I frowned, wondering whose prayers she'd been listening to. Pastor Ledbetter could send up a full, rounded one that covered all the bases, but the one she gave hadn't sounded anything like his. And I knew it couldn't be one of Brother Vern's, because he preached when he prayed. And the grace that Little Lloyd said at meals didn't come anywhere near the eloquence of the one she'd said.

"Whose did you use, Hazel Marie?"

"Well, you know that book of prayers Binkie has?" she said, biting her lip. "Well, I kinda borrowed it and copied from it. I know I shouldn't've done it, Miss Julia, but I get so nervous when I have to pray out loud with everybody listening. My mind just goes blank, and I tried to write out one of my own, but I didn't know what to say. So I used that book, and now Emma Sue thinks I'm just about a saint or something."

"Oh, for goodness sakes, Hazel Marie. You mean you used a prayer from the Episcopal Book of Common Prayer?"

"I didn't think it was so common. I thought it was beautiful, and it said what I wanted to say but didn't know how to. I know it was wrong. . . ."

"I declare, you worry about the most unnecessary things. The prayers in that book are *supposed* to be used. Why do you think they're there in the first place? And let me tell you something else: Every one of their preachers or priests or rectors or whatever they call them use them every day that rolls around. They don't rely on the first thing that pops into their heads, like we do. So you're not the only one to lift a few from that book, and if Emma Sue is so impressed with what you said, well, we'll just let her go on being impressed. And if she does find out about it, it won't hurt her to know that Presbyterians haven't cornered the market on praying."

A smile lit up Hazel Marie's face. "Then you think it's all right . . . ?"

"I certainly do. Now I want you to put all your worries to rest. Forget about Emma Sue. We need to concentrate on getting Wesley Lloyd sent off for testing. That's going to solve all our problems."

Then she said something that nearly stopped my heart in midbeat: "Oh, I hope it will."

Before I could get my mouth open, the doorbell sounded downstairs. I waited, thinking that whoever it was would go away, but it rang again, longer and more insistently this time.

"Unpack that thing, Hazel Marie," I said, pointing at her suitcase. "I'll go see who it is and hope it's somebody with better news than I've been getting."

Chapter 44

To my dismay, it looked to be bad news, or at least disturbing news, in the form of Pastor Ledbetter. He stood at the door, shivering from his dash across the street in the cold drizzle.

"Come in, Pastor, and put that umbrella in the stand. It's a cold day to be running around without an overcoat."

"It is that," he said, stepping in and brushing raindrops from his shoulder. "But I have to talk to you, Miss Julia, for time is drawing short. I won't stay but a minute. I know it's getting late."

Motioning him to a seat on the sofa, I walked around, turning on the lamps to brighten the room. Then I took a seat some few feet away from him. "It's always a pleasure to see you," I said, trying to compose myself. But I was feeling an inner turmoil that threatened to erupt all over the place at any minute. I didn't have the time nor the inclination for church business or for spiritual instruction, if he was feeling led to give me some.

"Miss Julia," he began, leaning forward on the sofa, his arms on his knees and his hands dangling down. "I have to have your decision, and I hope you've made the right one. We have to get the names of the nominees for the session in the bulletin this coming Sunday. But before you say anything, let's have a prayer so you'll be led in the right direction."

"Pastor, I . . ."

"Wait," he said, holding up a hand. "Don't tell me yet. I want you to know that I have had this matter in constant prayer ever since it came up. Be aware, Miss Julia, of what your decision can do to our church." He bowed his head, and I thought he was about to call on the Lord. But he was just gathering steam. "I've been led to a decision myself, which I've told no one, not even Emma Sue. But I have to share it with you. I cannot, in conscience, bring myself to continue working in the Lord's vineyard here if a woman is voted onto the session. It would go against everything I've learned and believed in, and I want you to know that before you give me your decision."

I almost smiled. What an easy way to be rid of him and call another pastor, who'd be more amenable to the way I thought a church should be run. But did I want to be

440

an elder? Did I want to tangle with a group of men every month who didn't want me in their midst? Did I want to be a spiritual leader of the church and have to watch every word out of my mouth and every step I took and be an exemplary model for every soul in the congregation? Not that all the current elders were, but that was their problem.

Lord, I'd hardly given it a thought — too busy with more urgent matters close to home. But I couldn't tell the pastor that my decision had not been uppermost in my mind, especially since it had been in his.

I bit my lip, wondering what I should do.

Pastor Ledbetter, picking up on my hesitancy, leaned closer. "I think we need to pray, or maybe you need a little more counseling?"

"No," I said, holding up my hand to stop him. "I've had my fill of both here lately. Pastor, it's like this. I know it'll upset the church, but I've decided that . . ."

"Wait, Miss Julia, you can't. You don't know what this will mean. You can't imagine how you will tear up the church. Do you want that on your conscience? I beg you, please don't run, because I know you'll win a seat on the session and it'll mean the end of the peace I've worked so hard to maintain."

The man was sweating. As I watched him struggle to come to grips with what he assumed would be my decision, I almost felt sorry for him. He was convinced beyond any reasonable argument that my presence on the session would mean the end of our reformed, Biblically based congregation of faith. I didn't know I had such power just by being a woman.

"Put your mind at rest, Pastor," I said, "because I do not choose to run. I don't want to be on the session and have nothing but church wrangling on my mind for the next however many years."

He stared at me in wonder, then collapsed against the back of the sofa. A tiny smile hovered around his mouth, as he murmured, "Thank you." He may not have been speaking to me.

"But if you think," I went on, "that this is going to keep the peace, you are wrong. A lot of people will be unhappy with me because they wanted me to run, and unhappy with you because they'll think you talked me out of it. You've escaped having a woman on the session this year, but over half of the congregation will not be stopped. You might as well come to terms with it and prepare yourself for next year. No telling what I might do then."

He sprang from his seat, relief spread all over his face. "Tomorrow will take care of itself. Miss Julia, with the Lord's help, you have made the right decision. Bless you, and may the Lord keep you and make his face to shine upon you."

"Amen," I said, getting to my feet. "Now, Pastor, I hate to rush you, but I have matters of some urgency to take care of." Then hearing a car turn into the driveway, I went on. "That's probably Lillian and Little Lloyd now. I know Emma Sue has dinner waiting for you, so I won't keep you."

Having gotten his way, he had no reason to linger. So he left with a smile on his face and, if I wasn't mistaken, a song in his heart. He forgot his umbrella, but I doubt a raindrop touched him.

I started toward the kitchen just as I heard a jumble of voices and laughter come through the backdoor. Out of the commotion, one unmistakable high-pitched little voice pierced the walls of the house, and I knew Lillian's great-granddaughter, Latisha, was among us.

Before I got in the kitchen good, Lillian began explaining. "I had to bring her, Miss

Julia. That after-school place she go to closin' early 'cause of the weather. But she gonna mind herself, ain't you, Latisha?"

"Yes, ma'am, I am," Latisha said, as sure of herself as she ever was. Her neatly braided hair bobbed up and down as she nodded her head. "I always do, even when I don't 'spes'lly feel like it."

Lillian snorted as she began turning on overhead lights, hood lights, and undercounter lights. The dusk outside blackened the windows, but it was now bright and warm inside.

I smiled at Latisha, noting again how tiny she was even with a heavy sweater and boots that looked a size too large for her. She was no bigger than a minute, but she could eat Sam under the table any day.

"It's good to see you again, Latisha," I said. "What did you learn in school today?"

"I got my numbers learned up to a hunderd and two," she announced, "but I don't never say 'em on weekends."

I could only smile at that, and turning to Little Lloyd, I asked, "And how was your day, honey?"

"It was okay," he said, then grinned at Latisha, who was hunched over, covering her mouth with her hand.

Laughing behind it, she said, "She call you honey. You don't look like no honey to me. You look like a big ole boy what need a snack. Like I do."

Lillian said, "Well, come on over here, an' I give you some grapes."

"I don't b'lieve I want no grapes," Latisha said, swinging her little pink book bag back and forth. "I b'lieve I ruther have a b'loney sammich and a big ole glass of milk. With some cookies to go with it."

Little Lloyd laughed. "Latisha, you'll ruin your supper. Come on, let's have some grapes, and go upstairs. I'll show you that video game I told you about."

"Well, okay. But I tell you right now, they ain't nothin' gonna ruin my supper." She accepted a napkin filled with grapes from Lillian, turned it around in her hand, and eyed it suspiciously. Then, on the way to the back staircase with Little Lloyd, she turned to me. "Thank you, Miss Lady, for lettin' me come play an' eat at your house." Then she cut her eyes at Lillian. "How's that, Great-Granny? Is my manners gettin' any better?"

"Your manners are perfect, Latisha," I said, forestalling comment by Lillian. "And we're always happy to have you. Now, you two run on up and play, and

Lloyd, don't disturb your mother. She's had a hard day and needs her rest. Run on, because Lillian and I have some things to talk about."

"Well, I can put off playin' for a while," Latisha said, " 'cause I'd like to lissen in on what y'all talk about."

"Latisha!" Lillian said. "Get on up them stairs. Lloyd, honey, take her on up an' keep her there till I get my cookin' done."

Little Lloyd was so tickled by this time that it was all he could do to urge Latisha up the stairs. Her boots clomped on each step, as her voice reverberated down the stairs. "It's black as pitch up here. I can't see where I'm goin'."

"We'll turn the lights on in my room," Little Lloyd told her. "But we don't want to wake up Mama, so be real quiet."

As their footsteps receded above us, Lillian looked at me. "What us got to talk about?" she asked, frowning, her hands propped on her hips. " 'Sides Miss Hazel Marie an' why she have a hard day, an' where Mr. Sam and Mr. Pickens, an' what that Brother Vern do when he here, an' about two dozen other things that nobody tell me about?"

"Oh, Lillian," I said, leaning against a counter. "There's something we have to do that is just beyond belief."

"Oh, my Lord, what you got to do now?"

Taking a deep breath, I reached out to her. "Prepare yourself, Lillian, because it looks like we have to exhume Mr. Springer."

"Zoom him! What you mean?" Lillian's eyes about popped out of her head.

"No, I mean, . . . well, I mean we're going to dig him up."

Her mouth fell open and a look of horror spread across her face. "No, you not. That's not right, Miss Julia. Don't be 'sturbin' a man what been put in the ground. No tellin' what you stir up, you go foolin' with the dead." Then, as she thought more about it, she frowned and asked, "What you gonna do with him when he dug up?"

"We have to test his bones to prove that he's Little Lloyd's father."

"Who say he ain't?"

"Brother Vern, that's who. And he's found a man he thinks will swear that *he's* the boy's father. And you know what that would say about Hazel Marie."

"What it say?"

"Think about it, Lillian. It would tear us all up if Little Lloyd's not who she says he is. So we have to prove he is. And the only

447

way to do that is to compare whatever the child's made up of with whatever Mr. Springer's made up of, and to do that we have to get him out of the ground and test him. But don't say a word to Little Lloyd. He doesn't know anything about this."

"Well, I don't neither, but look like you come up with something better'n a dead man what oughtta be left molderin' in his grave, like he 'spose to be."

"I wish we could. Lillian, I tell you, I've beaten myself over the head a dozen times because I threw away everything the man owned. If only I'd kept some things — things he personally handled — we could've used them instead of having to take this drastic step."

She studied on this for a while, a concentrated look on her face. "You mean, Mr. Springer could of rubbed hisself off on his b'longin's, an' if he did, you wouldn't have to go robbin' his grave?"

"That's what they tell me. Well, not on just anything, but he could be lingering on some things." Which was why I hadn't wanted to keep his belongings in the first place, although at the time I hadn't known quite how scientific I was being.

Lillian cocked her head to one side, her eyes moving slowly back and forth, a look of concentration on her face. I could tell she was in awe of the extraordinary measures I was willing to take in order to preserve our family. Makeshift though it was.

"Well, Lord he'p us," she mumbled. "I never heard the like."

Chapter 45

After calling Mr. Pickens on his cell phone and learning that he and Sam were drinking coffee at McDonald's, I expressed my displeasure in no uncertain terms.

"Lillian, I declare," I said, hanging up the phone. "Here I thought they were out searching for Hazel Marie and Brother Vern, and they've been sitting around wondering what to do next. Well," I went on with a shrug, "at least they found each other, which I guess is something to celebrate."

"Talkin' 'bout celebratin'," Lillian said, her back to me as she worked at the sink. "It comin' up Christmas pretty soon, an' you oughta be puttin' yo' mind to it. Y'all be eatin' all day long what with folks droppin' in an' all, an' I need to know what you want me to fix."

"I can't think about a menu now. Not with this heavy burden hanging over me. Lillian," I said, collapsing in a chair and leaning my head on my hand, "I feel as if I'm between a rock and a hard place. We could leave Mr. Springer in peace, accept Hazel Marie's word for it, and hope Brother Vern can't get his hands on Little Lloyd's assets. Or we can create a public spectacle by digging up Mr. Springer — because even if it's done in the dead of night, people will find out about it. But that way there'll be no doubt, no doubt at all. So my quandary is, is exhuming Mr. Springer worth it to have complete peace of mind?"

She didn't answer, which was all right because I was mostly talking to myself, anyway. Instead, she turned off the water in the sink and began to dry her hands with a dish towel.

"When Mr. Sam an' Mr. Pickens get back here?" she asked.

"Any time now. They were going to stop by the sheriff's office first and tell them that the lost have been found, then come on home. And when they get here," I said with determined resolve, "I'm going to tell Sam to get that disinterment order, because I have made up my mind. There is no need for us to have to live with a cloud over our heads. We're going to settle this once and for all, even though I'll have to explain to everybody my renewed interest in Wesley Lloyd Springer." I looked up as

Lillian started to walk out of the room. "Where're you going?"

"I got to get something."

And out she went, leaving me somewhat taken aback at her lack of interest in my worries. I heard the run-down backs of her shoes flapping on her feet as she walked through the dining room and down the back hall.

In a few minutes she was back, holding a shoe box carefully in both hands. "Miss Julia," she said, her face creased with concern, "I know you tole me to th'ow ever'thing what Mr. Springer own in the trash, or give 'em away, or do what I want with 'em, but I didn't, an' I know you might get mad at me, but I save some things for that little boy, 'cause I don't think it right he don't have something from his daddy."

My eyes got big, and my heart leapt in my chest. "You saved something? Oh, Lillian, I can't believe it."

"Yessum, I know. I ain't never do what you tell me not to do 'fore this, but maybe it he'p you outta the hard place you in now. Seein' how you say you wish you didn't th'ow it all out."

"Oh, my Lord," I cried, wanting to fling myself on her and hug her to death.

"Lillian, you are the most wonderful person in the world. Bless your heart, and God love you. What's in the box?"

"Jes' some things what ought to go to Little Lloyd, even if you don't want 'em to."

She put the box on the table, and it was all I could do not to snatch the lid off. "I don't care about that anymore. He can have anything he wants. Where've you kept it all this time?"

"Round an' about. I move it when anybody look like they gonna start plunderin'. It been way up on the top shelf of the linen closet goin' on three years now, back of the Windex an' the Johnson wax. I know you never get in that, so it been settin' there with nobody botherin' it."

I let that slide, too intent on the contents of the box to remind her that I did so do some occasional cleaning. "Let's see what's in it."

I took the lid off and saw several small jewelry boxes and tissue-covered odds and ends inside. Lifting out a box and opening it, I couldn't help showing my disappointment. "His gold and onyx cuff links. They won't work, Lillian."

Opening another box, I came across a gold tiepin that I recalled had been given to Wesley Lloyd by the bank employees one year for Christmas. He'd never worn it. Then there was a box filled with ten-, twenty-, and thirty-year pins for faithful Sunday school attendance. I stirred the contents and saw his gold college ring with a garnet stone, which he rarely wore, and the plain gold wedding band, which he might as well have never worn. I snapped the box closed and discarded it. Unwrapping a tissue-wrapped oddment, I saw three handkerchiefs, all nicely ironed and folded.

"Why did you save these?" I asked. "You can purchase handkerchiefs anywhere."

"They got his 'nitials on 'em, an' they same as Little Lloyd's, so I save 'em."

"Huh," I said, ready to sling them aside. Then I stopped. "Lillian, this could be the very thing. Sam said the laboratory could use any kind of bodily fluids. If Wesley Lloyd blew his nose, which he did a dozen times a day, and used these, why, they could be the answer to our prayers."

"Well, I don't know," she said, frowning. "He have to blow real hard, 'cause I soak 'em in Clorox 'fore I put 'em up."

"Oh," I said, discouraged again. "Well, who knows what modern science can do. What else is in here?" I opened a black, hard-shell case, giving her a sharp look at the same time. "Why in the world would you save his reading glasses?"

"They got gol' rims," she said. "An' I save ever'thing got gol' on 'em."

"They Lord," I murmured, putting aside the glasses. "But it was thoughtful of you, and I'm sure Little Lloyd will be glad to have them. But, Lillian, I'm not sure any of this will work for testing purposes."

"I put Mr. Springer's Bible in here, too," she said, lifting out a small, leatherbound King James version with onion-skin pages. "He carry it to church a lot, so maybe it pick up something offa him."

"Not unless he sneezed on it. Or maybe he licked a finger when he turned a page, except that'd probably be too old and dried out by now. But we'll show everything to Binkie. She'll know what's testable and what's not." I wadded up tissue paper that had been stuck in the corners of the box. "Is there anything more?"

"This the last one," she said, handing me up a square leather box.

I opened it and saw Wesley Lloyd's gold pocket watch and chain that had come down from his daddy, and his granddaddy too, for all I knew. He'd worn it every day of his life, the gold chain strung across his vest for everybody to see. It was so much a part of the man's attire that the funeral director had urged me to allow it to be displayed on Wesley Lloyd's chest during the viewing. The watch and chain had been given back to me when the casket was closed, since Wesley Lloyd had no longer had any use for them.

I smoothed my fingers over the ornate engraving on the back of the watch, recalling how Wesley Lloyd had taken such inordinate pride in removing it from his vest pocket. He would pull it out with a dramatic flourish, as he consulted the time, the fob attachment dangling from the chain.

"Well, Lillian," I said, handing the timepiece to her and sinking morosely into a chair. "It was a good thought, but there's not a thing here that'll do us any good. It's all come down to having to dig him up, and I'm just sick about it."

Lillian carefully placed the watch back into its box and smoothed out the chain alongside it. "You mad at me for savin' Mr. Springer's gol' pieces?"

"Goodness, no. I couldn't be mad at you if I tried. No, Little Lloyd'll be happy. . . . Lillian!" I sprang from my chair and snatched the box from her. "I just thought of something!" Fumbling with the catch on the box, I said, "I can't get this thing open, and there might be . . . Oh, I hope. Look!"

I pulled out the watch and held it up by the chain, peering at it as it twirled and sparkled in the overhead light. Then grabbing the fob, or charm, or whatever it was that was attached by a tiny gold link to the chain, I said, "Look here, Lillian! You know what this is?"

Lillian shook her head. "No'm. Look like a gol' tooth to me."

"It is! It's a tooth that he had dipped in gold." I held it up in my fingers, both repulsed and delighted by the find. "Have you ever heard of such a thing? So vain, carrying around a gold-plated wisdom tooth strung across his midsection on a watch chain! The man put an immoderate value on anything pertaining to himself." Except his wife, I could've added, but didn't. "Lillian, I know they can test teeth for DNA, Mr. Pickens said so. And that means we may just be in business." Relief spread throughout my system until I thought on it a little more. "But I'll tell you one thing, if the gold plate he put on this tooth has ruined it, I'm going to be vengeful enough to dance on his grave. Right before they prize him out of it."

Chapter 46

It didn't come to that, thank goodness, since my dancing days were all but over anyway. Wesley Lloyd remained undisturbed in his grave, and only a few knew we'd ever contemplated getting him out of it and sending him to a laboratory to have his insides examined for proof positive of Little Lloyd's paternity.

So I was glad that we were able to avoid such extreme measures, not because I had any lingering attachment to Wesley Lloyd's person, or what was left of it, but because it would've meant coming up with a believable explanation, acceptable to every bridge, garden, and luncheon club in town. Hazel Marie didn't need speculations running rife, and neither did I.

But that night, just as I was looking with wonder and increasing joy at the roots of Wesley Lloyd's gilded tooth, and offering up thanks that it hadn't been impacted, then splintered, during extraction, Sam and Mr. Pickens came in.

"Oh, Sam," I said, "I'm so glad. . . ."

"Where is she?" Mr. Pickens broke in, his brows drawn together in a worried frown. "Is she all right?"

"Yes, and upstairs, but look at. . . ."

"I'm going up," he said, walking right past me and making no apologies for his abrupt behavior. "I've got to be sure she's okay." And off he went toward the back stairs.

"Wait, I need to ask . . ." I started after him, but he was halfway up the stairs before I got to the foot. "Well, all right, but turn on some lights. It's black as pitch up there." Then I stuck my head up the stairs and called to him, "And don't close the door."

"Julia," Sam said, beckoning me. "Let him go. He's been beside himself all day because we couldn't find her."

I went to Sam and leaned against him, relieved to have him home where he was supposed to be. "I have to ask you something, Sam. While you were out gallivanting around and not letting me know anything, Lillian and I have about solved everything. Look at this, and tell me if it'll work."

I held the watch up in front of his face so he could see it twirl on its chain. I smiled, waiting for him to realize the importance of the dangling appendage.

He frowned as he looked closer. "I'll bite. What is it?"

I opened my mouth to tell him I was in no mood for jests, when an unearthly shriek split the air and echoed through the house. Lillian's hands flew up and so did a three-quart saucepan. It fell, clattering to the floor, as she whirled around, yelling, "Latisha!" I gripped Sam's arm, struck with fear as we all started toward the stairs.

"They's a man up here!" Latisha screamed. And down the stairs she came, shrieking and slipping and sliding and half tumbling until she landed with a bound in the kitchen. Terror stricken, she ran to Lillian and hid behind her.

"Oh, my land, chile," Lillian said, nearly collapsing in relief. "They's not no man up there. That jus' Mr. Pickens."

Latisha buried her face in Lillian's skirt. "Well, he come outta the dark," she said, half sobbing. "An' I runned into him, an' he like to scare me to death."

Sam started laughing, and when I could breathe again, so did I. Upstairs, doors slammed open and feet thundered down the stairs, the commotion sounding like a herd of horses on the loose. Hazel Marie and Mr. Pickens rushed into the kitchen,

Little Lloyd, his glasses askew on his face, right behind them, yelling, "What happened? What happened?"

Mr. Pickens, breathing hard, stopped short. "Where is she? Is she all right?"

Hazel Marie's eyes were still swollen, but she seemed somewhat resurrected with fresh makeup and a change of clothes. Catching sight of Latisha peeking around Lillian, she leaned over to brush away the child's tears. "Oh, Latisha, are you hurt, honey?"

Latisha shook her head as she buried it deeper in Lillian's skirt. Mr. Pickens squatted down beside her. "I didn't mean to scare you, little girl. But you know what? You scared me out of a year's growth, and I can't afford to get old that fast."

Latisha peeked out at him, the beginnings of a smile on her face. "You already ole, 'cause you got gray hairs on yo' head."

"You got me there," he said, and began to coax her out from behind Lillian.

"First thing tomorrow," I said to Sam, "Carpet is going on those stairs."

With the fright over and my pulse rate easing off, I quickly slipped Wesley Lloyd's watch, chain, and tooth into my pocket and slapped the lid on the shoe box. This was not an appropriate time for Little

Lloyd to be viewing his father's remains.

Turning to Sam, I whispered, "We need to talk. Let's go back to our room."

Slipping out of the kitchen while the others were taken up with Latisha, we found privacy in our bedroom. "Sam," I said, holding out the tooth to him, "tell me this thing has DNA in it, so we won't have to go mining the cemetery to get some."

Sam took it from me, turning it around as he examined the roots and the surfaces of a molar that, as far as I could see, had not increased Wesley Lloyd's level of wisdom by any degree whatsoever. "Whose is it?" he asked.

"Why, Sam, it's Wesley Lloyd's. Who else's tooth do you think I'd have? And if it hadn't been for Lillian going against my explicit instructions, I wouldn't have that. Now, will it suffice to lay this matter to rest?"

"It might." Sam looked at me, a broad grin spreading across his face. "It just might. We could ask Pickens, but maybe we'd better stick with Binkie. If she doesn't know, she can find out. Even so, it might take a few weeks before we know for sure, and it'll probably cost an arm and a leg."

"I don't care what body parts it'll cost — an arm, a leg, or a tooth — it's one and the same to me. Just so we get at the truth and can hit Brother Vern over the head with it. But *weeks*, Sam? How're we going to keep him quiet until the results come back?"

"Once we tell Puckett that DNA testing is being done, I think he'll be confident enough to want to wait." Sam held the tooth up to the light, shaking his head in disbelief. "Who would've thought it?" Then he looked at me, a troubled frown appearing between his eyes. "What about Whitmire? You heard anything from him?"

"No, and I don't think we will. I think he'll want to stay as far from Hazel Marie as he can get." And I went on to tell Sam of our visit to the American Dollar store and the change Hazel Marie and I had made in his outlook. "I gathered from what he yelled after us that money was involved in some way, and he was being paid to tell tales on Hazel Marie. But, Sam, you should've seen how he backed down when Hazel Marie lit into him." I bit my lip, recalling the scene. "I have to tell you, though, there might've been more between those two than I want to know. But — and I'm firm about this, and from Hazel Marie's attack on him, she was, too — he didn't have a thing to do with that child's conception. Besides, he was a married man at the time."

Sam and I looked at each other. We didn't have to say what we were thinking. Namely, that somebody else had also been a married man at the time, and it hadn't stopped him.

I bypassed that and went on to tell Sam about Brother Vern's visit and how it had undone Hazel Marie, and how I'd promised her that we'd leave no stone or grave unturned until we'd proven beyond a shadow of a doubt that Little Lloyd was a Springer through and through. Excepting, of course, the Puckett strain he got from his mother.

"So, Sam, I am depending on this tooth to dig us out of the hole we're in. And if it doesn't, I don't want to know about it. And I don't want Brother Vern to know about it, either. I want to see a test result come back here that leaves no room for doubt, and I intend to have it that way if I have to fix it myself. It's remarkable what you can do with a little Wite-Out and a copying machine."

"We won't have to resort to that, Julia," Sam said, as he turned the tooth around. "I think this is going to do the trick."

Then he gazed at me with what I took to be wonder and pure wide-eyed admiration. "In fact, it looks to me like you and

Lillian have saved the day."

"Well," I said, a smile as broad as his spreading across my features, "what's new about that?"

Chapter 47

We called Binkie the very next morning, and she explained the ins and outs of DNA testing and what laboratory to contact and how to collect and send off the samples. Would you believe you can get everything you need through the mail? As long as you have a credit card, it's just like ordering from Neiman Marcus.

Then there was the problem of getting a DNA sample from Little Lloyd. We couldn't just ask him for it, because we'd been bending over backward to keep him from knowing he had an identity crisis. I certainly didn't want him to find it out at this late date. And I couldn't take him to a doctor to get it, because we'd have to explain to the doctor why we wanted it, and that would be just one more person in the know.

Binkie said she could swab his mouth as well as anyone, since she had the whole do-it-yourself kit right there in her office. But Little Lloyd would've known exactly what was happening as soon as Binkie came at him with a Q-tip. He's smart as a whip, you know.

So I was about at my wit's end. Here we'd managed to find that tooth with Wesley Lloyd's DNA in it, saving us the trouble of digging him up, and you'd think it would be clear sailing from then on out.

"Julia," Sam said one evening, after several days in abeyance while we tried to figure out how to scrape the inside of the child's mouth without him knowing it. We were alone in the living room, fretting over the problem. "Julia," Sam said again, "let's just tell him. We'll assure him that *we* aren't questioning who his father is, but that it's a legal measure to prevent any question later on."

I was shaking my head all through his little discourse, but before I could say a word, he went on. "We can tell him it's necessary because Wesley Lloyd never legally recognized him as his son. Stress *legally,* because we don't want to stir up any doubts in the boy's mind. That would work, wouldn't it?"

"No, it wouldn't." I sprang from the sofa because I couldn't sit still. "You don't understand how sharp his mind is, Sam. He'd know in a minute that we were questioning his mother's word and her morals, because he is well aware that his mother and father don't have the same last name. He's already concerned about his own name."

"Well, then we're right back where we were before Lillian unearthed that tooth."

I shuddered. "Let's don't talk about unearthing. We escaped that by the skin of our teeth, thanks to her. But, think, Sam, there must be some way we can sneak around and get his DNA."

"Plenty of ways to get it, but doing it without his knowledge is the problem."

I paced the living room floor back and forth, trying to think of something. "Why do we have to fiddle around in his mouth, anyway? Didn't you say they can get DNA from all sorts of places? We're already using a tooth, for goodness sakes,"

Sam looked up from under his eyebrows, smiling. "I don't believe we can pull a tooth without him noticing. But," he went on somewhat more seriously, "you're right. Blood, skin cells, hair — which, by the way, has to have a root on it, so we can't just snip some off — all of that can be tested. But the easiest and least intrusive way is to swab the mouth. That's the way the lab kit's set up, and since they're going to have a hard enough time with Wesley Lloyd's tooth, we ought to follow their instructions for Lloyd."

"Well, of course you're right," I said, about half done in because he usually was. I took another turn around the room, turning the problem over in my mind.

"Well, Julia," Sam said, slapping his hands on his knees and getting to his feet. "It's past my bedtime. Let's sleep on it and maybe things'll be clearer in the morning."

"I hope so, because Brother Vern's not going to keep quiet much longer." I snapped off a lamp and walked across the room to turn off another one. "I'll leave one on for Hazel Marie, although no telling when she'll get in. I declare, you'd think they'd keep earlier hours, what with Mr. Pickens having to go to work in the morning."

Sam laughed. "He pretty much works when he wants to."

"Yes, and that's the trouble with him. If he'd buckle down and *settle* down, he'd be a lot better off." I fluffed up the pillows on the sofa and straightened the girandoles on the mantel. "I'm going to check on Little Lloyd, then I'll be in."

"Don't be long," Sam said, as he headed down the back hall toward our bedroom.

I tiptoed up the stairs, noticing a light from the child's room spilling out into the hall. I bit my lip in dismay, fearing that he'd been awake and listening to what we'd talked about.

I crept toward the door of his room and peeked around it. Every light in the room was on, but he was sprawled out in bed, sound asleep. I smiled with relief and carefully walked in to turn off the lamps.

As I approached his bedside and looked down, my heart melted at the sight. There is nothing sweeter or more innocent than a sleeping child. I stood for a minute just to watch over him, as he rested there on the pillow, his wispy hair a disheveled mess and his mouth open, breathing in and out with little gurgling noises.

I smiled, thinking how I would tease him about snoring as he had teased me on occasion. Then I stood stock still, stunned by a sudden realization. Turning on my heel, I hurried out and down the stairs, nearly crippling myself in my haste and in the effort to make no noise.

Rushing into our bedroom, I hissed, "Sam, Sam, get up. Quick, we've got to do it right now."

Sam jerked upright in bed. "What is it? What's the matter?"

"Come on. Hurry." I dashed around the room, looking for the implements from the lab kit Binkie had given us. "Where's that

Q-tip? Get up, Sam, I can't do it. You'll have to."

When I told him my plan, he laughed all the way up the stairs, until I told him he'd be mortally sorry if he woke the child. He held his hand over his mouth, doing his best to muffle himself, as he tiptoed behind me.

When we got to Little Lloyd's door, I let Sam take the lead. I pressed behind him, clutching a handful of pajama top. The bedside lamp I'd left on gave us a clear view of the child, still in deep and noisy slumber. Sam crept to the far side of the bed where the boy lay, with me making each step with him.

"See how his mouth is open?" I whispered. "Just scrape that thing in there, and let's get out of here."

Sam leaned over the bed, and I leaned over him. He eased the stick into the child's mouth, touching neither lip nor tongue. He held it there, suspended for a moment, as Little Lloyd gently snored around it, unaware of what was being done to him.

I nudged Sam. "Do it," I whispered with some urgency. "Hurry, before he wakes up."

So he scraped the cotton-tipped stick

along the inside of the child's mouth, while I held my breath and watched. Just as Sam made one last swipe, Little Lloyd snorted and jerked his head away. I thought my heart would stop. Then he brought his hand up, and just as Sam retracted the stick, rubbed his nose fiercely. With a long moan, or maybe it was a sigh, he turned over in bed and curled up, fast asleep again.

Sam clicked off the lamp, and we scurried out, carrying the precious essence of Little Lloyd on a stick.

After carefully stashing our prize in a container, we fell in bed, congratulating ourselves and laughing our heads off.

Contrary to what I'd been led to believe, it took only a few days to get the results back. That's how it works when you go private and don't mind the cost.

Binkie called Sam and me to her office and went over the test results with us. They were as plain as the nose on your face. After deciphering the graphs and pointing out the statistical genetic odds to us, Binkie stacked the papers together and slid them into a manila envelope. "I can't imagine you'll ever need these," she said, "but if I were you I'd keep them in a safe place. That tooth is probably in a million pieces by now, so you won't be able to use it again." She stopped and squinched her mouth together. "I don't know what happened to the gold that was on it. You want me to call the lab and ask about it?"

"No," I said, "I don't want anything more to do with any of it. As far as I'm concerned the matter is closed, never to be opened again."

Sam and I met with Brother Vern at Sam's house that afternoon, and I don't mind saying that it gave me a great deal of satisfaction to wave those papers in his face.

"We have the proof now," Sam told him. "Irrefutable proof that the boy is a Springer through and through. You need to go on about your business now and leave Hazel Marie alone."

Brother Vern's face turned red as a beet, and I thought he might explode with frustration. He hemmed and hawed and expostulated, but all he could come up with was that science in all its forms, including evolution, would be the ruination of us all.

Sam tried to explain the test results to him, but Brother Vern was not interested in being enlightened. "All I know," he fumed, "is that Hazel Marie don't deserve what's come to her, and I won't ever believe any different."

"Well, frankly," I said, wanting to have my say, too, "we don't really care what you believe. We want you as far from Hazel Marie as you can get, and it's time you got started."

I waved the papers in front of him again to shoo him out. He straightened his shoulders and tugged down his coat, all the while giving me a mean look. Then, with a great swelling of his chest to show he was undeterred, he folded his tent and slunk away.

Those papers are safe now in my lockbox at the bank, and every once in a while I think of going down there and destroying them. The day is going to come when I will pass on to my reward, leaving the boy, who I hope will be a grown man by that time, with access to all my papers and possessions. I would purely hate for him to learn, sometime in the future when I'm not around to reassure him, that the issue of his paternity and his mother's veracity had ever come up. I want Hazel Marie to believe that she has my trust, and I want the child to know that he is who he is, without any question or uncertainty entering their heads, or anybody else's.

So I'll do away with those test results one of these days, but in the meantime, I like to have them available just to look at now and then. And, in case we should ever need them. You never know, do you? It's always good to have proof, signed, sealed, and paid for, to wave in somebody's face if the question ever rises again.

Of course, I don't need any tests or papers or official evidence to put my mind at ease. I never had any doubts about that child to begin with.

Miss Julia's

— Christmas Day Menu —

Breakfast

(SERVED IN THE
LIVING ROOM BY THE TREE)
Pigs in Blankets
Pecan Coffee Cake
Orange Juice   Coffee

Lunch

(DISPLAYED ON SIDEBOARD,
SELF-SERVE STYLE)
Oyster Stew
Oysterette Crackers
Waldorf Salad
Tea   Coffee

Afternoon

(OFFERED TO DROP-IN GUESTS)
Lillian's Fruitcake and Date-Nut Bars
Cheese-Nut Wafers
Fudge and Divinity Candies
Coffee Sparkling   Cider   Hot Spiced Tea

Dinner

Roast Turkey and Cornbread Dressing
Giblet Gravy
Broccoli with Curry Sauce
Creamed Onions with Almonds
Squash Casserole
Candied Sweet Potatoes
Cranberry Orange Congealed Salad
Cranberry Sauce
Lillian's Yeast Rolls
Maraschino Cherry Christmas Pie
Coffee   Sparkling White Grape Juice   Tea